Mary Stewart, one of the most popular novelists writing today was born in Sunderland, County Durham and lives in the West Highlands.

Her career as a novelist began in 1956 with *Madam, Will You Talk?* Since then, she has published numerous successful adult novels, including her Merlin trilogy (*The Crystal Cave, The Hollow Hills* and *The Last Enchantment*), concerning the legendary enchanter Merlin and the young Arthur, and her novel of Mordred, *The Wicked Day.* Her most recent modern novels are *Thornyhold, Stormy Petrel,* and *Rose Cottage* as well as *The Prince and the Pilgrim,* her first Arthurian novel for twelve years.

Her books for young readers, *The Little Broomstick, Ludo and the Star Horse* and *A Walk in Wolf Wood,* quickly met with the success of her other novels. In 1971, she was awarded the International PEN Association's Frederick Niven Prize for *The Crystal Cave,* and in 1974, the Scottish Arts Council Award for *Ludo and the Star Horse.*

Rose Cottage
Stormy Petrel
Thornyhold

Mary Stewart

CORONET BOOKS

Hodder & Stoughton

The Rose Cottage and other stories by Mary Stewart
copyright © 1999 by Mary Stewart
The Rose Cottage copyright © 1997 by Mary Stewart
Stormy Petrel copyright © 1991 by Mary Stewart
Thornyhold copyright © 1988 by Mary Stewart

First published in paperback in Great Britain in 1999
by Hodder and Stoughton
A division of Hodder Headline PLC

A Coronet paperback

10 9 8 7 6 5 4 3 2 1

A CIP catalogue record for this title is available from
the British Library.

ISBN 0 340 76725 1

Printed and bound in Great Britain by
Mackays of Chatham plc, Chatham, Kent

Hodder and Stoughton
A division of Hodder Headline PLC
338 Euston Road
London NW1 3BH

ROSE COTTAGE

To the gentle shades of Henry, George, Patsy, Nip, Rosy, Maudie and Muffin, and all the other friends whom I met again in my stroll down Memory Lane.

1

It is 1947, a calm, still day of June. On the wide spreading moorland the ling is dark and as yet unflowering, but the bell heather is out, and bees are busy. Sunday afternoon peace. A grouse calls somewhere, safe still for a few weeks from men and guns.

The weather has been fine, and the hillside is dry, but a little way down the slope the cotton-grass shows fluffy-white among the reeds and dwarf thickets of bog myrtle. A tiny burn drips and trickles down to where the bog water gathers in dark brown pools, to soak away gently towards the river that winds along the base of the strath.

Strathbeg, the valley is called on the maps, the small glen. To its few inhabitants it is just "the glen", and the big house, Strathbeg Lodge, to be glimpsed among its sheltering trees some way below, is simply "the House". Built originally as a shooting-lodge, it has belonged for some years to the Brandons, who used to come here each year in summer from their home in the north of England. From a distance the Lodge is imposing, with its baronial turreting and stepped roofing, its well-grown timber and its lawns reaching to the river with its series of salmon pools, but from nearer can be seen the signs of the neglect enforced by the recent war; the woodwork could do with a coat of paint, the rhones all too obviously need to be cleaned out, the lawns are no longer lawns, but pastures cropped by sheep. It is still not possible, two years after the end of the war, to find the labour and the materials necessary to restore the place to good order, but the family make the best of it, and the best, in fact, is very pleasant. After the traumas and shortages of the war years the glen is a haven of peace, and a steady supply of milk, eggs, fish, mutton and venison goes a long way to make up for threadbare carpets and unmended pipes and the eccentricities of the plumbing.

The family, what is left of it, came here to stay in 1940, when their English home was requisitioned by the RAF. Lady Brandon settled in with her married daughter and the daughter's two children. Sir James spent his war in London, only travelling north for brief leaves. The son, Gilbert, who was unmarried, was killed at El Alamein. Now that the war is over the son-in-law, Major Drew, is home, and taking over on behalf of his own small son, William, who is the heir. Sir James is home, too, but feels his age these days – he is well into his sixties – and the family seems to have settled happily enough into the quiet glen. Tod Hall, their home in England, having housed a series of high-spirited airmen dedicated to living the brief span of their doomed young lives to the full, has suffered so much damage that Sir James, without too much regret,

2

has decided to use the compensatory cash to turn it into an hotel, and himself retire for good into the peace of Strathbeg. A peace which, at this moment, one could believe never to have been broken.

The burn, lapsing in whispers, is, apart from the bees, the only sound in the day. Both are drowned in the sudden *hear ye, hear ye* preliminary whistle of a curlew, and then the sky is filled, it seems, with the beautiful long, liquid call that is perhaps the loveliest, the most thrilling of all birds" songs. "The silver chain of sound" was how George Meredith described the lark's singing, and poet after poet has added praise to the nightingale; but it would take all the poets, from Wordsworth down, to do justice to the curlew's call. I, certainly, cannot describe it, other than to say that every time that liquid gold pours and bubbles through the sky, my skin furs up like a cat's and my throat tightens with tears.

This was the effect that the song was having on the young woman who sat near the brow of the hill. She sat at ease on the heather, apparently with no other thought than to listen to the curlew's song. She was a tall girl in her mid-twenties, dressed in a tweed skirt that looked expensive, and a silk shirt. Her hair was dark and fashionably cut, slightly ruffled in the shifting hilltop air. Her eyes – dark, too – were fixed on the curlew which, suddenly falling silent, was gliding to the heather some two hundred yards away. It would land, she knew, well short of its objective, and make a long and circuitous approach to the hiding-place of its lurking, all-but-invisible young. It had, while pouring out that glorious, heart-piercing song, most certainly had both beady eyes on her, and would be watching her still.

As the thought touched her, she saw the foolish,

long-beaked head pop up against the skyline, then vanish again swiftly, as no doubt the scuttling babies were herded away to safety. She smiled, and with the smile her face – which in repose was perhaps too serious, too set with some sort of private effort at self-rule – lighted, as she had been told at various times that it did, to a kind of beauty.

As she had been told. As I suppose I may not say for myself, since the girl (who was getting to her feet and brushing the heather-dust from her skirt, in preparation for setting off downhill) was myself. Myself when young, some fifty years ago. Mrs Kate Herrick, aged twenty-four, widowed, well-to-do, and here in Strathbeg to visit her grandmother, who was employed as cook at the House.

Somewhere deep in the heather the grouse called again, "Come back! Come back!" And indeed Mrs Kate Herrick, who had been Kathy Welland, and who had helped in the kitchen and sometimes in the gardens of the House, had at last, and after more than four years, come back.

I looked at my watch. Gran would be awake now and, after the comings and goings of the morning, there would be time at last for that private talk. I had not arrived till late on the previous night, and still did not know why she had so urgently summoned me north "to have a real talk. No, not on the phone, hen, I'll tell you when you come." Then as an afterthought: "You do remember Rose Cottage, don't you?"

Of course I remembered Rose Cottage. It was one of the cottages on the Brandons' English estate, and lay some two miles from the village of Todhall. My grandfather as a young man had been a gardener at the Hall, and one summer, when the family (as the

4

Brandons were locally known) went north to their newly purchased Scottish estate, he went with them, to help with the recovery and re-making of the long-neglected garden. There he met and fell in love with Mary Campbell, the kitchen-maid. They were married the following spring, in Todhall. A year later their daughter was born. In an uncharacteristically poetic moment they called her Lilias, a name taken from one of the portraits of long-dead Brandons that hung at the Hall. Lilias was my mother. I barely remembered her, but the memory was all delightful. Deliciously pretty, full of joyous spirits and invariably kind, she danced her way up from scullery-maid to the heights of house-maiding at the Hall with a light heart and, as was found to my cost, what her eighteenth-century namesake would have called a light skirt.

I had never been told who my father was. My mother was of course banished from service at the Hall when she was found to be pregnant. Her parents, defying the customs of the time, took her in, and cared lovingly for her and, in due time, for her baby, while the Brandons, without a word on the subject, left their gardener and their cook to manage their own affairs. Which showed their good sense, since cooks as good as my grandmother were even in those days hard to come by.

When I was five years old, my grandfather died. I could barely remember him; a comfortable, earth-smelling giant who when my mother was elsewhere used to take me up to the walled garden and let me play – "helping Granddad," he called it – in the back premises behind the glasshouses. Soon after his death Gran's elder sister came from Scotland "to keep her company". This was Aunt Betsy, and with her came change.

Aunt Betsy was religious. Her religion, which kept her very strictly in the paths of righteousness, also obliged her to see that other people trod the same thorny path. Things which had never been said before, were said now, and frequently. (So much I did hear, later, from my grandmother.) Rose Cottage was no longer a place of kindness, but of Godliness with a capital G. My mother stood it for a year, then one night, soon after my sixth birthday, she left.

The room I shared with her was at the front of the cottage, over the kitchen, which was our main living-room. I was wakened from sleep by raised voices. Gran's, urgent with something that could have been despair or anger. My mother's, unwontedly shrill and tearful. Aunt Betsy's, high, hard, and assured. I slid down under the bedclothes and covered my ears.

A door slammed. I pushed the blankets back and sat up. Light footsteps on the bare wooden stairs. My bedroom door opening softly. My mother at my bedside, arms tight round me. A hand coming gently to stifle my questions.

"It's all right, love. All right. Mummy's going away for a bit, that's all. Be a good girl now, won't you?"

"Where're you going?"

"Just away. Not far."

"Can't I come too?"

"No, baby, no. But I'll come home soon, see if I don't, and then old Sourpuss'll get her cards, and we'll all be happy again." A giggle, then a swift kiss, which let me know that there were tears on her cheeks. "I've got to go. Mind your books at school now, Kathy. You're a bright girl, and you'll go a long way. See it's a better way than me. Go to sleep now, lovey, and don't forget your mum." A quick hug and another kiss. "Good night, baby."

I stood at the window and watched her go down the front path. The moonlight was strong enough for me to see that she had Granddad's battered old Gladstone bag in one hand, and in the other a bulging bass carrier of the sort that the family used for game and salmon.

I never saw her again. She had gone with the gipsies, Gran said. Every year they came to the same lane near our house for a few nights, and they were there on the night she left. But by morning the camp had vanished without trace, and there had been no way of getting in touch with her. From time to time she wrote, usually with the cards she sent for Christmas and for Gran's and my birthdays. Some two years later she sent news that she was going to be married ("so tell the old cat") and was off to Ireland where "Jamie" had been offered a job. She would write from there and tell us all about it. But she never did. She had been killed in a bus crash, she and her Jamie, somewhere in the west of Ireland. That was all Gran told me; it was Aunt Betsy, inevitably, who gave me the details. The couple had been the only passengers in the small country bus, when, in the dark, it ran into a stray bullock loose on the road, and plunged down a bank and burst into flames. The driver, "a good man, though no doubt he was a Catholic", had been thrown clear, but had been badly burned himself in trying to free the two passengers. "And it was to be hoped" (this was Aunt Betsy again) "that they were dead already."

I do not know what Gran would have said if she had known about this, but, childlike, I said nothing, and took out my grief and horror in nightmares. But when, a little time later, Aunt Betsy was found to be working a text in cross-stitch which said THE WAGES OF

SIN IS DEATH, my grandmother, normally the gentlest of women, tore it out of her sister's hands and threw it into the fire.

And for once Aunt Betsy never said a word.

2

When I was sixteen the war broke out. I was at the local grammar school. The only other girl from the village who went was the vicar's daughter, Prissy Lockwood. Our cottage lay almost two miles from the village, on the way to the station, and Prissy and I travelled together daily, two stops down the line. She was just about my only contact with the village in those days; there was very little to do in Todhall, and our relations with the Hall were hardly social. I worked there when I could – a shilling an hour – helping Gran in the kitchen. It paid my train fares, and helped a little here and there. At home I kept a good deal to my room, working most evenings at my school-books, to keep out of Aunt Betsy's way. My great-aunt was a good housekeeper, and I am sure that she was a help to Gran, who was working most days away at the Hall, but I knew that she still regarded me as the offspring – and probably the inheritor – of Sin, and things were never other than distant between us. I sometimes caught her watching me with what looked like positive dislike, but it is impossible to be accurate about such things, and her normal expression was, to say the least, sour and forbidding. She died in 1945, of a cancer that we had never suspected, and which she bore with the same ferocious strength that she had brought to her fight against Sin. By that time I had been away from home for nearly five years.

In 1940 the Hall was taken over by the RAF, and the family went north and asked Gran to go with them. She went with few regrets, her only worry being my future. Aunt Betsy (who in fact had not been asked to go) declined to leave Todhall; Gran would be "living in" at Strathbeg Lodge, and there were new tenants in the Campbell cottage there, so Rose Cottage must remain her home. Things looked bleak for me. But here the vicar and his wife intervened, having no doubt heard something of my situation from Prissy. For my final year at school I was to lodge at the vicarage, and Prissy and I would take our Highers together. Which is what happened. My results were rather better than Prissy's, a fact which she accepted with cheerful indifference: she had never had any ambitions beyond marriage and a family, and in fact, after leaving school, she only put in a year with me at a teachers' training college in Durham before marrying a young officer whom she met on holiday, and relinquishing her college place without regret. I finished my course and was then – to my grandmother's delighted pride – appointed to an elementary school in a small Yorkshire town. I found lodgings near at hand, and, since I spent my holidays in Scotland, where I was glad to earn a little extra by "helping out" at the House, I saw nothing of Todhall for the next few years.

Of my marriage I will say little except that it was a typical war-time affair, too commonplace in those days to be seen as tragic. I met Jonathan Herrick at a concert given by Yehudi Menuhin. In those days the great artists travelled the country, taking music to out-of-the-way places, playing sometimes even in village halls. Jon and I had seats next to one another. We were both in uniform – he was a Flying Officer, and I did part-time war service in the Royal Observer Corps, and had just come off duty – and in the intervals we talked, and after the concert we went out together and sat for hours over ersatz coffee in some small bar-café. We met again, took a bus out into the country and walked and talked. I don't remember what about; he told me little of himself or his family, and nothing of his work; I knew merely that he was flying bombing missions over Germany. I took to watching and listening for the Halifaxes on "bombers' nights", and, when I was on duty, painfully trying to track the numbers of aircraft going and returning, without ever knowing which missions he was on.

In a short time – time was precious in those days – and after a few more meetings, I found that I loved him. We married, a typically hasty war-time affair, at which not even Gran (who was temporarily back at Todhall nursing Aunt Betsy) could be present. Five weeks later, in the last months of the war, Jonathan was killed. I found, to my stupefaction, that he had been wealthy, the only son of well-to-do parents who were both killed when a flying bomb got their Sussex home in a direct hit. That, with all it had held, was gone, but there was a London flat, and a great deal of money, all of it apparently mine. No angry relative turned up to contest it; there was no one, and Jon, his lawyers told me gently, had been careful to make a Will a few days before we were married. So there was I, Kate Herrick (Jon had hated the name Kathy and never called me by it), wealthy, widowed, and quite content to throw up her teaching job just as soon as the war ended, and move to the London flat. Eventually, because I found it hard to do nothing, but had no desire to go on teaching, I went to work in a big plant nursery at Richmond, which was run by the widow of one of Jon's friends, whom I had met during the brief days of my marriage.

Then came Gran's telephone call.

I was working in the potting rooms behind the shop. We had just had a delivery of pot-plants, and I was unpacking them, when one of the young sales assistants came running in.

"Phone for you, Kate. Long distance, so hurry."

I set down the pots I was holding, and wiped my hands hurriedly on the tissue wrapping. "Who is it, do you know? The Dutchmen, I hope? Those bulbs should have been here a week ago."

"I don't think so. Moddom says it's private. It's in her office, and so's she." "Moddom" was the junior help's name for Angela Platt-Harman, the owner of Platt's Plants, and my employer.

"Oh dear," I said. We were not supposed to make or take private calls at work, but my apprehension was only a token, a kind of expression of solidarity with my co-employees. In the work-place Angie and I were always, carefully, employer and employed.

"It's all right, she didn't look mad." She hesitated. "I was in the office when she answered it, and she sent me to find you. It's Scotland. Doesn't your family live there? I hope it's not –"

I didn't wait to hear what she hoped it wasn't. I ran to the office.

Angie was speaking into the telephone. "No, it's no trouble. Quite all right, really. Ah, here she is now, Just a moment." She covered the receiver with her hand. "Kate, it's your grandmother, but don't worry, she says there's nothing wrong." She handed me the receiver and pointed me to the chair behind her desk. "Take your time. I'll see to the shipment." She went out of the office.

I sat down. "Hullo, Gran? How lovely to hear you. How are you? When they said it was Scotland, I was afraid there might be something wrong. Are you all right?"

"I'm well enough." It seemed to me, though, that there was a quaver in the old voice that told of some distress or urgency. "It's all a lot of fuss, nothing but a touch of flu, and you know how it goes to my stomach, and the fool of a doctor says I'm not to go back to work for a bit yet, but I'm fine now, and come the month-end I'll be back at the House. That Morag may fancy herself at the clootie dumplings and broth and such, but she's a lot to learn afore she can dress a fish properly, or put a dinner on when they've company."

"Don't you worry about that, Gran. They'll do all right at the House. Just get yourself better, that's what matters. But hang on a minute, I didn't know you'd been ill. What is it? You said stomach trouble? What does the doctor say?"

"Never mind that now. This is dear, phoning. I know I didn't ought to have called you at work, but I can't get to a phone in the evenings, and you and I've got to have a real talk, and not on the phone. What I wanted to ask you – Kathy, hen, when do you get your holidays?"

"When I ask for them. I'm due some time, anyway.

13

Do you want me to come up now, Gran? Of course I will! I can look after you if you're supposed to rest. In fact I'd love to come. London's horrid in June. Can they have me? Will I be in my old room?" My room had been a small attic at the House, with no mod. cons., but with a breathtaking view over the whole length of the glen, right to the distant gleam of the sea-loch.

"No, didn't I tell you? I've got my own place now. I've got Duncan Stewart's house, down by the burnside. You'll mind the one, with the wee garden that used to be the kailyard."

"I remember it. How lovely! No, you didn't tell me."

"Oh, well, you know I'm not much of a hand at writing, and it's a long way to the post office for the telephone, and my legs aren't so good these days."

"Are you phoning from there now?"

"No, from the hospital. Now don't fret yourself, I'm going home tomorrow, and Kirsty Macdonald – you mind her, she has the house next door – says she can look after me fine. But there's something I want to talk to you about, Kathy love, and something I want you to do for me. It's important, and it won't wait. No, not on the phone, hen, the girls at the desk hear everything. It'll keep till you get here. It's about Rose Cottage – you do remember Rose Cottage, don't you? Well, then, can you really come?"

"Of course I can. I'll go and see the boss now, and I'll be with you some time at the weekend. Take care, Gran, won't you? 'Bye, then. Love."

I cradled the receiver, then lifted it again and got the number of the Lodge. It rang for a long time before a woman's breathless voice answered it.

"Hullo? Strathbeg Lodge."

"Hullo. Is that Mrs Drew?"

14

"Speaking. Sorry to keep you waiting. I was out in the garden with the children. Who is it, please?"

"Oh, madam, it's Kate Herrick. Kathy Welland. I'm sorry to trouble you, but I was worried about my grandmother. She's just rung me up from the hospital, but she won't tell me much about it. I gathered it was some sort of gastric flu, but I did wonder if she was all right? Do you know about it?"

"Kathy, how nice to hear from you. Yes, your grandmother did have to go into the Cottage Hospital last week. She's been off colour for some time now, but she wouldn't admit to anything, so in the end Dr McLeod sent her in, really just for a rest, and he said while she was there they'd do some tests."

"Tests?" Somehow the word held a world of fearful speculation.

"Yes. These stomach upsets she's been having lately. Didn't she tell you? I think they were wondering about an ulcer. William, take that puppy out of here at once, *at once* – oh, hell, now see what's happened! Go and get a cloth. I don't know, ask Morag – no, do *not* ask Morag to do it, do it yourself. I'm so sorry, Kathy. I was saying. Your grandmother is coming home tomorrow, and I think we'll hear in a week or so if there's anything wrong. But really, she was just a bit tired and run down, with something like a mild flu, but Dr McLeod thought she should go in for examination. I don't honestly know any more, but if you'd like me to keep you in touch – you're coming up? Oh, great, that'll do her more good than anything else. Dear God, there's that puppy again. William! *William!* When will you get here, Kathy? Saturday night? I'll ask Angus to meet the train, shall I?"

"That's very kind of you, madam. Is her ladyship well?"

"Very well. We all are. I'll tell her you were asking. And do come and see us. Mother will be so pleased."

So it had been arranged. Angie had been kind, the train had run on time, Angus had met it with the pony-trap, and I had found Kirsty in capable charge at Gran's cottage, with Gran herself in bed, and so relieved and happy to see me that she had gone almost straight to sleep. In the morning, with a visit from the district nurse and calls from two neighbours on their way home from the kirk, and Kirsty's busy presence, there had been no time for any private talk with Gran. The nurse, when I questioned her, was so professionally discreet that I was sure she knew nothing. Kirsty went back next door at lunch-time and I took Gran her soup and toast, but she looked tired, so when I went up to collect the dishes I smoothed the quilt over her, drew the curtains, and left her to sleep.

Then walked up the hill to sit in the sun and listen to the curlew's song.

3

Gran was sitting up against her pillows when I went upstairs after washing the supper dishes and saying goodnight to Kirsty, who had eaten with us.

"Well, and did you have a nice walk?"

"Lovely. How are you feeling now, Gran?"

"I'm fine. Now pull that chair up where I can see you properly. Hm. Very smart, I'm sure. Where'd you get that skirt, London? So they have tartans there now, do they?"

"England's pretty civilised these days. But you've had me worried, you know. What's it all about? If you say you're not really ill –"

"I'm not. I'll be up and about again in a wee while, but I can't say I'm not glad of a bit of a rest just now. It's a lot of standing, cooking, and my legs aren't as good as they were. Once this stomach's settled, I'll be as good as new, forbye a bit of the rheumatism when the weather's

17

no' right." A trace of her girlhood's accent had come back, I noticed, to mix quite kindly with the familiar North-country lilt.

"You want to go back to work? Truly? You don't have to, you know."

"What would I do with myself if I didn't? Nay, lass, we've had all this out and settled, so say no more. I'm as well here as I'll ever be, with folk I know, and with you coming home when you get your holidays, and the family for ever in and out of the door. It suits me fine, for all I miss Todhall and the folks there. Now tell me about yourself and this grand London job, for all I'd have thought you should have something better than working in a shop."

It was plain that, whatever she had to say to me, she would say it in her own time, so I stifled my curiosity and told her as much of my London news as I thought would interest her. I had only seen her once since my marriage, a flying visit in the summer of 1945, as soon as term ended, to tell her about Jon and that I was giving up my school job and going, at any rate until our affairs were sorted out, to London. I had offered to stay with her at Strathbeg, but, predictably, she would not hear of it. I must make a new life for myself now among my new friends (she meant, but did not say, "better myself") and try to let time heal the wounds of war. Not that she put it like that, but once again I knew what she meant; "stay where you're more likely to meet somebody else when you've got over it."

I knew she was hoping that this would be my news, but she bore very well with the daily doings at Platt's Plants, and then in her turn she brought me up to date with the happenings in the glen, and the affairs of the family at the House.

"I phoned them," I told her, "and Mrs Drew asked me to go over and see them."

"Well, of course you have to. Her ladyship's always asking after you. She'll tell you about it herself."

She was not looking at me as she spoke, but at something beyond the bedroom window. Not the blue hilltops of the summer evening; something further away even than they.

We had come to it at last. I said gently, "Tell me what?"

The roughened hands moved on the quilt. "It was something I heard not long syne. Something the family are doing at Todhall."

"Yes? Do you mean them turning the Hall over into a hotel? I heard that, too; in fact, I think they've already started."

"Aye, they have. Annie Pascoe wrote me. Jim and Davey are working there." Jim Pascoe was the Todhall carpenter, and Davey was his son. His wife, "Aunty Annie" to me since childhood, was my godmother.

"Do you mind very much, Gran?"

"What's the use of minding?" Recovering herself, she was brisk. "It was a nice house, and I liked my kitchen – better than the one I've got here – but it had to come, and I'm well enough myself back here in the glen, and now with my own home. No, it's not the Hall, it's the house. Our own house. Rose Cottage."

"What about it? Do you mean they're altering that as well? Or are they selling it?"

"Not selling it, no, not yet. But there was talk of converting it – making one of those hotel places where folk fend for themselves, I forget what they call them."

"Annexes? Self-catering cottages?"

"That would be it. Like a hotel, but you do your own cooking. So if our cottage has to be made over, they'll be making big changes there, too."

"I suppose they'd have to, yes, surely. There'd have to be a better bathroom, and I dare say they'll put an electric cooker in, and a few other things, like a fridge and a washing-machine? But Granddad always said the building was sound, so they won't have to pull any of it down, will they?"

"That'd be enough, the electric stove, I mean. They'll be taking the fireplace out for it, or if they make the back-place into one of those wee kitchens – kitchenettes, they call them" – the word held a world of scorn – "they'll surely take out my old kitchen range and put a sitting-room fireplace into the front room."

"I suppose so. Gran, do you mind very much? I think – yes, I think I'll mind, a bit. And it was your home and Granddad's for all those years. You weren't hoping to go back one day, were you?"

She wasn't listening. A hand moved, briefly, to touch my knee. "So that's it, Kathy. That's why I asked you to come."

"I don't see –"

"Listen. You never knew it, and nor, thank the good Lord, did your Aunt Betsy, but just aside the fireplace, on the left near the mantelshelf, there's a cupboard let into the wall."

"Is there? Really? I never saw one."

"No, you wouldn't, not without you knew where to look. Not to look, at that, but feel. It's tiny, no more than a tin box built into the wall, and it's been hidden – papered over – these many years. Do you mind the time we put that pretty paper on, with the autumn leaves and berries?"

20

"Not really. Was it – yes, wasn't it soon after Grand-dad died, just before Aunt Betsy came to stay? You and – you did it yourself, didn't you?"

"That's right. Lilias and I did it together." A silence, that I took care not to break. After a while she said, heavily, "For all that your Granddad was gone, that was a happy time."

I waited. When she spoke again she was answering, I knew, what had not been said.

"And then Betsy came. She was a good woman, your great-aunt, make no mistake about that, for all she was never one to be easy with. Nor to share secrets with, neither. So she never knew about the cupboard."

"Gran, you said to the left of the fireplace. Do you mean behind the picture there?"

"I do. A holy text. Your aunt thought a lot of that text." A twinkle. "She was a tidy body about the house, your Aunt Betsy, and a good enough cook, but she was never great with the mop and duster. You might say that she dusted kind of reverent, without disturbing things, nor lifting them about, so she never noticed it. But I made sure. I only opened it up again the once, when she was from home, to put –" – a pause – "to put Lilias's bangle away. You'll remember that. They sent it over from Ireland after the accident. It was all there was, and I didn't want Betsy to see it, and maybe ... Oh, well, never mind that. So then I made a real job of it, plastered it over nice and flat and matched the paper up, so if she ever did lift the picture down she'd not see anything, forbye a bit of a bubble in the pattern, where the keyhole is. Oh, it was safe enough, even at the spring-clean, or when we had to paper again. That's what your granddad used to call it, 'the safe'."

I said slowly: "I'm getting there, I think. There's something there still, in the 'safe'?"

"That's right. In all the clamjamphrie of the flitting, and giving the family a hand with their gear, I never thought about it. Nor at the time when your Aunt Betsy was took. The district nurse came most days, and Annie Pascoe helped out when I needed it, and what with one thing and another I never gave a thought to the safe. Maybe I was still thinking we'd be back there one day." A sigh, and another look through the window at something far away and long ago. Then back to me. "So what's there will still be there – that is, until they start pulling the fireplace out and find it."

"What is there, Gran?"

"Family things. Not valuable, except maybe for the five golden sovereigns that Sir Giles, as was the Squire then, gave your Granddad on our wedding day, and which he'd never dream of spending, but all things I'd sorrow to lose. My ring that your Granddad gave me when we were promised, and the brooch my lady gave me for a wedding-present, lovely it was, you've seen it, pearls and those green stones, I misremember the name."

"Peridots."

"That's it. And there's your Mum's bracelet like I told you, and the letters your Granddad wrote me from France when he was fighting, if letters you can call them; one of them was written on a bit of cardboard torn off a box, and it got to me just as if it had been in a proper envelope, and registered at that. And his medals, he got two, and his watch and his wedding ring and a whole bundle of papers – my marriage lines, and your Mum's birth certificate and – well, all that sort of thing."

"My birth certificate, you mean?"

A silence.

"It's all right, Gran dear. I've seen it."

"You've seen it?" She was sharp. "How?"

"A copy, that's all. I wrote to Somerset House for a copy. I wanted to see it for myself, and make sure. You see, I'd told Jon all about us – my family, I mean. I showed it to him. You do understand, don't you?"

"Aye," she said, "I do. And you did right." The clasped hands shifted on the coverlet. "Well, then, I don't need to tell you you'd get nothing from that. He's not on it."

"No." A pause, then I leaned forward to touch the old hands, lightly. "Gran."

"Eh, what now?"

"Look, Gran, I'm not sixteen any more and still at school. I've been married and widowed, and I'm twenty-four, and people think differently, anyway, since the war. I know you've always said you didn't know who he was, but if you're just trying to save me from hearing something I won't like –"

"Kathy love, don't. It's true I don't know. You have to believe me. She never told me. And guessing doesn't get you anywhere."

"Guessing? You can guess?"

My voice must have been sharp. She glanced up at me, then with a little gesture as if smoothing the air, said uncertainly: "It was nothing as anyone knew. Nothing to tell you."

"What was it? Gran, dear Gran, you must tell me, you really must. I've a right to know anything, anything at all."

"It's true, you have," she said, then, as if reluctantly, "all right. All I can tell you is what they said in the village at the time. There was gipsies camped in the lonnen – you remember Gipsy Lonnen?"

"Yes." It was a lane near Rose Cottage, a short cut to the station that the village rarely used.

"They were there that time, when she left. In the lonnen, with tents and a caravan. And they'd gone next day. So folks said she'd gone with them."

"They would. Maybe she did. But that doesn't mean it's anything to do with me, with who fathered me, I mean. I was six years old when she left."

"Yes. Well. The tale went that it was one of them, that she went with him some time when they'd been there before, and that when she left she went back to him. That's all. I told you it was nothing. Folks will say anything, and next time round they'll believe it." She touched my hand again. "I'm sorry, love. That's all there is. And now that she's gone, we'll never know."

Silence again. I stood up and went to the window. It was still light, the tranquil blue-grey twilight of the Highland summer. Somewhere a thrush was singing. I turned and spoke gently.

"Ah, well, it hardly matters now. I'm myself, and owing no one, except you and Granddad and Jon. Thanks for telling me, and let's forget it." I went back to the chair and sat down. "Okay, Gran. Now, have I got this right? You want me to go to Todhall and get your things from the safe before someone else finds them."

"That's it. But there's more."

"More?"

"Aye. Now I've got my own place here, I'd like fine to have the rest of my things sent up. The furniture, I mean, and some of the stuff that I left for your Aunt Betsy to use. Not all the furniture, I've neither room nor need for the beds and such, but there's my sideboard, and the good bits and pieces in Betsy's room, and some of the pictures and ornaments, and my rosebud tea-set, and his rocking-chair. I don't need the table, there's a good one here, and plenty chairs . . .

I'll make a list. I've talked to her ladyship about it, and you're welcome to go there and take what you want. She's sent word that the men are to keep away till she tells them. So you'll go, won't you?"

"Well, of course I will. I'll go just as soon as you like."

"And keep a good eye on the movers, lass, there's not one of them I'd trust an inch not to break my rosebud china."

"I'll watch them, never fear."

"There's just one thing –"

"Yes?"

"The safe's locked," said Gran, looking guilty, "and I misremember where the key is."

I laughed. "That's useful. If I have to get one made to fit – is Bob Corner still at the smithy?"

"He is so, but whether he can turn his hand to anything as wee as that . . . Ah, well, I'll try to think on about the places I might have put the key, and you could look about. But it might take you a day or two."

"That's all right. Can I stay in the cottage, sleep there? I don't want to have to stay at the Black Bull and walk two miles each way."

"It's all right, you'll do fine at home. It's just as your Aunt Betsy had it, and your room's still as it was. Annie's been in to keep it aired and decent, but you'll be sure to air the mattress –"

I laughed. "Don't worry. I'll have the place liveable-in in no time. But what on earth is the village going to say when I arrive on my own out of the blue and open the cottage up?"

"It's that far from the village that they mayn't even notice. Not that I'd count on that while the Miss Popes are still there, nosy old bodies. And Miss Linsey, who's no better, and daft forbye. But" – a twinkle as she looked me up and down – "I'm wondering if they'll connect this smart young lady Mrs Herrick with little Kathy Welland that always had dirty knees and her hair in a fine tangle. If you keep yourself to yourself for a few days –"

"I'll do just that. And I didn't have dirty knees when I was sixteen, and going to the Sec! No, they'll know me all right, and they can think what they like. Now look how late it is. You ought to be asleep, and so should I. Would you like a hot drink or anything?"

"Seeing as I'm here on my native heath, as the saying is," said Gran, primly, "I'll take a wee dram, and you'll find the bottle at the back of the press there, where Kirsty won't find it without I see her."

"Okay. I'll get a glass. Two glasses, if I may?" I got to my feet. "And don't worry any more, Gran dear, I'll get your treasures safe for you, and anything else you want from home. You just think on, and we'll make a list in the morning."

I walked along to the House next morning.

I went, as I had always done, past the stables and the walled garden and into the yard behind the house, where a stout, middle-aged woman was pegging some tea-towels out on the line. This must be Morag; Gran had told me that the only other "help" now was a girl of sixteen who came mornings, and I could hear the vacuum cleaner going somewhere behind an upstairs window.

Morag, who was new since my last visit to Strathbeg, did not look in the least like the apprentice that Gran had described to me; she was well into her forties, looked immensely capable, and I thought I would have backed her clootie dumplings against anyone else's *haute cuisine* anywhere.

She turned as I approached.

"Good morning," I said. "I'm Mrs Welland's grand-daughter Kathy. You must be Morag? I'm sorry, but I don't know your other name. It's Mrs –?"

"Morag'll do fine. So you're Kathy." We shook hands. She looked me up and down, not rudely, but with a sort of cautious appraisal. "You're welcome, I'm sure. Her ladyship said you might be coming down."

"Is it convenient now? I really just called to see – I could come later, but I may be going south again tomorrow."

"It's all right, come away in. You might as well come this way now you're here. It's through the kitchen."

"I know. It's the way I'm used to."

She gave me another look where I thought I saw a touch of sour approval. "Aye, well . . . And how's your grandma?"

"Glad to be home again. Hospitals are good places to get out of. You know, this feels a bit like home to me, too. The kitchen looks just the same, and you've been baking . . . It smells good."

A tightening of the lips that might be meant for a smile. "Scones. I'd a mind to send some up to Mrs Welland, but she'd maybe no" think they were good enough."

"She'd like it fine, I'm sure, and I'd certainly appreciate them, if you'd let me take them up. Thanks very much." I tried a touch of diplomacy. "It's nice that she can be so easy in her mind, with you here. Do you come from somewhere in the glen?"

"No. I'm from Inverness, but I like it fine here in the summer. The winter's another thing, but there's a while to go yet before that. Well, if you'll bide a bit while I see to the oven . . ." She lifted the baking-sheet out and began to set the delicious-smelling scones out on the rack to cool.

"The house is very quiet, isn't it?" I said. "Where are the children? I'd have liked to see them. William wasn't much more than a baby when I was here before, and Sarah was in her pram. Are they out?"

It seemed that they were. "Himself", as she called Sir James, was down by the river after the fish, and the Major was along with him. Mrs Drew had gone up to the village to meet the Bank – I would mind, said Morag, setting the last scone in place, that Monday was the day the Bank came to the glen – but her ladyship was in her room writing letters. I'd mind the room? The wee sitting-room by the side door? I did? Then did I want to go through now, or would she tell her ladyship I was here?

I hesitated. "Would you mind telling her, Morag? I don't like just to walk through if she's busy."

That nod of approval again. She wiped her hands on her apron, took it off, then led me along the well-known passage to the green baize door, that traditional barrier between the back and the front of the house. I could not guess what Morag had heard about me, nor what she had expected, but it was obvious that, in her view, I had quite properly kept to my own side of that barrier.

Going through the green door was like going back in time. It was all just as I remembered it. There was the wide hall, carpeted with worn and faded rugs which had once been valuable, and cluttered, rather than furnished, with enormous cupboards and chests rather in need of polishing, and a long table littered with gloves and newspapers and copies of the *Scottish Field* and a gardener's trug of hand-tools. Against the once-crimson walls hung pictures in heavy gilt frames, painted it seemed mainly in shades of sepia and Vandyke brown. All familiar; I had dusted or polished every item. Familiar, too, was the big bowl, full of water for the dogs, that stood on the floor by the drawing-room door. I had refilled it scores of times, carrying it carefully from the cloakroom by the front door. But never, I thought, as carefully as I would carry it now that I could recognise it for what it was, an immensely valuable piece of blue-and-white Ming. Beside it lay a half-chewed bone, presumably left there by William's puppy.

The sitting-room door was ajar, and Morag pushed it open to let a shaft of sunshine through onto these dim splendours.

"It's Kathy Welland, m'lady."

Lady Brandon turned and laid down her pen, then got up from her writing-table and came, smiling, to meet me.

"Oh, Kathy, good morning. Thank you, Morag. Kathy, how nice to see you, and how well you're looking. Come in. What a lovely day, isn't it? Sit down, my dear, and tell me how your grandmother is."

For all the years that had passed, and all that had happened in them of change, both in myself and in the world at large, I felt awkward as I went forward to shake hands. Last time I had been in that sunny little room it was to clean out the fire and do the dusting. But Lady Brandon, easy and kind as always, and of course vastly experienced, saw us both smoothly through the moment, and soon had me settled with her in the sunshine of the bay window, answering her questions.

She was a slightly built woman, too thin for her height, but with the elegance that this gave her. I noticed with wry amusement that she was dressed very much as I was, silk blouse, tweed skirt, woollen jacket. Uniform, almost, this side of the baize door. It didn't stop me feeling tongue-tied, and wanting to sit on the edge of my chair, but as she talked on, charmingly, about Gran, I found myself relaxing into naturalness and even ease.

"I'm hoping to call and see her soon," she said. "Perhaps this afternoon? Do you think she's up to it?"

"I'm sure she'd love to see you, my lady. She looks a bit thinner than I remember, and for once she admits to feeling tired, but she keeps saying there's nothing much wrong with her, except what the flu left behind." I hesitated. "I can't help wondering – this talk about tests at the hospital. She won't say anything to me, but I did wonder, do you know anything about it, I mean, if there might be something serious?"

"I'm afraid I don't know anything about that, but I do know that Dr McLeod isn't worried about her."

"He said so?"

"Yes. So I think you needn't be too anxious. I don't think your grandmother will be an invalid for very long. Were you planning to stay and look after her? I'm sure she'll love having you here. How long can you stay?"

"I've got a fortnight due to me, though I could take longer if I needed it. But actually I'm going south almost straight away. You see" – at her look of surprise – "it's Rose Cottage. Because of the plans to alter it, I mean. She's a bit anxious to get the rest of her things sent up, now that she's got a place of her own here. She wants me to go down straight away to see to it."

"I see. But is there any hurry about it? They won't do anything at the cottage until we give them the All Clear. I promised her that."

"Yes, I know. But – well, there's something she's worried about, and she wants me to see about it, and I think that – I mean, if her mind was at rest –" I faltered into silence. I did not think I could explain about Gran's "treasures" lying forgotten in their hiding-place.

I need not have worried that she would pursue it.

31

She said quickly, "It's all right, my dear. It's your grandmother's affair, she must do as she wants. Of course she would like her own things about her, and it's good that she has you to see to the move for her. Moving house, even only half a house, is a frightful job."

"It is only half a house, anyway – less than half what's there, I think. We made a list, and I've brought it for you to see, because she says she can't remember just what was already there – belonging to the Hall, I mean, when they moved in. Things like the big press in the back kitchen, and the table and chairs – she's leaving those anyway – and, well, here's the list. That's as much as she can remember of what's hers. If you would look at it, please, my lady, and see if it's right?"

"I'm sure it is. There's no need – very well, as you've gone to the trouble. Let me see it."

She took the paper. A brief silence as she studied, or pretended to study, the list we had made, and I looked around me at the familiar room. Pretty, washed-out chintzes and a Chinese carpet. A big bowl of flowers on a stand, and more in a vase on the mantelpiece, beside an assortment of fragile-looking china that I remembered all too well. Photographs everywhere, in silver frames. There were various ones of the children at different stages of growth, and of their mother, Mrs Drew, as a girl, as a debutante, and then as a bride. Beside her, on the bureau, was one of her brother, the dead son, Gilbert, young and smiling, in uniform, dark-haired and dark-eyed. Like me. Like an older brother. And indeed, he had been the nearest I had ever had to a brother; he had sometimes come down to the gardens when I had been there with Granddad, and I had been allowed to follow and admire him as his own sister never would – to retrieve the ball when he practised his bowling at the makeshift nets, to watch when he climbed the big cedar by the tennis court, to wait with the net while he fished the beck beside Rose Cottage . . .

I tore my eyes from the photograph and my mind away from what I was thinking. Had thought before; had tried not to think. Lady Brandon was folding the paper and she handed it back to me. "Well, please thank your grandmother for letting me see this, Kathy. I'm sure it's absolutely right. To tell you the truth I've quite forgotten what's there, and I don't know if an inventory was ever made, but please tell her that she's welcome to anything she wants to take."

"And it's all right for me to stay there while I'm seeing about the moving?"

She assured me that it was, and I thanked her, and said how much Gran appreciated having her own place here in Strathbeg, and how well she seemed to get along with Kirsty, and then for some minutes more we talked about the new plans for Tod Hall, and what might happen to Rose Cottage. I gathered that nothing had been settled there; the cottage might simply be re-let, if there was a ready taker, or even sold, "always providing that your grandmother doesn't want to go back there. I know how one feels about a place that has been home for so many years."

I thought that there was some personal feeling there for her, but said nothing.

She smiled at me, as if reading my thoughts, and added: "I don't know if your grandmother knows, but we're not leaving the place entirely. I've persuaded my husband to keep part of the south wing, the bit that overlooks the rose garden, and we're having a kitchen put in there – you remember the old flower-room? The joiners are working on that now. The main conversion is to be done by a big contractor, of course, but we did want to give our part of the work to local people, and the Pascoes always do such a good job."

"I'm sure the village will be pleased you're still there." I said. "The Hall will be missed, I know."

"I have such memories," she said. There was a short silence, and I wondered if I should go, but then she smiled at me again, and said, gently: "I haven't said, Kathy, how very sorry I was – we all were – to hear of your loss. It has been hard for you, I know." I made some sort of response, and then she asked me about my work in London, and whether I planned to go back to teaching, and the conversation slipped easily back to everyday things.

She went on to offer me coffee, but this I declined, more to save Morag's feelings than for any other reason. So I merely thanked her, took my leave, and went back through the green baize door to have coffee and newly baked scones in the kitchen with Morag.

5

At seven minutes to three on a warm June afternoon the train from Sunderland rattled into Todhall station and stopped with a jerk and a long, sighing puff of steam. On the platform was a porter I didn't recognise, a youth of perhaps sixteen, who would have been a small boy when I was last at home, but the old station-master just emerging from his office, watch in hand, was Mr Harbottle, who had been there for as long as I could remember. He did not see me, being busy consulting his watch, and nodding over it with satisfaction. The two-fifty-three was, as usual, exactly on time.

"Toddle!" shouted the porter, though no one but myself was alighting in the sleepy afternoon, then, "Toddle, miss?" as he opened the carriage door for me, and reached a hand out to take my case.

Coupled with his engaging grin and outstretched hand, it made a tempting invitation, but I controlled myself, saying merely, "Yes. Thank you," and stepped down to the platform. I handed him my ticket, and turned to speak to Mr Harbottle, but he was already on his way along the platform with his green flag at the ready, to exchange some no doubt vital information with the engine-driver whom he only saw four times a day and would not see again until five-fourteen, when the Earl Grey (as the stubby black and green engine was rather grandly named) pulled its coaches back to Sunderland.

Mr Harbottle looked at his watch again, the flag was lifted, the engine blew another noisy cloud of steam, the couplings clanged and strained, and the train chugged off. Without another glance in my direction, Mr Harbottle put his watch away, picked up a spade which was leaning against a pile of sleepers, and went back to what he had presumably been doing before the train came in – digging his new potatoes up and sorting them lovingly into an empty fire-bucket.

So much for Kathy Welland's homecoming. At my elbow the porter said, rather anxiously: "It's all of two mile into the village, miss. No bus nor nothing. Didn't they tell you when you booked?"

"It's all right. I haven't much to carry. I don't need the big case straight away. Can you keep it here till I can send for it? I can manage the other one easily." I had brought a light holdall with what I needed for the night.

"Easy. It can stay in the office." He swung it up and I followed him along the platform, past the chocolate machine (it was empty; I wondered if it had ever been refilled after Prissy and I took the last piece out six years ago), and the penny-in-the-slot Try-Your-Weight machine, and the flourishing beds of geraniums and calceolarias and love-in-a-mist.

"You staying in the village, miss? If it's the Black Bull, they're sending a cart along to meet the eight-sixteen in the morning. They've got beer coming then. I could put your bag on it if you like?"

The Black Bull was the village's single pub, four doors up from the vicarage, and next door to Barlow's shop where Prissy and I had spent our halfpennies on liquorice bootlaces and gobstoppers. The pub's loaded cart, I knew, would not want to turn aside down the steep lane that led from the high road to Rose Cottage.

"No, not the Black Bull," I said, "but don't you worry, I can get it picked up tomorrow. Thanks all the same." I gave him sixpence, which was twice the normal tip, but worth it for that smile again, as, with a cheerful "Ta, miss," he carried my case through the door marked "Station Master" and flanked by tubs of geraniums and lobelias.

As I went out into the sunny roadway I saw Mr Harbottle, still busy with his spade, getting on with his day's work at the far end of the platform. No doubt he was preparing, as he had done every year since long before I was born, to scoop most of the Firsts at the local Agricultural Show in July. Meanwhile Todhall would come, as usual, high on the Commended list for the county's best-kept station . . .

Memory Lane. Well, I still had two long, hot miles of it to go, if I went by the road, but I knew all the bypaths and short cuts for miles around, and had come comfortably dressed for the walk. I followed the road for perhaps a quarter of a mile, till I reached a field gate giving on a track that showed the triple ruts of the farmer's horse and cart. The track, shaded by an overgrown hedgerow, led along the side of a hayfield almost overdue for cutting, and deep in flowering grasses. A couple of hundred yards further, and I came to a gap in the hedgerow which had been roughly blocked by a criss-cross of hazel stems.

It was no more than a token barrier, easy to step over. I stepped over, and picked my way carefully down a steep bank into what had once been a lane, but was now little more than a path between high banks overgrown with ferns and weeds, and overshadowed by the rampant hedges. It was a deep, secret place. Gipsy Lonnen, the gipsies" lane.

It had changed, with time. Years ago it had been an open, grass-grown lane where sometimes the travelling gipsies would pitch for a few nights, nights when we, the village children, were strictly forbidden to venture out after sunset. We had obeyed, frightened into obedience with tales of children stolen away by the gipsies, tales which somehow got mixed up in my childish mind with the legendary abductions of Kilmeny and the little changeling boy and other creatures of poetry and fairy-tale.

Even by day, when no gipsies camped there, the lonnen had been a scary place. At some time in the past a caravan had been abandoned there. A frightened horse, possibly, had backed it sharply into the bank, and a wheel had broken adrift, and the shafts with it. The wreck, abandoned, had rotted and fallen still further apart, but it retained the shape of the caravan, and to our childish minds it was a place where the wicked gipsy ghosts of fiction lurked, ready to pounce. The boys, when we girls were watching, would dare one another to run up the lonnen and touch the shafts or the steps of the van, but only the hardiest spirits ever did this. The rest of us, cowards all, thought ourselves brave enough if we climbed down through the gap with the hazel-boughs and then ran hard along the half-mile of stony grass to the stile and the field above Rose Cottage. The only time that Gipsy Lonnen lost its terror for us was in bramble-time, when adults and children together took their baskets and buckets into the lane to harvest the blackberries.

Now I was an adult myself, and it was mid-afternoon, and there was no sign of gipsies. And the lonnen saved almost a mile. Somewhere out of sight to my right, presumably hidden now under the overgrowth of bramble and sapling, lay the remains of the gipsy van. I turned the other way. There was still a narrow path reasonably clear between high banks embroidered with wild roses and the white bramble-flowers. Campion and ragged robin showed everywhere among the crowding ferns and Jack-by-the-hedge, and the air was filled with the fresh, lovely smell of wild garlic, late-flowering in the shade.

The sense of smell is the hair-trigger of memory. I walked through the scented half-dusk full of garlic and fern and briar, trying not to think too much about what Gran had told me of the village gossip. Lilias and a gipsy? My young mother running off that night, with her Gladstone bag in her hand and tears on her face, to some vagrants' camp in the lane? At least, I thought, I need not be haunted by the broken caravan; that could have had nothing to do with her. It had been there as long as I could remember. Or had it? I had been six when she went. Had our childhood games gone as far back as that? Or was that the haven she had run to that night? Whose had it been?

I managed to thrust the thoughts out of mind, and walked on. Another half-mile along that nostalgically scented lane, then came the next gap in the bank, and the stile. I climbed over, back into sunshine and a freshly moving breeze, and the open, sloping field where, as children, we had come every Easter-time to roll our hard-boiled eggs in a sort of version of the conkers game played in autumn with horse-chestnuts. At the foot of the Pace-Egg Field, as we had called it, was another stile. This, too, led into a lane, but an open sunny lane that sloped gently down towards a stream crossed by a wooden foot-bridge.

And a few yards upstream from the bridge, snugly set in what had once been a lovingly tended garden, was Rose Cottage.

> *I remember, I remember*
> *The house where I was born,*
> *The little window where the sun*
> *Came peeping in at morn . . .*

I believe that anyone returning to their childhood's home is surprised to find how small it is. It was only seven years since I had lived there, but even so, Rose Cottage had shrunk. It was tiny, a genuine cottage, two-and-a-half up and two down, with a "back place" built out behind, over which a diminutive bathroom had been added. The two-and-a-half up had dormer windows projecting from the thatch, and the little window of what had been my bedroom had not allowed the morning sun very much of a peep. The garden showed every evidence of the past years' neglect, in a joyous riot of overgrown rose-bushes and weeds and summer flowers, but someone – presumably one of the Pascoes – had cleared the front path, and the windows and curtains looked fresh and clean.

I dumped my holdall in the porch, inserted Gran's key into the lock, and pushed the front door open.

It opened straight into the living-room, the kitchen as we had always called it. This was a smallish room, some twelve feet square, with an open grate flanked by metal trivets, with the oven alongside. Inside the high fender the hearth had been freshly holystoned, and Gran's old plate-warmer still stood there, a curious affair of turned wood, like a giant caltrop. All was just as I remembered it, the hearthrug made of hooked rags, warm and bright, with Granddad's rocking-chair to one side, and a rather less comfortable chair opposite; the solidly made table, which, scrubbed daily till the grain of the wood stood up like ribbing, was used for everything, baking, ironing, eating from, but which between jobs was covered with a red chenille cloth bordered with bobbles. The sideboard, backed by an ornate mirror, was covered with a long runner edged with crocheted lace, on which stood a pair of vases, much admired by me as a child, with a design of richly sprawling roses and forget-me-nots. Between the vases stood a rather lovely old oil-lamp, set aside as an ornament after "the electric" came to the village in the twenties. Above the sideboard hung a framed text, THOU, GOD, SEEST ME, and a flight of china ducks soared on a slant up the wall.

All this I took in at a glance, also that the place was as tidy, as newly dusted, as if it was still lived in. Mrs Pascoe, whose work, of course, this must be, had also been kind enough to leave a bottle of milk and a loaf on the table, with the bonus of a poke of tea and a note which said, "Welcome home and I've told the milk. Bottle in bed. Be down later. A. P."

No difficulty in interpreting this very real welcome-home, but I made no immediate move to fill the kettle or unpack any of the stand-by provisions I had brought. I would have been less than human if my eyes had not gone straight to the wall at the left of the fireplace.

Another text hung there, one that had been infinitely

more inhibiting to a small, highly imaginative child. It said, in large capitals: CHRIST IS THE UNSEEN GUEST AT EVERY MEAL: THE SILENT LISTENER TO EVERY CONVERSATION. I remembered my own childish surprise that Aunt Betsy had dared to speak as she did sometimes with the Unseen Guest sitting right there and taking in every word.

I lifted the text down.

"You can't see it," Gran had said. "It's tiny, no more than a tin box built into the wall, and it's papered over."

It wasn't papered over. Someone had cut cleanly along the edges of the door, removing both plaster and paper, and there, stark against the small pink roses and faded grey trellis of the wallpaper, was Gran's safe, just a small metal box cemented into the brickwork, with a keyhole showing, but no key.

I must have stood there for some minutes, staring blankly, before it occurred to me to try to open the metal door. I did not waste time looking for the key, which, as Gran had told me after much thought, might be in any of the drawers or vases or other hiding-places in the kitchen or anywhere else. I found a table-knife and inserted it, with some difficulty, into the crack by the lock, and tried levering the door open. It would not budge.

So, it was still locked. In some relief I stood back. Perhaps after all the safe hadn't been broken into: it must be quite a few years since this paper had been pasted on, and it was possible that Gran herself had cut it back to put some later treasure into hiding, and then had forgotten about it, as she had forgotten the whereabouts of the key.

The key. I peered into the vases on the sideboard. The first one appeared to hold nothing but two hairpins, a halfpenny, and a dead moth. The other was a quarter full of papers, and the assorted small rubbish of years. Well, later would have to do. No point in starting to worry tonight. I hung the text back in its place, and – the first really important action of every homecoming – went and put the kettle on.

6

I finished my tea, put away the iron ration of food that I had brought to last me till morning, then, spreading a sheet of newspaper on the table, I tipped out the contents of the second vase.

A clutter of papers, a couple of clothes-pegs, a toffee rather past its best, three safety pins and a thimble, and that was all. No key.

The sideboard drawers next, with the same result. No key.

I looked around me. The table drawer. The big cupboard in the alcove to the right of the fireplace. Two more vases on the mantelpiece, and a hundred other places where a tiny key might lie hidden. And then there were the back premises and the bedrooms.

It would have to wait. I had, in any case, a strong suspicion that Gran had taken the key with her to Strathbeg, and forgotten all about it. It was just the sort of thing she would have tucked away in some pocket of the enormous holdall she called her handbag, that held everything from her purse and essential papers like ration-book and identity card, along with her pills and her spectacles and her knitting and her prayer book, and other necessities of her life.

I picked up my own holdall and opened the door in the wall opposite the fireplace, which gave on the steep, enclosed staircase. My steps rapped, echoing, on bare boards. At the top was a small landing where Gran's beloved clock stood; a miniature long-case, the kind they called a grandmother clock. I remembered its gentle chime punctuating the long days of childhood. I would set it going, I thought, before I went to bed.

My room had certainly shrunk. Two steps from the door to the foot of the iron bedstead that stood against one wall. Three from the bedside to the window sunk in the alcove under the slope of the ceiling. It was hard to believe that I had shared it with my mother. It had been her room until Aunt Betsy came to stay, after which I had moved in with her, while Gran, giving Aunt Betsy the larger of the two front rooms, had taken over my little room at the back.

I dumped the bag and went to the window. I had to stoop to see out. There was a stool in the alcove, and I knelt on that and pushed the window open to look out.

Beyond the weedy garden with its riot of rose-bushes, nothing had changed. The beck, wide here and quiet, slid past below the bridge. Willows and wild roses, cuckoo-pint and king-cups, and a wood-pigeon crooning in the elms.

And someone crossing the bridge to approach the garden gate.

It was someone I knew well, my godmother Mrs

Pascoe, who had been my mother's friend and had "helped out" at the Hall when there were guests to stay. She was a little older than Lilias would have been, somewhere nearing her fifties, I guessed; a capable, comfortable woman who never seemed to be either fussed or short-tempered – a valuable quality in the sometimes stressful world of a crowded kitchen.

I went downstairs and opened the door to her.

"Aunty Annie! How lovely to see you!" We embraced warmly. "Do come in! And thank you for the welcome home. I had tea straight away, thanks to you, but the kettle won't take long to boil up again if you'd like a cup –"

"No, dearie, no. I'll be going home soon. I just came over to see if you'd got here. I thought you might be on that train. Well" – following me into the kitchen – "let's have a look at you. You look well, Kathy. You've changed a bit, but then how many years is it? Six? Seven?"

"Nearly seven, I'm afraid, but you haven't changed at all! Not a day older! How's Uncle Jim? And Davey?" Davey was their son, who worked alongside his father. He was about my age, and had been in my class at the village school, and later at the Sec.

"Oh, they're all right. Nothing ever ails them. But what about your Gran? She didn't sound so clever when she phoned me."

"I'm afraid she's had a bad time, flu and then some gastric trouble. They took her into hospital for treatment and tests, but we hadn't heard the result when I came south. Did she phone you from the hospital? Well, she's home now, but she's keeping her bed for a bit. Look, won't you sit down?"

"Well, thanks, but just for a minute. I only came along to see if you had all you need."

"I'm fine, thanks. I brought enough for tonight, and I'll go up to the village tomorrow. Thank you for the milk and the tea – Gran did tell me that you were coming in to fix the place up, but it was just wonderful to get here and find everything so lovely. You wouldn't know we'd ever been away! I hope it wasn't too dirty."

"It wasn't so bad. I've been coming down about once a month to open up and stop the place getting damp, so there wasn't all that to do, bar a few spiders to chase out, and a fall of plaster over by the fireplace there. But nothing to worry about, and you can see there's no damage to the ceiling."

I looked where she pointed, but it wasn't the ceiling I was thinking about. I was remembering the plasterless state of the square of wall behind the Unseen Guest. Presumably she hadn't lifted the picture down to see that. And possibly – a less comfortable thought – the plaster had been chipped away during the last three or four weeks, since she had last been in to air the cottage . . .

"How long d'you reckon you'll want to stay?" she was asking.

"What? Sorry. Oh, not long, just enough to get Gran's things sorted and the ones she wants packed up. I suppose you knew that she'd decided to stay up at Strathbeg? I doubt if she'll ever come back here."

"She didn't say much, but I thought that would be how it was. I suppose she feels at home there. Oh, well. Look, dearie, can I change my mind? I'll take a cup, if you'll have another with me yourself?"

Over the fresh brew of tea I told her about Gran's new house in Strathbeg, and the furniture that was to be sent north. She already knew something about it from Gran herself, and had talked it over with her husband.

Mr Pascoe knew a good firm of carriers in Sunderland who would do the moving, she said, and she and Davey, when he could, would help me with the packing.

"They're working at the Hall now, aren't they? Lady Brandon told me the family were keeping some rooms for themselves."

"That's so. It'll be a nice place for them when it's done, and it'll be good to see them back here again. Todhall isn't the same without the family. The word goes that Sir James isn't likely to come back much, but my lady always loved this place, and I dare say Miss Margery'll be here with the children."

"Have you heard anything about the plans for Rose Cottage?"

But she had not. A firm of contractors from Darlington were being called in to do the main work of the hotel conversion, but the Brandons had made it a condition that local tradesmen should be employed there, too, whenever possible.

"Stands to reason," said Mrs Pascoe, "that there's nobody knows more about that old house and its fixings than my Jim, and when it comes to the plumbing you can't get better than Peter Brigstock." She set down her cup. "Now, how about you? I should have said sooner, I was sorry about your trouble, we all were. An airman, wasn't he, your husband?"

"Yes. Bombers. He'd nearly finished his tour, only another four missions to go. Ah, well, that's the way it went. It seems a long time ago now. We didn't have very long, but we were happy while it lasted."

"It was a terrible thing. We were that sorry when we heard. But your Gran said he left you all right – comfortable, I mean? Well, that's a bit to the good. And you're living in London now, with a good job?"

"Well, it's a job. A friend offered it to me, and

it's pleasant work, in a big plant nursery. Not very well paid, but I enjoy it, and luckily that's all that matters."

"You didn't go back to teaching, then?"

"No. I didn't want to, but I had to do something." I didn't elaborate. I had never wanted to admit, even to myself, what a vacuum Jon's death had left in my life. With marriage had come a feeling of belonging, plans for the future, a sense of identity, of being. The satisfying, perhaps, of something primitive in every woman; the need for a warm cave-place of her own, and the family round the fire. Quite apart from the grief of it, his death had pushed me, so to speak, back on the world again, with my own solitary way to make, and not much idea of which way to go.

I put the thought aside, and asked about the people in Todhall that I remembered.

"Will I find the place much changed?"

"Not really. The village was lucky in the war. Your Gran would tell you about it, I don't doubt."

"She told me Arthur Barton lost an arm, and about Sid Telfer being killed. How's Mrs Telfer making out? There were three children, weren't there?"

"There were. And there are five now, so the less said about her the better." She must have remembered then that she was talking to another child of shame, because she pushed the empty cup back rather hastily and got to her feet.

"I'd best be getting along. I had a word with Ted Blaney yesterday – you remember the Blaneys at Swords Farm? – and he'll stop by with milk tomorrow. If you have a word with him he'll bring what you need from the village."

"Or give me a lift in? He always used to."

"I dare say he might still," she said, and suddenly

smiled. "If you change to something a bit less London. His cart's usually half full of straw, or even a hen or two in a crate. Not but what you look very nice, at that. So, I'll be getting back to the Hall. I go up there most days while the men's working. It's just Jim and Davey there now, and you'd be welcome if you want to come by and see what's going on."

"I'd like to, very much. Thank you."

I went to the front gate with her, and stood while she made her way back across the bridge. There was a sort of secondary driveway there, which led up through the woods that edged the park and then past the walled garden and into the back quarters of the Hall. It was the way my grandfather had walked daily to his work, and where I, as a small child, had so many times gone with him.

I turned back into the cottage, hesitated for a moment by the hidden safe, then, shrugging, left it for tomorrow, and went up to my bedroom to unpack.

7

Try as I would, I could not set aside my curiosity about Gran's safe. As soon as I had unpacked my few things, and refilled the hot-water-bottle in the freshly made-up bed, I went out to the toolshed which stood under the lilac tree behind the cottage.

The toolshed had always been my grandfather's special place. It was small, a wooden hut with a window in one side, under which stood a sturdy bench, and on the other wall a row of six-inch nails from which hung his garden tools. If he had needed any special implement, he borrowed it from the big collection up at the Hall; here he kept only the basics, spade, fork, hoe, rake, shears, and, in a wall-rack beside the window, the hand-tools such as trowels and secateurs. A metal tool-box under the bench held chisels and screwdrivers and boxes of nails and so forth. The barrow was kept outside under a lean-to. There was no lawn-mower; we had no lawn.

The shed had always been kept tidy, but when I saw it that day it was tidy indeed. It was empty. All the tools had gone, including the tool-box. I checked the door, which had been locked, and which I had opened with the key that hung in the back kitchen. No sign there of tampering or damage. I looked outside; the barrow was there. But all that could be carried away had gone.

It was possible, of course, that Gran had got rid of the things, sold them or given them away when she went north. It didn't concern me much, except that I would need something rather stronger than a kitchen knife to tackle the door of her safe. Feeling suddenly impatient, I glanced at my watch. Half past five. I would walk up to the Hall and borrow the tools I needed. If there were still gardeners employed there, they would have gone off at five, and the gate into the walled garden would probably be locked, but I knew where the key was kept. I got my jacket from the cottage, and set out for the Hall.

Across the bridge, up through the belt of woodland that edged the park, and then a short cut through a landscaped glade to the high wall of the vegetable garden and the archway with the beautiful iron gate that had been made, nearly a hundred years ago, in the smithy next door to the vicarage.

I did not need, after all, to feel up behind the Virginia creeper for the key. Just before I reached it the gate opened, and a young man came out, wheeling a bicycle. A workman, by his clothes, and what my grandfather would have called "a well-set-up young feller". He looked to be about my age, a capable-looking young man with brown hair and grey eyes, where I thought I could still see the quiet, clever seventeen-year-old who had been in my class at school.

He checked when he saw me. "Were you looking for someone? I'm the last. Everyone knocked off at five."

"I – it's Davey, isn't it? It *is* Davey?"

"Aye, but – ? Hang on a minute. You're Kathy, Kathy Welland. Mum said you were here. We-ell!" The last syllable was drawn out with a world of meaning as he looked me over from head to foot.

"Wouldn't you have known me?" I heard, in my own voice, a kind of wistfulness. Here in the place where as a child I had spent so many hours with my grandfather, where I had learned so much of what I needed to carry into the world, and where I had sometimes played with this very boy when his father had been working at the Hall, something in me was responding strongly to the scents and sights of a happy childhood, and Davey, standing there so changed, and looking at me with a mixture of friendly surprise and reserve, was part of it.

I could hear, too, that my voice had taken back, as a kind of echo, some of the country sounds it had rejected. Kate Herrick or Kathy Welland? Which was I? Which did I want to be?

"Sure I'd have known you," he said. "The sun was right behind you there, and you spoke different, but now I see you, yes, I'd know you anywhere." He gave a nod. "Good to see you back, Kathy. You okay at the cottage?"

"Fine, thank you. Were you going that way?"

"Yes. I'm going to the station to pick up a package for my Dad. I'll walk down with you if you like. Were you wanting something up here, or were you just out for a walk? Mum said you might come up some time, but she went home when Dad left with the van."

"I really came up to see if I could borrow a hammer

and chisel. All the tools have gone from our shed. If you'll wait a minute while I get them –"

"No need to bother going in there. I've got my tools with me. I can lend you what you want. What's it for? Mum didn't say anything needed doing." I saw then that a satchel of tools was strapped behind the bicycle. As he spoke he busied himself pulling the flap open, then turned with a chisel in his hand. "This do? What d'you want it for? I'll come in if you like and fettle it for you."

I took it from him. "Well, thank you, but –" I stopped. The chisel looked familiar, and yes, there on the handle, burned into the wood, were the initals H.W.

I looked up to see Davey grinning. It made him look years younger, and very like the boy I had known before time and the war years had taken and changed us both.

He gave a nod. "Yes, that's where they all went. You might've guessed. Your Gran told me to take the lot, 'and see you make good use of them, my lad,' she said, you know the way she talks. But you're welcome to any of them if you need them. Goes without saying."

"No, no. Just for the one job, and –" I made a decision. "And yes, Davey, I would be glad if you'd help me. If you've time, that is; I don't know how long it may take. I'll tell you about it on the way down."

We went together, Davey wheeling his bicycle, and as we went I told him about the safe, and something of what Gran had said. "There are things like Granddad's watch and medals, and some jewellery of Gran's, and some family papers. I never even knew about it, and I honestly believe she'd forgotten all about it herself till she heard that they might be going to alter the cottage."

"We'll get them out, no bother. But wasn't there a key?"

"Yes, but of course she's forgotten where she hid it. That's the other thing. I had a look at the safe, Davey, and the plaster's been cut away from the door. Someone's been there, but whether the door's been opened or not I can't tell. If it has, then it's been opened with the key. There's no sign of forcing."

"Hm. Sounds queer to me. No wonder you're in a hurry to take a look at it." A frowning pause. "I suppose your Gran couldn't have been at it herself some time back, and forgotten that as well?"

"I thought of that. But your mother told me just now that there was a trace of plaster on the floor there when she was cleaning, and that must have been pretty recent."

"It's loose stuff. Even if the wall was broken some time back, the plaster might still be flaking. Don't you worry yourself about it, we'll soon see. I suppose you did look for the key?"

"Yes. I've not had time yet for a real search, though I've looked in the obvious places, but it must be very small – the keyhole's tiny – and it could be anywhere, so I thought I might as well try and lever the door open somehow, just to set my mind at rest. Break it open, even. Gran's not likely to be using the place again."

We had reached the bridge. He paused with the bicycle hoisted half up the steps. "So it's true what Mum said? You're leaving Todhall for good?"

"Yes. Gran seems to want to stay at Strathbeg, and I've got a job in London now that I like, though if it came to that I'd be quite happy to give it up and go north to look after her. Anyway, they're selling our cottage, or making it over or something, aren't they?"

"Nobody seems rightly to know what's to be done

with it. In any case" – he heaved his bicycle up over the steps and wheeled it across the bridge – "busting your Gran's safe open won't hardly matter. Or if you like I can ask my Dad? It sounds to me as if he, or my Grandpa even, must have put that hidey-hole in, and there may be another key. But if you're in a hurry," he added, cheerfully, as he propped the bicycle beside the cottage gate, "we can break it open now. Soon see, when I've had a look at it."

"What time do you have to be at the station?"

"Doesn't matter. The package'll be left in the office, and there'll be someone there till the last train." He followed me into the cottage, dumping his tool-bag on the table, and watched while I lifted down the Unseen Guest.

"Hm, yes." He looked thoughtfully at the cleared piece of wall, and the metal square framed by paper and broken plaster. "And my Mum said there'd been a fall of plaster here?"

"Yes. Davey, could there be anyone local who'd know about the safe? I mean, if it has been opened, it's been done with a key, and –"

I stopped. He had swung round on me, in a way that reminded me sharply of the young Davey squaring up to a fight in the school playground.

"You listen to me, Kathy Welland! I told you, if your Granddad had this put in, it would be my Grandpa he'd get to do it, and if it was meant to be private, you can bet that my Grandpa never told anyone. My Dad may know about it, because he has all the shop records, but he never told me, and he would never tell my Mum either. And if he does have a spare key –"

"Davey! It didn't occur to me! Please! Truly it didn't. Why on earth should I think any of your family would go prying about here? It really could be that Gran did this herself ages ago, to put something away or get something out, and forgot to tell me that I'd find the paper already cut away."

"Not likely." But he sounded mollified. "This wasn't done all that long ago. Look at the edges of the plaster." He was running a thumb along the cut edge as he spoke. Dry plaster-dust floated to the floor.

"Ye-es, I see. Look, Davey, if you think your father might have a key, wouldn't it be easier to wait and ask him?"

"You reckon?" And, with his sudden grin at me, we were once again on easy terms. "You'd never last till morning. We'd better find out now. Let's go right ahead and bust it open."

"All right, let's."

He set to work with the chisel, but after a while stood back, shaking his head. "The fit's too tight, I can't get the blade in for leverage. I'll really have to break it. Okay by you?"

"Yes."

It looked easy. He laid the blade of the chisel against the door's edge nearest the keyhole, and gave two sharp blows with a hammer. There was a crack, and the little door came open. Davey said something under his breath, and stood back.

"What is it?"

"Look," he said.

I looked. Predictably, but still shockingly, the safe was empty.

Davey put into words what, after his recent outburst, I didn't care to say.

"Well, so that *was* opened with a key."

"Perhaps Gran really did – oh, no, there's the plaster. Well," I said, uneasily, "it's obvious what's happened, isn't it? There's been someone in here, squatters, perhaps, dossing in the empty house, and they came across the key, wherever she left it, and tried the safe door."

"They'd have to have known it was behind the picture."

"They might just have found it if they hunted about."

"Covered over with wallpaper?"

"Oh. Well, no. Oh, dear, this is awful. What am I to say to Gran? What are we to do?"

"Better not say anything to your Gran yet. But I reckon," said Davey slowly, "that we'll have to tell Dad about this." I noticed that he had accepted my "we" as natural. "Look, I'll ask him first thing if he knew about the safe, and if there was another key, and I'll find out from Mum if that plaster on the floor was dry."

He pushed the door as far shut as it would go, then hung the Unseen Guest back in its place. "And you can forget about squatters. I've come this way on my bike two nights out of five the last month, with a job I'm doing at Swords Farm, and there's never been anyone about. And Mum would have seen signs if people had been in the house. So you don't need to be scared, but if you are –"

"I'm not. Truly. Just worried, and just wishing I could think of some explanation. I mean, if it was a thief they'd have taken the valuables, but they'd surely have left the papers, or just chucked them in the fireplace or something. Hang on a minute" – and I was on my knees, destroying Mrs Pascoe's carefully laid fire – "No, only newspaper. And they were so tidy, weren't they? They cleared most of the plaster away, and the torn wallpaper . . ." I got to my feet again. "Oh, well, there's nothing we can do for now, is there? But thanks for everything, Davey, and don't worry about me. I'll be fine, really."

"If you're sure. Good night, then."

After he had gone I sat for a while, thinking, before getting up to re-lay the fire and put a match to it. The bright blaze brought the room alive, and even made a kind of company. Home. It was a long time since I had sat by this fire, but it felt like yesterday. I got myself some supper, then found the Penguin I had bought for the train journey and read for an hour or two without thinking more than fifty times about the empty safe, and finally, when the grandmother clock said eleven, went up to bed.

8

Next morning I was up very early, but had barely finished my coffee when I heard the sound of trotting hoofs coming down the lane from the road.

I went out to meet the farmer, a wiry middle-aged man with a face carved out of sunburned teak, who jumped down from the cart and came up the path carrying his wire basket of milk-bottles.

"'Morning. Nice to see you back. How're you keeping?"

"Good morning, Mr Blaney. I'm fine, thanks. And you?"

"Mustn't grumble. And Mrs Welland?"

"She's had flu, but she's mending. I'll tell her you asked."

"You do that. How many?"

"Do I have a choice? We're rationed in town."

"Not here, you're not. A pint do? And two-three

fresh eggs if it suits you? I've got some in the cart.
And I've got your suitcase there, too. I picked it up
at the station. Mr Harbottle said I might as well bring
it down home for you."

(Home? *I remember, I remember.* But I was only
here in passing, to pack up and then abandon the house
where I was born, however much it seemed to want to
wrap me around with familiar things. I had a job, a
place elsewhere that I would soon go back to. There
was nothing here for me now, not for Kate Herrick.)

I thanked Mr Blaney, and accepted his offer of
eggs, while he asked a bit more about Gran and her
new house (how had he heard that?) and whether
or not she meant ever to come back to Todhall. He
seemed to be in no hurry, and I saw why. His mare,
left to herself in the lane, had trotted on to where
it widened near the bridge, and there, with a couple
of expert heaves of her rump, she turned the cart
neatly and came back to the gate, ready for the return
journey.

"She hasn't forgotten her old round, then," I said.

"Rosy? Never forgets anything. Dunno how I'd do
without her. If I was to miss a call on my round,
she'd take me back there and refuse to shift till I'd
done it. Dear knows what I'll do when she gets her
cards."

"She must be pretty old now? I remember her – oh,
for years back."

"She'll be about seventeen. What I reckon, when she
looks like going, I'll get myself one of those motor
vans. I can't see myself starting over again with a new
horse."

"And Rosy?"

He was offhand, turning away. "I reckon she's
earned her retirement. She'll finish her life at grass."

"I'm so glad. I hope she knows!"

He laughed, not attempting now to conceal the affection in his voice. "Wouldn't surprise me. If she didn't before, she does now. Look at her. Hears every word. I'll get the eggs for you, and fetch your case up. No, it's no bother."

He started down the path, but, I could see, without much hope of getting near the cart. The old mare was standing with her forefeet inside the cottage gate, blocking the way, and staring fixedly, ears pricked, towards me. Mr Blaney paused and turned, trying to sound apologetic. "I told you she never forgot. Mrs Welland used to give her a piece – a bun or a bit of bread."

"Oh, dear. Of course! I should have remembered. Would a biscuit do?"

"She wouldn't say no. Come up, lass." He backed Rosy up a pace, heaved my case out of the cart and carried it up to the door.

I took it from him. "Thanks very much. I'll get that biscuit now. How much for the milk and the eggs, Mr Blaney? I may only be here for three or four days, so perhaps I'd better pay as I go."

"Never mind that. You can let me know the day before you leave."

"I wondered – could you give me a lift up to the village, please?"

"Well, of course. Like old times, that'll be."

So it would. I thanked him again, and hurried back indoors, snatched up my jacket and the basket and purse I had left ready, found a biscuit among what remained of my stores, and ran out. As I shut the front door I hesitated. We had never locked it, but perhaps now –? I locked it, pocketed the key, then delivered the biscuit to Rosy, who took it with velvet lips, tossed her head, and was away with the milk-cart almost before I could jump aboard.

The road to the village ran, deep between its flowering hedges, through a mile or so of pasture and woodland. The only dwellings on the way were two small houses, just too big to be called cottages, which nestled at the edge of a wood. They were still occupied (Mr Blaney shouted it above the rattling of the cart) by the same people. A pair of sisters, the Miss Popes, lived in the first house, with next door a single maiden lady, Miss Linsey. The village had dubbed the place Spinsters' Corner.

Rosy stopped at the first gate, and Mr Blaney got out. There was no sign that anyone was about yet, for which I was thankful. I remembered the Miss Popes as being deeply interested in all that went on in the village; at least, that was how they would have put it; the village called them, briefly and with adjectives that varied according to the station of the speaker, interfering old tabbies. This may have been true in a sense, but Miss Mildred, the younger sister, interfered only with the kindest possible motives. One gathered that the elderly sisters had been brought up in an era of soup and advice for the deserving poor. In spite of my mother's dubious goings-on, our family had been in that category, and sometimes glad of it, but even so I had always liked Miss Mildred, whose gentle charity of mind had even included Aunt Betsy. The older sister was a more practical character, and indeed held down some sort of key post with a charitable organisation in Sunderland.

Rosy moved on to the second gate, and put her head down to the roadside grass. No biscuit expected here, and the curtains were still drawn. Miss Linsey's house. Miss Linsey was in a different category from the ladies next door. She was a mystic. She was to be seen communing (as she would tell you) with the trees and the clouds, and she laid claim to a fairly powerful kind of second sight. As a child, I had been afraid of her, and on the way home from school had always run like the wind till I was well past her doorway. We children had had our own name for Spinsters' Corner, a name which carried its own terror; we called it Witches' Corner.

Soon we were trotting briskly past the cemetery wall, to pause at the first of the outlying houses of the village. I thanked Mr Blaney for the lift, patted Rosy, who ignored me, biscuitless as I was, then I walked briskly across the village green towards my first port of call, the vicarage.

Todhall village was a community of about two hundred souls, gathered round a village green with the church at its centre. It boasted one pub, the Black Bull, a post office, a general shop, the vicarage with the smithy close by, and above the smithy the carpenter's workshop which belonged to Mr Pascoe. To either side of the green the houses straggled in no sort of order, so that what we called Front Street was in fact a wide oval of green set about with a sprawl of dwellings, gardens and small-holdings. The only modern touches (and therefore, perhaps, the less picturesque features of the place) were at the southern end of the village where the milk-cart had set me down – the school and the church hall, with the raw brick wall of the cemetery alongside. The church, the proper centre-piece of the village picture, was late Norman, with (as I had known all my life, without understanding why it mattered) all the right stonework and a perfect horseshoe chancel arch. There were wild roses sprawling over the stone wall that surrounded the old graveyard, and some lovely elms lending their shade. A couple of goats and a donkey were tethered grazing on the green, and a gaggle of white geese sunned themselves near the pond.

As it was in the beginning ... Nothing seemed to have changed. Nothing ever would. And, as I had done so often in the past, I made straight for the vicarage gate.

Nothing had changed there either, except that here, certainly, the house did not seem the huge mansion it had appeared when the Lockwoods had lived there, and little Kathy Welland had first gone to play with the vicar's daughter. It was a low, compact house, squarely built but made attractive with whitewashed walls and green window-shutters and a trellised porch covered with jasmine. The garden walls were almost completely hidden by ivy, and as I passed the front gate with its glimpse of a pretty garden, a blackbird flew scolding out of a tangle of leaves where, as I knew, there had been a nest every year, time out of mind.

The front gate was not, had never been, my way in. I pushed open the back gate and went into the yard where the motor house stood, and beside it the hen-run, and the cage where Prissy had kept her rabbits. The rabbits had gone, but the hens were there, busy still over the morning feed. I would have lingered for a minute, remembering, but there was someone at the scullery window, and she had seen me. As I reached the back door it opened, and a girl looked at me inquiringly, wiping her hands on her apron.

She was, I supposed, about sixteen. I did not recognise her, nor, obviously, she me.

"Oh, miss. Did you ring at the front? I'm sorry, I never heard no bell –"

"No, I didn't try the front. It's all right. I know I'm

68

early, but is the vicar in, please? It's Mr Winton Smith, isn't it?"

"That's right, miss. But he went out a bit since, visiting up the village. Mrs Foster at the post office. She's been poorly. But Mrs Winton Smith's down the garden somewhere. Shall I get her, or maybe you'd like to go yourself? It's through that gate by the hens."

I hesitated. "No, I'll come back later. When do you think he'll be home?"

"I couldn't say. Sometimes he stays out till dinner, that's at twelve o'clock. But I'll tell him you came – what name is it, miss?"

"Herrick, Mrs Herrick. I think he'll know who I am. So I may see you later. What's your name, by the way?"

"I'm Lil Ashby."

The Ashbys were farmers a few miles along beyond the station. I remembered Mrs Ashby, who had called sometimes on Gran, and had supplied the Hall, and us along with it, with eggs and poultry.

"Well, Lily, thanks for your help."

"It's not really Lily. It's Lil, short for Lilias. Mum called me after someone she knew. Real pretty, she said, like the name." A cheerful giggle. "And the name's the prettiest thing about me, she says that, too. What is it, miss? Is there summat the matter?"

"No, no. Yes, it's a very pretty name, and it suits you. Well, then, tell the vicar, and I'll be back later. Goodbye."

Outside the gate I paused. A little way to the right a farmer's cart stood upended by the road, shafts in the air. The horse was presumably in the smithy being shod. I could hear the clink of the hammer and the clatter of hoofs and a "Hup there!" from the smith.

I went that way. I had always loved the smithy. To

me, as a child, it had been a mysterious dark cave, with the fire at the back roaring up from time to time under the bellows, and the rhythmic clang and clatter of hammer and anvil mixing with the hiss of the iron plunged to cool and the smell of the smoking hoof as the shoe was tried. I had loved it all; the old smith with his leather apron and hard hands that could be so gentle; the great mild horses, their skins as glossy as licked toffee, their quiet eyes, the way they heaved their feet up at a word and never seemed to feel nail or hot iron, their soft flickering nostrils that nuzzled and breathed down the smith's neck as he worked. A whole world. A world whose ways, sadly, must soon vanish for ever.

The smith was busy over the hind hoof of an enormous Clydesdale, his back wedged under the chestnut rump, his knees gripping the powerful leg. He shot a glance upward as my shadow paused in the doorway and spat out a nail to let him grunt something that sounded like, "Nice mornin'."

"Good morning, Mr Corner."

Another glance, as he tapped in the last nail, then he checked the shoe's hold, lowered the horse's leg, patted the chestnut flank, and straightened himself. "Well, if it isn't little Kathy Welland! Long time since you were in these parts. Your Granny here with you?"

"No. She's still in Scotland, and I think she'll stay there now. She sent me down to get the rest of her things from the cottage."

"Ah. Well, I'm sorry to hear that, but it's nice to have you home again. You be here long?"

"Only till I get Gran's things seen to. It's lovely to be back. Everything looks just the same. How's Mrs Corner?"

"Fine, fine. What about your Granny? Annie Pascoe said she hadn't been too clever."

"That's right. She's on the mend now, but she's feeling her age, she says."

"Then I'd best be watching out for mine," said the smith with a bark of laughter. "Ah, here you are, Jem. She's ready now, done all round, and that should keep her for a canny bit."

I waited while the young man – a stranger to me – settled with the smith and led the mare away, then said: "I was wanting to see Mr Pascoe. Is he upstairs in the shop?"

"Nay, lass. Him and Davey, they've been and gone. They're working up to the Hall. There's a lot of alteration there, turning the place into a hotel, but you'll likely know that."

"Yes, I did hear. I saw Davey yesterday. I wanted to ask you – do you make keys, or is it only big things, gates and such?"

"Anything in iron, I can make," said Mr Corner simply. "But keys? They don't come my way often. I once made a spare for the church tower when old Tom Pinkerton – you'll remember him, he's still sexton – dropped her down the well. A big old key that was, near as old as the church."

"This would be a small key, very small, a bit like a cash box key, I would think. No? Then what about a door key, the old-fashioned sort, quite big. Like this." I showed him the Rose Cottage key. "I wondered if anyone had asked you to make one lately?"

He regarded me for a moment under those bushy eyebrows, but said merely: "Nay, lass. Anything like that, they'd go to a locksmith. Baines in Durham's the nearest."

"I see. Thanks. Well, you're busy, and I'd better be going. It's lovely to see you again, Mr Corner."

"Good to see you, lass, and if you was dressed for it

I'd give you a job the way I used to, you and young Pris. You been to the vicarage? Thought I saw you come out, but I didn't know you, my eyes not being what they used to be at a distance."

"I was wanting to see the vicar, but he's out. The garden looks nice. Is Mrs Winton Smith the gardener?"

"Aye. Always at it, she is. Well, if I cannat set you to work, I'll be getting on myself. I've a wheel to fettle next door." Next door was the shed where he did his wheelwright's work. "Come back and see me before you go, lass. Or better still, come up to the house and get a cup of tea. The missus'd be real pleased to see you. Any day about six, and I can run you home in the trap."

"That would be lovely. Thanks very much."

And at any time after six o'clock today, I reckoned, as I went out into the sunshine, everyone in Todhall would know that Kathy Welland was down home at Rose Cottage, packing up her grandmother's things to send away to Scotland, and asking about keys. Like any other village, we had a very efficient grapevine. So, would use it for myself. Perhaps someone, somewhere might know if anyone had been hanging around Rose Cottage and might have broken in and rifled Gran's safe of her treasures.

9

The village shop lay about a hundred yards beyond the smithy, and looked out across the duckpond. The geese had left the water, and were marching purposefully across the green towards a farmyard we had always known as Scurr's, though it had been many years since anyone called Scurr had lived there. Their place on the water had been taken by a small fleet of ducks, mostly white Aylesburys, but with a visiting mallard in convoy, and one water-hen. A nondescript terrier sat at the edge of the water, wistfully eyeing the flotilla.

A shrill whistle from just behind me jerked me round, startled, and jerked the terrier, too, from his post. He came running to the shop doorway, which had opened to let a young woman – a girl of about sixteen – out onto the step.

She saw me and stopped in the doorway. "Oh, sorry! I never saw you. Come here, Muffin! You leave them ducks alone! Were you coming in the shop? He'd love to get them ducks, but he's frightened of the water. You can't blame him, can you, all that mud and the weed and all. A fair disgrace I call it, and no one does a thing about it. Come in, then. I'm Jinnie Barlow, Mrs Barlow's niece, from Ashhurst, and keeping the shop while she's on holiday. I haven't met you yet, have I?"

"No. I'm Kate Herrick. Nice to meet you, Jinnie. Will Mrs Barlow be away long?"

"Only a week. She's gone over to Hartlepool, to her sister's, my other Aunty's. She's just out of hospital, my other Aunty, that is, so I said I'd come and mind the shop, and the cat and dog. The shop's the least of the troubles." She laughed merrily. "Whose are the ducks?"

"I don't know. They probably belong to Scurr's, like the geese. I think they're used to dogs – anyway, I'm sure they'll know Muffin quite well. I wouldn't worry about them."

"I won't. What can I get you, then? Is it the rations?"

"Yes, please. Here's the book."

"Ta. Makes it easy, this does. This is only my second day, and I've not quite got the hang of Aunty's shelves yet, but the rations are easy, and I've got some of them made up ready anyway."

She chattered on as she served me. Ashhurst, where she lived, was about five miles away, and before this visit, she told me, she had done no more than call occasionally on her aunt, but she was enjoying this temporary job because one of her friends from home was working at the vicarage.

"Lil Ashby?" I said. "Yes, of course. Their farm's over Ashhurst way. You'd be at school with her?"

I spoke absently, watching all the while through the

glass of the door to see if I could catch a glimpse of the vicar coming away from his call on Mrs Foster at the post office on the other side of the green. Mrs Barlow's absence was disappointing. She was a great gossip, and since most people who visited the village found their way at some time to the shop, I had hoped she might have some information for me.

"That it?" asked Jinnie, putting the last of the packages into my basket. "We've got some tins of Spam, if you'd like one, and what about flour?"

"Oh, no thanks. I've got all I need, and I don't want a lot to carry. It's a long way to Rose Cottage. This'll do me very well. How much is it?"

She told me and I paid her. As she counted out the change she asked, with the first sign of curiosity, "Rose Cottage? Isn't that the place away down the station road? Where the old lady died and the sister went up north to stay? I heard about that."

I hesitated, then put the question I had wanted to ask Mrs Barlow. "Did your aunt say if there'd been any strangers seen about there lately, or maybe asking about it?"

"Not that I remember. Here, don't forget your ration book." As she handed it to me she caught sight of the address on the cover. "Richmond, Surrey? Oh, you're not from Todhall, then? And you're lodging down at Rose Cottage? On your own? Isn't it lonesome there?"

"Not really." There was the vicar now, shutting Mrs Foster's gate and setting out to cross the green. He appeared to be making for the church.

"Are you just there on holiday, then? Related, maybe? Aunty did tell me –"

"Excuse me. Someone I want to see. I must catch him. Thanks again, Jinnie. Good morning." Snatching my basket up I made hastily for the door, tripping over Muffin, who was waiting to be let out again, presumably for further contemplation of the ducks. In the ensuing scuffle as he was caught and held and apologised for, I made my escape from further questions and headed back down the green towards the church.

When I let myself in through the south door, there was no sign of the vicar. A woman was there, below the pulpit, with a bucket full of flowers and branches beside her, and a couple of big brass vases on the floor waiting to be filled. I recognised the massive vases that stood to either side of the chancel arch. On festival days my grandfather used to bring boughs of blossom or leaves from the Hall grounds. For ordinary Sundays the vases usually had to stand empty.

The church, the eternal centre of the village, was unchanged, not shrunken like Rose Cottage and the vicarage. The same yesterday, today and for ever. Just as it should be. I supposed – fleetingly, as I slipped into a back pew to say the brief prayer that was one's civil greeting to the church's owner – that the timelessness was the quality all churches shared; a matter admittedly, to some extent, of shadows and carvings and high groined ceilings and dim religious light, but also of the years of use, the words, the thoughts, the griefs and joys of countless people through the years. Here in Todhall there had been some nine centuries of them.

I got to my feet and approached the flower-arranger. She had not looked round as I entered the church, but now she stood up and greeted me. She was tall, thin rather than slender, with brown hair that showed a hint of grey tucked back uncaringly under a felt hat. She looked to be somewhere in her sixties, and wore an elderly skirt topped by a cardigan over a white shirt blouse. She greeted me with a poise verging on condescension. Her voice was educated.

"Good morning. A lovely day, isn't it? Are you interested in our church?"

"Good morning. You must be Mrs Winton Smith?"

"Yes?"

It was a question, and she waited for an answer. I said: "I'm Kate Herrick, Mrs Herrick. I called at the vicarage earlier, but the vicar was out. There's something I'm rather anxious to ask him about, and I thought I might catch him here. I was over there in the shop just now and saw him come across the green. I suppose he's come in by the vestry door? Do you think I might go in there and have a word with him?"

"I didn't hear the door, but he may be there, he did say something about looking out some papers this morning, and I do know that he is very busy. But" – she was gracious – "perhaps there is something I can do for you? You're a stranger to the village, aren't you? If it's the church you're interested in, there's a very good booklet written by the last vicar. It's down there on the bench by the font. I'm afraid we charge threepence, but churches do have expenses."

She must be practised, I thought, at defending her husband against time-wasters. I had to find some way through the defences. I looked down at the bucketful of flowers. "What lovely flowers. Do you grow them yourself?"

"Yes. They're all from the vicarage garden. Are you a gardener, Mrs Herrick?"

I smiled. "In a way. I work for a nursery firm in Richmond."

"Are you visiting friends here?"

"I'm just here for a day or two. Staying at Rose Cottage. You must know it, it's down –"

"Oh yes, I know it." She had stooped over a vase again, and now looked up. "But surely you're not there alone? Aren't you nervous?"

"Not a bit. You're the second person today who's asked me that. Why should I be?"

"All I know is, when my grandchildren came to stay for their half-term, they wouldn't go near the place. Someone had told them it was haunted."

"Haunted?"

"Yes. I don't know who by, something to do with gipsies. They used to camp there, I believe, and they were something to do with the people at Rose Cottage, some dreadful family that lived there, and some scandalous goings-on. Before our time, of course, the scandal, that is. Welland, that was the name. Welland."

A conversation-stopper if ever there was one. And that was the moment when the vicar chose to come bustling out through the vestry door. In sharp, and rather unkind, contrast to his wife he was a chubby, kindly-looking man with a thick mop of white hair and bright blue eyes peering over a pair of half-moon spectacles with gold rims, which had slid almost to the end of his nose.

He pushed them up absently, and they slid down again. "Ah, Muriel. I thought I heard voices," he said, and then to me: "Good morning. A beautiful day, isn't it? A beautiful day."

"This is Mrs Herrick," said his wife. "She is visiting the village, and is interested in the church, and I think she wanted to talk to you about it, but I told her that this was a busy day for you, Wednesday, with the evening service to prepare for, and –"

She was interrupted. The vicar came hurrying down the chancel steps with his hand out in greeting. "Mrs Herrick? Mrs Herrick, is it? How do you do? How do you do? I was speaking with Lady Brandon on the telephone only yesterday, and she mentioned that you were coming to visit your old haunts. Indeed, indeed. So, you wish to talk to me? Of course, a pleasure. If you like to come over to the vicarage now we can talk there." He turned to his wife. "Mrs Herrick, my dear, must know this church better than either you or I. Her folk have lived here for a very long time. She was a Welland before her marriage. Kathy Welland, wasn't it, from Rose Cottage?"

I said nothing. Mrs Winton Smith said nothing. The vicar said: "Shall we go?" which seemed an excellent suggestion. We went.

10

The vicar's study was much as I remembered it, a small room to the right of the front door, with a bow window from which, sitting at his desk, he could see who was approaching the house. Beyond the ivied wall of the front garden the church tower seemed very near.

There was a fire laid, but not lighted, in the grate. Above the mantelpiece hung a large engraving of an Oxford college, and on the mantelpiece itself were two silver cups and a college crest mounted on a wooden base. The other walls were lined with bookcases. It would have served nicely, I thought, for a stage set of "clergyman's study". It looked, in fact, exactly the same as it had in his predecessor's time, save that Prissy's father had been to Cambridge, and there had been an oar hung above one of the bookcases. There were even the same two baggy leather armchairs. Mr Winton Smith gestured me to one, himself taking the swivel chair at the desk, whirling it so that he faced into the room. Probably a practised manoeuvre; it put him with his back to the window, and on a higher level than his visitor. Understandable; this room must have seen quite a few difficult or delicate interviews.

But I didn't see that this would be one of them. Nor, apparently, did he. He picked up a box of cigarettes, offered me one, and when I shook my head said, "Wise girl," smiled, and took one himself.

I opened the batting. "You said you had spoken with Lady Brandon, vicar, and that she told you I was coming here to Todhall?"

"That is so. Yes. I understood from her that you were to stay at Rose Cottage, and that she had asked Mrs Pascoe to open it up for you. I trust all is well there? It has been empty a long time."

"It's fine, thank you. I don't – that is, I didn't – expect to be here more than a couple of days."

"Indeed, indeed?" A look, disconcertingly quick, over the top of his glasses. "Does that mean that you plan now to stay longer?"

"I may have to. There's something – that's why I came to see you. Did Lady Brandon tell you what I was here for?"

"Certainly. She said that your grandmother had decided to stay in Scotland and make her home there, and had asked you to come here to clear the cottage and arrange for the rest of her furniture to be sent north. I must say, Mrs Herrick, that I was sorry to hear it. Your grandmother was a great character, a great character, and I always enjoyed my visits there."

"She wasn't a very great churchgoer – at least I don't remember it." I smiled. "She used to pack me off, though, regular as clockwork, church, Sunday School, the lot, but she hardly ever went with me. Aunt Betsy did, though, sometimes."

"Ah. Yes. A worthy lady," said the vicar cautiously.

His expression of reserve was so marked that I laughed. "Don't say you didn't know that she used to sit outside in the churchyard till the service was over, in case the true faith – hers, that is – was contaminated? Surely someone would tell you – in fact I'll bet she told you herself!"

"And you would win. She, ah, she tended to make her opinions very clear. But at least you say she brought you, and fairly regularly, too."

"Only because she wanted to make sure I didn't have any fun – that is, get into mischief."

Another of those shrewd glimmers from above the half-moon glasses. "Indeed, indeed. The sins of children. Well, you were going to tell me why you were planning to stay longer. I hope there's nothing wrong? I believe you said that all was well at the cottage?"

"All's well with me, certainly. But a worrying thing has happened. There were a few small things that Gran had put away in a private hidey-hole, and they've gone."

"Gone?"

"Disappeared. Been taken. Things she specially asked me to take back to her."

"Oh, dear. I'm sorry to hear that. How very disturbing. I take it you've had a thorough search?"

"Not yet, no. But they should still have been where she'd hidden them, and there's no sign of them."

"Your grandmother couldn't have been mistaken? Forgotten just where they were?"

"It's not very likely. This was a secure, locked cupboard, built into the wall, and papered over, and she'd hidden the key away somewhere. She *had* forgotten where that was, and I haven't had time yet to look for it, but when I saw the cupboard last night it had been uncovered. Someone had cut back the wallpaper and the plaster to clear the door, and the cupboard was empty."

"Dear me. This is bad, very bad. Does it mean – do you think that the thieves had found the key?"

"They must have done. They had certainly used a key. They'd taken everything, and locked the cupboard again."

"It was locked? But if you yourself had no key –?"

"I broke it open. At least Davey did. Davey Pascoe. He was with me. Finding the wall stripped like that, we had to see if Gran's goods were still there, and it was the only way."

"Yes. Yes, I see. Well, I really am sorry to hear this, Mrs Herrick." A pause, while he swivelled his chair to face the window, then swung back to me. "The missing items. How valuable are they?"

"Intrinsically, not very. Things like medals and a ring or two and a brooch, small value, but the sort of thing you don't want to lose. I suppose the most valuable item was five gold sovereigns. Apart from that it was mostly family papers, you know, birth certificates, marriage lines, all the things one keeps."

"I see. Yes, I see. How very upsetting. Have you any – well, suspicions as to what may have happened?"

"None. The only people with any right of access to the cottage are the Pascoes, and they're hardly suspects. The family, too, of course – the Brandons, I mean – but you could say the same for them, and anyway they're not here."

"Hm." He stubbed his cigarette out, frowned down at the ash for a moment, then turned back to me. "I take it there's something you want me to do? If I can help you, of course I will, though I don't quite see how."

"I was going to ask you if you'd heard of anyone who'd been seen hanging around the cottage, a tramp, perhaps, or some other stranger. But you'd have told me already if you had. So all I can do for the moment is ask if you would – oh, there is one thing, have the gipsies ever been back? They used to camp in the lonnen not far from the house, but for years before I left they'd never been there. Has there been any sign of them?"

"None. I know the lane, and it's been overgrown ever since I came here. But you were going to let me know what I can do for you?"

"Yes, please. I wondered if you would let me look at the parish registers? All the family records must be there in the church, mustn't they?"

"Some of them, certainly. Not the records of birth, of course. Those – and the deaths – would be at Somerset House. They would supply copies of the certificates if you wanted them. I can give you the address to write to."

"Thank you, I already have it. But you'll have records of the baptisms and funerals and marriages – one does get a certificate of baptism, doesn't one?"

"Why, certainly," he said, and from the gentleness of his tone it was apparent that he, like his wife, had heard all there was to hear about the dreadful Welland family. But his reaction was different, and not, I thought, a purely professional one. "Of course you may look at the books. But we can do more than that. I can make copies for you of all the entries relating to your family. Those losses need not worry you. I'll do it with pleasure."

"Can you really? I didn't know. Thank you very much."

"I wish I could do more. Regarding the other items, the brooches and so on – your neighbours, I would have thought, would be the ones to talk to. The Misses Pope" – the suspicion of a smile " – don't miss many of the village comings and goings. They may have seen something."

"Yes, I'd thought of them. I'll call in today." I returned the smile. "And perhaps Miss Linsey may be guided for me."

"Indeed, indeed." His favourite exclamation was obviously a cover for thought. Once more he swivelled the chair half round and back again to face me. "What I might suggest, under the circumstances . . . Would you like me to have a word with Bob Crawley?"

"Bob Crawley? I don't think – who's he?"

"Since your time. Our policeman. Old Mr Bainbridge retired two years ago. He went to live with his daughter at Ferryhill. Bob Crawley has his house now, you'll know the one, the police house up at Lane Ends. If it would make it easier for you –?" He paused on a question-mark.

"Oh, yes, thank you. Thank you very much. If you would? Now I've taken up enough of your time, and I know how busy you are – I gather that you still have a service on Wednesday evenings – you do? Then thank you again for seeing me. About the copies of the certificates – when would it be convenient for me to come back?"

He got to his feet as I rose. "The easiest thing would be if you could make a list, with dates, of the papers you think have disappeared. Can you ask your grandmother? No, I can see that you don't want to have to trouble her before you've had time to find out more about this business. Well, then, just the records that you know would be held here in the church, weddings and funerals and yes, we do record baptisms. If you can let me have the dates of those, it will save a lot of searching. Where do you suppose they start?"

"I'm not sure. I suppose with Gran's wedding, and I can't remember just what year – oh, I've had an idea. If it's still there, she had an old photo album, and the dates might be in that. If I look tonight – is there a time tomorrow when I could let you have them?"

"If you send the list up with the milk-cart, then I can have the pages found if you come to see me later on. I've a christening at" – he glanced down at a diary on the desk – "yes, at four o'clock. So, half past three, say, at the church?"

"Thank you, that'll be great. I'll see you get the list first thing."

As I crossed to the door I glanced out of the window just in time to see the front gate open, and Mrs Winton Smith, back from the church with her empty trug, letting herself into the garden. I braced myself to meet her, but she managed, with perfect dignity, to vanish round the side of the house just as her husband ushered me out of the front door.

Two faces saved. But I wondered, as I let myself out through the gate into the sunny roadway, why I cared, and for whom I was doing the caring. Lilias? Aunt Betsy? Gran? Myself?

Lilias, from all I knew or had heard of her, would not have cared a rap. Besides, she was dead. Aunt Betsy had certainly cared, quite terribly, but she was dead, too. Gran had lived with the slur of "shame" all too long, and was now a long way away. Which left me. I had cared as a child, when people had let slip in my hearing remarks about my mother, or had too openly pitied my fatherless state. At school I had had to bear the thoughtless questions of the other children, and sometimes teasing, but this had come to an end on the day when Billy Comstock, the ten-year-old bully from Lane Ends, had found a new word, "bastard", and tried it out in school playtime, until Davey, aged nine, had flown at him and fought him till he yelled for help, and the two of them, streaming with blood, had to be pulled apart by the teacher. I was never teased again.

But that was a long time ago, and I had, perforce, worked out my own philosophy of living. It had to be what you were, not who you were, that mattered. I had taken life as it was dealt me, loved my home, and been happy. Would be happy again. So the person to be sorry for here was Mrs Winton Smith, a snob who had dropped a social brick, and who, being what she was, would obviously care very much about that.

Muffin was sitting by the pond again, but I doubted if he would be there for very long. The geese were on their way back from Scurr's yard, and the gander did not suffer dogs or children gladly. I would have liked to linger to watch the confrontation, but there was a lot to do. I turned for home.

11

The younger Miss Pope, Miss Mildred, was busy in her garden when I got to Witches" Corner. She was almost always busy in her garden, which was immaculately kept and extremely pretty, though Miss Mildred knew little or nothing about gardening methods, or even about plants. I had heard my grandfather talking often enough about her – "a real green thumb, that one has, and not knowing what on earth to do with it." The comment had stemmed from the time when he had stopped at her gate to ask her about some plant, a rareish species, which was growing rampant on her garden wall, and her reply, full of enthusiasm, had been, "That pink thing? What did you say it was? I've always called it my dear little rockery plant."

"She never prunes her roses, either," Granddad had said, "and look at them! Real beauties, all of them, and flowering two full weeks before mine at the Hall. Where's the justice?" Then he had laughed, starting to fill his awful old pipe, and said indulgently, "But there, it's a matter of love. Beats manure any day, that does."

But by whatever method or lack of it, Miss Mildred's garden was enchanting, a real cottage garden full of all the things it should have held, delphiniums, lupins, pinks and violas, with roses and honeysuckle on the rampage on every surface they could find. The house and garden were purely Miss Mildred's territory; her elder sister Agatha was the man of the house, the breadwinner, travelling by train daily to Sunderland to her work.

When I paused at the garden gate Miss Mildred was visible only as a flowered cotton rump sticking up among the lupins. I opened the gate and called her name, and she up-ended to her full five feet three inches, peered out between the lupins (which were taller than she was), and then broke out into delighted exclamations.

"It's Kathy! Well, my goodness, if it isn't little Kathy Welland!" She was a dumpy little creature, with the pink cheeks and blue eyes of a long-faded prettiness, and wispy grey hair that was rather the worse for its morning among the lupins. "Come in, my dear, come in! How lovely to see you! Annie Pascoe said you were coming, and here you are! It's like a miracle!"

Briefly wondering if this made Mrs Pascoe a liar or a prophet, I accepted Miss Mildred's fervent double hand-clasp and feather-light kiss and let myself be drawn into the garden, to answer as best I could all her eager questions about Gran, the family at the Strathbeg house, and then myself, my war work and marriage, and my life in London since my husband's death. It was a demonstration of what the village said, that "the Miss Popes knew the inside of everything." One could see how, but the eager questions were so full of real interest, with a total lack of criticism or any shade of unkindness, that one found oneself answering readily and in detail. As

Granddad had said of her garden, with Miss Mildred it was a matter of love. There was about her a rare and genuine innocence – in the most literal meaning of the word – that made it impossible to take offence, however personal her questions and comments.

"So you were left nicely off, well, that's a mercy, isn't it? I mean, that's *something* . . . And what a lovely job you've got, working with flowers. I suppose" – with an absent eye on the lily-buds shouldering their way up through carnations and roses – "they get all sorts of special flowers in those big London places? Flown in from Africa and India and the South Sea Islands and such-like?"

"Yes, they do. Some of them are lovely, but not a patch on yours, Miss Mildred! Your garden's gorgeous, it really is, just as I remember it."

"Well, we're having such a beautiful summer." Having so to speak passed the credit on, she turned back to me. "Are you here for long? You must come and have supper with us when my sister's home. She won't want to miss you."

"I'd love it, if I can, but I don't quite know yet how long I'll be here. Mrs Pascoe would surely tell you why I'd come?"

It was a very mild shaft, and it went wide. "Oh yes, she told me all about it. And she says that Jim and Davey will help you, and I suppose they'll get Caslaw's to do the move. Which bits does she want, your grandmother? She'll want the old sideboard, I'm sure, and the rocking-chair, and is the table hers, and the other chairs? It'll be nice for her to have all her own things around her again." A pause and a quick intake of breath. "Oh, goodness, of course –"

"What is it?" I asked, as she stopped.

"So stupid of me to forget, but seeing you suddenly like this, and then the garden, always so much to be done . . . I meant to come and tell you, but now you're here . . . Come over here and we'll sit down." She led the way to a seat set back under a rustic arch predictably laden with pink rambling roses laced through with purple clematis. We sat.

"It was talking about your grandmother's furniture and things that reminded me, though how I could have forgotten I don't know. Sister said I must tell you if I saw you, but I did wonder if it would scare you, staying down there alone at the cottage."

She paused, looking a little anxious. I said quickly, "Being alone doesn't scare me. Really it doesn't. Do go on."

"Well, if you're sure . . . It was Monday, just the day before you got here. Sister had told me she would get home late, because there'd been a muddle at the office, with someone being ill the week before, so she would get the later train, and she would bring the papers home to do in the evening. And she goes to the market on a Monday as a rule and gets what we need for the week, things you can't get in the village or from Barlow's van. So I knew she'd have a lot to carry, and there isn't usually anyone else getting off here from that train, so I thought I'd walk down to the station to meet her. Well, I was a bit late starting, so when I got to the Rose Cottage lane-end I thought I might take the short cut by Gipsy Lonnen. It was getting dark by then – just dusk, really – but I know the way so well, and it does save a lot of time."

Another pause. I prodded gently. "So you went by the lonnen?"

"No. I didn't get as far as the stile. I was about half way down the lane from the road when I saw it. At least, I think I saw it, but Sister says –"

"Saw what, Miss Mildred?"

"A light in your cottage garden. Round the back. A light that moved."

I stirred. "Well, but couldn't it just have been Mrs Pascoe? She's been coming down from the Hall when the men were working there, to put the place right."

"At that hour? Anyway, Annie Pascoe goes to the Mothers' Union meeting on a Monday night, and she went that night, because I asked her. I asked her if anyone else had a key, and she said no, certainly not."

"What time was this? The last train? Could it have been reflected moonlight, maybe, from a window?"

"No. And I told you, the light moved, like someone with a torch."

I was silent for a moment. In my mind's eye I was seeing the framed text hanging on the cottage wall, with the rifled safe behind it. It was one thing to trust the vicar with the truth, but I wasn't yet ready to broadcast it to the village via Miss Mildred. So I said merely, "How horrid for you. No wonder you asked if I minded being alone there. What did you do?"

"I am not myself afraid of the dark," said Miss Mildred, "but I don't like meeting strangers in it. I knew the cottage was empty, but there was nothing there that thieves would want to take, and anyway, I didn't want to be late for Sister's train, so I went. Not by the lonnen. I went back up the lane, and to the station by the road."

"I don't blame you. But – was the light all you saw? Nobody moving about?"

"I didn't care to go close enough to look," said Miss Mildred, with dignity. "And I couldn't wait to see if anyone came round into the front garden. I had to hurry. By the time I got to the station the train had gone, and I met Sister on the road."

"Did you tell her about the light?"

"Oh, yes. She said it would be silly to go and look, but we must tell Bob Crawley. That's the policeman, he's new since you were here. Such a nice young man, and with two dear little children, twins, a boy and a girl, and so keen on his garden, Bob, I mean, not the twins, and I was able to give him a lot of nice plants when they first moved in, and he has really got it beautiful now, even though it is mostly vegetables."

"And you told him what you'd seen?"

"Yes. That is, young Freddie Smart – you'll have met him, the porter at the station – came by on his bike; he goes home after the last train, and we asked him to call at Lane Ends on his way home, and tell Bob. And Bob went down to Rose Cottage straight away. He went past while we were having supper. He went all round and he came in on his way back and said nothing was disturbed that he could see, except that someone had been digging round the back, near the toolshed. So you see, I must have been right."

"Digging?" I said blankly. It had already occurred to me that what she had seen might just have been Davey fetching the tools, but then what would he have been digging for, and after dark, too?

"That's what he said. Digging, just by the toolshed. Bob did ask Davey Pascoe about it, because he knew Davey had got your grandfather's things from the shed, but that was last week – you did know about that, dear? That your grandmother had said Davey might take the tools and things from the shed?"

"Yes, I –"

A piercing shriek startled us both to our feet. It came from behind the hedge that separated Miss Mildred's garden from the one next door, where Miss Linsey lived. As we both hurried to the hedge to see what violent crime was being committed behind it, a head appeared over the top, and said in a voice that would have made a fortune for a tragic actress, "I've found him!"

12

I had not seen Miss Linsey for some years, but she had not changed at all. She was of middle height, middle age, medium build, but nothing else about her was medium, except perhaps in the professional sense of the word. She had a thin face, with a prominent aquiline nose, and myopic, rather mad-looking eyes, and she was in the habit, probably because of the myopia, of poking her head forward and fixing you with a fiercely intent stare, much as a large hawk stares down its beak at the prey it has marked down. Her hair was pepper-and-salt, fair turning grey, and was usually frizzed out into an old-fashioned coiffure rather like a bird's nest, but just now it was straggling in a wild tangle, as she had, quite literally, been through a hedge with it. She was holding something up in both hands, and repeating in triumph, "I've found him! He was just coming back through the hedge! He's been in your garden all the time!"

"Who has?" asked Miss Mildred, looking bewildered.

"Henry! If he's had your sweet peas I'm sorry – he does so love sweet peas, and when they're so near the fence – such a temptation! I did put wire netting right along there, but he finds a way through anything. Naughty, naughty Henry! Oh hullo, is that Kathy Welland? Annie Pascoe said you were here. I'd love a little talk with you, but I can't ask you in to coffee because I've run out, and I've no biscuits, but some other time soon, perhaps –"

"Thank you, I'm on my way home now, anyway. Do tell, who is Henry?"

"Oh, well, half a mo, I'll come round. Really, Mildred, I'd have thought you'd have seen him, he's been gone nearly a week, and . . ." The voice trailed away as its owner turned and vanished once more behind the hedge. We heard the clash of her gate and then she reappeared at Miss Mildred's. She was carrying a tortoise.

"Henry?" I said.

"Yes, the naughty boy! I found him just squeezing back through the bottom of the hedge. I was so afraid he was lost this time. If they stay out till winter, you know, they die." The light intense gaze fixed itself on me. "So you did come. They were right. I knew it. It's not always easy to tell, but this time I was sure. You must actually have been on your way at the time. It's like a miracle."

Somehow, this was a rather different sort of miracle from Miss Mildred's. I groped for some kind of sense. "What do you mean, Miss Linsey? Who were right?"

I might as well not have spoken. Waving the tortoise

vaguely in the direction of the village, she went on, "And when Annie Pascoe said you'd got off the train yesterday I felt like saying, 'Well, of course,' and if she hadn't told me I would still have known it had to be you, even though you haven't been back here for all these years, and you've changed so much, a young lady now and so well spoken –"

"Bella –" Miss Mildred started a protest, but Miss Linsey was not to be put off. She waved the tortoise at her, but kept her eyes fixed on me. "You're not really at all like your mother, are you?"

"I'm sorry?"

"Oh, I don't mean to be rude. You're very good-looking, you must know that, but you're dark, and she was so fair, really golden, when she was a girl, wasn't she, Mildred?"

"Yes, but, Bella, really –"

"Of course those looks don't last, but she carries her age very well. I saw her only a few days ago."

Miss Mildred made a little movement of protest, and I said under my breath, "It's all right," adding, aloud, "when was this, Miss Linsey?"

"The other night. I forget. Nights are all the same. People come and go. Some of them are dreams, but some come back in daylight. It's hard to tell. The man who was with her – I don't know who that was. He looked like a gipsy. She went away with a gipsy, didn't she?" She paused, but not for an answer. There was no shred of malice in look or voice. She gave me a smile, making another large gesture with the long-suffering tortoise. "But you mustn't let it trouble you, my dear. There's never any need to be afraid of them. The spirits, I mean. Believe me, I know. They only come back if they are lonely, or if they have something to tell you. They never harm anyone."

"On the other hand," said Miss Mildred, firmly bringing the conversation back to earth, "your Henry has been doing quite a lot of harm to my border. I hadn't noticed till now, but just look down there." She pointed to a patch of very pretty dwarf campanula, which certainly showed signs of damage. "Look at that! My little blue bells, I call them, and all squashed and nibbled. It must have been Henry, but perhaps the poor little soul was hungry. Why don't you take him home, Bella, and give him some of that lettuce I gave you, and then come back and have a cup of coffee here? I baked this morning."

"Just a minute," I said, stooping. Something white showed among the little blue bells, an elongated oval shape, something over an inch long, tucked in among the campanula leaves. I stood up with it in my hand. It was recognisably an egg, though strangely shaped, and with a tough-looking, matt, slightly uneven shell. I held it out on my palm. The two ladies regarded it with curiosity and slight repulsion, the tortoise with indifference.

"That's what Henry's been up to," I said. "Henrietta. She was laying an egg."

"An egg?" Miss Mildred sounded lost. "An egg? But – he's not a bird. How can he lay an egg?"

"A reptile. They lay eggs. I saw one like this once before somewhere. It's a tortoise's egg."

Miss Linsey looked from the tortoise to the egg with something like pride. "Well, would you believe that? Henry! And they leave them to hatch in the sun, don't they? Do you suppose we could actually *hatch* it? In the airing-cupboard, perhaps, or over the stove?" Quite suddenly, it seemed, Miss Linsey was back with us in the real and daylight world. She gave Miss Mildred a look where I could see a kind of indulgent affection. "Wouldn't it be fun to bring up a dear little baby tortoise? What do you think, Kathy?"

"I don't know. You could try. But – well, does Henry live on his own, or does anyone else in the village have a tortoise?"

"No, I've never heard of another one here, and I've had him for three years. Oh, well." And Miss Linsey dropped the egg into her pocket. "All right, Mildred, thanks. I'll take him – it's far too difficult to say 'her' all of a sudden – I'll take him home to his pen, and I'd love some coffee, thank you." Then to me, "You'll be staying, too, Kathy?"

"I can't. I must get back, but I hope I'll see you again before I leave. Perhaps –" But she had already disappeared back to her own garden. We could hear her admonishing Henry as she went.

"Er – Kathy, my dear," said Miss Mildred, low-voiced, "what she was saying about your poor mother – all that was just her way, you know. It doesn't mean anything. She sees things. She was telling me just the other day that our dear father had been here, working in the garden, and you know he's been gone for nearly fifteen years, and he never was a great gardener. I don't know if you remember how she talks sometimes –"

"Yes, I do." I also remembered what I had heard about the old tyrant of a father who had never lifted a spade in his life, and who had been lovingly cared for by his daughters until any chance of living their own lives was long past. I said gently, "I know. Just one of her dreams. Don't worry. It didn't matter."

"That's all right, then." Relieved, she turned the subject, moving with me towards the gate. "Well, my dear, if you must go. How very strange about Henry, isn't it? The egg, I mean. And wouldn't it be nice –

and kind to dear little Henry, too – to try and hatch it? Do you think perhaps one of Mrs Blaney's hens – I'm sure she said she has a broody just now."

"I don't think it would hatch. If there's no other tortoise in the village –"

"What difference does that make?"

A startled glance at her kind, inquiring face, and I fell back on a cowardly kind of truth. "The hen wouldn't sit long enough. They take ages, tortoises. It – well, believe me, Miss Mildred, it wouldn't work."

"Oh? What a pity. Ah, well. Now don't you worry about Bella's dreams and visions. She does get so mixed up. She's a dear girl, but you could say a little *unworldly*. You really can't stay for coffee?"

"No, thank you. There are things I've got to look out, and there's a lot to do, getting Gran's things sorted ready for the carrier. But I'd love to come again to see you – and Miss Agatha too – before I go. Goodbye, then, Miss Mildred."

Feeling rather like Alice emerging from Wonderland, I set off for home.

13

It was true. At a point about half way along the side of the toolshed, someone had been digging. The turned soil had dried out, but it still appeared fresh.

I stood looking at it, while the recent words of the ladies at Witches' Corner ran a chilly finger up my spine. Ghosts, spirits, darkness and shifting lights, digging . . . The word they combined to suggest was *grave*. Even on that sunny day the word was cold.

Then I took a pull at myself. A grave? The disturbed patch of earth was roughly two feet square, no more. If something really was buried here, it could not be anything much bigger than a cat.

Buried. This time the word held none of the chilling connotations of "digging". The word that went with it was "treasure". People buried treasure. And a treasure of a kind had been stolen. I could think of no reason at all why anyone should rob Gran's safe and then bury the proceeds a few yards away in the garden, but I had to find out if that was what had happened.

And of course I had no spade. Davey, as I was being reminded with tiresome frequency, had all the tools. But this time I was not prepared to wait till he came by, or to go up to the Hall for him. There ought to be a shovel in the coal-house. Awkward and heavy, but it would have to do.

I went to get it, half expecting to find that it, too, had gone with the rest. But no, it was there, propped just inside the coal-house door. I hefted it to one shoulder and went back to the shed. As I poised the shovel for the first stroke I noticed two things; there was dried earth on it, mixed with the residue of coal dust, and now that I looked, there were traces of coal dust in the soil of the "grave".

So Miss Mildred's intruder, whoever he was, had had to use the coal-shovel, too. She had seen the light on Monday, and the tools had been taken the previous week. It fitted. She could be right. I dug.

I dug for twenty back-breaking minutes. That wretched shovel got me down to nearly one and a half feet, and then I struck undisturbed clay. And nothing else. Nothing was buried there.

So the hunt was still on for the missing treasures. I put the shovel away and went in to wash and make myself some lunch.

At least there was no difficulty about finding the photograph album. There had never been many books at Rose Cottage; Gran read weekly magazines, which she called "books", and very little else, except the Bible. This lived in the bottom drawer of the sideboard, and the album was there with it. It was more than an album, it was a sort of family record book;

besides the photographs there was an envelope full
of old, yellowed news-clippings, mostly, as I saw
at a quick glance, about prizes Granddad had taken
at flower shows, or cuttings from the local paper
about the doings of the family at the Hall. About my
mother's flight from home, or about her death, there
was nothing. Either she was not news enough even for
the *Echo*, or my grandmother had not cared to keep
the record. I found ballpoint and writing-pad, and sat
down to make the list of dates the vicar wanted.

I doubt if it would be possible for anyone, who has
not seen it for some years, to work quickly through an
old family album. It took me well into the afternoon to
find all the relevant dates, then, after a pause for a cup
of tea, I turned to Gran's list, and busied myself with
looking out the small things she wanted, and ranging
them, ready for packing, on the sideboard or the table
in the back kitchen.

The evening was shading to dusk, and I had finished
my supper and got the dishes washed and put away,
when there was a soft rapping at the door. Wondering
who could have come here at this hour, I went to
open it, to find Miss Linsey outside. The light from
the window, outlining her against the growing dusk,
made her look almost ghostly. She had on some kind
of cloak, grey and shapeless, which she clutched to her,
and above it her hair looked wilder than ever.

She spoke in a whisper, with a glance over her
shoulder so nervously furtive that I found myself
looking about to see if anyone else was lurking near.
But garden and lane were empty.

"It's only me, Kathy. May I come in?"

"Well, of course. How nice to see you again, Miss
Linsey." I stood back, holding the door for her. "I'm
afraid I haven't lighted the fire, but please –"

"No matter, no matter." She slid, rather than walked past me as she spoke.

"Will you let me take your cloak, or would you rather keep it?"

The polite commonplaces didn't seem to have the desired effect, of taking out whatever drama she saw in the situation. She went into the kitchen in a kind of breathless rush, looking to see that I had shut the door safely behind her. Then, still clutching the cloak round her, she rotated slowly, as if to check that no one besides ourselves was there in the little room.

"Your door wasn't locked." The whisper was a little stronger, but it was still a whisper.

"Well, no. We never used to lock it. Have things changed hereabouts?" I smiled, trying to give the reassurance she seemed to need. It was difficult not to whisper back. "I did ask the vicar if the gipsies had been here again, but he says there's been no sign of them. And even when they were here –"

"That's it. That's just it. They have been back."

I was reaching up to the mantelpiece for a match to put to the fire. I stopped in mid-action and turned. She nodded, with a glance to left and right, and I thought her eyes looked not so much mad as distressed.

"Just let me get the fire going," I said, "and sit here in the rocking-chair. That's it. It'll soon be warm, and then we can talk."

The fire, which I had relaid after a fashion, caught, flickered, then burned up into a cheerful blaze. Miss Linsey subsided into Gran's chair, let her cloak slip back, and spread her hands out to the warmth.

"You'll take a cup of tea." I didn't wait for an answer, but went to fill the kettle. When I returned with the tray bearing the tea-things I found that she had the album on her knee, and was slowly turning the pages.

I set the tray down. "Milk and sugar?"

"No sugar, thank you." Then as I put the cup on the oven-top beside her she said, on a faint note like a sigh, "Ah. Yes. It was. I knew it."

I looked at the open page on her knee. It held four small photographs, in faded black and white. They had been taken, I knew, with the cheap little box Brownie camera that Granddad had treasured. The prints were not more than two-and-a-half by one-and-a-half inches, but the focus was sharp, and the detail pretty good. There was one of Gran sitting outside the cottage door, with her lace-pillow on her knee. I remembered how years ago she had made the delicate lace to sell. Another of her down near the gate, picking beans, and with her myself, a very small girl, bare-footed, in a print dress with a cotton bonnet on my head, and a basket for the beans held in both hands. One of me on the step of the front porch with my arms round the neck of our old dog, Nip. The fourth was a delightful snap, taken in a lucky moment, of a slender, lovely girl, standing just inside the garden gate with an armful of flowers. She was laughing. In my memory, except when I had last seen her, she was always laughing. My mother, Lilias.

"They're good, aren't they?" I made my voice as prosaic as possible. "I was just checking some dates. The album's a bit heavy, isn't it? Let me."

I took it from her and put it back on the table, then sat down on the opposite side of the fire.

Before I could speak again she leaned forward, the eyes fixed again, intense. "You would hardly remember her, I suppose. How old were you when she left? Five? Six? But I knew her well. And she wasn't someone you could forget very easily, she was such a pretty creature. So very pretty. Poor girl. If only I had known in those days what I know now, I could have warned her ... But then it would have been so different, wouldn't it?"

"I suppose it would. But Miss Linsey, you were saying that the gipsies had been back. Did Miss Mildred tell you what she told me this afternoon?"

"Not if it was anything important," she said, sounding all at once surprisingly normal. "She never does. I think Sister" – the word came out in a fair imitation of Miss Mildred's slightly tremulous falsetto – "warns her that I'm not reliable, because she can only see what's there in front of her eyes, and Millie can't even see that. She's a dear creature, but very unworldly, of course." She sipped tea. "Do you know, I don't think she even knows what the bees are doing to her precious flowers?"

I laughed. "Henry?"

"Yes. She spent half an hour this morning trying to persuade me to hatch that wretched egg, even when I told her that I'd had Henry here alone in my garden for three years. But she's such a dear, and at least she doesn't try to put one *down* the way Agatha does."

Remembering Miss Agatha, I knew what she meant. That efficient business lady would have no patience with what she had called (according to Gran) "airy-fairy goings-on, and why doesn't she set up as a fortune-teller and make a little money with a crystal ball or some such rubbish, instead of living on bread and greens and whatever my soft-hearted little sister gives her?"

She put her cup aside, settling back comfortably into the folds of her wrap. The hunted look had gone, but she still looked troubled. "I'm sorry to disturb you so late, Kathy, but I couldn't really get away till now without Millie seeing me, and I thought she might try to stop me. You saw what happened this morning. I did try to tell you then, but there was all the fuss about Henry, and to be honest, I think dear Millie changed the subject deliberately."

"She may have done, but she had just told me something herself, and I think she may have been afraid of making me nervous. You said you'd had a dream about my mother, and about the gipsy she ran off with." I showed a hand. "It's all right, it's a long time ago, and everyone knows the story. It's all over, and nothing to do with me now."

"But that's just it. It's not all over. It started with something I saw. It may have been a dream, I don't know. I did see her, and the gipsy with her. They had a light, a lantern, and they were in the lonnen, where that old caravan is – you know the one I mean?"

"Yes, but Miss Linsey – no, please listen! I know you have the Sight, and I do believe that you see things that other people can't, and that you dream things and then they come true. I remember what Gran told me about it, and when I was little we all knew." I tried a smile. "We were a bit afraid of you. We thought you might be a witch. But this about seeing my mother – she's dead, and Jamie – that was the gipsy's name – is dead, too. And that old caravan, well, if it is still there, it'll have dropped to pieces by this time. What would anyone go there for?" I added, gently, "It must have been a dream, Miss Linsey."

"But there was a light. I saw a light."

"There was someone down here the other night with a light. That's what Miss Mildred told me this afternoon. Monday night. She thought she saw someone out there by the toolshed, and when I got home I looked around, and it's true that someone has been there, digging, but I can't think why. There's nothing there."

"That would be Davey Pascoe." She spoke impatiently. "He took the tools. That's nothing to do with it. And it wasn't Monday when I saw them, Lilias and her gipsy. I know it wasn't Monday. And I didn't say they were down here at the cottage."

She turned that light, bright gaze on me again, but I had the uncomfortable feeling that she was not seeing me. "The caravan – perhaps you are right about that. That was a different time and yes, now that I remember it, the lantern shone through the trees, and the caravan wasn't broken at all, and there was a horse grazing, and she came running up the lonnen with a bag in each hand –"

"Miss Linsey –" I spoke breathlessly, but she took no notice. She swept on, still looking past me as if the cottage walls had melted into the dusk.

"And then they weren't there. They weren't there. That's right. That was a dream. Mildred's wrong. They were in the lonnen, not at the cottage."

I said nothing. A coal fell in the grate, and the little noise seemed to bring her back, and to rebuild the firelit room round us. She turned to me.

"But the other time wasn't the same. They were in the cemetery. And they didn't have a lantern then. He had a torch, an ordinary electric torch. He was shining it down on the grave."

That frisson again at the word. I didn't speak. Her eyes focused on me, disturbed and disturbing still, but not mad. Certainly not mad.

She gave a nod. "You do understand. It isn't always easy to keep the two kinds of reality apart. So please forgive me, and forget it if you can, the dream about the caravan. Even if it happened like that, it was a long time ago."

"I know."

She set her tea-cup aside and leaned forward. She had abandoned her whispering, and the normal, everyday tones somehow helped to enforce belief, as if she really had come out of her dream-country to the reality of every day.

"But this was real, Kathy, and it happened on Sunday. I do always go to the cemetery on a Sunday, after the evening service, to tend Albert's grave – my brother, you never knew him – and Mrs Winton Smith had kept me talking, something about the Sunday School Treat, where I always help, so I was late, and when I got to the cemetery it was dark, but the light from the torch was reflected from a white headstone, that marble angel with the Bible, and I recognised her."

"But Miss Linsey, please! I'm not sure – are you really trying to tell me – what are you trying to tell me? That you think you saw –" I hesitated. "I don't know what you think you saw. But in any case it's nearly twenty years –"

"I know." Still that practical, everyday tone of voice. "That's why I said she was carrying her age well. Still so lovely, and in that light . . . I suppose my vision of her at the caravan – call it a dream if you find that a more comfortable word – my dream had reminded me of what she was like, but I was sure."

"I –" I took a deep breath. I found my heart had quickened uncomfortably, and I had to make an effort to keep the disbelieving protest out of my voice. "Look, Miss Linsey, all right. But if you were so sure it was, yes, let's put it into words – if you were so sure it was my mother, still alive and back here in

Todhall, why didn't you *say* something? Call out, or go closer and speak to her – at least ask her what had happened and what she was doing there?"

"I tried to," she said simply. "I did say something, and I tried to hurry, but I tripped over a kerbstone and dropped my flowers, and when I got up they were gone."

"'They'? You said 'they'. Who was with her?"

"I couldn't see him very well, and of course I never knew him, but he was tall and dark, like the gipsy, the one at the caravan."

"And when you tried to speak or approach them, they disappeared? Just vanished?"

She nodded, but as if answering a question I had not asked. "Yes, I know, my dear. You're kind, and you have good manners, and you listen, but you still don't believe. Well, I don't understand it any more than you do, and perhaps I was mistaken, but I had to tell you. I do believe that I saw them there, both together, on Sunday, by the grave."

"By your brother's grave?" I said, blankly.

"Oh, no! What would they be doing there? It was your Aunt Betsy's."

She went soon after that, refusing my offer to see her as far as the road. She had never been afraid of the dark, she told me, with something of a return to her earlier manner; night was more interesting than day. On this note she floated off, a shapeless ghost muffled in cloak and scarf, to vanish into the shadows of the lane.

Interesting indeed. I retreated rather smartly into the comforting firelight of the cottage kitchen, trying to think sensibly and coolly about what she had told me. It could not be true. It obviously could not be true. But, perhaps illogically, the very fact that her vision of the young Lilias's flight into the lonnen was apparently so accurate, bade one believe that her tale of the couple in the cemetery might be true, even if her interpretation of it was not.

I added the album to the goods laid ready for packing, then rummaged in the drawer for an envelope, ready for the list of dates for the vicar that would go up with the milk in the morning. As I folded the notes and sealed the envelope my mind raced away again, putting together the odd things that had happened. The light in the cottage garden. The empty safe – robbed by someone who had a key. The digging by the toolshed. And now this weird and unlikely story of Lilias and her gipsy at Aunt Betsy's graveside . . .

Comfortingly, none of it added up to anything believable. Lilias back from the dead, and not getting in touch with Gran or myself? Not going near anyone in the village? Coming back from a long silence of some sixteen years, during which time neither her mother nor her daughter had had a word from her? Coming back, apparently, simply to visit the grave of the woman she had, with reason, hated, and then vanishing like a ghost at Miss Linsey's approach?

I got briskly to my feet, propped the envelope behind the empty milk-bottle in the porch, along with a biscuit for Rosy, then I raked out the remains of the fire, and locked both doors before going up to bed. I didn't want any more of Miss Linsey's interesting things to happen while I was alone at Rose Cottage.

14

I was wakened next morning by the sound of Rosy's hoofs in the lane. I had not found it easy to get to sleep. The night had been quite silent and uneventful, but I kept thinking about Miss Linsey's ghosts. If Miss Mildred's story of the light at the cottage, and the digging, was true – as seemed to be proved by the disturbed patch near the toolshed and the state of the coal-shovel – then it was possible, just possible, that Miss Linsey's story of the couple with the light at the site of the old caravan might have some truth in it as well. As for her "seeing" of the young Lilias running up the lonnen with a bag in either hand, that was a story known by this time to everyone in the village, and she had admitted it to be merely a dream, but I was well aware that she had not been called a witch for nothing. I could think of at least two occasions when her prophetic "dream" of a disaster had been right, and on one of those occasions a life had been saved. So it might at least be worth looking into.

But her story of the couple encountered in the cemetery was harder to explain. Her Sunday evening visit to her brother's grave must have been real enough, but the encounter with the ghostly couple was surely a trick of the imagination, suggested, perhaps, by the other dream? For Miss Linsey to recognise Lilias, a Lilias last seen almost twenty years ago, and now glimpsed at some distance in the evening dusk, and then to have her and her gipsy companion vanish when approached – it had to be a dream, and dreams, as all Todhall knew, were Miss Linsey's stock-in-trade.

But what had so disturbed me about it was the fact that she had not enjoyed telling me. Had been, if not frightened, then deeply uneasy. So could there be some sort of "message" here for me? Some sort of ghostly getting-in-touch, like those prophecies of hers that the village still remembered with respect?

Which was nonsense, I told myself. And maybe I had missed a chance to solve my own mystery. With Miss Linsey in soothsaying mood, I should have asked her where Gran's treasures had vanished to . . .

On which robust note I turned over and went to sleep, and woke to the sound of the milk-cart and the creak of the garden gate.

I flung back the bedclothes and ran to the open casement.

"Good morning, Mr Blaney! I'm sorry, I slept in. Just a pint, please, and I wonder if you'd be good enough to leave that envelope at the vicarage? The vicar's expecting it."

"That's all right. No bother at all. Lovely day, isn't it? You staying on till the weekend? Well, don't you trouble yourself, you just get your sleep, and I'll leave you one tomorrow, and it'll be two on Saturday. We don't do a round on a Sunday."

I noticed the "we". Sunday wouldn't be his day off, farmers didn't have them. It was Rosy's. I had forgotten that. I smiled. "Yes, thank you. It looks as if I'm to be here at least till Monday. And that's Rosy's biscuit under the envelope."

He took it, pocketed the envelope, waved the empty bottle in salute, and went off.

Somehow his simple kindness made the worries of the night seem trivial. Cheered and soothed, I dressed and had breakfast and then, after finishing the morning's chores, went out to gather flowers for Granddad's grave. That I chose to visit the cemetery this morning was, I told myself, nothing to do with Miss Linsey's story. I had intended to go one day while I was here, to take flowers on Gran's behalf and for myself, and to check, as she had asked me to, that the sexton was earning the small fee he got for keeping the grave-plot tidy.

That was all. Nothing to do with ghosts, or a witch's dreams.

I didn't bother to find an excuse for what I did after I had gathered the flowers and packed them carefully with some damp moss into a basket. The cemetery lay at the south end of the village, and the shortest way would of course have been by the lane. The other route was by the lonnen, which reached the main road a good quarter of a mile beyond the cemetery wall.

I went by the lonnen.

There was a stronger breeze today, and the birds were still busy with their morning songs. Deep in the lane the air was still, full of the scents of fern and dead leaves and wild garlic and the musk of Herb Robert trodden underfoot. High overhead the treetops rustled and soughed, but where I walked it was like being at the bottom of a deep, still stream. The only movement was the sudden whisk of russet-brown as a squirrel scudded up a tree-trunk, and the flight of a blackbird cutting low across the path with a beakful of food for its young.

The remains of the caravan were still there, some little way above the gap where I had entered the lonnen on my way from the station. Elder and brambles were growing round and into it, and everywhere there were nettles, those jackal plants that follow humans and take over their deserted homes.

One wheel lay flat, barely visible in long grass. The other was still held, at a crazy slant, by a rusted bolt. The wood of both was almost rotted away, held only by the decaying iron rims. The van itself was a rotten shell, its roof fallen in and its sides sagging. The shafts, the whole front rig, had come adrift and was in pieces on the ground.

It was a long-forgotten wreck which could not possibly have anything to tell me. Nevertheless I set my basket down and prodded about among the crumbling wood and the undergrowth, picking up a few nettle-stings and a scratch or two from the brambles, but no message from the past. Nothing left by the ghosts of Miss Linsey's vision. Just a host of memories, my own ghosts, remembered with amusement and a kind of sadness, the ghosts of the children who had played in this lane, and for whom this derelict gipsy-van had been at once romantic and terrifying, and a goal of challenge and delight.

A sound brought me round, my heart suddenly thudding, as if the place had not wholly lost its terror. A sound which in any other place would hardly even have made me turn my head. A breaking twig, and the slither of a footstep on the bank above me.

The sun, blazing through a gap at the top of the bank, was blinding me. Against it, at the head of the bank, stood a man, gigantic against the distorting brilliance, body bent forward to stare down at me. He grabbed a branch, swung himself through the gap, and came down the bank at a run, and it was only Davey Pascoe, in his working overalls, and not looking in the least like the menacing gipsy giant that my nerves had conjured up. In fact, so wrapped had I been in my memories that it came as a kind of shock to see him there, a young man with the same thatch of light-brown hair and the same grey eyes as the child whose ghost, a moment before, had been playing there.

I let my breath out. "Damn you, Davey! You frightened me!"

"Did I? Well, you disappointed me. I heard something moving about down here, and I thought it might be a badger. There's a sett further up, and they do sometimes come out in daylight."

"Really. Well, I'm sorry. But what were you doing here anyway?"

"I've been at Swords. The job's finished, so I thought I'd come back this way and see how you were getting on. I'm not working this afternoon, and I thought you might be starting to sort the stuff out for packing."

"Well, thanks, but I haven't done much yet." I indicated the basket of flowers. "I was going to the cemetery with those."

"Why this way? It's quicker by the lane." He grinned, and it was the grin I remembered. "Or did someone dare you?"

"Who'd do that? I never took the dare anyway. No,

I came because I wanted to see –" I stopped. I was not sure myself just what I had wanted to see.

"See what?"

"I don't know. It sounds silly. The van, I suppose. I've wondered, sometimes, if there's any way you could tell where it was made or who owned it. You know, like a number plate on a car."

"After all this time? Even if there was, it's gone long since." He was frowning now. "Look, Kathy, it's past history. You'll do yourself no good by trying to rake it all up again now. Can't you let yourself see that it's past?" He finished it deliberately. "Past and dead and gone."

The three syllables fell like stones. I turned and picked up the basket.

"Yes. I know. I've accepted that long ago. I've had to. Don't worry about me, Davey. I don't want to rake anything up that's better left alone. But we've got this mystery on our hands, Gran's things being stolen, and I thought – well, something happened last night that set me wondering, and I came along here to check it out."

"Last night?" he said sharply. "What happened? Has anyone been bothering you at the cottage?"

"No, no. Nothing like that. It was Miss Linsey. She came to see me, and told me some very queer things."

He laughed. "Old Linsey-woolsey? I'll bet. Such as?"

"Oh, it's a long story, and it'll sound queerer still in daylight."

"Well, queer or not, I'll listen. Here, give me that basket. I'll go back with you, and you can tell me about it."

*   *   *

His bicycle was at the head of the bank, propped against a stump. He slung the basket over the handlebars and, as we walked up through the field towards the road, with Davey wheeling the bicycle, I told him about Miss Linsey's visit.

His reaction was, I suppose, predictable.

"Silly old bat, saying she didn't want to scare you, and then doing her best to give you nightmares! Well, you can forget all that about your mum running up the lonnen. I could've said all that to you myself, there's no one in the village that hadn't heard all about her taking off like that, and, I might say," he added, "there's no one who blames her, running away from that old catamaran – well, speak no ill, and there's two sides to everything. But this tale of old Linsey-woolsey's about the couple at the graveside – that might be interesting, seeing what else has happened. I mean, there's been someone at the cottage, that's for sure, and it might just be that – Oh, well, leave it for now. Here we are, and we can go in by the side gate. Your Granda's near it, you'll remember, a little way along."

There was a door set into the high brick wall of the cemetery. Davey leaned the bicycle there, retrieved my basket for me, and pushed open the door.

15

The cemetery was large – two fields taken over from Low Beck Farm when the old churchyard became too crowded to be serviceable – and surrounded by a high wall. My grandfather's grave was about midway along on the west side, a large plot, to leave space, as I remembered Gran saying, for late-comers. Among the flowers I had brought for him were clusters of his favourite rose, the cottage rose, Old Blush, which he had planted in every available space at home, because, he said, they wouldn't let him grow "the real roses" at the Hall, just "those coloured cabbages they breed nowadays, all size and no scent".

"You'll want water for those," said Davey. "The tap's over near the main gate, and there's usually a can there. I'll get it for you." He went off, leaving me to go to the grave-side alone.

I had stooped to set my basket down at the kerbside

before I realised that, when I had gathered the flowers that morning, I had not even thought about taking any for Aunt Betsy. Admittedly, she had never expressed a preference for, or even an opinion of, any flower or plant, except to complain about the scent of the wild garlic in the lane, but even so –

I need not have troubled. On the grave-space next to my grandfather's there were already flowers, masses of them, arranged with some care in a couple of metal urns. Not roses, but a mixture of garden and wild flowers, lupins and delphiniums and Canterbury bells, along with dog-daisies and cornflowers, and trails of ivy and wild honeysuckle. The wild flowers were all dead or dying, but the others were fresh still.

Even in the presence of the quiet dead it is not easy to control one's thoughts. My first one was, who in the world would have done this for that very unpopular old woman, my great-aunt? My second was that she herself would have called it a sinful waste, and Popish at that.

So who? Miss Linsey's ghosts? My dead mother and her long-dead gipsy, creeping after dark into the cemetery with this charming tribute to someone whom, in life, she had disliked, even hated, whose viper's tongue had driven her from home? If there was any sort of truth in Miss Linsey's tale of lights and people at the grave, no ghosts had put these flowers there. Then who? Not Gran; she had known that I would visit the grave-plot, and she surely would have told me if she had asked anyone else to bring flowers.

A sudden breeze stirred the grasses by the wall, sending a couple of petals floating to the ground, and bringing with it the scent of roses, and with the scent, a vivid memory of a garden crammed with roses and lupins and all the flowers of summer. Miss Mildred's garden. Miss Mildred, the one person I knew whose simple loving-kindness would have embraced even Aunt Betsy. Whose loving-kindness put me to shame.

I detached a sprig of the cottage rose from the bunch in my basket, and laid it on her grave, then turned to give the rest to Granddad.

He, too, had been visited. In the vase near the headstone was a bunch of roses, chief among them the silvery pink of his beloved Old Blush.

"Who in the world?" I asked. "Miss Mildred?"

"Might be," said Davey. He had returned with a can of water, and we had puzzled over it together. There was no card or message. "But I've not seen flowers here before. Well, we can ask her, but I doubt it's not her."

Another "we", and in its own way as comforting as Mr Blaney's. I smiled at him, and knelt to replace the fading roses in the vase with the fresh ones I had brought. "Then who?"

"Dear knows, but you see what it might mean? Look at those flowers. The garden ones are still okay, but the wild ones, the cornflowers and such, they're all dead. Which they would be, if they've been there since Sunday."

I sat back on my heels, staring up at him. "Then you really think that? Miss Linsey's ghosts?"

"I reckon so. Who else? It fits. Somebody brought them. Somebody's been here. It could be folk your aunt had known at home in Scotland, maybe, visiting nearby, and they came over, and old Linsey-woolsey saw them."

"But Davey, they vanished. She said they just disappeared."

He pointed to the door we had come in by. "She'd have come in by the main gate. If her two ghosts came

123

in the way we did and left the door open, it's only a couple of steps out to the road, and they'd gone. It was pretty dark Sunday night."

"Ye-es. Yes, you could be right. But who? And if it was friends of the family, Gran's family, why didn't they go into the village, to see your mother, perhaps? Or to Rose Cottage –" I stopped.

"Yeah," said Davey. "That's what it comes to, isn't it? They did go to Rose Cottage. They may have come to see Mum as well, but there was nobody home at our place last weekend. Look, let's not worry about it now. If they came to leave flowers here, they mean no harm to you and yours, that's for sure. And if you're thinking what I think you are, stop it."

"I – I don't know what to think."

"Then don't try. Have you finished your flowers?"

"Yes." I stood up, watching while he tilted the can to trickle water into the vases. "Look, why don't we stop by Witches' Corner and ask Miss Mildred if she brought the flowers. Get that bit clear, at least."

"No good. She's not home. She went into Sunderland this morning, and it's my guess the two of them'll go to the pictures and get home late. There, I needn't have bothered to get the water. There's plenty. Hang on while I tip the rest out. Those pansies could do with a drop, and that rose bush by the wall. That's it. Okay. Tell you what, we'll go home, and Mum'll give us some dinner, and maybe talk some sense into us."

As it happened, Mrs Pascoe did not get the chance, as, by unspoken consent, neither Davey nor I mentioned Miss Linsey or the riddle of the cemetery. We told her merely that we had met in Gipsy Lonnen, and that he had gone back with me to put flowers on the graves. and brought me home for dinner.

"If that's all right?" I said. An unexpected guest could pose problems with food rationing.

"Lord bless you, child, of course it is. There's plenty, and you're welcome. Davey, get her a knife and fork, and go and call your father."

She refused my offer of help, told me briskly to sit down, and began to dish up a large chicken pie. "And had old Tom been doing a good job on the graves?"

"Mr Corner told me he was still sexton, and I could hardly believe it! Does he do it all himself still? I used to think he was about a hundred, and that's years ago."

"Eighty-two, and won't even talk about retiring. He does get help with the grave-digging, though."

"Well, the place was very tidy, and the grave looked fine." I hesitated, then asked her merely if Miss Mildred was in the habit of taking flowers to the cemetery. She knew nothing about that, she said, with a kind of snort, but she did know that poor Miss Mildred wasn't even welcome, these days, to take them to the church, since the vicar's wife fancied her own stuff so much, and looked down her nose at other people's.

"And now there's none coming in from the Hall – here, Jim," as Mr Pascoe and Davey came in, "yours is ready." She set his plate down, and spooned potatoes. "Have you washed your hands, Davey?"

"Yes, Mum," said Davey, and winked at me as he took his place.

Mr Pascoe greeted me as he sat down. He was a quiet, mild-mannered man, who was known for miles around as an excellent craftsman. He was, in looks, an older version of Davey; an inch or so shorter, perhaps, and with the thicker body and greying hair of middle age, but the same grey eyes and indefinable poise of self-belief that marks the man who knows his limitations, but who also knows what he is good for, and expects – and receives – the respect it brings him. It was a dignity which, I supposed, carried over from the other part of his profession. He was, of course, the local undertaker.

"Davey says you've been to see the graves? They'd be all right, old Tom does the grass every Friday, rain or shine. By the way, Kathy, I've been on to Caslaws, and they'll do your move for you Monday at latest, but there's a chance of Saturday, so you'd best be ready. Davey can take time off to give you a hand."

"Thank you very much."

"You're welcome, you know that. Give the girl some more of those potatoes, Mother. She'll be on short rations down there at the cottage."

"No, really, I've got plenty. The pie's lovely, Aunty Annie."

Mrs Pascoe primmed her lips, looking pleased. "Well, eat up," she said, and sitting down she began to ask me about the Brandons and Gran's new house, while Davey and his father ate busily and, when they spoke at all, exchanged brief comments about the work they were doing at the Hall.

I helped clear the plates, and while Mrs Pascoe was dishing the pudding – a hearty syrup sponge – I asked her, "Was there much damage done at the Hall in the war? Gran said it was a mess, though I suppose you can't blame the boys. The RAF, I mean."

She gave me a quick, sideways look. "Nobody blames them, poor lads. We all know what they did for us, and if that's any comfort to you, it's the truth."

"Thank you. These two plates for the men?"

"That one was for you. If it's too much, give it to Davey. No, the Hall wasn't too bad, really, just scratches and chips everywhere, and the floors a bit of a mess. Nothing that can't be repaired, with a bit of plaster and a lick of paint and some polish to bring it up lovely again. No real harm done. We'd moved some of the breakables down to the cellar, and the carpets from the drawing-room, and the pictures, and things like that. The books are still down there."

"Is the kitchen still the same?"

"The big kitchen, yes. They put a modern stove in the servery, and the cooking was mostly done there. The library's the worst. That's where the bar was."

"I can imagine."

She primmed her mouth again, but looked amused. "Well, they had a dart-board there. Where old Sir Giles's portrait used to be."

"Oh dear."

"But the billiard room's all right. Someone must have kept their eye on that."

"Billiard room?" said Davey. "You talking about Toad Hall?"

Mrs Pascoe tut-tutted, and I laughed as I got up to help her with the dishes. I had forgotten the name which, inevitably, had stuck to Tod Hall once *The Wind in the Willows* reached our classroom. Our elders, afraid of the Hall's reaction, had tried, but in vain, to stop us using it.

"I'm taking the van across this afternoon," said Davey, to me. "Want to come over with me?"

"I thought you said you weren't working this afternoon?"

"I'm not. But Dad wants some tools bringing that he left there, and there's some timber needs carting over as well. Wouldn't you like to see the place?"

"Well, yes, I would. I'll be writing to Gran tonight, and I know she'd like to hear what's going on."

"If you're writing to your Gran —" said Mr Pascoe.

"Annie, lass, there's that paper the masons sent. Can you think on where we put it?"

"It's behind the clock on the mantelpiece. Get it for your Dad, Davey."

"Give it to Kathy," said Mr Pascoe. "There you are, Kathy, maybe you'll send it to your Gran, if you're writing. I'd have asked her about it myself, if she'd been on the phone. They want to know about the text for the stone."

"The stone?

"Your Aunt Betsy's headstone. Well, it's the same stone, of course, your Granddad's. There's space left, as you know. The masons have taken long enough, they always do, but I wrote a while ago to ask them what was keeping them back, and they said they were still waiting for the text. You know how most folk like something from the Bible put on the stone, and your Gran did say something about it, but I reckon she's forgotten."

"Well, I'll ask her, but she probably didn't want one." I thought of the Unseen Guest, who would have been welcome, I was sure, in this kindly house. "I think she had enough of them at home. But I'll ask her, certainly."

"And tell her we were asking after her."

This, being translated, was "give her our love". I promised, smiling, and was interrupted by Davey, sounding impatient.

"Are you coming? If we go now I can get you back in plenty of time for your date with the vicar."

I glanced at Mrs Pascoe as I hung the tea-towel to dry above the fireplace.

"You go on," she said. "I'll be quicker putting the things away myself. I know where they go."

As she turned to stack the clean dishes away in a cupboard, I thought she was smiling.

16

Davey drove the van round to the back of the Hall, and under the archway into the courtyard. This was a wide, cobbled square, with the old mounting-block at its centre, and on two sides the stable doors and the archways of the coach-house. One of the other sides had held offices and quarters – now mostly storerooms – for those servants who had lived in, and on the fourth side were the back premises of the Hall itself.

I remembered the courtyard as a peaceful place, where doves strutted and cooed, or flew up in mock alarm when the stable clock struck or a gardener wheeled his barrow across the cobbles. But today it was very different. Evidences of the proposed conversion were everywhere, piles of bricks, a cement-mixer, ladders, buckets, timber, and an unattractive collection of bathroom fittings still pasted up with strips of gummed wrapping. And there was something else that was new, or rather, unexpected after the gap of years. The smell of horses. The stable half-doors and the old tack-room door stood open, and outside was a pile of manure sweepings ready to be carted off, presumably, to the garden heap.

"Horses?" I said to Davey. "Who's got horses here now?"

"It's a riding-school, has been for nearly two years now, and the family thought it'd be a good idea to have riding here for the hotel. You remember Harry Coleman?"

I remembered Harry Coleman, a good-looking boy a couple of years older than myself, who had been in the senior class at school. For one long blushful year I had been one of his worshipping admirers. One of the crowd. He went up to the secondary school two years before me, and was there, ready to receive our homage once more, when Prissy and I were enrolled. He was kind to us, unbending from the height of his achievements in the sports field, and our greatest privilege had been to travel back to Todhall with him in the same carriage, and carry his school bag to his home gate. Luckily his home gate had been very near the station. His father farmed Low Beck, which belonged to the Hall.

"Handsome Harry?" I said. "Running a riding place here?"

"Aye. Doesn't make much out of that yet. The schoolteacher goes there, and a couple of boys from Fishburn way, but he keeps horses there, at livery he calls it, for some of the locals – Mr Taylor's got one, and Jim Sands, and the Blake girl from Deepings. They hunt with the South Durham. It was Harry thought of it, and his Dad put the cash up, so the family let them have the stables. They reckon it'll be an extra draw once the hotel gets going."

"I remember Harry was always keen, and his father kept a good horse for him. I was there when he won the cup at Sedgefield. He used to talk about Olympia, but of course there was the war. Did he ever get there?"

"Not that I ever heard, and if he had we'd have all heard," said Davey drily. He swung down from the cab and turned to unlash the timber from the roof of the van. "I'll get this stuff stacked in the coach-house under cover. D'you want to go into the house now? Here's the key."

"Yes, I'd like to. How long will you be?"

"Not long, but there's no hurry. I'll come and fetch you."

He shouldered some of the timber and tramped off towards one of the coach-house archways. I made for the back door. It opened on a long passage floored with stone flags. There was evidence here, too, that work was being done, but when I reached the kitchen I found it much the same as I remembered it.

For a house built in the early nineteenth century, the kitchen was a good one. It was on ground level, and the big, barred windows, though they faced north, looked out over the walled kitchen-garden. There were few concessions to modern living, so I supposed it was inevitable that, to make it viable as a hotel kitchen, the working premises would have to be stripped and totally rebuilt.

Why was it that one always regretted change? Things were not made to stay fixed, preserved in amber. Perhaps the only acceptable amber was memory. I had "helped" in this kitchen so many times. I could remember when the table-tops were above my eye-level, and I shared the floor under the table with the dog, waiting, both of us, for the piece of cake or biscuit to be handed down and shared. The kitchen, the heart of the house, with its warmth and its wonderful smells of baking, or the delectable smell of roasting meat, and the sizzle and spit as the joint was speared and turned in the pan. The clashing of pots and dishes and the cheerful chatter of women's voices. A whole world, once. And now changed, and soon to be changed again. And, surely, for the better? One had to believe that the world was changing for the better, or else why live? That, arguably, was one of the facets of what Christians called faith?

I left the empty kitchen and once again went through the green baize door that shut the servants' quarters off from the main house. That first door led to the dining-room, where sometimes I had helped Alice, the parlourmaid, to set the table. The big room was empty now, echoing, stripped and waiting for the contractors.

No stab of regret here, no memories. I shut the door on it and went along to the hall. This – the great hall, as we called it – was a room in itself. The front door opened into it, and there was a huge open fireplace to one side, usually protected by screens from the draughts that were everywhere. The main staircase was opposite the door, a wide flight rising to a landing, where it divided, the twin stairs leading to the two wings of the house. The landing was lit, grudgingly, by a stained-glass window. The only time, Gran had said, that the hall had been habitable – in fact the only time I had ever been in it – was at Christmas, when we schoolchildren had come carol-singing with the vicar, and there had been a fire in the vast fireplace, and a tree, and a mince pie and an orange for each child.

The drawing-room lay on the south side of the hall.

The big double doors were shut. I hesitated for a moment, then, feeling as guilty as if I were invading Bluebeard's chamber, I pushed them open.

A blaze of light met me, from three big floor-length windows that threw sharp patterns of sunshine slanting across an acre or so of unpolished parquet floor. A pair of Chinese carpets, presumably restored from their place in the cellars, lay in front of the twin fireplaces, with chairs and sofas disposed here and there. There was a grand piano, covered and, it was to be hoped, undamaged. A writing desk. A big breakfront bookcase, empty of books. Not much else in the way of furniture, but pictures, lamps, and a couple of vast Chinese jars on carved pedestals, all back in place. It was a beautiful room still, a room that looked as if it had only been temporarily abandoned, and could be lived in, and loved, again. Even its owners were still there; above the fireplaces hung the portraits – done presumably soon after they took over the Hall – of Sir James and Lady Brandon.

I stood looking up at the portrait of the young Sir James.

Immaculate in riding clothes, he was pictured with horse and dogs beside a tree in the park, but, I thought, put him in uniform and make him smile, and he could have sat for the photograph of his son Gilbert that I had seen in Lady Brandon's sitting-room at Strathbeg. It was the same boy, dark-haired, dark-eyed, and handsome . . .

"Changed a bit, hasn't he?" asked Davey, behind me.

"Well, don't we all? You have."

"And you," said Davey.

"Yes. Well, it's been a long time." I turned away towards a window. "I was just thinking how like him

Gilbert was. Not that I saw him after he'd gone away to school – except at a distance, I mean – but there was a photo of him at Strathbeg, and it could be the same person. Poor Gilbert."

"It was a long war," he said, and then, with a hesitation that was unusual in him, "I didn't like to say anything before, but, well, you getting married and then losing him like that. I'm sorry."

"Thank you. It – well, it seems a bit like another life now. I was lucky to have what I did. And you, Davey? I'm surprised you're not married."

"Never got round to it. Never seemed to have the time."

"What sort of war did you have?"

"Oh, joined up as soon as I was eighteen – the DLI, of course, you were allowed your choice then if you were a volunteer. You'd just gone to college in Durham. There were four of us from the village, Arthur Barton and Pete Brigstock and Sid Telfer and me. You knew about Sid?"

"Yes."

"The four of us stayed together right through training, then we were drafted, and our battalion – the 16th, it was – was in Algiers by 1943. That's where Sid got his, at Sedjenane."

"I remember the news from there. It was rough, wasn't it?"

"Well, it wasn't a picnic. Pete got through it all without a scratch, and ended up in Italy, having a great time, according to him, en route to Greece." He laughed. "You should hear some of the things he has to tell, or come to think of it, maybe you shouldn't! To hear him now, it makes me sorry I missed out on the Greek bit."

"So don't miss out on what did happen. I know about Arthur. Do you mean you were wounded, too?"

"Nothing much." He was dismissive. "I was back on active service in a matter of weeks, in time for D-Day. After that it was Normandy till the end of the war. Demobbed early this year. End of story."

"Yes. End of story." I was silent for a minute, remembering how lightly, almost, Davey and I had spoken of change. If the almost domestic traumas of my war had made something so different of me, what, then, of Davey? Back to Todhall and home and the old life? End of story?

I said, "Do you remember the shows Mr Lockwood used to put on in the village hall when we were little?"

"The magic lantern? Yes. They were great – at least we thought so then. Why?"

"I was remembering that slide he had, the kaleidoscope, where you turned a handle and all the bits of coloured glass got shaken up, and then fell into another pattern, a different one each time. Like the war. Shaking all our lives up into a different pattern, so different that we don't quite know what the pattern means."

He gave me a quick look I couldn't interpret, then he smiled. "We got shook up, no mistake about that, but I wouldn't worry too much about what the pattern is. Maybe it has changed a bit, but if you think about it, it's the same bits of glass every time."

"And that's a comfort?"

"It's meant to be, but take it or leave it."

Feeling, for some reason, vaguely lightened, I looked around me again at the big, calm beautiful room. "At any rate, this is still here, even if this sort of thing" – I lifted a hand – "is changing, too. Has changed already, everywhere."

"This sort of life, you mean? That's true. But this room isn't to be touched, just done up again. No change. Her ladyship's made sure of that."

135

"I'm glad. It's lovely, even though it's so grand – and so neglected. Do you know, I've never seen it before. I was never allowed in, even to dust."

"I'm not supposed to be in here now," he said cheerfully. "Come on. It's not worth going up into the south wing, it's still just a mess, and you can't really see what it'll be like. We haven't got much of a start yet. I'll just go up and get Dad's tool-bag, and I'll see you in the courtyard, and get you back for your date with the vicar."

We went back through the green baize door together.

17

As I went out into the sunshine of the courtyard, I heard the clatter of hoofs and the sound of a girl's laugh.

A few moments later two riders came in under the clock-tower arch, a man and a young woman. Neither of them, busy with their talk, noticed me, but I recognised the old flame of my childhood. Handsome Harry was still handsome, and his riding clothes, whipcord breeches and a yellow shirt with a silk cravat, suited him well. The girl was a good-looking blonde, beautifully turned out, who sat her horse well. A match for her escort, I thought, in more ways than one; she had a sort of smooth polish to movement and manner that could easily deal with men more worldly than Handsome Harry.

Before he could get round to help her dismount, she had thrown her right leg forward over the pommel and slid competently to the ground. He bent to loosen the girth, with some remark in an undertone, but she replied briefly and turned away, to see me sitting on the step of the mounting-block.

To my surprise, after a moment's fixed staring, her face lit up. "Kathy? Kathy Welland? It is Kathy, isn't it?"

I got to my feet. "Yes. But I'm afraid –?"

Laughing, she pulled off the peaked riding-cap and ran a hand through the fair hair. Harry had turned when she spoke, but she took no notice of him other than to throw him the reins of her horse. "Well? Now do you know me?"

"Prissy? It *is* Prissy? Oh my goodness me, where did you spring from?"

We flew together and kissed. The embrace was warmer than any we had exchanged in girlhood, but five years is five years, and there was a lot of time to make up. We clung to one another and laughed and asked questions and both talked at once while Harry, with the reins of both horses looped over one arm, hovered nearby, tapping his crop impatiently against a boot.

"Kathy Welland? Hullo, there!"

"Hi, Harry." I threw it over my shoulder with a smile. "Nice to see you! Davey told me you were running the place here. It looks great. But Prissy, what on earth are *you* doing here in Todhall?"

"Just visiting, honey, just visiting! We're staying near Bishop Auckland with friends of Gordon's, and I don't play golf, so when someone said that Harry had started the stable up here, I came over on spec. But you, I might ask the same of you! What in the world brings you back here? I thought you'd shaken the dust off your feet years ago!"

I started to tell her, but at that moment Davey, with a tool-bag slung over one shoulder, came into the yard and made for his van. He gave Harry a nod, then glanced across at me, hesitating.

"He's giving me a lift back," I said to Prissy. "It's Davey Pascoe, you remember Davey?"

"Of course I do. I was here on Tuesday and I saw him and Mr Pascoe then. Hullo, Davey, how's it going?"

"Slowly. The hotel's supposed to open for Christmas, and dear knows if it will, but that's not our problem, and our bit of the job should get done all right. Nice to see you again, Pris. D'you want a lift now, Kathy, or do you want to wait and get Pris to take you back?"

"Oh, God, I can't," she said. "Kathy, I'm sorry, but I'm due to join them at the Golf Club and we're going on to drinks with some people the Heslops know, and I've got to get back to change. Look, I've just got to see you, masses to talk about. You're a rotten letter-writer and so am I. How long are you here for and where are you staying?"

"I'm at Rose Cottage, but I'll only be there a day or two, just over the weekend."

"I could come there. I suppose you're not even on the phone? No? Well, then, we'll have to fix it now. What about tomorrow?"

"I thought you were coming riding again," put in Harry.

"Well, I'm sorry, but I can't. It'll just be the two days I owe you for. But thanks for today, it was great."

"Why don't you both come?" he persisted. "The day after tomorrow? Saturday? We could go out by Low Beck, and get a good canter –"

"I can't ride," I said.

The familiar, charming smile. He really was very attractive. "I could teach you. I'd give you Maudie, she's very quiet, and we can forget the canter. You'd enjoy it." Then under his breath, but quite audibly, "And so would I."

"I'm sure I would. But I can't, thanks all the same." I turned back to Prissy, raising my voice above the sudden clatter as Davey threw the bag of tools into the back of the van, and slammed the doors shut. "And it's no good for us, either, I'm afraid, Pris. I'm packing the place up for Gran. She's at Strathbeg now, did you know? and she's decided to stay there. I've really only come to Todhall to get her stuff moved for her. Uncle Jim's fixing it with the movers for me, and he said something about Saturday, but I don't know yet. I'll be packing up tomorrow. So how about Monday? If the movers do come, we'll be a bit short of furniture, but we'll have a table and chairs and something to cook on, and what more do we want?"

"Sorry," she said, "I can't. We're leaving on Saturday. Tell you what, I'll come over tomorrow and give you a hand, and we'll go and eat somewhere good –"

"Such as?" I said, and laughed. "Spam sandwich at the Bull? You've forgotten, haven't you? Come over at lunch-time, anyway, and we'll eat at home, if I can remember to keep back some knives and forks. It'd be lovely to see you, and don't worry about the packing. Davey's going to help with that."

"Sure. Whatever you say. I'll be there."

Harry started to say something then, but just behind us Davey started up the van's engine, which was a noisy one.

"I've got to go," I said. "Nice to see you, Harry, and I hope things go well. You've a lovely place here. Tomorrow, then, Pris, any time you like, and that'll be wonderful. Okay, Davey, sorry to keep you waiting."

I climbed into the van, and we were off.

"Did you know Prissy Lockwood had friends at Bishop Auckland?" I asked him.

"Yes. Her husband and Major Heslop served together in the war. In Burma, I think. They go over there quite a bit, but this week's the first time I know of that she's been back to Toad Hall." A sidelong look that took me straight back to primary school. "Quite an Old Toddlers' Reunion, wasn't it? Do you think she came over here for Harry? She was always a bit sweet on him."

"Be your age, Davey, that was centuries ago, and anyway, it was just kids' stuff."

"For you, too?"

"For heaven's sake, I was in my teens, and as silly as they always are!" I rounded on him. "If it comes to that, what about you and Peggy Turner? You used to trail about after her like a puppy dog, and what you ever saw in her –!"

"Okay, okay, skinch!" *Skinch* was the local children's word for "pax", and I hadn't heard it for at least ten years. I laughed and, quite suddenly and for no reason that I knew of, felt like crying. I turned quickly to look out of the van window. The park stretched away, summer pasture studded with big trees, their lower branches, grazed flat by the cattle, stretching smoothly parallel to the ground. Each tree made its own island of shade, where sheep and cattle clustered. No change here, not yet. The same yesterday, and today. But tomorrow?

Davey said no more as we turned out through the main park gates and rattled along the half mile that led to Lane Ends, the northern limit of the village street. No one was about. The place drowsed in the sun. The geese had disappeared, and Muffin was back by the pond. Cause and effect, no doubt.

141

"What time are you seeing the vicar?" asked Davey.

"Half past three, at the church."

"It's getting on for three now. If you like, you can wait at our place."

"No, no, I'll be fine. If you just put me down at the shop, I'll see what I can get for Prissy's lunch tomorrow, and then I'll sit in the sun till he comes."

"Okay. This do?"

"Yes thank you. Thanks again, Davey, I enjoyed it."

"Don't mention it. Do you still want me to come down and help with the packing-up tomorrow?"

"Yes, of course, if you have time."

"I'll have time. And if you come by the workshop after you've seen the vicar, I'll run you home."

"Well, thank you, but –"

"See you," he said, and drove off.

I stared after him for a moment or two, then said something polite to Muffin, and went into the shop to see what I could find to feed Prissy on the morrow.

18

It was almost a quarter to four when the vicar at last came hurrying across the green into the churchyard, where I was sitting on the warm stone of the wall, waiting for him.

"I really am very sorry, Mrs Herrick, but we were over at Sedgefield for lunch, and then my wife needed the car, so I came home by bus, and the bus was late, and then there was someone waiting for me at the vicarage, and I simply couldn't get away. Have you been here long?"

"Not really, and anyway, who minds waiting on a day like this? I've enjoyed sitting in the sun."

"It is a lovely day, isn't it?" But he had hardly the air of anyone noticing. He wore his cassock, and carried a clean surplice over his arm. "Shall we go inside? The papers are in the vestry."

I slid from my perch and went with him. Inside the

vestry it was cool and dim. He laid the clean surplice carefully over a chair, then took a key from a pocket and unlocked the old-fashioned safe – little more than a metal cupboard with a padlock – that stood in one corner. I caught a glimpse of books, registers, I supposed, stacked inside, and some objects wrapped in green baize that were presumably the Communion silver, and a cash box. He turned with a long manila envelope in his hand.

"Copies of what records we have," he said. "There may be others, but I looked up the dates you gave me, and came up with these."

"That's wonderful." I took the envelope. "Thank you very much."

"I was glad to be able to help. I did speak to Bob Crawley, by the way, and he told me some tale he had heard from the Miss Popes about a stranger at Rose Cottage this last weekend, but apparently he went all round the place and saw no sign of a break-in."

"I knew about that. Miss Mildred told me she thought she saw something, but that was all. I don't think it was anything to worry about."

"I'm glad to hear it." An inquiring look over the half-moon glasses. "Have you any clue yet as to what happened to the missing objects?"

"None at all. I've been asking around, but no one knows anything, and I'm sure the thief wouldn't be anyone local. Even if someone broke in and pinched the coins and medals and so on, they'd hardly take the papers, once they saw that the envelopes didn't hold cash. Well, thank you again, vicar. Is there – I mean, I think there's something called a search fee?"

"Indeed, indeed. I must charge you an exorbitant fee for my very valuable time." He smiled. "Six and eightpence, if you can manage it, and would be good enough to put it in the poor-box at the south door?"

"Of course. But if I may – there was just one more thing while I'm here –"

"Yes?" He had already turned away to pick up the surplice. Through the half-open door leading to the chancel I could hear sounds of people coming into the church. The christening party, presumably. I said quickly: "My grandfather's gravestone. My great-aunt is buried there, but they haven't yet put an inscription up. I wondered – they seem to have taken a very long time. I did wonder if my grandmother had forgotten to make arrangements for it, or if there had been a hold-up of some sort? I understand that the – well, the wording has to be approved by you?"

He stopped, with his head protruding from the neck of the surplice. With his hands sticking out of the sleeves he looked like a travesty of someone in the stocks. His spectacles had slipped right to the tip of his nose. Above them his eyes, unfocused, looked puzzled and, uncharacteristically, vague.

"I have no recollection of any letter from Mrs Welland, but I may be wrong. It is certainly some time since Miss Campbell died, and I would have thought ... Oh dear. How remiss of me not to have followed it up sooner." A wriggle, and the surplice drifted into place. He pushed the straying spectacles back into place and straightened, in all the dignity of his robes.

"I think I hear the christening party now, so I must leave it, but if you like to go over to the vicarage and ask Lil to give you Paterson's address – it is beside the telephone in the hall – you can find out what, if anything, has been arranged. In fact, I seem to recall Lil saying there had been an inquiry quite recently,

145

so you may find that your grandmother has been in touch with Paterson herself. Or Mr Pascoe might know. Paterson is the stone-mason, and I am afraid he tends to be . . . shall we say dilatory? Please use my telephone if you wish – I know you have none at Rose Cottage."

I started to protest that there was no hurry, and that Mr Pascoe had already asked me about it, but he had turned away to gather his things together, with his eye on the vestry door, and his mind already on the party waiting at the font, where the star of the show could be heard already yelling blue murder. "Oh dear," he said, "one of those. Now if you will excuse me, Mrs Herrick –?"

"Of course. Thank you again. You're very kind. I won't forget the poor-box. Good afternoon, vicar."

I left by the outer door, amused to find myself automatically turning right off the gravel walk, following the rough grassy track that wound through the ancient gravestones to encircle the church. Another flicker of memory, rolling the years back. Coming out of Sunday School, ready for the long walk home – in those days one had run almost all the way – we children had always turned that way. One walked round a church clockwise, never widdershins. Just as one never stepped on the joins of paving-stones. And never forgot to cross one's fingers while telling a lie. And cried "skinch" to stop being teased or bullied . . .

Old Toddlers' Day.

The poor-box was in the south porch. I folded a ten-shilling note and pushed it through the slot. The child who had run all the way home to Rose Cottage had never seen a ten-shilling note in her life. So? That was then. This was now. I brought myself sharply back to the present and walked across to the vicarage.

I had not thought it worth telling the vicar that the stone-mason's number was on the letter-head of the paper Mr Pascoe had given me, but I wanted to see Lil, and preferably while there was no chance of coming across Mrs Winton Smith.

Lil was in the back yard, feeding the hens. She greeted me cheerfully, and I told her what the vicar had sent me for.

"Paterson's?" she said, looking surprised. "Your Auntie's grave? Well, yes, the number's there. Will I get it for you?"

"Don't bother, Lil, thanks. There's no hurry after all this time, but there was something else the vicar said, and I wanted to ask you about it."

She stood there in the sunshine with the bowl still half full of the hens' corn clutched to her breast. "Ask me?"

"Yes. He told me that there'd been someone else inquiring about the gravestone, fairly recently, he said. Do you remember?"

"Yes, I do. I was just thinking that it was funny, with her being buried all that time ago – I mind that, because she died just before I come here to work, and that was straight after I left school – and now you've come asking about it, when only last Sunday there was a man here asking the same thing."

Absurdly, in spite of the heat of the sun, I felt a shiver go over my skin. "Last Sunday? Do you know who he was? What did he want to know? I gather he didn't speak to the vicar?"

"No. He just come to the back door here. He didn't want to see the vicar nor the mistress, he just talked to me. I don't know who he was, but he was a foreigner."

"A foreigner? Do you mean a real foreigner, or just a stranger to Todhall?"

"A real foreigner. He spoke funny. He was a tall chap, thin, with a short kind of coat, and –"

"He didn't give you his name, or say where he was from?"

"No, miss."

"Could he – did he look like a gipsy?"

"Oh, no, miss. Well, I mean, he was kind of sun-burned, but his hair was grey, and cut short, and his clothes ... well, they were foreign, too, but they looked good, and he was a gentleman, for all he spoke funny." She added, as if to prove the point, "He come in a car."

"What did he say?"

"He asked what the vicar's name was, and I told him, and did he want to see him, because he was over at evening service and wouldn't be back till late, and so was the mistress, but he said no. Then he asked who lived next door, and I said the Pascoes, but they were away for the weekend to a wedding. I said did he know them, and he said no again. Then he said about the grave, why wasn't there anything carved on it, and I said I didn't think anything had been arranged because there was nobody left to see about it since the old lady died and her sister had left and gone back home to Scotland. That was all, miss. Are you all right, miss?"

"Yes, thank you, I'm fine. Was there anything else?"

"I don't think so. I asked if I would tell the vicar and he said it didn't matter."

"And he never said where he was from, or what his interest was in the grave? Did he say ... Did he mention Rose Cottage, for instance?"

"No, miss."

"And he was alone?"

"Well, I didn't see no one else, but I think there was someone in the car. He had a car outside the gate, and

I thought I heard him talking to someone before it started up and drove away."

I was silent for so long that she began to look worried as well as curious, but then the cockerel created a diversion by flying up to grab food from the bowl she was carrying, and in the ensuing scuffle I took a pull at myself and managed to say, easily enough, "Well, thanks very much, Lil. It's certainly a bit odd and I'd love to know who the gentleman was, but he'll probably be in touch again, and if he knows I'm at Rose Cottage he can come to see me there. No, I won't come in. It doesn't matter about Paterson's, I'm sure their number's on the letter Mr Pascoe gave me. I'll not keep you, and thanks again. Goodbye."

And, parrying the offer of a cup of tea, I managed to get away and head for the workshop next door.

It was a long room, which had been a hay-loft in the days when the vicarage had owned and run its own farm. It was lighted mainly from windows let into the roof, but at one end there was a double door, used formerly for loading and unloading, and this was open, letting in air and light. The floor was carpeted with shavings and sawdust, and the place smelled deliciously of pine and cedar and other woods, with undertones of varnish and linseed oil.

Davey was there, busy with a plane over a long piece of timber gripped by the vices on the bench that ran down the centre of the loft.

He glanced up when my shadow crossed the light, but without checking the smooth run of the plane along the plank's length. The sliver of wood, paper-thin and silvery, curled up and back, then floated down to join the sweet-smelling carpet on the floor. Davey straightened and turned.

"Well, did you get what you wanted from the vicar?"

"Yes. And something rather interesting from Lil at the vicarage."

"Oh?" He laid the plane down. "What was that?"

I told him about Lil's visitor, and he listened, head bent, while he ran a finger absently along the smooth surface of the planed wood. When I finished he gave a grunt and was silent for a few moments, then he said:

"And someone else in the car, eh? The lady?"

"Of course. And I am thinking what you're thinking."

"Such as?"

"Only that they went down to Rose Cottage and found it empty, and so they broke and entered. This man saw Lil during Sunday evensong, she says. So later, when Miss Linsey paid her visit to the cemetery, they were there."

"Again."

"Again?"

"Aye. They surely must have been at the grave earlier, before they came here to ask about the gravestone. Then they went back."

"Taking flowers for Aunt Betsy?"

"There's that, isn't there?" He turned and put the plane up on the tool-rack that ran along one wall. "When your Mum was killed, was that gipsy with her?"

"I believe so. All I ever heard about it was what Aunt Betsy told me. I do know she said he was going to marry her, but Gran never knew his name, except she called him Jamie. There's nothing about the crash among the cuttings in her album."

"We could find out if we had to, I reckon. What I was thinking was, if he survived her, or if they'd parted before she died, then it's likely he'd marry again. Do gipsies 'talk funny'?"

"I've no idea. But if this was Jamie, and he'd come back for whatever reason to Todhall – to show it to the new wife or to look in the safe that my mother had told him about, or whatever – why, again why, the flowers for Aunt Betsy? And why take the papers from the safe? Why not just rob it?"

"From the sound of it, he'd not need to go stealing a few poundsworth from your Gran," said Davey. He reached his jacket down from its peg by the door. "We'll get no further by chewing things over now. Seems to me that what you need's a bit of time to see what the vicar's turned up for you, and then maybe start thinking about your Gran's packing."

"I suppose so."

"Whoever this chap is, if he's really bothered about anything in Todhall, he'll be back, and it would clear a whole lot of things up if you were there to talk to him ... Prissy's coming to see you tomorrow, isn't she? Well, I'll be along in the afternoon to give you a hand, so don't try shifting anything, just get the small stuff sorted ready. Coming?"

I came.

19

He took me back through the park, and set me down by the bridge, refused the offer of tea – "I'll get mine at half-six when I've done" – and then drove off.

As soon as I was in the house with the door shut I sat down at the table and pulled the vicar's envelope out of my pocket.

It was a meagre crop, though I supposed it was worth six and eightpence of the vicar's time. The first was the copy of my grandparents' marriage certificate: Henry Welland, gardener, to Mary Campbell, domestic servant, witnessed by Jeremiah Pascoe, carpenter, and Giles Brandon, farmer – "farmer" being the accepted label for the owners of the land, the gentry. I had heard it all from Gran, of course, how Sir Giles had not only attended the ceremony, but had made a speech at the wedding breakfast in the village hall, and given the young couple the tenancy of Rose Cottage, which had "just been done up lovely" after the death of its previous occupant.

Then, a decent year and a half later, the certificate of baptism of Lilias Mary, their daughter, with the god-parents duly noted, Margaret and Jeremiah Pascoe.

Why I should have hoped for anything from the next slip of paper I do not know. It was some years now since I had drummed up my courage and written to Somerset House, and I had my own copy of my birth certificate, but I sat there staring at the vicar's careful copperplate as if something might be written there between the lines. It was the certificate of baptism of Katherine Mary, daughter of Lilias Welland. Father unknown. And the godparents, friends to the third generation, James and Annie Pascoe, with Sybilla Lockwood, the vicar's wife.

And that was all. I bestirred myself at length. I got up and went to lift the Unseen Guest down from the wall and push the papers into the safe.

I had barely readjusted the framed text when there was a knock at the door.

I suppose I stood there for a full ten seconds, my hands still on the frame, tightening till the knuckles showed white. My first thought was, *It's the foreigner, the gipsy, he's here already, the stranger who's been asking questions about my family – now perhaps I'll find out some of the things I want to know.* My second, *I wonder if I want to hear them after all?* And finally, as I pried my hands loose from the Unseen Guest and turned to the door, *And Davey's back at home by now, and a good two miles away . . .*

I opened the door.

It was no foreigner, though the woman who stood there was something of a stranger. I had not seen her for some time, but she never seemed to change. The elder Miss Pope, Agatha. And behind her was Miss Mildred.

"Well, how nice to see you, Miss Agatha!" I said, and relief must have warmed my voice into such a delighted welcome that she looked surprised. "And Miss Mildred, too. How good of you to call! Do please come in."

"I know it's not Friday," said Miss Mildred, following her sister into the room.

"She means," said Miss Agatha, "that normally she only walks to meet my train on Friday. But we've been in Sunderland to the pictures, and Sister persuaded me to come here with her on our way home because she was worried, and wanted to talk to you."

"Oh?" I said, at a loss. "Well, please sit down, won't you? I'm sorry the place is a bit untidy, but I've been trying to sort things out for the movers. Would you like a cup of tea? It won't take a minute, I was just going to put the kettle on anyway."

"No, thank you. We always have high tea when we've been into town, and it is all laid ready." She sat down, still holding her handbag firmly on her lap, as if ready to go at any moment. I took my place by the table again, and she fixed me, much as the Ancient Mariner fixed the Wedding Guest, with her glittering spectacles. Miss Mildred, perched on the edge of the rocking-chair, made a little chirping sound like a nervous young bird. I began to feel a little nervous myself. Perhaps the strange foreigner would have been a little less alarming.

Miss Agatha spoke in her deep, rather pleasant voice.

"My sister wanted me to come with her to tell you," she said, "though I have no idea what she is talking about. It's very difficult, but I always say that when a thing is difficult or unpleasant one had better say it at once."

155

I'll bet you do, I thought, and said aloud: "Oh, dear. Well, you're probably right. So what is it, please?"

"Only that Miss Linsey is insisting now that she saw your mother here in Todhall last Sunday night. In the graveyard," said Miss Agatha, and shut her lips tight on the word.

A twitter from Miss Mildred, then I said, "But I know that. She told me herself."

"My sister was afraid –" began Miss Agatha, but Miss Mildred rushed in, the blue eyes filling with tears, the kindly face flushed.

"Poor Bella. Her dreams, it's those wretched – I mean those dreams of hers she thinks are visions. She lets them upset her so . . . Well, you remember I told you that I thought there had been someone here, at Rose Cottage, with a light, on Monday night?"

"Yes, of course I remember."

"Well, I wasn't thinking, and I told Bella what Bob Crawley had said, about someone digging there near the toolshed, and I said, 'Perhaps it was your ghosts, Bella,' quite without thinking, and she looked so queer, and said, you know the way she does, 'A warning. It could be a warning. Sometimes even the unenlightened are used to warn of a death,' and she just put her cup down and went without another word. She was having tea with me at the time."

"When was she not?" said Miss Agatha, under her breath.

Miss Mildred swept on without pausing. I thought I could acquit her of wanting to pass on disturbing news, but if it had to be done, then she would get it over as quickly as possible. "I'm afraid I put it out of my mind, because, well, you know Bella, but it kept coming back to worry me, so I told Sister, and she said it was far better to tell you ourselves than for

Bella perhaps to come down here frightening you with her tales."

"As a matter of fact –" I began.

"Go on. If you're going to tell her, tell her," said Miss Agatha firmly, with a brave disregard for both her sister's feelings and mine.

Miss Mildred gulped, then said distressfully, "It's just that I had this feeling" – she waved a hand somewhere near what I was sure she would have called her bosom – "that it was all my fault that Bella got the idea that someone was here digging a grave, as if it wasn't bad enough for you to have to listen to all the other" – a pause – "the other *stuff* about your poor mother in the cemetery."

For Miss Mildred, the word was an expletive. And with it she had apparently shot her bolt. She sat back, dabbing at her eyes. I gave her a smile which she didn't see, but Miss Agatha looked suddenly interested.

"You knew this already." She made it a statement, not a question.

"Yes. Thank you for coming to tell me, it was kind of you, but actually Miss Linsey did come here last night, and we had a talk. We – well, we got her dream sorted out, I think."

"Well, really!" Miss Agatha's deep voice went deeper. She added, rather unfairly, "If that isn't just like her! Anything to get something frightening off her chest and onto yours! I never did hold with all that nonsense of Bella's. She'll be breathing ectoplasm next."

"I don't think one actually – that is, never mind, but look, Miss Agatha," I said hurriedly, "whatever Miss Linsey thought it might mean, or whatever Bob Crawley said about the digging, there's nothing to it, really. I went and took a look myself yesterday. It's true that someone has been digging there recently, over by the toolshed, but –"

Another tiny sound from Miss Mildred, and a deep, "Really?" from her sister.

"Yes, but it's not a grave, nothing like one, it's just a small patch that's been dug over. Nothing there. I told Miss Linsey that, and she seemed quite ready to dismiss it. Dismiss it, I mean, as not being anything to do with her vision, or dream, or whatever you like to call it . . ." I turned a hand over. "But not, I'm beginning to think, not nonsense, Miss Agatha."

"Indeed? Well?"

I leaned forward in my chair. "Look, let's get one thing clear. It's obvious that whatever these dreams of Miss Linsey's may mean, it's nothing to do with my mother or with me here and now. She died years ago. And it's even longer since she was here in Todhall. Even if she were still alive, and came back here, would anyone recognise her straight away like that, and in the dark, too?" I drew a breath. "Listen. There's something I think I ought to tell you, but for the present, please may we keep it between ourselves till I find out more about it? I heard today that a man called here recently, at the vicarage, asking about my grandfather's grave-stone, and he had a friend with him."

"Ah!" That was from Miss Agatha. "A woman?"

"I don't know. It could be. If so, it's possible that it was that couple Miss Linsey saw in the cemetery."

"Do you know who he was?"

"No. A stranger to Todhall, apparently. It was Lil who answered the door to him."

"And she's not been here very long herself. A stranger to the village? So what was his interest, do you suppose, in your grandfather's grave?"

"It's Aunt Betsy's, too." In face of that intelligent,

unwinking stare I did not feel like taking the thing any
further, and said merely, "Davey Pascoe and I went up
there today with flowers, and there were some already
on Aunt Betsy's grave. They could have been put there
on Sunday."

"Connections of Betsy Campbell's. I see. Yes." A
final, summing look at me that apparently decided her
to leave the subject. "Ah, well." And Miss Agatha,
stiff, deep-voiced, still braced with disapproval of the
whole world of dreams and visions and ghosts from
the past, sounded resigned, rather than relieved. "Well,
Mildred, it seems as if Bella may have been right, even
if misguided."

"Poor Bella. She has been so distressed." That,
tremulously, from Miss Mildred, and it brought a
snort from her sister.

"Then she might at least have kept it to herself! It's
a mercy that Kathy here has so much sense."

"Don't worry about me," I said. "But I must say I
hope Miss Linsey isn't going around telling her story
to everyone in the village!"

"I doubt if she will. She is in some ways," finished
Miss Agatha, with (I thought) considerable restraint,
"a difficult neighbour. But I think I can assure you,
Kathy, or should I call you Mrs Herrick now?"

"Kathy is fine."

"I can assure you that this won't go any further. We
only came to tell you about it because Millie here has
been so upset, and we did not know what Bella had
already said to you. And you need not worry that she
will go about repeating her nonsense in the village –
for nonsense it is, whether true or not," she finished
robustly. "I have spoken to her myself."

And I'll bet that puts paid to any more dreams for
a fair while, I thought, then was afraid I had said it

aloud, because Miss Agatha smiled suddenly, her eyes twinkling behind her spectacles. "I'll see that it does," she said. "And I'm sure you are far too sensible to lose any sleep over it. Come, Millie."

They went.

Sensible or not, I did lose a fair amount of sleep that night, but morning came safely at last, and brought Prissy, elegant, laughing, and laden with goodies for lunch.

20

She had brought smoked salmon and some fresh rolls, and a bag of peaches.

"I didn't think Barlow's shop would be stocking these quite yet," she said cheerfully, dumping them on the kitchen table. "And I won't tell you where I got them. The blackest of markets, needless to say, but it's my conscience, not yours, and I've had more practice with that than you, being a vicarage child. I keep my conscience in my stomach these days, anyway. Here, I brought a lemon, just in case. There's a tin of ham, too, but since you'd asked me to lunch I thought I could leave the main course to you. You used to be a good cook before you went up in the world."

"Stewed rabbit," I said, and then laughed at her carefully expressionless face. "No, don't worry. There's no one to shoot the poor little beggars now. It's chicken."

"Well, thank goodness for that! I thought that heavenly smell couldn't be rabbit! So there's a black market here in deepest Todhall, too?"

"Only pale grey. I was lucky. I remembered Mr Blaney used to do a poultry round on Fridays, and I got a spare. Oh boy, this salmon looks wonderful! Thank you! That makes it a feast. Drink first? I scrounged some reasonable sherry from the Black Bull. Now, canny lass, sit thisel' doon, and for a start, tell me how you got that gorgeous figure, Podgy Pris?"

"Doing without smoked salmon and roast chicken. Years, just *years*, my dear, of disgusting things like raw cabbage and carrots and home-made yoghourt. But it's worth it in the end. It's Slim Scilla now. Thanks. Cheers." She raised her glass and sipped sherry. "Not bad, for Todhall! Yes, Gordon won't have me called Prissy any more, I'd have you know." She laughed. "I went up in the world too, my girl! I didn't see it like that at the time, because I fell for Gordon in a big way before I knew anything about him, but marrying a wealthy banker is definitely a step up from any vicarage you care to name!"

I laughed. "I believe you! Scilla? It's pretty. Same with me. I'm Kate to all Jon's friends, but somehow now I'm back here Kathy comes more natural. And so, I'm afraid, does Prissy."

"Fair enough. So long as you forget the Podgy bit!"

"How could I even think it, seeing you now? Hang on a minute while I look at the chicken ... Yes, it's about ready. Now, we've a lot to catch up on. Tell me all about it. I know you got some sort of teaching job after Gordon was sent overseas, and then the school was evacuated to Canada. When was he demobbed, and are you settled over here now, and where are you living? Heavens, we have lost touch, haven't we?

Your mother and I keep up, of course, Christmas and birthdays and such, but I don't really know a thing about you, except that you're happy, and now that you and Gordon are together she's dying to enter the Granny stakes. Any hope for her?"

"Not up and running yet, but her name's down." She laughed, stroking a hand down over her flat stomach. "Podgy Pris will soon be with us again."

"Well, that's wonderful. When?"

"Oh ages, Christmas, and you will be. godmother, won't you? We mustn't lose touch again. You're surely not thinking of living here? I heard about Aunt Betsy, but I don't know – I mean, how's your grandmother? Is she –"

"Still alive? Sure. She went back to Scotland after Aunt Betsy died. She's fine, at least she's in bed just now getting over the flu, but she'll be with us, please God, for a lot of years yet. Look, shall we start on the salmon?"

"I brought some brown rolls. They're in that bag. I hope you've got some butter, or is it still Gran's marg?"

I laughed as I set the dish on the table. We had always been able to say things like that without offending. "Here you are, ma'am. They make their own at Strathbeg, and Gran gave me some to bring. Help yourself, there's a whole half-pound."

It was a delightful meal. There was five full years' news and gossip to make up. She knew only the barest facts about my marriage, and, cut off as I had been from my childhood's friends, I had never talked about it before, that brief, frantic span of my life, when I had spun from rapture (I had loved him dearly) to dread, the nights that were not passed with him spent wakeful, listening for the planes overhead, trying, uselessly and without comfort, to count them, the number going out, the lesser number returning. And then the final grief, the long-expected, numbing blow that stops the pain and brings a kind of relief. Life had stopped. Life would have to go on. Life went on, and in time the unbelievable began to happen; pleasure and happiness came back, and even joy. But love? Not again. I said it very firmly. Not again.

"Not anyone?" she asked.

"It's just that I don't think that could happen to me again. It would be different now, love would, I mean. I'm older, and want different things. Coffee? It's Barlow's best, which isn't exactly fresh-ground, but it's quite okay."

After coffee we washed up, then wandered outside into the sunshine, down to the gate and on to the bridge. The sun was hot on our backs as we leaned elbows on the railing and gazed down into the clear, sliding depths below.

"There's one! Look over there, in the shadow of that stone. Do you remember when we came looking for eels, and Davey Pascoe fell into the beck and broke your grandfather's rod, and got thrashed for it?"

The flood of memories, as deep and clear as the stream below us, took us well into the afternoon, till Prissy, looking at her watch, said reluctantly, "I'd better be going, I suppose. We're leaving tomorrow. Gordon has to be in London for two or three nights. How long did you say you'd be here? And will you go back to London, or up to your Gran's?"

"I'll go north first, to see her settled with all her stuff, and I'll stay, if she'll let me, till she's out and about again. Look, won't you stay a bit longer, and have some tea?"

"I really can't."

"Well, come back in and get your bag, and we can exchange addresses. Would you like some flowers?"

We had been making our way back as we spoke, and she had paused at the gate, where the roses and honeysuckle had gone wild along the fence.

"Love some. Hotel bedrooms are kind of soulless, and I haven't been back in England long enough to get used to these heavenly gardens."

"Half a minute while I get the scissors."

When I got back into the garden she was over by the toolshed. "This rose! Isn't it just lovely? Would it last if I took some?"

"Not long, but it's worth it. I'll cut it in bud, and that should get it to London with you. Take care, it's pretty prickly, and I'm not sure if these scissors are strong enough. Ought to have secateurs, really, but they've gone. Gran gave the tools away to Davey."

"Well don't bother, then. It's a sweet rose, and they must have been pretty fond of it. They're all the same in this corner, even the one that's been dug up. There's the label, look, under those weeds." She picked it up and handed it to me.

I took it. A small metal label, embossed with a name, CHINA: OLD BLUSH. A label that had presumably fallen from the bush when it was dug up, and which had been flung aside among the weeds when I, in my turn, had dug in the same spot.

I stood there, staring down at the thing in my hand. So that was it, the solution of Miss Mildred's mystery, the light in the cottage garden, the man digging. That laborious job, done with the clumsy coal shovel, was not a grave, for buried treasure or anything else. He had simply been digging up a rose-bush.

Why?

I knew the answer, of course, even if I could give no

reason for it. To take it to the cemetery and replant it on the grave.

"And if he shifted it at this time of the year, no wonder it looked as if it was dying for lack of water."

"What was?" asked Prissy curiously. "What are you talking about?"

"I'm sorry. I was thinking aloud. It's nothing, just a sort of mystery that keeps cropping up, but probably doesn't mean a thing."

"Well, if it doesn't, it seems to worry you just the same. You looked for a minute there as if you were sleep-walking. Want to tell me?"

So I told her, standing there by the toolshed, and turning the little label over and over in my hand.

She only interrupted once, to say, "Huh! Witches' Corner! Doesn't change, does it?" when I got to Miss Linsey and the sisters, but when I had finished she was vehement.

"Well, of all the silly old cuckoos! What do they think they were doing, coming down with you here on your own, to chew it all over again? Were you frightened? I'd be scared witless, anyway, sleeping down here by myself."

"No, I'm not scared, I like it here. Confused certainly, and maybe a bit nervous, but I don't honestly think there's anything to be scared about. All it comes to is that this man, presumably, must be the one who broke in and took the things from the wall-safe. Heaven knows who, or why. And if he really did dig up one of these roses and take a whole lot of flowers over for Aunt Betsy —" I dropped the label back on the weeds, and dusted my hands together. "Well, it's another piece in the puzzle, and no doubt they'll all fit in in the end."

"I hope so, I must say!" said Prissy. "It's all a bit

weird, but I think you're right, it sounds pretty harmless to me, and so do old Linsey-woolsey's fancies. So forget them. Anyway, you'll soon be away and out of it all." A shrewd look. "Am I right in detecting a bit of nostalgia, a bit of the Old Toddler, about you? Well, it's been fun, but forget it, chum. Get back to London, and central heating and telephones, and get on with your real life. There's nothing for you here."

"You may be right. But I'm here for a day or two anyway. And I'm sure there's nothing really to worry about. Mysteries don't go well with Todhall and Granddad's roses."

"If you're sure you're all right –"

"I'm sure. If I do get scared I can always go to the Pascoes. You've got my addresses – London and Strathbeg? Great. It's been lovely, Prissy, and don't let's lose touch again, especially with your interesting news coming up! Take care, and thanks again for everything. 'Bye."

21

Davey came down soon after Prissy had gone, with the information that the removers had telephoned to his mother to say they would come next day.

"Saturday?" I exclaimed. "I didn't think they could possibly come before Monday!"

"Seems they have an urgent delivery at Sedgefield, so Mr Caslaw told them to save a journey and do the pick-up here on the way home. Costs him no more, and they don't mind, getting time and a half. So they'll be here tomorrow morning, and we'd better get going."

He had brought a packet of coloured stick-on labels, and while I made tea he toured the kitchen and back-places with Gran's list in his hand, affixing the labels to the things that were to be removed. It was left to me to finish sorting out the small objects that were not on the list, but which I thought she might want, so, after clearing away and washing up our tea-cups, I did a final rummage through drawers and cupboards, and then turned my attention to the contents of the cupboard under the stairs.

"Not much to go from upstairs," said Davey, scanning the list. "You'll still have somewhere to sleep. And not much from your Gran's room either. I suppose she took her best stuff up when she left?"

"I don't think so. No furniture, at any rate. She was sleeping at the Lodge to begin with. Anyway, the beds and things aren't worth taking. They've been here since the Flood. Aunt Betsy had the best of the bedroom furniture."

"She would."

I laughed. "To be fair, Gran did her room up before she came. There are one or two things there that came from the Hall, and they're good. They're on the list."

"Yeah." He was studying Gran's rather uncertain writing. "Here we are. 'B's room. Wee table with gate leg by the bed. Chest of drawers. Chair with green velvet. Glass vase. Pic of the Hall. Mat beside bed. Landing clock.' What on earth's a landing clock?"

"The clock on the landing, what else?"

"As you say, what else? Well, I'll go and mark them, shall I? Which was her room?"

"Second left at the top of the stairs. The clock's beside the door."

"Okay."

I finished with the stair-cupboard, then turned to emptying out what was left in the sideboard drawers, with a view to repacking in them as many as possible of the small things that Gran had not thought to list, but which I knew she would like to have. The candlesticks from the mantelpiece, the rose vases, the china ducks; all these, carefully wrapped in newspapers and old tea-towels, went to join the tea-set, the "best"

170

cloths, the half-dozen silver teaspoons that had been a wedding present from the Pascoes. I was tipping the contents of the bottom drawer out on the table when I became, gradually as it were, conscious of complete silence from upstairs.

I stopped work and listened. No movement, nothing. I had just taken breath to call out when his voice came:

"Kathy."

"Yes?"

"Come here a minute."

"What is it?"

"Just come up here."

I went with some reluctance. I had not been into the big front bedroom since I had been back at Rose Cottage. But I need not have worried that anything of Aunt Betsy's presence would be left there. The room was stripped and clean, and smelling of the polish Mrs Pascoe had used. The bed was bare, covered only by the mattress, the only soft furnishings being the cotton curtains and the "mat beside bed", which was, in fact, a worn but still lovely Oriental rug, that had been a gift from Lady Brandon. This was lying, folded as small as it would go, on the bare mattress, and beside it was one of the drawers from the chest. This was empty. Davey was sitting on the bed, with a paper in his hand. Not the list; this had floated to the floor by his feet. It was a ragged slip of paper, yellow with age.

"Davey? What on earth is it? You look queer."

He got to his feet, lifting the empty drawer, and sliding it back into its place. "I feel queer. Sit down. I've found something you'll want to see."

I sat down on the bed. I knew already what was in his hand. It could only be a newspaper cutting, the paper whose absence from the family chronicle was so remarkable. I put out a hand and he gave it to me, then turned and went over to the window, where he stood with his back to me, looking out.

It was indeed a cutting, from a West of Ireland newspaper. The date, 12 January 1931. The heading, *Two Die In Bus Crash*, then, told in the bare local-news style, the story of a country bus trundling home late on a dark night, empty of all but its last two passengers as it neared the end of its journey, and colliding with a bullock that was straying, black and invisible in that black night, across the unfenced road. The bus had swerved, skidded, then plunged down the steep roadside bank, where it had overturned, and burned. It was (said the report) no fault of the driver's; he was new to the route, and in spite of a broken arm and multiple bruises he had done his best to drag his passengers from the burning bus, but they were beyond help. Mr and Mrs Smith, said the *Sligo Advertiser*, had only recently arrived in Ireland, where Mr Smith was employed at the stables of the well-known Flaherty brothers. Mr P. Flaherty himself had identified the remains, and the relatives in England had been informed of the tragedy.

And that was it.

"Smith's a gipsy name, isn't it?" I said at length. "And no address for them except the stables. Maybe they'd settled down to live there, after they left the travelling people. Yes. It happened two years after she left home." I took a breath, with something like relief. "So they were still together, and he did marry her. That's something, isn't it? And it tells us something else, too. The 'foreign gentleman' at the vicarage wasn't my mother's gipsy after all. So we'll still have to wait to find who he was. Well, I'm glad to have this, Davey. Where did you find it?"

"At the back of the drawer. The chest's empty, so I thought I'd pack the small stuff into the drawers.

The linen and stuff that she wanted from her own room, and –" he turned from the window towards me. I couldn't see his face properly, but his voice sounded flat and strained – "it was in an envelope, and stuck to the back of the drawer. Deliberately stuck, I mean. Meant to be hidden."

"Well, I'm glad you found it. I've wondered why there was nothing about the accident in Gran's album. Maybe she didn't want to be reminded. If that's the case I won't tell her about it, but I'll keep it anyway." I tried for a light tone. "Have you ever read *Northanger Abbey*, Davey?"

"No."

"The heroine in that thinks she's in the middle of a 'horrid mystery', and she finds a paper in a cabinet in her bedroom, but it's only a laundry list. At least this paper's part of our mystery, even if it doesn't tell us –"

"There's other papers."

His tone, as much as the words, struck the breath from me, and the words from my mouth. He took two strides across from window to bed and was standing over me.

"Here," he said, and laid a torn, dirty envelope in my lap, then went quickly from the room, and I heard him go downstairs two at a time. The front door opened and shut.

I sat there in the silence for what seemed like half an hour or so, but was probably only a minute. Was this, at last, the fact I had tried to search out? Something known to Aunt Betsy, but kept from Gran, and used to drive my mother, the despised sinner, out of the Christian home, and prevent her from corrupting her child? I found that my hands were shaking as I drew out the contents of the envelope.

They were letters, one of them still in its envelope,

held together by a twist of what I recognised as Aunt Betsy's embroidery wool. It was rotten, and snapped easily, and I dealt the papers out onto the mattress in order, as one might deal Patience cards.

The first letter was in a flimsy envelope with an American stamp. The address on the back was, one could guess, a boarding-house. The letter was not dated, but the postmark was clear. July 1932.

More than a year after the bus crash.

So here at last were the first lines of the story that was later to come clear, a story of spite and bigotry, too mean and petty to be called tragedy, but tragic for all that.

He had married her, the gipsy boy, and they had had a couple of years together, living any way they could, until there had come the chance of the job in Ireland, and they had left the travelling folk and Jamie had landed the job at the Flaherty stables. Until that move, as I knew, she had tried to keep in touch, cards at Christmas and birthdays, then, after the date of the bus crash, silence.

The letters told why.

In the first of these she told of their journey to Ireland, along with another young couple from "Jamie's folk", their friends. The friends had not been so lucky with a job as Jamie, but Jamie stayed with the Flahertys for less than two months. A visiting American racehorse-owner had liked his way with horses, and had offered him a good job "back home", fare provided. Jamie, gipsy that he was, had not troubled to see out his notice. He and Lilias had faded into the night and taken the next ship across, telling no one of their plans except Jamie's friend, who was still looking for a job.

So much for the facts that could be gleaned from the letter. The rest could be guessed at. The couple in the burned-out bus must have been the other gipsy pair, perhaps hoping to pick up Jamie's job. Unknown in the district, unrecognisable anyway, the burned bodies were, probably naturally, assumed to be Jamie and Lilias, taking that last bus home.

There were four more letters. In the first of these she told of her marriage, not long after Jamie's death in 1934 from a virus pneumonia, to an American businessman – "very respectable from Ioa". It was his third marriage, and there were two children at home. From the brief sentence at the end – "Ive not told him nothing" – it could be gathered that the very respectable gentleman from Iowa did not yet know of his pretty wife's previous slip-up. Me.

The next letter was the shocking one.

"Dear Mum,
   I got your letter aunt B wrote for you and I wish I hadnt. I know you think I am wicked and not fit to be near Kathy but it is hard to be told never to see you again. I wish you had writen me after Jamie died. He wasnt much but he was good to me and now Im married again to Larry a good man and he does not know what I did and you dont have to worry as I am living in America and rich. Please give Kathy a kiss from me and tell her to grow up a good girl and not like her mum and take care. I wish I could see you again but I know you are right that I musnt show my face in Todhall ever again as Kathy has to grow up respectable.
      Your loving Lil."

The next was very brief, just to ask why her mother had

not replied, and the last was the same, a sad little missive with a ring of farewell about it. She understood, and just wanted her mother to know that she was happy, and got on well with her husband's family, and to forget her. She did understand, and it was for Kathy's sake, and please give Kathy a kiss . . .

I sat for a long time with the letters in my lap, thinking about it, and how it could have happened. Aunt Betsy, obviously, had intercepted the letters. Keeping house here at Rose Cottage, with Gran working daily up at the Hall, she could easily have done so. Even the postman could not have guessed that the American letters, labelled as they would be with Lilias's married name, were from Gran's "dead" daughter.

That first letter from America must (I thought) have come like a bomb. The sender's name on the back – Mrs L Smith – would be enough to set Aunt Betsy guessing, and must have led her to open the letter, to find that against all reason Lilias was still alive and well. What to do? Pass on the glad news and then wait for the prodigal's welcome home? Or keep quiet for the moment, and wait?

To start with, she might only have been concerned to keep Lilias the sinner away from Gran and me, but it was also possible that she was afraid – with reason – that if Lilias ever should come home, she herself would be turned out. So she had kept quiet, and waited.

Then the second letter came, and with it, no doubt, relief. Jamie was dead, but Lilias was still in America – in those days a safe enough distance away – and had remarried and was settled there. Aunt Betsy must have thought that there was no longer any risk of her "coming back to life", and perhaps returning to Todhall to usurp her, Betsy's, place. She had made sure of it; she had written, as she sometimes did for Gran, to tell Lilias that she would never be welcome at home again; that Todhall wanted none of her; that as far as her home was concerned, she was dead. And through it all, Gran had been allowed to believe that her daughter had in fact died years ago.

I got up from the bed slowly, moving like an old woman, and went downstairs. Davey must have been watching for me. He came in, and without word or pause, walked right up to me and put his arms round me tightly, patting my shoulder. It was a brotherly sort of comfort, and I assured myself that it was exactly what I wanted.

"It's all right, love," he was saying, "it's all right."

"Davey, you read the letters."

"Yes."

"It's – I haven't taken it in yet. But did you see what's written on the back of the envelope?"

"No."

He let me go, and I showed it to him. Aunt Betsy's writing. *The Wages of Sin Is Death*.

"But it isn't," said Davey, robustly. His hands came out again to take me by the arms and shake me gently. "That's just what it isn't! It's all good news, couldn't be better, so never you mind what that wicked old woman got herself up to! What all this really means is that your Mum is still alive! I know you've been having thoughts about it, with all these queer happenings lately, and so have I! And now it's true. D'you get it? Alive! Alive and kicking and somewhere near Todhall! Come on, Kathy love, dry your eyes! You got a hanky?"

"Yes. Yes, I know. I know. That's twice you called me love," I said, into the hanky.

"What?"

"Nothing," I said, rubbing my eyes dry, and smiling at him.

"Listen, then! Work it out, now that we know. She's been here, back to Todhall, with the American husband, the foreigner. They come here – this is Sunday night – find the cottage empty, and your Gran gone. So they make for the village, and on the way they stop at the cemetery to visit your granddad's grave, and there's another grave, and no name yet on the stone. What d'you bet she thinks it's her Mum, and then that girl at the vicarage puts the lid on it –"

"That's it!" I exclaimed. "If she said what she said to me – 'The old lady died and the sister went back home to Scotland' – then they might easily take it that it was Gran who'd died and Aunt Betsy who'd gone back north. I noticed myself the way she put it, because Jinnie at the shop, Lil's friend, used the same turn of phrase, and it sounded odd to me."

"She could easily take it that way. If my folks had been at home she might have come to our house, and saved us a deal of trouble." A short laugh. "But they weren't, and your Mum maybe didn't want to show her face in the village yet, so she stayed in the car and he did the asking, and got put on the wrong tack by Lil Ashby."

"Well," I said, "we got one thing right – she'd never have taken flowers for Aunt Betsy."

"I doubt if she'll ever get any now after this. But she did get a bit of what she deserved, if you think about it."

"What? You mean that my mother got married to a respectable gentleman in the end?"

"That he was rich," said Davey briefly. "She says so, doesn't she, in one of those letters?"

"So she does. My poor Mum, she can't be very happy right this minute, coming back here after all this time, and thinking her mother's died."

"All the better, when she finds the bad news isn't true after all," he said cheerfully. "So there's the story, all but the end. They came down here from the vicarage, and cleared the safe out – she'd know where your Gran kept the key – and then they got some flowers for what they thought was your Gran's grave –"

"And dug up one of Granddad's roses," I said, and told him about it.

"With the coal-shovel," he said, and laughed. "Her rich American gentleman. I'd have liked to have seen that! But hang on a minute. If they robbed the safe – it must have been them – they didn't do that till Monday. Why not?"

"Because 'Davey Pascoe has got your Granddad's tools.' I quote. I've been told that every ten minutes since I got home."

"And they couldn't cut the plaster without them. Right. So they went and got something to do the job with, and came back next evening. Yes. That's it." He paused, seemed about to say something else, then repeated, "Well, that's it."

I sat down by the table and stared at him over the litter of stuff from the sideboard drawer that I had tipped there. Shock, amazement, relief, anxiety and a cautious happiness – a rush of contrasting emotions had left me confused and exhausted.

"And now they've gone. How do we find them again? What do we do?"

"Wait," he said, cheerfully. "What else? Wait here. There's still you. You can't tell me she'll give up without trying to find you. And Todhall's the only starting-point she has. What's the betting that if you sit tight here she'll be back again?"

"Yes," I said. "Yes, of course. I – I can't grasp it, Davey. I – if she comes back here . . . And then there's

Gran. We'd better not say anything to Gran yet, till we know for sure." I shook my head as if to shake my brain back into action. "Oh, heavens alive, if it is true, how on earth do I tell Gran?"

"If I was you," he said, "I'd stop thinking about it and get myself some supper. Have you got some food, or will I take you home again?"

"No. There's plenty. We had a chicken for lunch. Davey –" I hesitated.

"I know. You want a bit of time to yourself. That's okay. Just remember, this kind of news doesn't kill. Your Gran'll be out of her bed and skipping like a spring lamb, just like you'll be yourself once it's sunk in. But till we're sure, say nowt. Don't worry, I'll not tell Mum and Dad yet ... Well, if you're sure you're all right, I'll get along. Okay?"

"Yes. But Davey –"

He turned in the doorway. "What?"

"Thanks for everything. I don't know what I'd do without you."

"You don't have to," he said. At least, that is what I thought he said, and I thought he added "Love", as he wheeled abruptly away and went down the path. The gate creaked shut. The van door slammed. The engine coughed into life and the van moved off.

I went to cut myself some of the cold chicken for supper.

22

The cottage felt very empty after Davey had gone. It seemed to give off an echo like that in a long-deserted house.

Well, I thought, as I finished my solitary supper and washed the dishes, what now? Prissy had been adamant in urging me to go back to London, to "life" as she called it, as soon as the furniture removers had been, but now, of course, I would have to stay. If Davey and I were right about the mystery, and my mother was really still alive and somewhere in the vicinity, she would surely come back to Rose Cottage again.

Part of me longed for her coming, with a kind of uncertain excitement, but another part was afraid. Afraid of time, of change, of what had happened to us both in the lost years. And, however joyfully the news of her daughter's reappearance must come to Gran, I did not know how to break it to an ailing old woman, especially when it involved telling her about her sister's part in the tragic years of bereavement.

Aunt Betsy. That, as well. There were too many people who had been touched by the tragedy of her making. Lilias, too, must believe herself bereaved, that her mother was dead, and buried in the cemetery here. I sat down at the still cluttered table, and tried to think.

If Davey's and my guess at what had happened was correct, then what would Lilias (I thought of her by name, as Gran had always spoken of her, rather than as the Mum of my childish memory) what would Lilias and her husband have done next, after their visit to what they thought of as Gran's grave? Gone back to wherever they were staying, and let Lilias take time to absorb the shock of her mother's death? Gone back to Iowa? Whichever, I had no way of tracing them. I leafed hurriedly through those pathetic letters again; there must originally have been an address, the one Aunt Betsy would have written to, but in the irritating American way, there was no heading to the letters, and the envelopes – deliberately destroyed, perhaps? – were not there. So, no direction except "Ioa"; no mention, even, of the respectable gentleman's surname. No way, in fact, for me to trace my mother.

What I suppose I hadn't sufficiently taken into account was that I, too, had suffered a shock. The events of the past two or three days, the confusion of the mystery, the sudden throwback into a forgotten way of life that nevertheless seemed to enfold me like a comfortable old coat, all these, I thought suddenly, must have addled what brains I had. Davey had seen it. I had only to think myself into Lilias's place, and it was obvious what she would do next.

She would look for me.

I found I was staring at the Unseen Guest. Or rather,

clear through the picture and the metal door behind it, at what had apparently been the contents of Gran's safe. If in fact Lilias had taken the papers from the safe, had there been anything there from which she could get my London addresses – Jon's flat, or my place of work? I thought not. Gran, with the super-accurate memory of the semi-literate, would never have troubled to write them down, and my marriage-lines were in London. With a twist of wry amusement I realised that my mother was in the same boat as I was; she did not know my married name; could not, even, know that I had been married. She herself had spoken to no one in the village, and since I had arrived here after she and her husband had left, she must have no idea that I was due to come to Rose Cottage.

So what would she do? Come back to have another look at the cottage, to see if a more determined search would turn up a clue to her daughter's whereabouts? Possibly. It was more likely that she would try again to see the Pascoes. Even if, as it seemed, Aunt Betsy's letter had persuaded her that they had joined with the village in their condemnation of her, she might approach them now, with her husband's support, if her need to find me was strong enough. And so she would find out that I was here.

For the time being, then, I would have to stay. But as I put Lilias's letters back into the safe I wondered if, come morning, I would find myself wanting to dodge the issue. How in the world did one face a situation like this? The only precedents were on the stage, and even there domestic melodrama had been out of date for a long time, and had never had much connection with real life. There were no precedents. In actual fact, I thought, as I busied myself clearing the last of Gran's things off the table and packing them into the sideboard drawers ready for the removers in the morning – in actual fact there was as much sheer embarrassment as joy in the idea of such a meeting. What did one say? How act? For both of us, the eighteen years would be a yawning gap, a gulf, both of years and experience.

There was a coward's way open to me. I would of course have to wait for the removers, but once the cottage was cleared I would be free to leave. Would it help both Lilias and me over a difficult moment if I just went? I could write to her, leave a letter here to break the news about the grave in the cemetery, and tell her of Gran's present whereabouts, and that we would both be waiting for her there at Strathbeg. I could send my heavy case back north with the removers, and, once they had gone, walk to the station and catch the five-fourteen train. With any luck I might be at Strathbeg before Gran's things got there . . .

Which was nonsense. A cowardly fantasy, dreamed up in the aftermath of shock. To do any such thing would be both stupid and cruel. Stupid, because even if I dodged the meeting here, I would have a possibly even more difficult one to face with Gran. And cruel to allow Lilias, who had come home to an empty house and (as she thought) the news of her mother's death, to come home a second time and find the cottage empty and stripped of furniture, and nothing but a note from the daughter who apparently did not want to meet her.

Telling myself sharply that I should be ashamed of even thinking about it, I wrapped up the last of the brass candlesticks, tucked it neatly into the drawer, and slid the latter back into place. It was no use trying to think what to do, what to say. Take the time instead to think what this meant to Gran, and what it would certainly mean to me. *Take life easy, as the grass grows on the weirs.* I had had my weeping time; this was a gift, take it as such, and take it easily.

I was half way up the stairs to bed before I remembered the other mystery that had been in the background all my life. The one person who would surely know the answer to that would be Lilias herself.

I went down and unlocked the front door, leaving it on the latch in case my mother should come home.

No one came.

No one, that is, until the morning brought Mr Blaney and Rosy with the milk, and the information that the removal van was already there, and waiting at the head of the lane till he was clear of it.

"You manage to get everything ready, did you?"

"Yes, just! I'll see you on Monday anyway, Mr Blaney, and I may be staying on a day or two after that. I'm still not sure of my plans."

He beamed. "There now! Wasn't I just saying the same thing to the missus? Once she's back here with her own folks, I said, she'll likely stay a bit longer than she thought to. So if you're to bide for a bit, you'd like a couple of eggs again Monday?"

"I'd love them, thanks. Here's Rosy's biscuit. Oh, and the chicken was lovely. Would you tell Mrs Blaney?"

"I will, and you're welcome. She was saying it was good to have you home."

Rosy whirled him smartly up the lane, with the word almost echoing in her wake. Home.

The echo was dispersed, promptly and noisily, by the removers. They were cheerful, quick and reasonably tidy. Shortly before noon the big van backed cautiously away up the lane, and I heard the gears grind as she turned into the road and trundled off. I went back into the cottage and looked about me.

Home. A different echo now. The table was still there, and the four upright chairs, but the rocking-chair had gone, and Gran's fireside chair, and where the sideboard had stood there was its ghostly shape outlined in unfaded wallpaper festooned with dusty cobwebs. The mantelpiece was bare of its ornaments, but the fender was still there, and the fire-irons, and the cracket – the stool that had been my fireside seat as a child. The rug had gone, and the exposed edge of the lino in front of the fender was frayed and ugly. On the bare wall the shapes of the flying china ducks were like little ghosts.

Even a very minor move is somehow drastic. The place looked dead, and though I had done little through the morning except check with Gran's list and tell the men where to find the items that Davey had marked with the coloured stickers, I felt drained and depressed. At least, I thought, staring round me at the desolate remains of my home, it gave me something to do, a way to fill the waiting time. For my own comfort, as well as for Lilias's sake, I would do my best to get the place clean again, and at least reasonably comfortable.

But first, lunch. (Call it dinner, Kathy, you're home now.) Whatever it was called, it was a good meal, cold chicken and a tomato, with bread and butter and one of Prissy's peaches. I took my cup of coffee out into the sunshine and drank it sitting on the seat under the kitchen window. The scent of Granddad's roses filled the air, and the beck ran sweetly over its washed stones. Birds were singing everywhere. It was very peaceful.

No one came.

I went in and started work.

*　　*　　*

At half past four I stopped for tea, reasonably satisfied. The floors were clean, the fire relaid, the exposed walls and skirting swept clear of cobwebs, and the windows bright. I went up to my bedroom, brought the bedside rug downstairs, and laid it in front of the fireplace. It was too small, and the colours had faded and worn to various shades of grey, but it covered the frayed edge of the lino, and was a distinct improvement. Even so, the room looked deserted and pathetic, with its bare walls and empty mantelpiece. I supposed that pictures and ornaments, even things like the brass candlesticks and the china ducks, gave life and spirit to the place, because they were someone's choice, they were loved. The Unseen Guest, which was still there, did very little to help. Home is where the heart is, and the heart had gone out of Rose Cottage. Soon, now, it would be a shell of its old self, waiting for the builders to "improve" it ready for its new tenants.

I still don't know what made me, at that moment, do what I did. There on the table beside me lay my pen and the writing-pad with the list for the removers. I tore the list off and threw it into the fireplace, then sat down and started to write a letter.

Not to my mother. To Lady Brandon. To ask if she would reconsider her plans for the cottage, and would either let it or sell it to me. I was still not too sure of my plans, I told her, but since coming back here I had realised that I would very much like to keep my old home. If she preferred to let it to me, I would do my best to put it in good order and keep it so, but I would really like to buy it. I would be very happy to let her see any plans I made for its improvement . . . and so on. I had not yet, I wrote, mentioned this to my grandmother, but I would be coming back to Strathbeg soon and would, if her ladyship would like me to, come and talk to her and Sir James about it. I did very much hope that they would see their way to letting me have the cottage. I was . . .

I hesitated. I would normally have been theirs sincerely, Kate Herrick, but somehow the words weren't there. I finished the letter as I might have finished it ten years ago: *Yours faithfully, Kathy. (Mrs Herrick.)*

The signature was in its way an omen. I was a cottager again.

I looked up from addressing the envelope, my heart jumping. The garden gate had creaked.

Someone was coming up the path.

23

Not Lilias. Just Mrs Pascoe, coming in a hurry, carrier-bag in hand.

"Oh, Kathy! You've never been and done it all yourself! I meant all along to come and help clear after they'd gone, but I didn't think they'd be here so early. Ted Blaney said they nearly beat him to it."

"It's sweet of you, but there wasn't a lot to do. They were pretty good. There was only Aunt Betsy's room to clear upstairs. I shut the door on the others." I was watching for an indication that Davey had changed his mind and told her about our findings, but she gave no sign of it. She dumped the carrier-bag on the table and looked about her.

"Looks funny without the sideboard, doesn't it? She'll be glad to have her things round her again, though. She was always fond of that sideboard. Did you pack her tea-set, the one with the rosebuds?"

"Yes. Everything I thought she'd like, whether it was on the list or not. Did you come over from the Hall?"

"Yes. The men are real busy today. The plumbers have come – and not before time – and there's a lot to get sorted. Jim had to come home to pick something up, so I got a lift back with the van. They won't get home for their tea till late, so if there's any more clearing up to be done, I'll give you a hand. I brought my apron along."

"Thanks very much, but I've done all I mean to do, for the time being anyway. There's only Aunt Betsy's room to do upstairs, and I've shut the door on that, too. I was just knocking off for a cup of tea, if you'd like one?"

"Never refuse a good offer," said Mrs Pascoe comfortably, "and here was I hoping you'd say just that. Here," fishing in the carrier-bag, "I've been baking, and I brought you some gingerbread. I mind how you always liked my gingerbread. And after tea, if you like, I'll turn your Aunt Betsy's room out for you."

"Well, thanks, that'd be great. Pretty nearly everything's gone from there."

"Your own room's all right? Davey did say you'd got all you need, but you know you're welcome to come up to us if it's more comfortable for you."

"Yes, he did ask me, but thanks all the same, I'll be fine here."

"You're staying on for a bit, Ted Blaney says?"

Ted Blaney seemed to have said rather a lot. "Yes. One or two more days, perhaps. I've no definite plans yet." I poured tea. "The gingerbread looks gorgeous. Fancy you remembering that."

"There's not much I could forget about you, nor about your poor mother either." She looked round the bare little room, and to my discomfort I saw her eyes brim with tears. She sniffed, smiled, and batted the back of a hand against her eyes. "There I am for an old fool. It's seeing the place like this, when it's been a friend's home for longer than I can remember." She drank tea, her eyes seeming to follow the flight of the shadowy ducks up the wall. "You're young yet, but you'll find it. You go through your life thinking things never will come to an end, but they do. It may be a comfort to those in pain, but it's a sore thing to know that things you've loved will be gone before you are."

"I'm sorry."

She set her cup down and turned to face me, dry-eyed now, but with some kind of strain showing in her normally cheerful, plump face.

"Well, I dare say that's why the good Lord gave us the gift of memory. But it comes hard. It was bad enough all those years ago when your mum left, poor lass, and she the nearest thing I've ever had to a real friend, but I never would have thought your Gran would go. I've been telling myself all this time that she'd be home, maybe, at the back-end, but dear knows there's nothing for her to come back for." A pause, but before I could speak she said, so abruptly that it sounded like an accusation, "And now you."

"Me?"

"Yes, you. Clearing the place out and then leaving."

"But I'm not leaving."

"Not for a day or two, you said. But that's not what I was meaning."

I smiled right into the troubled eyes, and pointed to the letter which lay on the table. "I've just written to Lady Brandon to ask if I may rent Rose Cottage, or better still, buy it. I hope she'll agree."

"Well! Well I never! That's good news, and I'm sure

she'll jump at it. I know she didn't want your Gran to leave. You mean you're going to live here again, and maybe persuade your Gran to come back?"

"I don't know. It's just that I feel the way you do about the cottage. It's my home, and I don't want it to change or disappear. But there's something else."

"Oh? What's that?"

I set my cup down. The little click it made in the saucer seemed to finalise a decision already half made while Mrs Pascoe had been talking. If, as I had surmised, Lilias and her husband were to come back to Todhall and go to see the Pascoes again, Mrs Pascoe ought to be prepared for it. Even if our guesses were to be proved wrong, it was a mistake for Davey and me to keep our discovery a secret.

"There's something I have to tell you." I spoke slowly, wondering quite how to put it. "It's the reason why I'm staying on, at any rate for a time. Davey and I agreed not to tell anyone, but I think you and Uncle Jim should know. I'll have to wait and see how to break it to Gran." I pushed my cup and saucer aside and turned to face her. "Something happened yesterday that's changed everything."

She had been waiting with what looked like eagerness. The sad look had gone, so that I wondered if, after all, Davey had let out some hint. Her face lit to a delighted smile, and her cup went down into its saucer with a rap that could almost have cracked it.

"Kathy, dearie! I've been hoping! If you knew how I'd hoped! And when you came back, and things happened the way they did, I was sure. It's lovely news, lovely! But when did you – I mean, he's said no word to me?"

"We – well, we agreed not to." I hesitated, confused.

"You were hoping? Do you mean you suspected something? But – for heaven's sake, how on earth did you guess?"

"Oh, I've known for long enough. He didn't need to say ought, but I'm his mother, and I've known all these years, and never a look at anyone else, let alone walking out with them, and I'll not soon forget what he was like when we heard you were married. He was on leave then, and that was the only time – it was Polly Walker from Fishburn, but it didn't last even till the end of his leave, though he might have done worse, she's a nice girl. Maybe I oughtn't to have told you, but I know you'll understand, and it's just between ourselves."

"Of course, but look, you've –"

"And then when we heard you were coming back here he – all of us – were afraid you'd have changed, and wanting different things and different ways –"

"Aunty Annie, please, it isn't –"

"And when I laid eyes on you I thought, no, he can forget it, but then you were just the same, for all you've been away so long, and I've been hoping, aye, and praying, too. I've missed your mother something sore, but now, maybe, with him and you settled here in Rose Cottage –"

"You've got it wrong," I said desperately. "Listen, please! No, listen! It's nothing to do with – with what you think. I'm sorry. It's something quite different, not about me, or Davey, at all. It's something we found when we were packing Gran's things up yesterday. It's about my mother."

"About Lilias?" The colour had rushed up into her face as I spoke, but the last word brought her up sharply, her embarrassment forgotten.

"Yes. Davey found some letters upstairs in Aunt Betsy's room. They were hidden away. She may have meant to destroy them, but obviously she forgot, or didn't have the chance. I understand she was taken bad very suddenly at the end."

"That's so. But, letters? What letters?"

"Letters my mother wrote, and Aunt Betsy intercepted. And" – I swallowed – "this will be a shock, but not a bad one. I promise you, not a bad one. They were written, all of them, *after* the date when she was supposed to have died."

A staring silence. A hand up to her mouth.

"Supposed to?"

"Yes." I reached a hand across the table to cover one of hers. "She's still alive, Aunty Annie. We're sure of it. And we think she and her husband have been here in Todhall recently, just this last week. I know" – as she started to say something – "I'm sure they'd have come to you, but it was last weekend, when you were away somewhere at a wedding."

"Wedding?" She was looking dazed. "Last weekend?"

"Yes. It's pretty certain that they came here, too; they would, of course, but they found the cottage empty, so they've gone, I've no idea where, but I think they're bound to come back to find some trace of me, and you'd be the person they'd go to, I'm sure. So you see why I had to tell you, and why I have to stay here myself till she comes, or till we're proved wrong?"

The flush had died from her face and she was very pale. She shook her head, not looking at me. "I can't get it. I can't see . . . Why? What happened? You say you're sure, but now you say you might be wrong? Kathy, love, you wouldn't say all this without you were certain, would you?"

"No. It's quite certain that she didn't die in that accident, and that's the main thing. The rest is a guess,

194

but it honestly looks like a good guess. She's been here, and if that's so, she'll be back." I got to my feet. "Look, just sit quiet for a minute while I make a fresh pot of tea, and then I'll tell you the whole thing."

The story was told, the questions, speculations, and exclamations over. We lapsed at length into an emotionally exhausted silence while the sun, wheeling lower, sent the shadows of the big trees stealing across the edge of the cottage garden, and my grandmother's "evening thrush" began his song from the top of the nearest elm.

Mrs Pascoe got to her feet. I must have looked as she did, tired but lightened, and moving as one does in a dream.

"I've got to go. They'll be finishing soon. I'll see you tomorrow, then. Whatever happens."

"Yes. Will you take this letter for me, please, and put it in the post? Here, you've forgotten your carrier."

"I reckon I'm not thinking straight yet." She sounded spent, her voice as flat as if she was talking about the week's groceries. "And I never did get to help you with the cleaning. There's that wicked old woman's room still to do. It can wait. I couldn't bring myself to lay duster to it after this."

"Forget it. I told you I shut the door on it. If I do buy the cottage I'll have to get the vicar to do a spot of exorcism. I wonder if he knows how?"

It was a feeble attempt to break the emotional tension, but it did the trick. We laughed, and then hugged one another – something we had seldom done – and she went to the door, pausing on the threshold to say, hesitantly, "I don't somehow like to leave you alone."

"I'll be all right."

"I ought to be at home anyway, in case" – that flash

195

of joy again, this time for Lilias – "well, in case. But are you sure? Maybe I could ask Davey to come down – oh, no, maybe not." A pause, and then she went back to the question that still lay silently between us. "I got it wrong, didn't I? You and Davey don't have an understanding at all?"

"I'm afraid not."

"Then I'm sorry. I was hoping, and I let it run away with me. I can see it wouldn't be right for you."

I said quickly, "It isn't that. It just hasn't come up. I – I never thought about it. I had no idea he felt that way."

"Then for mercy's sake don't let him know I told you."

"Of course I won't!"

Another brief pause, then she suddenly reached up and kissed me. "Well, if it's not to be, it's not to be. But believe me, I'm as happy for you tonight, child, as I am for myself. Good night, and I hope she comes soon."

24

I scrambled eggs for my supper, and ate Prissy's two remaining peaches. It was a meal that took me back a few years, eaten as it was on the bare table-top, and with the "cooking" plates and cutlery which were all I had kept out for my own use. After I had washed up I did a leisurely tour of the cottage, ostensibly to check that everything had gone that should have gone, but in reality to do something – anything – to occupy me and keep my mind from turning over and over in the same treadmill of speculation.

If we were right. If she should come. If we were wrong, and no one came. If she did not come tonight, then when? How long to wait and wonder? If we were right . . .

And so on. By the time I knew that I had totally failed to fix my mind on anything else except the possibility of my mother's return I was back in the kitchen, where only the table and chairs and the Unseen Guest, along with the fireside tools and the cracket, remained to offer any kind of welcome.

Welcome? It looked, in the failing light, inexpressibly dreary. But it suggested something to do.

Flowers. That was it. Flowers, the loveliest ornament of all, guaranteed to charm any place to life. There was no vase to be had, of course, but a couple of Mr Blaney's milk-bottles would do very well. Flowers and a bright, freshly lighted fire. No better welcome anywhere.

I found the bottles and rinsed them, leaving them ready in the back kitchen. Then I went out.

It was nearing nine o'clock, and dusk was drawing down. Behind the trees the first star pricked out, low and brilliant. The light breeze of day had dropped, and the evening was very still. The stream sounded loud. I walked down to the gate and stood leaning on the top bar, enjoying the scent of the roses, and straining to listen for any sound from the lane or the road beyond.

There is nothing that wakes memory so quickly and vividly as scent. If my solitary supper eaten off the bare table-top had taken me back a decade or so, the fragrance of the roses took me back still further. Some of the bushes, I knew, had been in the old rosery at the Hall, which Sir Giles – the present baronet's father – had had cleared and replaced with the modern varieties that to his gardener were very much second best. My grandfather had brought a good many of the old bushes here to his own garden. Fashions had changed, in plants as in other things, and some of the roses were rare now, but not his favourite, the tough, ubiquitous old cottage rose that (if Davey and I were right) Lilias and her husband had dug up and taken to the cemetery for him.

If we were right. Back it came, the wearisome round of preoccupation. Would she come? Could we be wrong? And if we were right, then how, dear God, how to meet the situation? How cope with it?

Action again indicated. I went to gather the flowers, the still flourishing survivors of a season of neglect. There were lupins and irises, and some columbines soon to go wild, and, loveliest of all, the double white lilac that hung in scented clouds over the toolshed roof.

I was just about to make my way back to the cottage when I heard the sound I had been waiting for. A car turning in from the road and coming slowly down the lane. The toolshed was behind the cottage, so from where I stood under the lilac tree I couldn't see the lane or the gate. Nor could I see lights, though by now it was almost dark. I wondered briefly if it might be Davey, come down for some reason, but he would have used headlights, and this was a much quieter vehicle than the van. Clutching the flowers to me, I stood still, waiting.

The wheels stopped at the gate. The car door opened, and shut gently. Then came the click of the gate latch, and the squeak of hinges. Footsteps, almost inaudible on the weeds, but recognisably a man's, trod up the path. Then a tap at the cottage door.

I was just about to move to answer it, when I heard the door open, and after a moment, the sound of someone moving about in the kitchen.

The back window of the cottage, which faced towards the toolshed, showed a crack of light; the kitchen door must be half open. My heart thumping, I moved forward and peered in through the window.

There was nothing to see but that crack of light, and the movement of shadow across it as the visitor crossed

199

the room. A man's voice called, "Is there anyone there? Kathy?"

I pushed open the back door and went quickly through into the kitchen.

The visitor was a tall man, a total stranger to me, and he was standing by the fireplace, apparently examining the framing and stitchery of the Unseen Guest. As I entered he turned quickly, self-possessed and smiling.

"Well, hullo there! I guess you must be Kathy?"

I stared at him. Dark eyes, dark hair with a dusting of grey. Fifty years old, maybe; tall and thin, with skin tanned brown. American, by the voice and the clothes; light drill trousers, a casual, expensive-looking jacket, and a scarf knotted at the neck. He could have passed as a gipsy for Miss Linsey's "vision" at the graveyard, but more certainly he was my mother's respectable gentleman from Iowa.

I cleared my throat, but found myself unable to speak. I stood there, clutching the flowers to me, staring at him.

He spread both hands in a placatory kind of gesture. He might have been saying, "Look, I'm not armed." He spoke again, with a calming sort of social ease, obviously attempting to bring a bizarre situation under control.

"I hope you'll forgive me for walking in like this, Miss Kathy, and I'm sorry if I gave you a start, but I'm real happy to meet you. I don't have to ask if you're Kathy, do I? Yes, I think I'd have known you. I'd have known you anywhere."

I found my voice. It came out none too steadily, and with no attempt at all at bridging the situation.

"Is she here with you?"

His brows went up, but he answered readily in that pleasant drawl. "She certainly is. She's right there in the car. But –" this as I started towards the door – "no, please! If you'll wait just a moment? I guess she's just as nervous as you are, so she asked me to come in first and see if you were home, and kind of break it to you. But it looks like I don't have to? You were expecting this? You know already?"

"Not know. Guess. You're Larry, of course?"

"I am. Larry van Holden. I sure am happy to meet you, Miss Kathy."

He put out a hand and, rather bemusedly, I took it. I was wondering how much, in the end, she had told him about me. "Make it Kathy. You're my step-father, after all." I turned back from the door and put the flowers down on the table. "All right, then. It's not just an easy meeting, is it? Perhaps you're right, it might be better to clear one or two things up before my – before we meet. I found it out only yesterday, that my mother was still alive, I mean, and that she'd married you and was living in America. It was when Davey Pascoe – she'll have mentioned the Pascoes? Yes? – well, when we were clearing Aunt Betsy's room to pack things up for the removers, we found some letters, letters from my mother, hidden away. We worked things out from that, and from what we'd heard in the village, so we knew you'd been here. It was you who took the things from the safe in that wall, wasn't it?"

"It was." He hesitated. "I must tell you, we hadn't planned to visit here at all. It was my idea to come over to England, to look up traces of my mother's folks from north of here, near Hexham. The trip was a kind of holiday, and Lilias was two ways about it, a bit homesick, you can imagine, and wanting news of you and her mother, but being scared to come anywhere near the place in case she wasn't welcome. Then we saw something in a local paper, that the Hall here was to be made over, and this cottage fixed up as a rental, so Lilias began to wonder if her mother had moved away, or had maybe even died, and we hadn't heard a thing. So we came over – it had to be after dark so that no one would see her – and you know what we found. The cottage was empty, no sign of anyone, and poor Lilias – well, I don't have to tell you how she was feeling. So we went up to the village and she sent me to ask at the Pascoes' house, but there was no one there, so I went to the vicarage, and from what the girl there told me I took it that your grandmother had died, and your Aunt Betsy had gone back to her folks in Scotland."

"I knew about that. She said the same to me. 'The old lady died and the sister went back to Scotland.'"

"That's it. So we came back here. Lilias knew where the keys were, of course. No one had said anything about you being expected here. Lilias figured that your aunt hadn't known about the safe-cupboard, so she wanted to get the things from it, but we had no way of getting at it right then."

It was like coming alive again to feel that twinge of amusement. "Because the tools had all gone from the toolshed?"

"That's right. Why is it funny?"

"No reason. I'm sorry. Go on. You came back on Monday night?"

"That's right, we did, and we did our bit of safe-breaking. I've got the goods here." He dug into the pocket of his jacket and brought out a yellowed envelope which bulged with papers. He laid this on the table between us, and added to it, item by item, an assortment of small objects. I recognised Granddad's old turnip watch, the battered little box that held his medals and Gran's rings and the "Mizpah" brooch that had been his engagement gift to her.

I had been listening to his story with only half my mind; the other half was outside there, in the car at the cottage gate. The objects on the table, for so many days past an obsession with me, seemed quite irrelevant to what was happening now. I picked the envelope up, turned it over without seeing it, then put it down and opened the box. Two medals, a twist of paper holding five gold sovereigns, a thick old-fashioned wedding ring, a pretty, cheap-looking bracelet, a brooch of seed-pearls and peridots . . .

His voice said, gently amused, over my bent head: "They're all there. I don't know why I've been hanging on to them; we meant to leave them with your grandmother, but what with all that was going on there, I quite forgot. They've been in the glove compartment of the car."

I was hardly listening. I had picked up the bracelet. "But this?" I said. "This was sent back to Gran after the bus crash. It was on the – it was one of the things that identified Lilias. Her initials, see?"

"Yeah, I know. It certainly gave Lil a shock to see it. She'd never heard about the accident, you realise that?" He took the bracelet from me and laid it back in the box. "This made it sure it was Cora and Jackie, their friends, who'd been killed. She'd given Cora the bracelet as a keepsake when they left. And they weren't the sort, any of them, to keep in touch, so they never knew."

"The travelling folk? I suppose not. But my mother did try. She wrote to us several times."

He was putting the other objects carefully back into the box. "She did, poor girl. So that's how you knew who'd been here, and how you found out about Lilias? You knew my name, even." He laughed. "You sure had me wondering just now if your grandmother had found

203

the news too much for her. She promised to leave it to us to tell you, but I'd begun to figure that maybe she couldn't wait and had gotten herself to a telephone after all."

"What? *What did you say?*" The meaning of the quiet words, drifting past in that slow, even drawl, got through to me at last, and brought me up with a jerk. "Gran? What are you talking about? How would Gran know about this? I've never been in touch. What do you mean, Gran promised to leave it to you?"

"Just that. We've just got back from Scotland. That's where we've been since the weekend."

"Scotland?" I said blankly. "You mean you've been to Strathbeg?"

"That's right. When we left here on Monday night, thinking that Mrs Welland was dead, and that your Aunt Betsy hadn't troubled to let Lilias know, your mother was so mad that she just had to go straight up to Scotland to have it out, as we thought, with your Aunt Betsy, and find out what had happened to you."

"I see . . ." I took a long breath. "Yes, I do see."

I looked at him, at Lilias's rich, respectable gentleman, and, for the second time, found myself smiling. She'd have been upset enough, my poor mother, to face a dozen Aunt Betsys, and with Larry beside her she'd have found it easy. "It's a pity she didn't do it long ago!"

"It surely is. Poor Lil. All the way north in the car she was saying all the things she'd been wanting to say, and going over all the years . . . Well, she'll tell you herself, and it doesn't matter now, thank God, because when we got there, there was your grandmother, alive and well and not believing her eyes and ears." He showed a hand. "You can imagine."

"I'm not sure that I can."

"You can say that again. Well, I left them to it. I got to know that bit of Scotland real well in the hours I spent walking around the place while they talked. It's pretty, but kind of quiet, isn't it? And yes" – in answer to some questioning sound from me – "your grandmother's quite okay now, and she sends you her love and wants you back there just as soon as we can get you to go back north with us."

I didn't answer. I found I had sat down – collapsed, almost – into one of the remaining chairs, and put both hands to my face, as if the pressure on my forehead could steady the whirling confusion of thoughts and emotions. What did come with cool relief was the realisation that Gran's part in this was already played; she knew; she was happy, and according to Larry, well again. With that part of the tangle straightened out, the rest might not be so hard to deal with. What was left now was just between me and Lilias.

I found my voice at last. "It's wonderful. I – thank you for all you've done, Larry. It must have been, well, just wonderful for both of them."

He said mildly, "It was quite a scenario. But I reckon Lilias'll want to tell you the rest herself. Now look, this may be wonderful but it sure isn't easy. Are you okay?"

"Yes."

He went to the door and opened it. "I thought I heard someone – that's right, I did. There's a nice-looking young guy out there by the car, talking with her. I heard her laugh. She must be feeling better."

"It's Davey Pascoe. I thought he might come down. He's the son –"

"I know who he is. Well, that's great. There'll not be that much ice left to break, will there?" A kind look, as he paused in the doorway. "And I figure you can manage a bit of fancy skating if you have to. So what do you say I go talk to Davey, and walk about outside some more, while Lilias comes up here to you?"

25

There was a pause, while presumably he told her
what had passed between us, then, while he stayed
tactfully by the car talking with Davey, she came up
the path alone.

I got up. I had not even been trying to think of what
to say. There was no precedent for a meeting like this,
save perhaps in some old Gothic tale. I steadied myself
with both hands flat on the table, as she came up the
path and paused in the doorway.

She would be a year or two over forty now, and
the slender girl of the photos had put on weight, but
I still would have known her, and she was still one
of the prettiest women I had ever seen. On the fresh,
lively beauty the pictures had shown, and the flyaway
loving charm that I remembered, were superimposed
the assurance of security, and the gloss of American
grooming. A poised and beautiful woman, Lilias, even

in the crudely lit and barely furnished cottage kitchen, though the assurance, as she hesitated there in the doorway, did in fact seem a little fragile.

She stared at me, as Larry had stared, and then the smiles came, and with them the tears.

"Why, honey . . ." The phrase and the accent were recognisably American, but the soft voice was the same, and sharply, surprisingly, I remembered just how the dimple had come and gone, enchantingly, in her cheek. Remembered, too, the tears that had wetted my face on the night when she had kissed me goodbye.

"I – I thought you were dead," I said.

The dimple again, and she dashed a hand across her eyes. "Darn it, I'm happy," she said. "I'm not crying. Well, I'm not dead, never was, but you – you might as well have been, and Mother, too, but now – for goodness' sake, we ought to be rushing into each other's arms, but we'll skip that bit till we know one another better, shall we? Just say hello?"

She came into the room, still with her eyes fixed on me. "Yeah, well, he said you were a beauty, and you are." The little trill of laughter that, out of the past, I remembered. "But not a patch on your mother, he said, so how's that?"

"What I'd expect," I said, smiling back. Her light handling of the situation was making it easy. "It's hard to know what to say, isn't it? It's all come as such a shock, everything suddenly happening, coming right . . . I'm happy, too, but I don't quite know what to say, except that I'm so terribly sorry we lost you like that, and lost all those years, but it wasn't our fault, Gran's and mine."

"And don't I know it! Don't fret yourself, Kathy love, Mother and I got it sorted out, what that old witch

208

had done, and now Davey's been telling me how you'd got it worked out yourself from some letters of mine you found in her room." A side-glance. "I suppose you had to read them?"

"Yes. I'm sorry." I was still, rather helplessly, feeling around for what to say. "But we had to. I didn't know anything, you see. And it was so marvellous to find we'd been wrong all the time, even though it had been done in that beastly way. It was you and Gran who had the worst, I know that. I was just little, and I missed you terribly, but children get over things. But even so – all those years – to be without you . . ." It broke from me with the force of anger. "How could she? How could anyone do what Aunt Betsy did?"

"Jealousy," said Lilias, wisely. And looking at her, lovely, still young, beautifully dressed, moving with her graceful walk round the shabby kitchen, looking about her, touching here and there, as if to help her remember, it was easy to see how she could have wakened a hell of resentment in a narrow and barren heart. She said over her shoulder, "Take it easy, honey. It's over, and we're here, and there's a lot of life left for us all still."

"I know. It's okay. But it's hard to take. It's easy to see why she would want you out of the house, but once you'd gone, to cut you off, deliberately like that, from me and Gran, and for good –" I took a steadying breath. "Poor Gran. What did she say when she knew?"

"After the bells of heaven had stopped ringing and we came back to earth and thought about what had happened?" A smiling slant of the head as she lifted a corner of the cotton curtain and examined it. Her eyes came back to me, and were suddenly grave. "I'll tell you exactly what she said. I'll never forget it, and nor will Larry. She just said, 'Poor Betsy. She thought she was doing right, keeping sin away from Kathy, and trouble away from me. She was a good woman, Lil dear, in her way. Try to remember that.'" A look where mischief mingled with a kind of ruefulness. "When I told Larry, you know what he said? 'Then may the good Lord preserve me from good women!'" And the gravity broke up into that delicious laughter. "He has, too, and don't you and I know it!"

In spite of everything, I found myself laughing with her. "Do you mean that your respectable gentleman from Iowa – I read your letters, remember? – still doesn't know about – well, the truth about me? I've been wondering just where he thought I came in. He didn't seem surprised to see me."

"We knew you'd be here. Mother told us." She picked up a spray of lilac from the table, and was silent for a moment, brushing the scented flowers to and fro across her mouth. Above the white blossom the lovely eyes regarded me, I thought warily. "No, I know what you mean. Okay, you'll have to know. He thinks you're Jamie's daughter."

"I see."

She said quickly, "I didn't actually tell him that, but I know that's what people said at the time, and Jamie and I did get married later, so it was a fair guess, and I just let it be. The rest – of course I told him – well, maybe not everything, but most of it. He knows why I left home, and about that letter, the one Aunt B wrote, and why I was scared to come home, even though I wanted so much to see Mum again, and to find out about you." A pause. "I know that was the worst thing I did, leaving you, but with the kind of life I knew I'd have with Jamie, unsettled, I mean . . . well, it was best for you, the way I was thinking then. And I did mean to come back, if things changed, but it didn't work out that way. You do understand, don't you?"

"Yes."

"And you have to believe that I never stopped thinking about you, and Mum, and Rose Cottage . . . It's true. Larry guessed it, too. I truly think that's what he planned this trip for, not really to go back to his own family's roots at all. He's – well, it was something to me to find that people can be good, real strict with morals, I mean, and still be so kind."

"I'm glad. And of course I believe you. I could tell from the letters what it meant to you to be cut off from home."

"I reckon I'll have to see what was in those letters. Where are they?"

I nodded a head towards the Unseen Guest. "In the hidey-hole."

"Well, what do you say we light the fire and burn them up? I've got the key here in my purse."

She turned quickly away to the fireplace and reached up for the box of matches as if she had put it there herself only yesterday. She struck a match and stooped to set a light to the fire, then stayed there by the hearth with her back to me, watching while the paper caught, and the kindling burned up with a pleasant crackling blaze. Evasive action, I knew, but I could find no words for what I wanted to say, so I waited in silence, watching her as she watched the flames. She turned at length, but without meeting my eye, to pick up her handbag, which she had left on the table, but before she could open it I said, "Don't bother. It's not locked. Davey and I broke the box open."

"So you did. He told me. I forgot."

"Mother – Mum –"

It came out hoarsely, and I stopped.

"Make it Lilias, can't you? We're the same age now, and believe me, likely to stay that way!" This time the light tone didn't ring quite true. Her attempt at a laugh trailed away, and we stood there awkwardly, one to either side of the table, looking at one another.

I found my voice. "Never mind the letters. We've got to talk about it, you know that. I've got to ask."

"Ask what?"

"You know what."

"I suppose so."

"It wasn't Jamie, was it?"

She did not answer straight away, but pulled out the nearest chair and sat down at the table facing me. She seemed to do it in slow motion, as if approaching some barrier which would take calculation and then painful effort to surmount. Her face, which had been slightly flushed from stooping close to the fire, was pale again; paler, I thought, than before. For the first time I could see the faint, give-away lines that strain had sketched near eyes and mouth.

I found that somehow I, too, had sat down.

She was regarding her hands, folded together in front of her. Then she looked up to meet my eyes.

"No, honey. It wasn't Jamie."

"Then – please –?"

Colour came up in her cheeks again, making her eyes look very bright. She shook her head, and then said with the slightest quaver in her voice, "I know. I know. I have to tell you. You've enough to forgive me for already, but now you're going to have to forgive me all over again. You see – that is – darn it, I don't know how to start!"

I said abruptly, "Was it Sir James?"

That brought her upright in her chair, looking so

shocked that, nervously keyed as I was, I wanted to laugh.

"The master? What an idea! Of course it weren't!" It might have been the pretty house-maid of twenty-odd years ago, scandalised and protesting. Even her voice had slipped its careful accents. "How could you think such a thing? He wouldn't never – ever – have dreamed of it, and neither would I! That would have been a real disgrace! Oh, no, it was – there was no harm in it – or so we thought." A pause, and then, as memory came back, a hint of her enchanting smile. "I was only sixteen, don't forget, and he wasn't much older, your father, I mean, though somehow I never think of him that way. It was all quite innocent in its way."

"Then why have you never told anyone, Gran or me? Is it because it's somebody awful?"

"Give me some credit!" Another flash of the pretty Lilias, and this time I certainly saw the dimple flicker. "As if I'd ever – oh, well, I'm afraid – what I mean is – what I'm trying to tell you is, I know you've a right to know who your father is, but the truth is, I don't rightly know myself!"

That really did knock the breath from me. I tried for words, and only managed, crudely, "What do you mean, you don't know? Do you mean there were so many of them?"

"Give me some credit!" she said again, and now I was sure of the dimple. "Of course there weren't, not that could have been your father, I mean! I don't say I didn't always have plenty to choose from, but he . . ." She leaned forward, gravely earnest now. "You have to believe me! He was the first, and then the only one till Jamie. By the time I knew I'd fallen wrong – though that's a silly way to put it, since having you was the best thing I ever did in my life – he'd gone, and I didn't want to chase after him and maybe make a peck of trouble, and, well, there was no point to it. Do you see?"

"I – I suppose so . . ." I said awkwardly, then, on a rush, "but no, I don't see. How could I? If you've never wanted to get in touch with him again, neither Gran nor I are likely to try. So if he was your only, well, your only real lover, then why won't you still tell anyone who he was?"

"Because – oh, it all sounds kind of crazy now, but I swear it's true. Okay, I'll try to tell you how it was." Her hands fluttered, palm out, sketching a gesture of surrender. "That summer – I still remember every minute of it! It was gorgeous that year, and they seemed to have parties all the time at the Hall. Every weekend, seemingly, the place full of young folks, and cars, and tennis and dancing . . . You've never known what it was like in them – in those days. People had house parties, and dances, and there was always lots of young folks at weekends, and *fun*. It was such fun!" Wistfully. "And in the servants' hall we had fun, too. Oh, it was a lot of work, but nobody minded that – and of course the tips were good."

A pause. I didn't speak. After a few moments she went on. "I was house-maiding there, you know that. Well, one night when they, the gentry, were all at dinner I went up to help turn the beds down and carry the hot water – you had to do that in those days – and when I went into his room he was there. He hadn't gone down to dinner. He hadn't even started to change. He was just sitting on the bed in his shirt-sleeves with a letter in his hand, and he was crying."

Another pause, then she went on with the story.

It really was, as she had said, an innocent one. The young man – a boy of perhaps eighteen – had come back from the day out with the other guests to find that a letter had come with the afternoon post. It was from his mother, breaking the news to him of the death of his dog, at thirteen years old the beloved companion since he could well remember. The old dog had been run over by some brute who had driven away and left it to die in the road. His mother had given no details, but the agonising end could be guessed at, and his distress had left the young man quite unable to face the company downstairs. The rest followed naturally. He had tried to hide his tears, while she, in all simplicity offering what seemed natural comfort, had run to put her arms round him and try to soothe the grief away.

They sat side by side on the bed while he talked, and later she contrived, unseen, to get a tray of supper up to him. And the acquaintance thus begun had blossomed. Next day – her afternoon off – he had met her with his car at the end of the lane to Rose Cottage, and they had spent the rest of the day together. After one or two snatched meetings during her working days at the Hall, he took to driving down after dark through the Hall grounds to wait by the wooden bridge, and Lilias, whose parents went early to bed, found it easy to creep out to meet him.

"He stayed three weeks," she said. "Then we said goodbye and he left. I suppose we would have said we were in love, but we both knew there was no question of getting married, and we both knew it would never have done. But we had a lovely time together, and we *liked* each other, as well as being romantic, if you know what I mean. And it was a couple of months after he'd gone before I knew about you coming, and another few weeks before I dared tell Mother and Dad, and there'd have been no point in trying to chase him up and make trouble, and in any case he'd told me that he was trying to get a job abroad somewhere.

India, I think, or Australia. Somewhere like that. So you see?"

"Yes." It was somehow not a conversation one could have had with the mother who had brought one up, but we were, as she had said, on a level. Certainly I could not have asked the question that had been suggesting itself to me, irresistibly, as she told her story. "And are you going to tell me that I started life in the back of a car?"

She looked shocked, then she giggled. "It was a two-seater. There's some details you don't have to have! But if you want to know, it was probably up there in Gipsy Lonnen." A lift of the shoulders and a little laugh that told of tension relieved. "Oh, I knew I'd love you again, even with all the time lost, and all the changes!" She took in a long breath, and let it out in a sigh. "Oh, well, it's all a very long time ago, and if you're the wages of sin, Kathy love, all I can say is, it was worth it!"

There was another pause, then for the first time she made a move to touch me. Her hands came out, and mine went to meet them. She said nothing, but it was in answer to something unsaid that I told her,

"It's all right, it is, really."

"If you knew how I've dreaded this! It was the only good thing about being cut off from the family, but I knew I'd have to come back some day and get it over with. I've told you all I can, but look, Kathy, if it matters so much to you, there are ways of finding out the rest, what happened to him, I mean."

"No," I said. "I'm glad you've told me this much, of course I am, but I'd rather not take it any further. I mean that."

It was the truth. I felt nothing but relief, the lifting of a vague dread that had nagged me ever since I had come back to Rose Cottage. And I had spent the first ten minutes or so of the interview wondering if I was going to hear that my father had been some married man with a reputation and career to lose, or one of the visiting chauffeurs who hadn't cared to take the responsibility of a child. It came like a burst of sun clearing the mist away, that it didn't matter either way.

I smiled at her, and repeated it. "It doesn't matter at all. I think you and Gran and Granddad were right about that. I couldn't have had a better home or better folks than I did have, except for missing you."

That brought the tears, and with them at last the kisses and the final relief of spent emotion. Only for a minute or two, then my mother, recovering herself, reached for her purse and started on repair work, while I retreated to the fireside to tend the fire and dab my eyes dry unseen.

Still kneeling by the hearth I watched her for a few moments, then said, uncertainly, "Look, I'm sorry, but we can't leave it quite yet. Why did you say you didn't remember who he was, when actually you do seem to remember everything? We've agreed to do nothing about it, okay, but really, this is one thing I do have a right to know. *Who was he?*"

She sat back in her chair, while a look compounded of mischief, embarrassment, and sheer irrepressible amusement brought the sparkle back to her face.

"I only meant," she said, "that I don't remember his name."

"Lilias!"

"I know, I know! But it was such a long time ago, and in some ways it's gotten that it's not much more than a dream. All I remember is that he was handsome, and he was a real sweetie, and he stammered a bit when he was excited, and he had a red sports car with a copper exhaust pipe and a strap over the hood, and everybody – me, too – called him Bunny, but I think – I'm pretty sure – that his name was George."

Five seconds or so of complete silence, then I laughed.

Not quite the "proper" reaction, perhaps, and there may have been a touch of hysteria there at this ending to my long search, but it was a good ending, and, as I was fast discovering, I was my mother's daughter. So I laughed, in reaction, relief, and because it was funny. *Take life easy.*

Lilias stared, gasped, then giggled, and suddenly all was well, very well, and the lost years, the Aunt Betsy years, were past and done with, and the future was ours. America, Strathbeg, Rose Cottage, it didn't matter. It was ours.

My mother sat up, dabbing her eyes again. "Oh, Kathy, honey, I love you ... ! Darn it, I've got the hiccups now! Just let me put my face right again, and what do you say we tell poor tactful Larry and your handsome Davey to come in, and for godsake is there a kettle around here some place, and have you any tea?"

26

There was, and we had, and I boiled the kettle and
found some cups, while Davey shifted the chairs to
the fireside and pulled the cracket forward to act as
a side-table, then followed me through to the back
kitchen where I was hurriedly pushing the flowers into
the milk-bottles and a couple of the remaining slices of
bread into the ancient toaster.

"Okay?" was all he said, and I nodded.

"I came down just in case. You don't mind?"

"Of course not."

"He seems a nice chap, the American. Easy to
get along with. Seems he has a big business, selling
property. Real estate, he called it. That's all we talked
about, really, and cars. That's an Armstrong-Siddeley
he's hired, and he's quite keen on it. I thought you'd
like to know."

"About the Armstrong-Siddeley?"

"Don't be daft. You know what I mean."

"Yes, I know. It's all right, Davey, I'm all right. It went – it was okay."

He still lingered. "Kathy?"

"Mm?" The first two slices popped up and I put two more in and started the buttering.

"What d'you say I go home and tell my folks that she's here and it's all okay? Since you talked to Mum this afternoon she's been like a cat on hot bricks, wondering if it's all real. Can't rightly believe it."

I stopped buttering to consider it, knife in hand. "Better still, why not bring them down? It's getting late, and I doubt if Larry and Lilias plan to call anywhere else tonight, and they're going back north tomorrow. Tell you what, ask them, but I think that'd be great."

It would also, I couldn't help thinking, as the toast went on popping and I went on buttering, help to spread the burden, leaven the lump, whatever metaphor meant "make the situation less close and overloaded with emotions".

While the last two slices were toasting I carried the flowers through to set them on the mantelpiece, to find that Lilias, who had been reading the letters retrieved from the Unseen Guest, was making a kind of laughing ceremony of consigning them to the flames. But as the papers blackened and wisped away up the chimney I, from where I was by the mantelpiece, could see a faint reflection of the firelight on her cheek, as if a tear had spilled there. She caught my eye and smiled, then dusted her hands together and said, gaily, "There! That's the past disposed of, Kathy love, and the future to drink to. And in English tea!"

And presently, with tea and toast – the toast I would have had for my breakfast – the three of us settled round the fire with a fair assumption of cosiness, and put together what was left of the story – those parts of it which could, with Larry there, be told.

My story had to come first. Gran had told Lilias about the missed years of my girlhood, and what she could about my marriage with Jon and its rough ending on that April night over Pas de Calais. Later, I supposed, my mother would want to know more about those whirlwind months, but now she kept to easier topics, my life since that time, the London job, my home there and my friends, and what I thought of Todhall where, like Larry in Hexham, I was "rediscovering my roots".

This brought us home to Rose Cottage, and I had to tell the story of my house-to-house detective work, and my attempts with Davey to unravel the mystery. Lilias, half amused, half wistful, plied me with questions about the village and the people I had talked to, unconsciously betraying what Larry had told me about her home-sickness. He, listening half absently, as if to some fairy-tale, sat smiling, with his eyes on his wife's face, and – I noticed – leaving his tea untasted.

When I told them about Miss Linsey and her gipsy ghosts my mother laughed, and sent a sidelong look at her husband. "A gipsy? Well, I suppose he could be. They say you always fall for the same type, don't they? I'm Larry's third, and the other two were both blonde."

"And beautiful," said Larry, giving her the sort of fondly admiring look that Americans find it easy, and Englishmen impossible, to bestow.

Then it was America's turn, and I heard about Iowa, and their home there, and the two daughters ("sweet girls") who were both married now and lived not too far away; and this in its turn led to invitations and promises. I must go to Iowa and visit with them; in fact why wouldn't they take me right back with them when they left? I could make it right with my boss in London, surely? They had originally meant to fly back this next weekend, Larry told me, but it could easily be put off. He himself had to be home by the beginning of July, but if Lilias wanted to stay on, and maybe bring me back with her . . . ? But in the meantime I obviously could not stay here in this half-empty cottage, so, since they had promised Gran to drive straight back to Strathbeg, and take me with them –

"Tonight?" I said, startled into stupidity by a vague memory of American hustle during the war.

But no. Tomorrow. Tonight they would be going back to their hotel. Not the one in Corbridge, where they had been staying while Larry hunted up his Northumbrian ancestors; they called there on their way south and had telephoned ahead to book into a hotel in Durham.

"The Three Tuns, it's called," said Larry, "and I'm told that Durham's only about nine miles from here. When I called them I said we might be pretty late, but they'll hold the rooms. For you, too, of course."

"Well, thanks very much, and of course I'd love to go to Strathbeg with you, but if you don't mind, I'd rather stay here tonight. I've still got – well there are things to do, and . . . would it be all right with you to pick me up here tomorrow?"

I think he would have persisted, and I would certainly have found it hard to explain my reluctance to leave the cottage for the comforts of the Three Tuns, but I was saved by the noise of the Pascoes' van coming down the lane.

Lilias, jumping to her feet, ran to the door and opened it.

"Annie! Why, Annie!"

"Lil!"

They flew together, and the rest was lost in a flurry of greetings, and a long colloquy, mostly in whispers, held half way up the garden path. Then, both talking at once, they came back into the kitchen, with a grinning Davey in the rear. He pulled up an empty packing-case that the removers had left behind them, set it beside me and sat down on it.

"Your father," I said, "isn't he here?"

"No," still grinning. "He knew how it would be. Let them get it out of their systems, he said, and come and tell me about it later on. They'll be back, he said, and that'll be time enough. He takes life easy, my Dad."

"Like you?"

"I try. So what's the plan?"

"They're going to stay tonight in Durham, and drive back to Strathbeg tomorrow. They want me to go with them."

"Will you?"

"Yes. Apart from everything else, I'd like to be there when Gran's furniture arrives, though that's the least of it now! Larry did want me to go with them straight away, but I thought I'd like to stay here tonight. It's all a bit sudden, and a bit late, if you see what I mean."

"Yeah, I do. Sleep on it before you pull the roots up?"

I said, surprised, "That's exactly it."

"And you're going to? Pull them right up, I mean?"

I had been wondering if his mother had told him about my bid to buy Rose Cottage, but this answered me. As I hesitated over my reply I was saved yet again by an interruption from outside. Davey had left the door open – the fire, while providing cheer, had made the kitchen rather too warm for the June night – and outside in the dusk I heard again the creak of the gate. Someone was coming up the path.

I saw my mother, who was near the window, turn to look out.

"Who on earth's this? Some woman, with a shopping-bag?"

"Oh, heavens," I said, "it's Miss Linsey!"

"So it is! Larry, quick, look, that's the witch who saw us in the cemetery! The one Kathy's been telling us about. What on earth does she want here at this time of night?"

"Goodness knows," I said, as I went to the door. "Miss Linsey! How nice! Won't you come in?"

"Oh, Kathy, I hope you don't mind my coming at this hour, but I've been rather worried, and I did just wonder – oh!" as her eye went past me to take in the rather crowded kitchen. "You've got company. I didn't know. I thought you'd be on your own, and so I came down –" A scream, as Larry rose from his chair.

"That's him! There you are! I knew it was true! That's him! That's the gipsy!"

"And me," said my mother. "How are you, Miss Linsey?"

"Lilias Welland!" Another screech from Miss Linsey, as she thrust her shopping-bag at me and surged forward to seize my mother's hands. "I knew it was you! I told them you were coming back, and no one would believe me! They said you were dead, and I knew it wasn't true! I've seen you so many times in dreams, and then I saw you in the cemetery –"

I missed the rest. As the kitchen filled with a babel of talk and exclamations the shopping-bag wriggled in my hands and I screamed, too, and dropped it on the floor. Something shot out of it, and up the curtains to the rail, where it hung, fizzing. A kitten, small, tabby, and furious. It balanced there, glaring down at the scene.

"She's brought her familiar," said Davey in my ear, just as Miss Linsey, still clinging to my mother's hands, said over her shoulder, "I brought it for you, dear. It's one of Patsy's, and quite clean. I found homes for the others, and I meant to keep it, but it can't stand Henry, so I thought of you. Since you'll be staying here at the cottage I thought you might like the company."

"Well, thank you, it's very sweet, and I'd love to have it, but what made you think I'd be staying here? As a matter of fact —"

"It was my dream last night." The light intense gaze turned on me. "So I knew. I saw you here, it was Rose Cottage, I knew it, but it wasn't the same. There was —" a vague glance round at the denuded kitchen — "well, there was some furniture, and it looked as if —"

I saw her catch sight of Davey and she hesitated. I heard Davey say "Oh, no," under his breath, and, as she opened her mouth to go on I put in, quickly, "I'd love to keep the kitten, if someone can get it down from there! I'm going away tomorrow, as it happens, with my mother and Mr Van Holden. This is Mr Van Holden, my step-father. Larry, do meet Miss Linsey, one of our neighbours."

Larry shook hands, making gently courteous noises of greeting, and inquiries after her health, which, mercifully, turned her attention to him.

"You sound like an American. I met one during the war, and of course there are the films. I didn't know they had gipsies in America? Indians, of course, and hoboes, or do I mean bozos?"

A choking sound from Davey, and I saw hysteria in his eye. Lilias, over at the window trying to entice

225

the kitten down from the curtain-rail, stiffened, peered out at the dusk-filled garden, and clutched at my arm.

"Jumping Jesus," she whispered, but with complete reverence, "look there! Isn't that the other two from Witches' Corner? I'd know Miss Mildred anywhere, and Miss Agatha is surely wearing the same old hat." She turned to Larry, who, I could see, was making a great hit with Miss Linsey. "Larry, love, we seem to be holding a convention. More neighbours. The calling hours have changed some since I lived in Todhall, and will you for God's sake see if you can get that kitten down?"

Larry, reaching up from his six-feet-plus, detached the kitten gently, hook by hook, from its hold on the curtains, and lifted it down to a perch on his shoulder as I hurried to the door again. "Miss Agatha! Miss Mildred! How nice to see you. Do come in."

"It's not too late, is it?" began Miss Agatha, and Miss Mildred, pushing past her sister, leaned forward to say in a whisper, "Is she here? Is Bella here?"

"Yes. She came just a few minutes ago."

"Oh, you've got company." That was Miss Agatha, looking past me, as Miss Linsey had done, at the thronged kitchen. "There, you see, Millie, I told you it would be all right. There really was no need to fuss."

I must have looked puzzled, because Miss Mildred hurried to explain. "The thing is, my dear, Bella's been rather tiresome today, going on and on about things, you know how she does, and then she said she was coming down to see you again. Well, I thought you were on your own, and I was afraid she would upset you, even though you said it didn't bother you, all her talk, so I thought I'd come and see."

"I told her you had too much sense to let Bella's non-sense upset you," said Miss Agatha, "but she insisted, so in the end I came with her –"

"But with all these people here –" added Miss Mildred.

"It was quite unnecessary after all," finished Miss Agatha."

I said warmly, "It was sweet of you, Miss Mildred. Both of you. But everything's fine. More than fine. Won't you come in? There's somebody here who'd love to see you again."

27

It was Mrs Pascoe who saved the situation from getting completely out of hand. Pushing Davey and me in front of her, she herded us into the back kitchen.

"Now, Kathy, I know what's bothering you, and you needn't worry, nobody's going to say anything they shouldn't in front of Mr Van Holden. Whatever you may think of those ladies, they *are* ladies, and it's not likely they'll say anything that might give Lil a red face. So that's that. Now, where's the wine, Davey? I knew you wouldn't have any here, Kathy, so I brought a bottle along, to celebrate. It's my own elderflower champagne, and this was a real good batch. If Davey'll get it open, we can give them a glass each, and then we'll drive them home. That'll get rid of them with no hard feelings. I think you and Lil have about had enough."

"Good idea," said Davey, producing the bottle.

"Okay, Mum, this should fettle them. Get the glasses, Kathy."

"No glasses," I said, rather shakily.

"There's some jam-jars out in the toolshed. I saw them when I stole the tools."

"Behave yourself, Davey," said his mother. "Take no notice of him, Kathy. Come on, I'll help you rinse the cups out."

"Hold up, love," said Davey, to me. "No, don't tell me, you haven't got a corkscrew?"

"You wrong me, every way you wrong me, Brutus. That's one thing I have got." I had kept one back for Prissy. That pleasantly civilised lunch seemed a very long time ago. I routed it out, and while Davey wrestled with the cork Mrs Pascoe and I hurriedly rinsed out the tea-cups. We did not quite have to descend to jam-jars, as Larry, still clutching the kitten to him, quietly materialised beside us with a couple of elegant tumblers from the picnic basket in his car. These, with my tooth-glass, almost made up the quota, and Davey made do with a small, and it was to be hoped clean, jar that had once held fish-paste.

I saw that my mother, abandoning hope, had gone down under a wave of delighted chatter from Witches' Corner. If she had been afraid of some drawing aside of skirts among the Todhall neighbours she need not have worried. All parties seemed to have plenty to say, and said it at length, and all at the same time. Davey determinedly broke it up, wading in with the wine, which was received with pleasure, and then Larry, tea-cup in hand and kitten on shoulder, somehow got silence, and, standing there in front of the dying fire, prepared to make a speech.

"Well, now, ladies – and you, Dave – I am not going to make a speech. I am only going to say – Dear God!"

A fascinated pause as the kitten launched itself from his shoulder to the mantelpiece, by way of the top of the Unseen Guest. Larry, to the intense admiration of everyone present, simply reached a long arm, retrieved it, and held it to him while he went calmly on not making a speech.

"I would like to say," he said, "how very much my wife and I appreciate the welcome we have gotten here in Todhall. We have had the most warm and loving welcome from our lovely daughter, and now from all of you here tonight. It has been a great pleasure for me to meet you all, a very great pleasure. It's getting late, and Lilias and I will have to be going soon, but we'll be back here, never fear, and we'll hope to see you all when we visit again, as we certainly have plans to do. This darned cat has about sixteen claws to each foot. What are you going to do with it, Kathy?"

"Keep it, of course."

"But if you're coming with us tomorrow –" began my mother.

"We'll look after it for Kathy till she comes home," said Mrs Pascoe. I saw Lilias glance quickly at her, then at me, but she said nothing.

"You'll really keep him, then?" said Miss Linsey. "I'm so pleased. I do love them to get a good home. What will you call him, Kathy?"

I smiled at them all. My mother and her dear respectable gentleman; Miss Linsey, the true prophetess who had seen what I knew to be the future; the other witches, beaming kindly at me over Larry's picnic tumblers; Mrs Pascoe, who shared my secret. And Davey. With a sudden lift of the heart, I raised my tooth-glass in the toast.

"I'll call him George. Here's to George!"

"To George!" echoed everyone, and drank their

wine down. My mother was smiling mistily, looking very happy and, though I could see she was exhausted, as pretty as a picture.

Then one saw how she managed it. After one long, assessing look at her, Larry took charge. He handed the kitten over to me, then somehow, without seeming to hurry them at all, he had the three witches, taking cheerful farewells of me and the Pascoes, shepherded out of the kitchen and down the path towards the big car. My mother hung back, with a whispered word to Mrs Pascoe, then turned to say goodnight to me.

"Till tomorrow, then, sweetie. Isn't that wonderful? Till tomorrow."

A few more words and a kiss, and then she went, but slowly, to stop half way down the path and look back, as if to commit the scene to memory, the dim garden, the ghost of the white lilac, the shadowy bulk of the cottage with me standing in the lighted doorway. Then she went, and the gate creaked shut behind her.

As Larry settled her in the car Mrs Pascoe said, "We'll have to go too. The van's in their way. You'll have to back it up, Davey." Then to me, "You know that letter you gave me to post?"

"Yes."

"I brought it back. It's in my bag here. I thought, if you're going up to Strathbeg yourself, maybe you'd rather talk to Lady Brandon when you get there? She was on the phone just before we came down, and it was to tell me that they'd had an offer for Rose Cottage."

"Did she?" That was Davey. "Were they planning to accept it?"

"What's it to do with you?" His mother was dismissive. "Go and shift the van, Davey. He's got the car turned already."

"An offer for Rose Cottage?" I was surprised at the

force of my dismay. So short a time it seemed since my own hopeful net had been cast into the void. "But surely she'd never sell without telling us? Did she say if Gran knew?"

"Yes. She approved."

"But who on earth would Gran approve?"

"Me," said Davey.

We both turned to stare at him. His mother's hand went to her mouth, and she said nothing. He smiled at me.

"So you see it's got quite a lot to do with me. I was going to ask you about it, Kathy, but I didn't reckon on being rushed into it like this with half the village looking on and Mum rabbiting on about moving the van." He put out a hand and touched, not me, but the kitten, so that it purred and clung and butted its head into my neck. "I'll have to go. But I'll be down here early, before they come for you, and – maybe I can ask you then?"

"I'll be here," I said.

They had gone. Silence came back, broken only by the sound of the stream and the purring of the kitten in my arms as I walked down to the gate. The scent of Grand-dad's roses filled the air. An owl called from among the trees in the Hall grounds. Another answered, breathily, from somewhere in Gipsy Lonnen.

Gipsy Lonnen, where it had all begun.

Well, I knew now. As much as I would ever know. As much as I wanted to know.

Take love easy, as the leaves grow on the tree.

I would try. The quest, in the end, had been for myself, and I had been answered. It isn't the roots that matter to life, it's the flower. No more questions, no more looking back. I had found myself, and I knew

233

where I belonged. I was part of this place, and it was part of me. It was home.

I still had the tooth-glass in my hand, with a little wine left in it. I raised it towards the dim looming of the treetops at the head of Gipsy Lonnen.

"Whoever you were, and wherever you are, may God bless you, George," I said.

The kitten, no doubt assuming that I meant him, purred.

STORMY PETREL

Dedicated to
Culcicoides Pulicaris Argyllensis
with respect

1

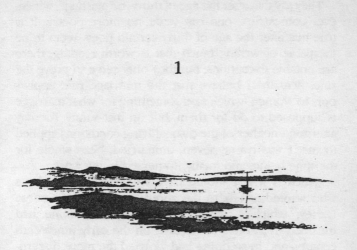

I must begin with a coincidence which I would not dare to recount if this were a work of fiction. Coincidences happen daily in 'real life' which would be condemned in a mere story, so writers tend to avoid them. But they happen. Daily, they happen. And on this particular day they – or rather it – happened twice.

I was working in my room, when a knock at the door heralded the entry of four second-year students. Usually I welcome them. They are my job. As English tutor at Haworth College in Cambridge I deal with them every day. But on this sunny afternoon in May, as it happened, I would not have welcomed any intruder, even the gyp with a Recorded Delivery letter announcing a big win on Ernie. I was writing a poem.

They say that after the age of thirty, or marriage, which-ever comes first, one can write no more poetry. It is true that after the age of thirty certain poets seem to be incapable of writing much that is worth reading; there are notable exceptions, but they only serve to prove the rule. Actually, I believe that the marriage rule applies only to women, which says something for what marriage is supposed to do for them, but on that sunny Tuesday afternoon neither of the disqualifying conditions applied to me. I was twenty-seven, unmarried, heart-whole for the time being, and totally immersed in my work.

Which is why I should have welcomed the students who wanted to talk to me about the poetry of George Darley, which a misguided colleague of mine had included in a series of lectures on the early nineteenth century, and in so doing had worried the more discern-ing of my students, who were failing to see any merit there. But I had been visited that morning by what was usually at this state of the term a rare inspiration, and was writing a poem of my own. More important than George Darley? At any rate better, which would not be difficult. As a struggling poet in the late twentieth century, I often thought that some early poets achieved publication very easily. But I did not say so to my students. Let them now praise famous men. They do it so rarely that it is good for them.

I said 'Come in,' sat them down, listened and then talked and finally got rid of them and went back to my poem. It had gone. The first stanza lay there on my desk, but the idea, the vision had fled like the dream dispelled by Coleridge's ill-starred person from Porlock. I re-read what I had written, wrestled with the fading vision for a few sweating minutes, then gave up, swore, crumpled the page up, pitched it into the empty fireplace, and said, aloud: 'What I really need is a good old-fashioned ivory tower.'

I pushed my chair back, then crossed to the open window and looked out. The lime trees were glorious in their young green, and, in default of the immemorial elms, the doves were moaning away in them like mad. Birds were singing their heads off everywhere, and from the clematis beside the window came the scent of honey and the murmur of innumerable bees. Tennyson; now there, I thought, was one of the really honourable exceptions to the rule, never failing, never fading even in old age, while I, at twenty-seven, could not even finish a lyric that had seemed, only a short while ago, to be moving inevitably towards the final tonic chord.

Well, so I was not Tennyson. I was probably, come to that, not even George Darley. I laughed at myself, felt better, and settled down on the window-seat in the sun to enjoy what was left of the afternoon. *The Times*, half-read and then abandoned, lay on the seat beside me. As I picked it up to throw it aside a line of small print caught my eye: 'Ivory tower for long or short let. Isolated cottage on small Hebridean island off the coast of Mull. Ideal for writer or artist in search of peace. Most relatively mod cons.' And a box number.

I said, aloud: 'I don't believe it.'

'What don't you believe, Dr Fenemore?'

One of my students had come back, and was hesitating in the open doorway. It was Megan Lloyd, who was the daughter of a Welsh farm worker from somewhere in Dyfed, and who had earned her place in College with a brilliant scholarship. Short, rather thickset, with dark curling hair, dark eyes, and freckles, she looked as if she would be most at home with dogs and horses, or with bared arms scrubbing a dairy down, and perhaps she was, but she was also very intelligent, highly imaginative, and easily my best student. Some day, with average luck, she would be a good writer. I remembered that I had promised to see her about some poems she had written and had nervously asked me to read. She looked nervous still, but half amused with it, as she added: 'Surely, *The Times*? It's not supposed to get things wrong, is it?'

'Oh, Megan, come in. Sorry, was I talking to myself? It's nothing, I was off on a track of my own for a moment. Yes, I've got your file here, and yes, I've read them.' I went back to my desk, picked the folder up, and gestured her to a chair. She looked back at me with no expression at all in her face, but her eyes were twice as big as usual, and I could see the tension in every muscle. I knew how she felt. Every time your work is read, you die several deaths for every word, and poetry is like being flayed alive.

So I went straight to it. 'I liked them. Some of them very much. And of course some not so much . . .' I talked on about the poems, while she slowly relaxed and began to look happy, and even, in the end, cheerfully argumentative, which, with Megan, was par for the course. At length I closed the folder.

'Well, there you are, as far as I'm able to judge. Whether some of the more, shall I say, advanced judgments of the day will concur is something I can't guess at, but if you want to try and publish, go ahead and good luck to you. Whatever happens, you must go on writing. Is that what you wanted to hear?'

She swallowed, cleared her throat, then nodded without speaking.

I handed her the folder. 'I won't say anything more here and now. I've written fairly detailed notes about some of them. I think it would be better – and we would both find it easier – if you looked at those in your own time? And of course if there's anything you don't under-stand, or want to argue about, please feel free. All right?'

'Yes. Thank you. Thank you very much for all the trouble. It was just that I – that one doesn't know oneself –'

'Yes, I know.'

She smiled, her face lighted suddenly from within. 'Of course you do. And in return, am I allowed to give *you* some advice?'

'Such as what?' I asked, surprised.

She glanced down at the empty hearth, where the crumpled page had fallen and partly unfurled. It would be obvious even from where she sat that the sheet con-tained lines of an unfinished poem, disfigured with scor-ing and the scribbles of frustration.

She repeated, with a fair imitation of my voice, but with a smile that robbed the echo of any sting of impertinence: '"Whatever happens, you must go on writing."' Then suddenly, earnestly: 'I can't read it from here, but I'm sure you shouldn't throw it away. Give it another go, won't you, Dr Fenemore? I loved that last one of yours in the *Journal*. Please.'

After a pause that seemed endless, I said, rather awk-wardly: 'Well, thank you. But in term time . . . One can't choose one's times, you see.'

'Can one ever?'

'I suppose not.'

'I'm sorry, I shouldn't have said that.' Suddenly embar-rassed, she gathered her things together and started to get to her feet. 'None of my business, but I couldn't help seeing. Sorry.'

More to put her at her ease again than for any other reason I picked up *The Times* and showed it to her.

11

'I was trying, you see. A Hebridean island – it does sound like a place where one could work in peace, and they have actually called it an "ivory tower". There, I've ringed it.'

She read the advertisement aloud, then looked up, bright-eyed. 'Mull? An island off Mull? You've answered this?'

'I was thinking of it.'

'Well, isn't that something? Ann Tracy and I are going to Mull this summer. Two weeks. She's fixing it up, I've never been, but her people used to spend holidays up there, and she says it can be fabulous, weather and midges permitting. What a coincidence! It sounds just the thing – like fate, really, after what you were saying. You will answer it, won't you?'

'It looks as if I'd better, doesn't it?' I said. 'I'll write this very evening.'

*

But fate had not quite finished with me. That evening my brother Crispin telephoned me.

Crispin is a doctor, a partner in a four-man practice in Petersfield in Hampshire. He is six years older than I am, married, with two children away at school. He would have preferred, I knew, to keep them at home, but Ruth, his wife, had overruled him in that, as she did in quite a few other matters. Not that Crispin was a weak man, but he was a very busy one, and had to be content to leave the management of their joint lives largely to his highly capable wife. They were tolerably happy together, as marriages seem to go, a happiness achieved partly by agreeing to differ.

One thing they differed about was holidays. Ruth loved travel, cities, shops, theatres, beach resorts. Crispin, when on leave from his demanding routine, craved for peace and open spaces. He, like me, loved Scotland, and made for it whenever he got the chance. There he walked and fished and took photographs which later, when he found time, he processed himself in a friend's dark-room. Over the years he had acquired real skill in his hobby, and had exhibited some of his studies of Scottish scenery and wildlife; his real passion was bird photography, and through the years he had amassed a remarkable collection of pictures. Some of these had been published in periodicals like *Country Life* and the wildlife journals, but the best had never been shown. I knew he had a private hope that some day he might make a book with them. When our vacations coincided, we often holidayed together, content in our respective solitudes.

So when he rang up that evening to tell me he was taking a fortnight's leave towards the end of June and what about a trip north as soon as term ended, I did feel as if the fates themselves had taken a hand.

'I'd been planning that very thing.' I told him about the advertisement, and he was enthusiastic. I let him talk on about harriers and divers and skuas and all the rare and marvellous birds that would no doubt be waiting around to be photographed, and then put in the usual cautious query: 'And Ruth?'

'Actually, no, not this time.' The usual casual answer. 'She doesn't like the Highlands, you know that, and she's got rather a lot on just at present. She's planning to take a holiday abroad later on, after John and Julie go back to school. But if you can get this place . . . It could be really good. Most of the young birds will still be at the nest, and if the weather lets up, we might get across to the

Treshnish Isles as well. Look, Rose, why not? It sounds great. Why don't you go right ahead and get the details, and then we'll be in touch again?'

And so it was arranged. I wrote that night to the box number.

And got my ivory tower.

2

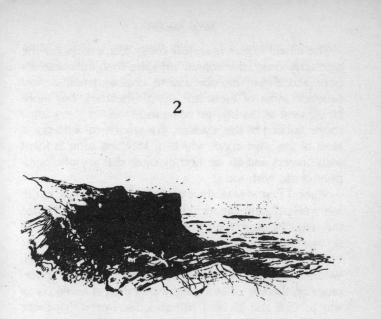

The Isle of Moila is the first stop past Tobermory. It is not
a large island, perhaps nine miles by five, with formidable
cliffs to the north-west that face the weather rather like
the prow of a ship. From the steep sheep-bitten turf at the
head of these cliffs the land slopes gently down towards a
glen where the island's only sizeable river runs seawards
out of a loch cupped in a shallow basin among low hills.
Presumably the loch – lochan, rather, for it is not large –
is fed by springs eternally replenished by the rain, for
nothing flows into it except small burns seeping through
rush and bog myrtle, which spread after storm into sod-
den quagmires of moss. But the outflow is perennially
full, white water pouring down to where the moor
cleaves open and lets it fall to sea.

15

The island's coast is mainly rocky, but, except for the northerly crags, the coastal cliffs are low, thrusting out here and there into the sea to enclose small curved beaches. Most of these are shingle beaches, but those facing west are sandy, the white shell sand of the Atlantic shore, backed by the machair, that wonderful wild grassland of the west coast, which in May and June is filled with flowers and all the nesting birds that any photographer could wish for.

When I first saw Moila it was on a beautiful day in the last week of June. My term had ended a few days before the start of Crispin's leave, so we had agreed to travel up separately, and meet on Moila itself. The island ferry, as I had discovered, sailed three times a week, on Mondays, Wednesdays and Saturdays; it went from Oban to Tobermory on the Isle of Mull, and then called at Moila on its way to Coll and Tiree. I had also discovered that there would be little, if any, use for a car on Moila, so both my brother and I had arranged to travel up by train.

It was a pleasant journey. I took the night train for Fort William, which stops at Crianlarich at seven in the morning. With a three-hour wait there, I ate a large breakfast, did a quarter of the day's crossword, then boarded the little local train that runs through Glen Lochy and past the northern end of Loch Awe, to finish at Oban on the west coast. The ferry for the outer isles was due to leave at six on the following morning, so I checked into the waterfront hotel where I had booked, then spent the day exploring Oban, and went to bed early. At half past five next morning I boarded the ferry, and was on the final stage of my journey.

The sea was calm, and Oban, caught in the clear light of a summer morning, looked charming and toylike, as we sailed sedately out between the islets and castle-crowned rocks, with sea-birds drifting in our wake, and everywhere, even over the smell of salt and wind, the scents of summer. Idyllic. Just the setting for an ivory tower.

Or so I still hoped. Nobody I had spoken to in the train, or on the ferry, had ever visited Moila, which must support, so I was told by one slow-spoken Highlander, no more than thirty folk in all.

'So you'll be right back to nature, and let us hope that the natives are friendly.' The twinkle in his eye was reassuring, but when we tied up at Tobermory and the purser pointed out to sea where a group of small rocks (or so it seemed) showed strung out on the horizon like a mother duck with her ducklings after her, I felt a cowardly twinge, and found myself wondering what the 'relatively mod cons' could be.

'Yon big island, see? That's Moila,' said my guide.

'And the others?'

'Och, they've all got names, but I could not tell you what they are. There's no folk there, only the birds.'

'Can you get to them?'

'Oh, aye, with a bit of luck, on a fine day. Parties do go out, folks with cameras to film the birds. You're one of these bird watchers, are you?'

'Not really. But my brother's very keen. He's coming to join me later this week. Do you know if we'll be able to hire a boat in Moila?'

But here he had to leave me to attend to stores which were being brought on board, and some twenty minutes later I could see the place for myself.

*

17

The ferry was not big, but she dwarfed the harbour – she had to stand off from the jetty and land us by boat – and indeed the village. As far as I could see, there were some eight or nine cottages strung out on a narrow road which circled the bay. The building nearest the jetty was the post office-cum-shop. A home-made notice informed me that it was kept by M. McDougall, who also did bed and breakfasts. Some fifty yards away was a white-washed building surrounded by a stretch of asphalt; the village school, I was to discover, where on alternate Sundays the minister from Tobermory came over to hold a service. A narrow river, little more than a stream, lapsed gently over its stones past the post office. It was spanned by a narrow hump-backed bridge of the picturesque variety that is guaranteed to damage any car that uses it. But, as I had been warned, there were no cars. One battered Land-Rover stood outside the post office, and leaning against the schoolhouse wall were a couple of bicycles. No other forms of transport. Nor, as far as I could see, did the road continue beyond the end of the village.

And my cottage, I had been informed, lay at the other side of the island.

Well, I had asked for it. I left my cases parked on the quay, and made my way into the post office.

Since the thrice-weekly visit of the ferry brought all the island's mail and supplies, and the post office was very small, the place was crowded, and the postmistress, busily sorting through a pile of mail and newspapers, while exchanging two days' news in Gaelic with the ferry's master, had no glance to spare for me. The little shop had been arranged as what I have seen described as a mini-hypermarket, so I found a basket and busied myself with collecting what supplies I thought I might need for the next couple of days. I was called to myself by the

echoing hoot of the ferry's siren, to find that the shop
had emptied of its crowd, and the postmistress, taking off
her spectacles, was hurrying round to the store counter
to look after the stranger.

'You'll be the young lady for Camus na Dobhrain? Miss
Fenemore, was it?'

She was a thinnish woman of perhaps fifty, with greying
hair carefully arranged, and very blue eyes. She wore a
flowered smock, and her spectacles hung round her neck
on a cord. She had the beautiful skin of the islands, with
hardly a wrinkle, except near the eyes, where the smile
lines puckered the corners. She was not smiling now, but
her look was full of a benevolent curiosity, and the soft
island voice, with the lilt of the Gaelic moving through
it like a gentle sea-swell, warmed me as palpably as
if the sun had come into the dim and cluttered little
shop.

'Yes, I'm Rose Fenemore. And you are Mrs McDougall?
How do you do?' We shook hands. 'And yes, I'm for the
cottage that the Harris Agency advertised. Is that the one?
I don't understand Gaelic, I'm afraid.'

'And how should you? Yes, indeed, that is the one. The
English for it is "Otters' Bay". It is the only place on Moila
that is to let. We're not just a metropolis, as you see.' She
smiled, busying herself with my purchases as she spoke.
'You'll not have been here before, then? Well, if the
weather stays fine you'll find plenty of nice walks, and
I'm told that the house at Otters' Bay is comfortable
enough these days. But lonely. You are by yourself, are
you?'

'Till Wednesday, at least. My brother's hoping to come
then.' I gave her all she wanted to know. I was part of
the week's news, after all. 'He's a doctor, from Hampshire.
He couldn't get away when I did, so I came up on my

own. Does the Wednesday ferry come in at the same time?'

'It does. You have not put any firelighters in. You will find it is much easier to get your fire going with one of those. Are you used to a peat fire?'

'No, but I'm hoping I can learn. Mrs McDougall, how do I get from here to the cottage? I'm told it's about two miles. I can easily walk to do shopping and so on, but I've got a couple of suitcases here now, and I certainly can't manage those.'

'No worry about that. I saw your cases there, and Archie McLaren will have them into the Land-Rover by this time. So will you perhaps be wanting a couple of bags, say, of coal to help with the fire? The house will be dry enough; there was a couple in it through the middle of May, and we have had good weather, but you would be better to stock up now for what next week might bring.'

'Yes, of course. Thank you very much. Two bags of coal, then, please, and the firelighters, and – yes, I think I've remembered everything else. Oh, about milk and bread. Can one only get it fresh when the ferry comes over?'

'We have fresh milk here from the farm, but you would be better to take some of the long-life with you. It's a long walk from Otters' Bay in the bad weather. Here it is. Two cartons, and it will keep a long time, even with no fridge. I don't know if you have one over there ... The bread comes with the boat. Will I keep you a loaf on Wednesday? And another at the weekend, or two then, perhaps? Mostly we make our own if we want it fresh. There, is that everything?'

'I think so, thank you. How much is that, Mrs McDougall?'

She told me, and I paid her. A young man, dark, short,

burly, in a navy guernsey and jeans and gumboots, came in and lifted the coal bags into the Land-Rover beside my cases. I picked up the carrier bag where the postmistress had packed my groceries.

'I don't imagine there's a telephone at the cottage, is there?'

'There is not. There is one here, and one at the House, and that is all there are. And the one at the House is cut off since the old lady died.'

'The House?' Somehow, the way she said it gave it a capital letter.

'The big house. It's not far from you, half a mile along the shore, maybe. Taigh na Tuir, they call it. That means House of the Tower. There is a small island off the coast just there, with the remains of a broch on it. I suppose that is the tower that the House was named for. It was built as a shooting lodge in the old days, and then the Hamiltons bought it, and lived there most summers, but old Mrs Hamilton, she was the last of them, died this February, so it's empty now, and likely to stay so.' She smiled. 'It's not everyone wants the kind of peace and quiet we have on Moila.'

'I can imagine. Well, I'm all set to enjoy it, anyway. And I don't really want a phone, except to make sure about my brother's coming. So I'll walk over here tomorrow and telephone him, if I may. What time do you shut?'

'Half past five, but if you want the telephone, then come to the house door. No, it's no trouble, it's what everyone does, and the cheap calls are after six anyway. Just you come. That's it, then.' She picked up the second carrier bag and saw me to the door with it. 'Archie will see you into the house, and if there's anything more that you need, you will let him know. And I'll look for you maybe tomorrow. Goodbye. Look after the lady, now, Archie.'

Archie was understood to say that he would. I got in beside him, and we set off. The Land-Rover had seen better days, and once we had left the village street and taken to the track – it was little more – that wound up from the village towards the moorland, conversation was difficult. After one or two tries, met by a nod or a non-committal noise from Archie, I gave up, and looked about me.

I suppose that there are very few places on Moila from which one cannot see the sea. The track, rough and strewn with stones, climbed, at first gently, through sheep-cropped turf bristling with reeds and thistles and islanded with stretches of bracken. Once we were out of sight of the village there were no trees except, here and there, thorns dragged sideways by the wind and shorn close by the weather. The track grew steeper, and twisted. Now to either hand was heather, at this season still dark and flowerless, except where patches of the early bell heather splashed their vivid purple across grey rock. The whins, those perpetual wonders, were blazing gold, and everywhere over the stretches of grass between the bracken spread the tiny white and yellow flowers of lady's bedstraw and tormentil. The very lichen patching the grey rocks was bright mustard-gold, like flowers. Away to the right I saw the flat gleam of the loch.

Nothing could be heard above the noise of the engine, but I saw a lark spring skywards out of the heather, and another, a few minutes later, sink to its rest. A pair of grey-backed crows – hooded crows – flew across the track, and then, as the Land-Rover topped the rise and started down into a narrowing glen, a buzzard soared up in leisurely circles, to be lost over the crest of the moor.

Then we were running gently downhill beside a burn, towards the distant gleam of the sea. Here, in the shelter that the glen gave from the Atlantic gales, the trees crowded close, and reasonably tall. Oaks, mostly, but there were beeches and ash trees, with birch and hazel everywhere, tangled with brambles and wild honey-suckle. Along the edge of the burn were thickets of alder and hawthorn standing knee-deep in foxgloves.

The track levelled out, the glen widened, and there below us was the bay.

Otters' Bay was very small, a pebbled crescent backed by a storm beach of smooth boulders. Thick black curves of dry seaweed marked the reach of the tides. To our left a high cliff cut off the view, and to the right a lowish headland jutted well out into the sea. Narrowing my eyes against the Atlantic glitter I could see the line of a path that climbed from the bay and on over the headland to the west. And beyond the crest of the headland, hazy with distance, the shape of a hill, smooth and symmetrical, like a drawn-up knee.

Then the Land-Rover came to a halt beside a rough jetty made of stacked boulders tied down with fencing wire, and there, backed against the cliff a short way above us, was the cottage.

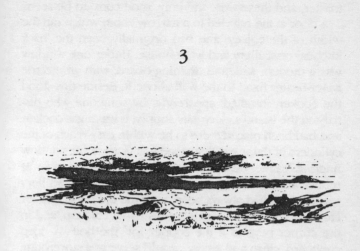

3

The cottage was bigger than I had expected. Originally it had been built on the usual pattern, a tiny square hallway, with doors to either side leading into the two 'front' rooms, and a steep enclosed stair up to the twin bedrooms under the pitch of the roof. But someone, fairly recently, had done a job of conversion; the two downstairs rooms were thrown into one, with the staircase half dividing them. The sitting-room, to the right, had a pleasant fireplace, and was adequately, if not well, furnished with a couple of easy chairs, a low table, and a doubtful-looking sofa pushed back against the staircase wall. The 'kitchen-diner' on the other side boasted the usual cupboards and what looked like home-made worktops, and a table near the window with four chairs drawn up to it. On the worktop stood an electric kettle and a toaster, and these were the only 'mod cons' to be seen.

A door at the rear led to a narrow room which ran the width of the cottage and had originally been the 'back kitchen' or scullery and wash-house. Under one window was a modern sink and draining-board, with an electric water-heater fixed to the wall above it. Beside this stood the cooker, installed, apparently, by someone who distrusted the island's electricity supply; it was a gas cooker, and had been placed there to be within easy reach of the cylinders of Calor gas that stood just outside the window under a lean-to, beside a stack of peat. That was as far as modernisation had gone: the other end of the scullery was just as it had always been, with the old deep sink for laundry, served by a single, presumably cold tap, and in the corner beyond it the copper for 'the boil'. A deep cupboard, clean and empty, would serve as a storeroom; another, beside the copper, held cleaning tools. No fridge, but the place would be cool even in summer; those windows never saw the sun. Peering out, I could see that there must once have been a garden or kail-yard between the cottage and the cliff; now the tumbledown wall enclosed nothing but a tangle of brambles and wild roses almost hiding a garden hut. Alongside the wall a narrow path wound between waist-high nettles to a small structure whose function one could guess at. The house agent had assured me that a bathroom and lavatory had been installed upstairs above the scullery; looking at those nettles, I hoped he had told the truth.

'I will take your cases upstairs for you,' said Archie McLaren.

'No, don't bother – well, thank you very much.'

I dumped the carrier bags of groceries on the kitchen table and started to unpack them. I heard him moving about upstairs, and it was a minute or two before he came down again.

'I was just' – he pronounced it 'chust' – 'taking a look. She had Robert McDougall over from Mull last year to do the bedrooms up. That is Mary McDougall's cousin from Dervaig. He always does a good job. I had not seen the upstairs rooms since they were finished, but I remember the job they had with the bathroom, and with this.' He looked about him with interest. 'It was very different here when the family had it. It was Alastair Mackay lived here, that was the gardener at the House. They only moved away two years ago, to the mainland, and then Mrs Hamilton did the place up for letting. When they took the old oven out, I brought the cooker down myself, and the fittings for the kitchen units. The timber and the bath and such came across by boat into the bay there, and a fine job they had dragging them up to the house.'

'I hadn't realised that the cottage belongs – belonged? – to Mrs Hamilton. Mrs McDougall told me that she had died recently.'

'That is so. She was a nice lady, and when her husband was alive he was a great one for the shooting and the fishing, though there is not much fishing here on Moila. He used to go north for the salmon every year, to the mainland, but she would stay here. She liked it, and then after Colonel Hamilton died she never went away at all, even in the winter. But this last winter was too much for her, poor lady.'

'What do you suppose will happen to the House – the big house, I mean – now?'

'I do not know. I think that there is a relation abroad somewhere, but that is all. It will be sold, I think, but who will buy it?'

'Someone who loves peace and quiet, I expect.'

'An ivory tower?'

I had been reaching up to put packets and tins into one of the wall cupboards, but this startled me into turning. 'A what?'

'Ivory tower. It was what Mrs Hamilton used to say. She was a writer, a real one who got books printed. When she was younger she used to write books for children. She said it was a poetic way of saying you wanted to be left alone.'

'I see. Yes, I see. I did wonder. House agents aren't usually poets.'

'What is that?'

'Only that the house agents called it that when they advertised it. Rather clever of them. That's what caught my eye. I wonder if they'll try to sell the cottage too, or if they'll go on letting it?'

'It has only ever been let in the summer, and no one has been here yet this year except the people last month, folk from Cornwall, I think. They came with a boat, and did all their shopping in Tobermory, so we did not see much of them at all.'

'I suppose a boat would make sense if one was here for long. Do you have a boat?'

'I do. If you should ever want to go fishing, or maybe to take a look at the bird islands, you will just let me know?'

'I certainly will. Oh, I nearly forgot. Did you unload the coal?'

'I did. It is out the back where the peat is kept. Just beside the door. Will I get some in for you now? No bother. Do you know how to make a fire with the peats?'

'Mrs McDougall asked me that,' I said. 'I don't know. I can but try. I might have to ask for help with that as well.'

'You will be welcome. But you will find plenty of

kindling and dry wood down on the beach. Then give the peats plenty of air. If once you get it going, it is a good fire.'

'I'll do my best. Thanks very much, Archie. Now, what do I owe you?'

I paid him and he took his leave, but in the doorway he hesitated, then suddenly, as if the question had forced itself out in spite of good manners, asked: 'Are you sure you will be all right here, all on your own? What are you going to do? It's a lonely spot, and if it's walking you want, Moila is such a small island, and once you have been round it, you have seen it all. There is nothing special about Moila, except maybe the birds on the outer islands, and they will be away soon.'

I smiled. 'I wanted an ivory tower. I'm a writer, too, you see.'

'Well, now . . . A writer, is it? Yes, I do see.' His tone and look said, clearly, that everything – any possibly lunacy – was now fully explained.

I laughed. 'I don't intend to write all the time, though there is some work I want to do. But I'm not really planning to be a hermit; my brother's coming over soon, and I know he'll want to go to the islands, so we'll be in touch. Thanks again.'

I watched the Land-Rover grind its way up the track till a turn of the glen hid it from sight, and in a few more moments the sound of its engine had faded to silence.

Silence? The wash of waves on the pebbled beach, the crying and calling of the wheeling gulls, the silver chain of sound from a lark above the cliff-top, and, as a final coda, the distant, breathy note of the ferry's siren as she drew away towards the west. The last link gone. Solitude. Complete and unassailable solitude. The sported oak.

I shut the front door gently, a symbolic gesture which

shut out what sounds there were, and went upstairs to
see what that nice lady, Mrs Hamilton, had provided in
the way of beds.

*

The beds were reasonable, the bedrooms tiny, tucked
under the slope of the roof, and charming, with white
paint, flowery wallpaper, a minimum of furniture, and of
course that marvellous view right out to the south-west.
Storm-direction, I supposed, and spared a thought for the
winter; but in June, surely, all would be well? The
windows were tightly shut, and the rooms smelled stuffy,
but not damp, though the drawers of the chest stuck as I
tried to pull them open. The solitary ornament in my
room was a faded copy of a Biblical scene by Gustave
Doré, sinners drowning in a rough sea. Rather too perti-
nent, I thought, for the place's original dweller, who must
have gone down to the Atlantic in a small boat on many
a stormy night. But today the real sea looked wonderful,
silken, with a gentle running glitter where the tide
moved, and here and there the tilt and flash of white
wings in the sunlight as the gulls sailed out from the
cliffs.

It would do. It would do very well. I would finish
unpacking, have a look at the cooker and set things ready
for supper, then I would take a walk out to look at the
sea, and gather kindling in case the evening turned chilly
enough for a fire.

*

There was, as Archie had promised, plenty of good kindling among the piled jetsam on the beach. I soon had an armful, then clambered up off the shingle to the better walking of the salt-washed turf where the burn, dividing into deep peaty runnels, cut its way to the shore. Sea-pinks were thick everywhere, with here and there patches of small shingle glistening with broken shells. An oystercatcher screamed from somewhere at the end of the beach, warning its young. Not far away I caught, from the corner of my eye, the flickering movement as a ringed plover scudded and ran among the sea-pinks. It went silently, dodging and hiding; it must have left its nest at my approach.

Any thought I may have had about finding the nest for Crispin's camera left me then. Gradually, over the last few minutes, I had become conscious of a growing discomfort, a tickling, burning sensation in the face and hands, and even in my hair a stinging sort of unpleasantness that suddenly became insupportable.

Midges. I had forgotten about the midges. The curse of the Highlands. The infinitesimal and unbeatable enemy. The serpent in paradise.

Tucking my load of sticks under one arm, and rubbing my free hand hard over face and hair, I scurried for the safety of the cottage.

After all, the evening stayed mild, so the fire never got lit. I made and ate supper, washed up, then watched the changing view of evening from the haven of the cottage window, and went early to bed.

4

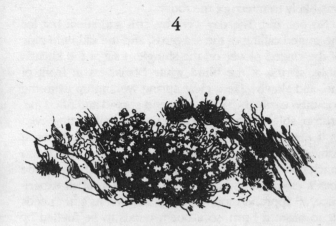

I awoke next morning to a brilliant pearly light, but when I went to the window, no sea was visible. Nothing, in fact, was visible. The world was shrouded in a curtain of mist. This was not the sort of fog one is used to in towns, but a veil of salt-smelling white, damp and mild, with all the soft brilliance of a thin curtain drawn between earth and sun. But view there was none. I could not even see as far as the mouth of the burn. So, no walk today, until I was a little more certain of my way. Even the main track to the village could be treacherous in this blinding, moveless white.

I was not disappointed. I told myself so, firmly, several times. I had all that I had wanted, peace and privacy, a day to myself before Crispin came, and an absolute compulsion to stay indoors and take another look at the poem that had been broken into by the tutorial in Cambridge. I would look at it again, and see if it had been totally destroyed. At least no person from Porlock was likely to interrupt me today.

No one did. The day went by, still and silent but for the muted calling of the sea-birds, and the sad little pipe of the ringed plover on the shingle. I sat at the kitchen table, staring at the blind white blankness in front of me, and slowly, like a clear spring welling up from the common earth, the poem rose and spread and filled me, unstoppable as flood water, technique unknotting even as it ran, like snags rolled away on the flood. When it comes, it is worth everything in the world. There is too much easy talk about 'inspiration', but at such times one sees it exactly for what it is, a breathing in of all experience, all apprehension of beauty, all love. As a fire needs air to make it burn, so a poem needs to be fuelled by each one of these. And the greatest of these is love.

When I looked up at last, it was to see the near cliffs bright with the afternoon sun, and the sea creaming calmly against the storm beach in the gentlest of high tides. The horizon was still invisible, but above the line of mist that hid it the sky was clear, with the promise of a lovely evening. An evening with a breeze; I could see movement in the bracken that edged the track, and cloud-shadows moved from time to time over the sea-pinks. So much for the midges, and it would be better at the head of the track and over the central moors. I would make myself some tea, I decided as I packed away my papers, then walk over to the post office to make my call to Crispin.

*

34

My sister-in-law answered the telephone, in the voice which, whether she means it or not, always sounds abrasive and resentful when she speaks to me. She was sorry, but Crispin was out on call. No, she did not know when he would be home. When did she ever? His train? Well, it now seemed that there was someone he wanted to see in Glasgow, so he was taking this chance to fit that in. He had booked on tomorrow night's sleeper, and would head up to Oban on Friday. Then, she gathered, he would get the ferry the next morning, Saturday. Would that be right?

'It could be. I was hoping he'd manage tomorrow's boat, but Saturday would be great. I've found out more about it now, so if you wouldn't mind giving him a message, Ruth? Have you got a pencil handy? Well, the ferry is the one for Coll and Tiree ... C.O.L.L. and T.I.R.E.E. ... Yes, they're two of the islands in the Inner Hebrides; Crispin will know. It leaves at six in the morning, and they want you on board soon after half past five. I stayed at the Columba Hotel, just near the quay. I'll make a reservation for him for Friday night. Oh, and tell him that Moila's too small for the ferry to dock, so he'll come ashore in a boat. I won't offer to meet the ferry – it docks at eight in the morning – but I'll arrange transport for him to the cottage. Did you get all that?'

'Yes. But wouldn't it be better if I got him to call you back when he comes in?'

I laughed. 'It would be difficult. There's only the public phone in the post office, and I've just walked two miles to get to that. But I'll give you the number –' I gave it – 'and if he wants to leave a message for me, Mrs McDougall will take it.'

'Mrs McDougall. Yes.' Now it was her professional voice, quick and cool, the doctor's wife taking another message down. Then she was herself again. 'Rose, what's it like? Two miles from the phone? And you had to walk it? I must say, it sounds just the sort of place Crispin would love.'

'He would. He will. It's quite lovely.' I added, in total insincerity: 'You really ought to have come, Ruth. The cottage is tiny, but it's charming, and the views are out of this world.'

'But what on earth would there be to *do*?'

'Well, nothing.' Nothing, blessed state for the hard-working Crispin, and for myself after the turmoil of exams and end of term.

'I,' said my sister-in-law, who never, I am sure, means to be offensive, 'simply cannot stand being idle. I'm going to Marrakesh in September. Marvellous hotel, bags of sunshine, and plenty of tours and fascinating shopping.'

'That sounds wonderful. Enjoy it. I'll have to go now, Ruth. I'll ring again on Thursday evening to see if Crispin's going to make it. Goodbye now.'

'Goodbye.' And she rang off.

Mrs McDougall was in her kitchen taking a batch of bread out of the oven. I paid her for the call, and stayed chatting for a while, answering her queries about the cottage and then telling her of my brother's expected arrival, and the possibility that he might telephone with a message.

'I expect I'll walk over this way every day anyway, and if he does come on Saturday could Archie be here, please, to take him down with his bags to the cottage?'

'He will be there. He always meets the boat. There are always goods to carry that have been ordered. Well, it will be nice for you to have your brother here, and we will hope for the best. I am afraid that there is bad weather forecast. I have just heard it on the news.'

'Oh, dear, is there? Really bad? Enough to stop the ferry crossing?'

'It has to be very bad indeed for that. Don't worry, your brother will get here. But you might find the cottage a bit draughty if it gets really rough.'

'I'll batten down the hatches,' I told her. She laughed, and we talked for a few minutes longer. When I left I had a bottle of midge-repellent in my pocket, and a loaf of new bread, still warm, in a plastic carrier. The loaf was a gift. The natives were friendly, after all.

*

I went slowly, and presently found myself walking towards a most spectacular sunset. Gold, scarlet and blazing flame I had seen before, but never like this, washing over the low clouds from below, and backed by the most delicate and limpid green which faded to primrose and then into the shadowy greys of the upper sky.

I stood to watch. To my right was the small loch, edged with deep reedy banks of moss and thymy turf. The water lay smooth as glass, polished with all the colours of the sunset sky. Then something moved, and the shining world broke up into arrowing ripples, as a bird slid across the water, no more than a shape of black against the glare. A duck? Too big. A diver? It was possible. I had never seen one, but my brother had talked of them, and I knew that he was hoping he might find one here. As I screwed up my eyes against the dazzle, trying to see the creature so that I might describe it to Crispin, it vanished. Duck or diver, it had dived, and, though I waited for long minutes, it did not appear again. I walked on, and down the hill towards the cottage which, already, seemed like home.

It is never quite dark on a clear June night in the Highlands. And never, in the long, light nights, do the sea-birds cease from calling and flying. I went outside again that night, just before bedtime, to look at the stars. Back in the city, or in fact anywhere that I had lived, the night sky was disfigured by street-lamps and the city's emanations. But here, in a clear arch of pewter-grey air, the stars were low and bright and as thick as daisies on a lawn. I picked out the Plough, and Orion, and the Pleiades, and of course the long splashing trail of the Milky Way, but that was as far as my knowledge went. Of one other thing I could be certain; the weather was changing. A wind was getting up, and even as I stood there, the lower stars were obscured by drifting darkness. The cries of the sea-birds, muted, seemed to change, too. And the soft murmur of the sea. It was perceptibly colder, and the wind smelt of rain.

I went indoors and to bed.

*

During the night the wind got up, and the morning dawned grey and blustery, with bursts of heavy rain. Thankful that I had taken the trouble to gather dry wood while it was fine, I lighted the fire, and soon had a cheerful blaze going.

And, once the chores were done, there was nothing to do but write.

It is time, I think, to make a confession. Though I was a student of literature and, I believe, a reasonably good teacher, and loved my work, and though I was, moreover, a serious poet who had gained some small recognition in circles even outside my own University, my writing life was not confined to poems and articles, or even lectures. I wrote science fiction.

Not only wrote it, but published it and made what seemed to a poorly-paid lecturer to be a very acceptable amount of money with it. Under another name, of course. The flights of Hugh Templar's imagination paid Rose Fenemore very well indeed. They also gave her a much valued safety-valve for an almost too-active imagination. The pure invention of these tales, the exercise of what at its best can be called the high imagination, allow the writer (in Dryden's phrase) to take the clogs off his fancy, and to escape the world at will.

So through that dismal day Hugh Templar sat at his kitchen table and pursued the adventures of a team of space-travellers who had discovered a world directly behind the sun, which was a mirror-image of our own Earth, with the same physical composition, but with a rather different kind of population, a race having strange and, I hoped, thought-provoking ideas about how to run their planet...

At ten o'clock the lights went out.

Though normally, in the Highlands, there is almost enough light at that time to write by, the storm-clouds that had thickened and threatened all day made it quite dark. The fire had died to cold ashes, but I felt my way to where I had seen a candlestick, left ready on the mantelpiece, presumably as insurance against just this event. I crossed to the uncurtained window and peered out. The wind was stronger than ever, and fistfuls of rain hurtled against the glass. A wild and nasty night.

I finished the section I had been writing – an idea left

in mid-paragraph tends to vanish very quickly – then took myself and my candle early to bed.

*

The walls of the cottage were thick enough to shut out the worst sounds of the storm's buffeting, and even the creaking of doors and rattling of windows could not keep me awake for long. But something, some sharper, unaccustomed sound, brought me out of my first deep sleep into listening wakefulness.

The storm was still raging, more fiercely now than before. I could hear the crash of waves on the shingle, and the intermittent shriek of the wind as it tore through the gaps in the kail-yard wall.

But the sound that had startled me awake was different. It came from within the cottage, a quiet sound, but cutting through all the noise from outside. The closing of a door; the back door, I thought. And then sounds from the scullery. A tap running, and the echo of metal as the kettle was filled.

Crispin? Against all expectation, all possibility, had my brother managed to make his way here, and cross to Moila in spite of the storm?

Too bewildered by sleep to think just how impossible it was, I slid out of bed, pulled on my slippers, threw my dressing-gown on, and opened my bedroom door. There was a light on downstairs, and as my bedroom door opened, all sounds ceased from inside the house. For a moment I thought I had been mistaken, and that perhaps I had left the switch on after the light failed, but no, I was sure I had switched off. And I had locked the back door. I ran downstairs.

He was just turning from the sink, kettle in hand. A young man, tallish, slenderly built, with dark hair dragged into a tousle by the wind, and a narrow, pale-skinned face. A good-looking face; blue eyes, straight nose, cheeks flushed with cold and wet with rain, and with tomorrow's stubble already showing dark. He wore a navy fisherman's jersey and gumboots, and a heavy anorak, shiny and running with wet.

I had never seen him before in my life.

I stopped dead in the doorway. He stood, rigid, gripping the kettle.

We both spoke at the same time, and, inevitably, the same words.

'Who the hell are you?'

5

He set the kettle down with a rap on the draining-board. He seemed even more taken aback than I was, and this heartened me. I said, with a reasonable show of calmness: 'You're welcome, of course, to take shelter from the storm, but do you usually walk into someone else's house without knocking? Or did you knock, and I didn't hear you? I thought the door was locked, anyway.'

'Your house?' He asked it without any apparent sense of its being a stupid question.

'Well, yes. Temporarily, anyway. I've rented it for a fortnight. Oh, I see. You know the owners? And you thought you could just walk in –'

'As a matter of fact, I thought it was my own house. I was brought up here. See?' He put a hand in a pocket and brought out a key, the duplicate of the one I had been given, which fitted both front and back doors. 'I'd no idea the place had changed hands. I'm sorry.'

'I'm sorry, too.' An awkward silence. He stood by the sink, dripping quietly onto the scullery matting. He showed no sign of offering to go, and, hearing the wind outside hurling fistfuls of rain about, I could hardly blame him. I cleared my throat. 'Well, this is a bit awkward, isn't it? The people who lived here moved away a couple of years ago, so I was told. I don't know where they went, but Mrs McDougall at the post office could probably tell you, if you wanted to get in touch again. I think she said the name was Mackay.'

'That is right.' Now in his voice I could hear, through the flattening cosmopolitan overlay, the unmistakable lilt of the islands. 'My father used to do the garden at Taigh na Tuir. My foster-father, that is.'

'You mean your *parents* lived here? Then this was your home?'

'That is right,' he said again.

'Well . . .' I stopped, at a loss for words. He smiled then for the first time, and the smile lightened his face to a sudden, vivid charm.

'A bit of a facer, isn't it? For me, too.'

'You mean you really didn't know they'd left? You just let yourself into your own home and thought they'd be upstairs asleep?'

'Just that.'

'But – but that's awful. You . . .' I stopped again. There was really nothing left to say. I finished, feebly: 'You're taking it very calmly. What will you do?'

'What can I do, but wait till morning?' The smile was still there, but behind it now was a hint of trouble, and more than a hint of tiredness. 'It wasn't quite such a shock as you might think. It certainly shook me when you came downstairs, but then I just thought my people might be away, and have let the cottage. Then I thought ... well, as it happens, I did know that the old lady – Mrs Hamilton – had died earlier this year, and of course that could have meant that Dad's job had packed up and they'd had to move. But then, when you said they'd been gone for a couple of years...' He paused and took his breath in. No smile now. He frowned down for a few moments at the damp patch on the matting at his feet, then he shook his head, as if ridding himself of some unwelcome thought, and looked up at me again. 'In fact, that's still what may have happened, isn't it? If she hadn't been well, perhaps, for some time, and had lost interest in the garden, and wanted to get the cottage done over for sale or letting, then she might have told them to go?'

He finished on a note of inquiry, but I shook my head. 'I wouldn't know. I've only just got here, and I really haven't heard anything more than I told you. But how does it happen that you didn't know they were leaving? All that time ago – did they never write?'

'I've been abroad. Moving around, and one loses touch, I'm afraid. I've only just got back to the UK.' He looked around him. 'I did notice the changes, of course, but I just thought the old lady had had the house done over for them – the parents. But she must have done it after they left; she'd have to, if she wanted to let the place. It wasn't much before, you can see.' A glance at the corner where the copper stood, then at the doorway behind me, where the light fell on the gleaming worktops and new cupboards. He lifted his shoulders and let them fall in a dismissive shrug. 'Ah, well, I can see now, they've made a pretty good job of it. I didn't really stop to look earlier – I was just so glad to get out of the weather.'

'I can imagine. You said you knew that Mrs Hamilton had died?'

'As it happens, yes. I hired my boat on Faarsay – that's a little island south of Mull – and they'd heard about Mrs Hamilton, but they didn't know my folks, so no one told me our house was let.'

'I – yes, I see. Well, I'm sorry you had to find out this way.'

A pause. There seemed to be nothing else to say. The water dripped steadily from his anorak to make a puddle on the floor. He looked pale and, I thought, tired and rather lost. I said crisply: 'Give me the kettle. You look as if you could do with a hot drink, and as a matter of fact, so could I.' I carried the kettle into the other room, plugged it in and switched on. 'What'll you have, coffee? Tea? Cocoa? I'm not stocked up with strong drink yet, I'm afraid. Why don't you take that wet anorak off and get the fire going again while I make the drinks?'

He did as I suggested, dropping the wet clothes into a corner by the back door. 'Well, God bless this house. It's very good of you to take it like this. I'm sorry if I gave you a fright. The coal's still kept just outside the back door?'

'Yes, but I brought some in earlier; it's in that bucket there, and there's peat there, too, and it's dry. I suppose you're used to peat fires? You can show me how. Are you sure cocoa will do?'

'If there's coffee, I'd rather have that, please. Yes, instant would be fine. Thanks.' He came in from the scullery with the coal bucket in one hand and in the other a fat metal cylinder. 'I'll certainly show you, but didn't you know about this?'

'Don't tell me it's a gas poker? How wonderful! Where was it?'

46

'At the back of the cupboard. We hardly ever used it, but it's a great standby, and very quick.' He dumped the cylinder down by the sitting-room hearth and knelt to stack peat and coal over the cold core of the fire. The kettle boiled and I made the drinks and followed him through to set the mugs down on the low table near the fireplace.

'Do you take sugar? Will that really burn?'

'Yes, please. Yes, indeed, given time, it will burn well. This always was a good fire. They have changed the fireplace, but the chimney will be the same, and it burns hot. You will see.'

'Incidentally, were you hoping to get a meal here? Because I'm afraid that all I've got at the moment –'

'No, no, that's OK. The drink will do fine. I've got this to help it, anyway.' He took the mug I handed him, then produced a flask from his pocket, and tipped a generous measure into his mug. He held the flask out to me, but I shook my head. The fire caught the peat and spread into a warming glow. Feeling as if I was still asleep and having a very curious dream, I settled myself on the other side of the hearth from the stranger and took a sip of cocoa. It is a simple drink, but wonderfully heartening.

'My name's Rose Fenemore,' I said, 'and I'm from Cambridge.'

'Mine's Ewen Mackay, from Moila, but it's a long, long time since I was here. You're taking this very well, Rose Fenemore. Some women would have come downstairs with the poker at the ready.'

'I might have done, only I'm expecting my brother to join me, I don't quite know when. I was too sleepy to wonder how he'd managed, at this time of night.' I glanced at the window. 'Did you really bring a boat across tonight in that?'

'Why not? Rounding the Horn is worse.' He laughed. 'As a matter of fact, the really nasty bit was when I was walking across here, coming over the head of the cliff there with the wind trying to blow me out to sea again.'

'Over the cliff? The headland? Then you didn't put into the bay here?'

'No. With the wind and the tide this way it's too tricky to bring a boat in here. There's a little cove about half-way between here and the big house – the Hamilton house. It's a safe mooring in any weather, and the nearest to home.'

The last word fell queerly in the little room, with the fire burning cosily and the insistent sounds of the storm at the window. I sipped cocoa, and wondered how and when I would be able to turn him out into the night again. Or even if. The windows, black as pitch, were streaming with water, and from time to time doors and windows rattled as if the cottage were under attack. I would not have put a stray dog out into such a night.

And the man, apparently, still regarded the place as 'home'. Well, Rose Fenemore, now might be the time to broaden your outlook a little. I could name at least three of my friends who would have been prompt to offer this undeniably attractive young man a doss-down on the sofa, and one of them who would have already been thinking of taking him upstairs for the night . . .

He was saying something about the Hamilton house, a question.

'I'm sorry?' I said.

'I asked if you had been over there yet?'

'No.'

'You should go. It's quite a good path over the cliff there, and the island with the broch is worth a visit. There's a nice bay there, too, very sheltered. You can take a boat in there most times, except at low water, but it can be awkward then, and in this weather ... Anyway, I tucked my boat in snugly at Halfway House – the cove – and walked over to Taigh na Tuir. That's what they call the Hamilton place.'

'Yes, I know.'

'I just wanted to see it again.' He reached forward to turn off the gas poker and add a couple of peats to the fire. 'Even though I knew there was no one there. And even if they hadn't told me, I would have known. She never slept well, and she used to read half the night. It seemed queer to me to see the windows all dark and the curtains still not drawn ... I don't think I believed it till then, that she was gone, I mean. You might say that Taigh na Tuir was as much home to me as this was. More. I was over there most days when I was a boy.'

'Mrs McDougall – no, I think it was Archie McLaren – told me that your father looked after the garden there.'

'My foster-father.' That emphasis again. 'I was adopted. Did they not tell you that? It was never a secret. Yes, he worked at the House, and so did my mother. But they – the Colonel and Mrs Hamilton – they had no family, only a brother who lived abroad all the time, and, well, they treated me like a son, or grandson, rather. It was the Colonel himself who taught me how to shoot, and I always went with him for the fishing. The way they were with me, I sometimes wondered –'

He broke off. A quick flash of a glance from those blue eyes, then he turned away.

'You wondered?'

'Nothing. Nothing at all ...' He stirred the peats, the Gaelic suddenly strong in his voice. 'But it's a strange feeling to be robbed of both homes all in the same wild night.'

49

Celtic twilight, I thought. Is he dramatising all this a bit, for sympathy and a bed for the night, or is this the normal way of the Gael? The chill little touch of criticism roused me. Stray dog or no stray dog, I wanted him to go. I sat up in my chair.

'I'm sorry. I really am. But –'

He smiled at me suddenly, the same flash of charm. 'And that was not a hint for you to offer me a bed for the night, Miss Rose Fenemore. You've been very kind, and I'm good and dry now, and I've slept on the boat many's the time before, and in worse nights than this. The wind's dropping a bit, anyhow, and she'll be all safe and snug in Halfway House. I'll maybe get round to the harbour in the morning, and have a talk with Mrs McDougall. Here, let me wash the mugs up for you first.'

'No, really, they're nothing. Give me yours.'

As I got up to take it from him, there was a sharp rapping at the front door. In the time it took me to turn my head, Ewen Mackay came upright, and a hand moved – incredibly – towards a pocket. It was a movement I had seen a hundred times on television, but never before in real life. For real life, visit Moila, the island of the ivory tower.

His hand dropped. I said, feebly: 'Would you answer the door, please? And if it's my brother, don't shoot him.'

He didn't smile. He gave me a sideways look that was curiously disconcerting, and went to the door.

It opened on a rush of air. Outside stood a young man in oilskins, the hood blowing back from a soaking tangle of brown hair blackened by the rain, and one hand gripping a duffel bag.

Ewen Mackay stood back for him to enter. 'Do come in. The kettle's just on the boil. Mr Fenemore, I presume?'

The newcomer came in on a gust of the storm. He

stood dripping on the rug while Ewen Mackay shut the door behind him. 'What?' he asked. He blinked at the light as if it hurt him. His eyes were bloodshot, presumably with the wind, and he looked dazed.

'Your brother made it after all,' said Ewen Mackay to me, but I shook my head.

'I've never seen him before in my life,' I said.

6

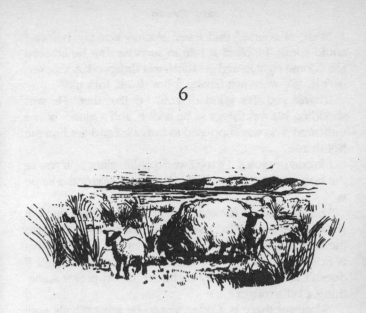

'I'm terribly sorry to butt in like this.' The newcomer looked from Ewen Mackay to me and back again. He was, understandably, taking us for a couple whose holiday idyll he had interrupted, though why we should be sitting by the fire at that hour, with me in a not very elegant dressing-gown and Ewen in stained jeans and a guernsey it would be hard to imagine. Something of the sort was getting through to him. He paused, and finished, uncertainly: 'My tent was blown away, and some of my stuff with it. I tried to chase it, but it was no good in the dark, and I went clear into a bog, and in the end I saw your light, so I picked up what was left and came along. If I might just wait here till the storm passes, till daylight, perhaps, and then try again to track my things down?'

'Well, of course,' said Ewen Mackay warmly, before I could speak. I looked at him in surprise, but he ignored me. 'Come right in and get those wet things off. A shocker, isn't it? We were just having a hot drink. Join us?'

'Thank you. It's good of you. I'd like that.' He was shedding his wet things as he spoke, and a glance at me indicated who was supposed to hurry off and get him the hot drink.

I found my voice. I gave Ewen a chilly glance. 'If you're the host, you make the drink. You know where the kettle is.'

The newcomer looked surprised, but Ewen took it without a blink. In fact, he smiled. 'Of course.' Then, to the other man: 'My name's Mackay, by the way, and this is Rose Fenemore. There's coffee if you'd like it, and it doesn't have to be totally harmless, if you prefer something a bit stronger?'

'Whatever there is. Coffee would be great. Thank you. It's very good of you.' He dumped his things on a chair near the door, and came to the fire, hands spread out to the warmth. 'My name's Parsons. John Parsons.' He spoke over my head to the scullery door, where Ewen was refilling the kettle. He obviously still took us for a couple holidaying together, and his embarrassment at intruding took the form of ignoring my presence.

I was busy wondering why Ewen Mackay, by playing host, had taken such pains to foster that impression. It was hard to see a reason. A stab of male vanity, perhaps? Discovered alone in a remote cottage with a young female whose brother had once described her as 'a don, alas, but a dish when she takes the trouble,' had he quite deliberately misled the newcomer? Or, to take it further, had he begun to have hopes for the remainder of the night, and so taken this means to get rid of the other man? My own vanity, such as it was, could not accept any of this; in that dressing-gown, and with my hair all over the place, I was hardly something that a chance-met man would want to lay claim to.

'Milk and sugar?' Ewen, still the charming host, was pouring hot water.

Mr Parsons had turned to stand with his back to the fire, the eternal male hogging the best place in the room. 'Great. Yes, both, thanks.' He accepted the steaming mug from the other man, then addressing him, and still ignoring me: 'Are you on holiday, or do you live here?'

I caught Ewen Mackay's swift glance as he resumed his place on the other side of the fireplace. His look was faintly apologetic. As well it might be, I thought. As an exercise, even of vanity, it had been pointless. Had he really thought that I would play along? Out of sheer curiosity I held my tongue, and waited.

He stretched out a foot to the fire, stirring the peats. 'I did live here years ago. I was brought up here. But just at present I'm like you, an orphan of the storm. Miss Fenemore gave me shelter, too.'

'Oh. Really. I see.' Mr Parsons looked down at me at last, and I could see a different embarrassment replacing the first as he met my ironic eye. 'Well, Miss Er, it's awfully good of you. Quite an invasion. I'm terribly sorry to be such a nuisance.'

'Think nothing of it. Where are you camping, Mr Er?'

For a moment I thought I had gone too far. In the grey eyes regarding me through the steam of the coffee I saw a spark that might have been amusement. It might equally well have been annoyance – John Parsons the macho male being quietly baited by the nonentity by the fireside.

Then it was gone and he answered mildly: 'On the

machair. But with the wind this way it's next to impossible.' Back to Ewen. 'You lost your tent, too?'

'Not a tent. I've a boat. I tied up in a cove west of here, just beyond the headland.'

I asked: 'Can you really see the lights of this cottage from the machair?'

A perceptible pause, as Mr Parsons turned and set his mug down on the mantelpiece. 'I doubt it. But when I saw it tonight I had just struggled as far as the road. Why?'

'I just wondered.'

'Whereabouts on the machair?' asked Ewen. 'Pretty exposed for camping, I would have thought. Or were you near the House?'

'Which house?'

'The locals – we – call it the Big House. Or just the House. The one opposite the island where the broch is.'

'Oh, yes, of course. I remember. Isn't that the Hamilton house?'

'That is right. Old Mrs Hamilton who lived there died recently, so the place is empty now. You know it, then? You've been to Moila before?'

'Yes, a long time ago, when I was a student.'

'I wondered . . .' Ewen Mackay had been staring hard at the other man while they talked. Now he asked: 'Perhaps we met then? I've been wondering if I knew you.'

'Perhaps. I don't think so.'

'So what brings you back here now?'

'I'm a geologist.' Mr Parsons sipped his drink placidly. He had accepted the addition from Ewen's flask. 'There was something I remembered that I wanted to look at, and I thought it would be an interesting place to spend my leave. I've been working in Sydney. I'm planning to move across soon to the broch isle. There's an igneous intrusion there, with fragments of garnet peridotite –

56

that's a rock from below the earth's crust – and I'd like to spend a bit of time there, though the rocks at the north-west end look pretty difficult to get at. But that won't interest you . . .' The conversation had long ceased to interest me. I was feeling the need to get back to bed and to sleep. From where I sat I could not see the clock on the mantelpiece. I got up to look, and something else caught my eye. Tucked behind the clock was a small sheaf of papers, old letters and bills, perhaps, pushed there and forgotten, presumably by the last tenants. An address was printed, and clear:

> J. R. Parsons, Esq.,
> at Otters' Bay,
> Isle of Moila, Argyll.

So 'John Parsons' was perhaps not genuine all the way? When Ewen Mackay suggested that they had met before, I had thought that the other man had countered with a faintly wary look. And Ewen himself, for all his outgoing charm, had certainly acted in a way that gave pause for thought. All else apart, I could not forget that movement of his hand to his pocket when 'Parsons' knocked at the door.

I carried my empty mug out to the sink, then stood in the doorway and regarded them. Neither of them had taken the slightest notice of my movements, except that Mr Parsons was already in my empty chair, and the two of them, with Ewen Mackay's flask of whisky now standing between them, were talking about salmon fishing. A subject which, I thought drily, afforded a good deal of scope for liars.

The next move was mine. Ewen Mackay had said he could sleep on his boat, but he had made no move to invite Parsons to share it with him. There might not be space for two, and I could hardly turn the other man out now. Safety in numbers. Let them both stay. I may be a dish, but I am also a don, and not prone to see emergencies where none exist.

I said: 'It's after three o'clock. I'm going to bed. The bedroom upstairs is all ready for my brother, and I'd prefer to have that floor to myself anyway. I see you've salvaged your sleeping-bag, Mr Parsons. I'll throw some towels down, and a couple of blankets, and you can toss for it who sleeps on the sofa and who gets the floor.' I added, out of pure malice, to Ewen: 'And of course you remember where the old loo is. Not more than twenty yards from the back door. Good night. Sleep well.'

7

The morning was calm and bright, with sunlight gilding the whins and sending a glitter across the bay. The sea still echoed the storm, foot-high waves breaking with a long *hush* against the shingle, but the sky was blue and clear. There was no sound from downstairs. I slid out of bed, put on my dressing-gown and padded out to the tiny landing. Still nothing. Downstairs there was silence, the unmistakable silence of emptiness.

I went down to make sure. Yes, they had both gone. The blankets and towels lay neatly folded on the sofa. In the scullery I found a note propped against a milk carton on the draining-board.

It ran: 'Many thanks for the hospitality. Hope you slept

well. Gone early to hunt for tent, etc. See you around, perhaps?'

It was unsigned. The reference to the tent meant either that 'John Parsons' had written it, and was hoping to see me around, or that they had teamed up on a declared truce. Whatever the case, my social life on Moila seemed to have begun.

I put a cautious hand to the kettle. It was warm. So they had managed some sort of breakfast, and without waking me. More thoughtful than either of them had seemed last night. It must have been a truce. I put the kettle on again for myself, and went upstairs to dress.

*

I dutifully spent the morning in outer space. Once Crispin arrived, I would want to be out and about with him, so I worked till lunch-time, and was rewarded by reaching the half-way mark, and with a new idea to carry me through the next section of the story. I wrote up the notes, made myself some scrambled eggs, then decided to walk over to the post office to see if my brother had telephoned last night with any message.

Mrs McDougall, busy behind the counter with cus-tomers, merely shook her head at me, and signed towards the rear door of the shop, which led through into her house, where the telephone was. I went cheerfully through, finding the coins as I went.

My sister-in-law answered, so quickly that she must have been right beside the telephone. She spoke almost before the first ring had finished.

'Yes? Is that the hospital?'

'No,' I said, 'it's Rose. Don't tell me something's turned up at this stage to stop Cris getting away?'

'Oh, Rose...' Nothing abrasive now about Ruth's voice. I heard her draw in a quick breath and swallow, and felt my hand tighten on the receiver as I said, more sharply than I intended: 'Please. Tell me. What's happened? Is Crispin all right?'

'Yes, he's all right. At least, he's hurt, but not badly. It's his leg – the ankle. They thought it was broken, then they said it was just a bad sprain, but apparently they want to do another X-ray, so I simply don't know what's happening. He tried to phone you last night, the number you gave him, but there was something wrong with the line –'

'We had a rough night. Ruth, please, how was he hurt? What has happened?'

'He was in that train, the one that crashed last night, the derailment south of Kendal. He was on it, the sleeper for Glasgow. I thought you'd have heard about the accident. Didn't you get it on the radio?'

'No radio. Go on. About Crispin.'

'He's all right, really. He phoned me himself. It wasn't a bad accident. There was a coach dragged off the line, but it didn't overturn, apparently, till everyone had been got out. Nobody killed, but a few people hurt. Cris tried to help, of course, but as soon as the ambulances came they sent him off to the local hospital, and that's where he is now. I did wonder why you hadn't called sooner –'

'Yes, well ... Have you got the Kendal number handy?'

'Yes, but he's leaving there today. I told you they want to do another X-ray, and they're sending him to Carlisle for that, the Cumberland Infirmary.'

'To Carlisle? But you said he wasn't much hurt.'

61

'No, he's not, don't worry. He sounded quite normal when he phoned, just annoyed about the holiday. He said he'd call again as soon as he heard the result of the new X-ray, but not to worry about it, it's just the extra fuss they make when there's a doctor involved. You know how it is. So we'll just have to wait and see. He won't be able to do much walking, of course, but he still wants to come.'

She finished on such a note of surprise that in spite of myself I laughed. 'He sounds all right, anyway. Try not to worry, Ruth. I'll ring off now in case he's trying to get through to you. But I'll come up here to the post office this evening, and call you again.'

'Fine. I'll get his number for you and you can call him yourself. What about you, though, Rose? Are you all right there, on your own? I don't see how he can make it before Monday, and that'll be a whole week.'

I was surprised, and touched. 'I'll be fine, thank you. The cottage is rather cosy, and I'm busy on a new story, so I'll have plenty to do even if the weather's bad. And when it's fine, well, it's a lovely little island, and I can have some bird-walks of my own. Give Crispin my love, Ruth, and I'll ring tonight and see how things are.'

'I'll tell him. Goodbye, Rose.'

'Goodbye.'

Mrs McDougall was still busy when I went back into the shop. I collected what I needed, and when I got to the counter I found that she and her neighbours were discussing the train accident. Mrs McDougall, with a quick, concerned look at me, took my basket from me and dumped it on the counter.

'I hope it was not bad news, Miss Fenemore? Did you not think that your brother might be coming north soon?

And from London, so it would be on the line where they had the accident, would it not?'

'Yes. And he was on that train, I'm afraid. No, no, thank you very much, it's all right, he isn't badly hurt, a sprained ankle, and they say it isn't serious, but it does mean he can't come north yet...'

They exclaimed and condoled, with – once I had assured them that nothing serious had happened to my brother – a rather charming mixture of sympathy for me and pleasure in the excitement of the news. I gave them their full due, repeating all that my sister-in-law had said, and told them that I would hear from my brother himself that evening, then paid for my groceries and made my escape.

I was half-way home before I realised that, with all the worry and talk about the accident, I had forgotten to ask Mrs McDougall about Ewen Mackay. Or, indeed, about John Parsons.

Not that it mattered, as I would probably not see either of them again, but the scene last night had been strange, and my curiosity was aroused.

Take Parsons first. He was, I was sure, an imposter. I refused to believe that he chanced to have the same name as the previous tenants of the cottage – unless he himself was the previous tenant, and had for some reason returned to Moila without wanting to be known? I remembered that, according to Archie McLaren, the family had used a boat, and done all their shopping in Tobermory, avoiding the islanders. An echo of Parsons' geological jargon last night sounded in my head. I had heard the word 'garnet'. Perhaps he really was a geologist. Perhaps he had discovered a seam – did you have a seam of garnet? – and had come back secretly to exploit it, and...

This was Hugh Templar taking over. Nonsense. Forget fantasy and look at fact. Take Parsons again. He had – possibly – lied about his name. He had certainly lied about seeing the cottage light. If he had been chasing his flying tent up from the machair on the west of the island, he might have got up as far as the bogland near the lochan, but surely the light from my cottage would not be visible until he had followed the road downhill past the curve and almost into Otters' Bay. Hence, his excuse for coming to the cottage was also a fake.

Now take Ewen Mackay. Maybe he had not lied, and in any case what he had said about the cottage being his home could easily be checked. He had known where the coal was kept, and the Calor gas poker, and he had had a key – which, now that I thought about it, I should certainly have asked him to hand over to me ... But there was that unmistakable and disquieting reaction to the knocking on the door, and then the pointless deception which followed; pointless, because he must have known he could not get away with it. Had it merely been a quick try at getting rid of the intruder? But why? Then there was the rather sharp bout of questioning, which had had, on both sides, a sort of wariness about it.

And finally, the note this morning, with its suggestion of a truce between the two men.

I stopped in mid-stride, so suddenly that an oyster-catcher, which had been guddling among the reeds at the edge of the lochan, took off seawards with a screamed complaint.

Supposing, just supposing, that Mackay and Parsons had arranged to meet at the cottage. The storm had been fortuitous, an extra. Mackay, key in hand (where had he really got it from?), had made his way to Otters' Bay, and had walked straight in, assuming the cottage to be empty.

I found it hard to believe that, even if he had been out of the country, his family could have moved away without his knowing. Unless, of course, they had not wanted him to know, and had seen to it that he had no address for them.

Which would say certain things about Ewen Mackay.

So, for some reason impossible to guess at, he and Parsons had arranged to meet. It was I, the unexpected tenant of the empty cottage, who was the joker in the pack. I had made them welcome, accepted their nonsensical stories because it didn't matter one way or the other, and then gone obligingly off to bed and left them to their meeting . . .

Something moved on the farther side of the lochan, something bulky and dirty white, caught in the bog myrtle, where it shifted and billowed in the breeze. John Parsons' tent? Could there have been that much truth in what he had said?

I dumped the carrier with my groceries down beside the road, and set off across the moor. Not that it mattered (I told myself again) one way or the other, but now that my brother's arrival was postponed at least until Monday, it would be good to have something of the story checked. And of course, if the object did happen to be the flyaway tent, its owner would need it back.

It was not a tent, nor indeed any sort of camping equipment. It was an old plastic sack, probably used by a farmer and left outside to blow away. And it could have blown a good distance in last night's gale. I regarded it with distaste, decided that the rain would have washed it reasonably clean, then dragged it clear of the bog myrtle and looked around me for somewhere to dump it out of sight.

A fox's earth, long abandoned, and not taken over by

birds or rabbits, provided the dumping-ground. I stuffed the sack down out of sight, and straightened, to see that my search had brought me above a cleft in the moorland through which a glimpse of the western machair could be seen.

It was a lovely stretch of shore, white sand and sheep-grazed turf backed by a stretch of flat, flowery meadowland. Even from where I stood I could see the white and yellow of dog-daisies and hawkear blowing in the sea-breeze like coloured veils over the green.

No sign of a tent, but over to the left, just showing, was a clump of trees thickly planted and apparently sheltered from the worst of the weather, and, standing up from among them, the chimneys of a house.

The Hamilton house, presumably. Taigh na Tuir. A big house, with no smoke rising from the chimneys. And – I walked another few yards and craned my neck to see – no sign of life in the little bay beyond, with its boat-house and jetty.

Across from the bay, beyond a narrow stretch of water, was a small island, an islet, rather. It was long and low, humped at the northern end and tapering to the south into flat rocks washed by the sea. Just below the hump I could make out – I have good eyes – the dark outline of what must be the ruined broch, and beside that, in its shelter, was a speck of bright, alien orange. A tent. He had found his tent and had already moved to the broch island.

The oystercatcher had come back, and was wheeling noisily over the lochan. 'So what?' I said to it. So what indeed. Whatever the facts, both men had gone about their affairs, and would presumably not trouble me again. Forget it; get back to something more reasonable in the way of fantasy fiction. Another chapter today would see me nicely into the second half of my story, and this evening I would talk to Crispin and get things sorted out with him. And tonight ... Well, I had noticed that on both front and back doors of the cottage there were stout and serviceable bolts.

As I squelched my way back round the lochan's edge towards the road, I saw the diver. Unmistakable, even though I had never seen one before; a big bird, brown and grey with a red throat, low in the water, where the wind-rippled surface managed to camouflage it in the most extraordinary way. When I had passed the lochan earlier, there had been no sign of it. It must be nesting, and now my near approach had driven it off the nest.

The thought had hardly occurred to me before the diver, with a weird-sounding cry, left the water in a noisy take-off, and flew seawards in alarm. And there, two paces in front of my feet, was the nest.

Two huge eggs, greenish-brown like the sedge, with a matt surface mottled like moss, lay in a shallow depression on the very edge of the loch, with a distinct sloping runway leading to the water, so that when alarmed the bird could slide invisibly off the eggs into a deep dive, to surface many yards away from its well-camouflaged home.

I glanced around me, quickly. No one in sight; of course there wasn't. No one to see my interest in this spot on the lochan's edge. I stooped quickly and laid the back of a gentle finger against one of the eggs. It was warm. She must just have got off, and she was probably watching me from somewhere high above the distant sea. I turned my back on the lochan and walked a dozen paces away from the edge before heading back towards the road.

A sound from overhead made me look up. The diver went over, high. I reached the road, picked up my groceries, and left her in peace.

*

I did not see Mrs McDougall that evening. There was a girl in charge of the place, a child of perhaps twelve, who told me that her name was Morag, and that her auntie had stepped out on a visit, but had said the young lady from Camus na Dobhrain might be there to use the telephone, and please to go through.

For what it was worth I asked her if she knew of a Ewen Mackay who might once have lived at Otters' Bay, but she shook her head.

'No.' She spoke with an accent so soft that it sounded as if an h was attached to each consonant. 'Not at all. There was a Mr and Mrs Mackay living there, yes, but they moved away, right to the mainland. My auntie would know. Alastair he was called, though, Alastair Mackay, that was gardener to old Mrs Hamilton at the big house.'

'Did they have any children?'

She hesitated, then nodded, but doubtfully. There had been – yes, she was sure there had been a boy, a long time ago, that would be. She had heard tell of him, but it was when she was very small, and she did not remember him. He would be a grown man now. She did not remember his name. Ewen? It might have been Ewen. Her auntie would know . . .

I supposed that it did endorse part of Ewen Mackay's story. Not, of course, that it mattered . . . I would ask Mrs McDougall next time I was here.

On which fine piece of mental self-deceit I thanked Morag and went to the telephone.

*

I got straight through to my brother at the number Ruth gave me, of the hospital in Carlisle.

'What's this about another X-ray?' I asked him. 'Have you had the result? Is it really only a sprain?'

'That's all, but it was – still is – badly swollen, and they insisted, quite rightly, on sending me here to have another look taken at it. The first X-ray showed what might have been a crack. But it's all clear. No crack. They've given me an elbow crutch, and I can make the journey perfectly well now, if I thought the blasted train would stay on the lines, but there's not much I could do once I got to Moila, is there, if I can't walk? What's it like?'

'I think it's lovely. The cottage is tiny, but it's got all we need, and there's just enough island to explore without transport. I'm afraid there's none of that – transport, I mean – except Archie McLaren's Land-Rover, the one that carries you from the harbour. You'd be a bit stuck. But would it matter? You'd be away from the job and the telephone, and you'd be resting. Unless – do you have to go back to a hospital with it, or anything?'

'No, no. There's nothing I can't deal with myself.'

'Well, Archie has a boat, and he says he can take us out to the bird islands, and I'm sure we could get him to take you somewhere in the Land-Rover where you can fish. Of course, if it's really painful, forget it. I'll be fine, and I'm writing, and if it gets a bit unlively I could perhaps find somewhere else –'

'No, why should you? I was only doubtful because of

spoiling your holiday. I can manage perfectly well, and I'd hate to miss Moila.'

'It would spoil my holiday far more if you didn't come,' I said. 'So risk the train, will you? And do you want me to ring the Oban hotel and tell them what's happened and change the booking? You have? That's great ... It really is lovely here, and – well, I didn't want to over-persuade you, but I found a red-throated diver's nest today, perfectly lovely, two eggs, and I didn't bring a camera. Didn't think we'd need two, and mine's not nearly as good as yours, even if I could take half as good a picture.'

'And you don't call that over-persuading? I'll be there,' said my brother. 'Expect me on Monday's ferry, then. If I know anything about it, I'll be well and truly mobile by then.'

'Physician, heal thyself,' I said, laughing, and rang off, with a lightened heart.

8

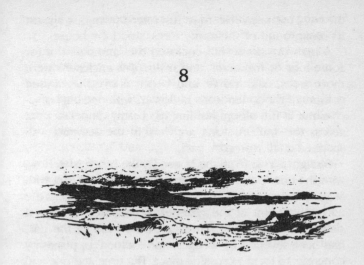

Next morning was fair and sunny, with a breeze, but I
journeyed duly into outer space, to tackle the problems
of my party on Terra Secunda. Their difficulties were
rapidly threatening to become too much for them, and
consequently for me, too. In those circumstances I have
always found it wise to abandon effort and leave the
subconscious mind to sort things out while the conscious
mind does something quite different. Goes for a walk,
for example, and takes a look at the Hamilton house and
that delectable stretch of milk-white sand bordering the
machair.

I followed the cliff path which led steeply up out of
Otters' Bay and then westward over the headland for
something less than half a mile, to bring me in sight of

the bay I had seen yesterday. Just inland from this, against its background of sheltering trees, stood the house.

A high dry-stone wall enclosed the land round it for some four or five acres, and inside this enclosure were more trees, oak and fir and beech above the massed colours of rhododendrons in flower, with one big horse-chestnut in full bloom holding its creamy candelabra out across the wall. A stone archway in the seaward wall spanned a tall ironwork gate.

Straight across from the house lay the broch islet. Now, with the tide low, the causeway connecting the islet with Moila's mainland was high and dry, running across at the narrowest point of the channel. It consisted of natural slabs of flattish stone which at some time in the past had been levelled by wedges, and 'helped' in places by concrete, to form a crossing-place. But time and tide and neglect had eaten away at the structure so that even at low tide, with the slabs fully exposed, crossing would be tricky.

To either side of this causeway was a tumble of half-exposed rocks, glossy with black seaweed, where the water rose and fell, barely stirring the weed. Apart from this crossing-point the channel seemed, even at this stage of the tide, to be fairly deep. Deep enough, at any rate, for a boat to get in to the boat-house which was tucked in under the cliff at the southern end of the bay, below the path where I stood. Beside the boat-house a jetty thrust out into the water, and from this a weedy, once-gravelled path led along above the beach to the stone archway which was the garden gate of Taigh na Tuir.

I made my way down into the bay. That alone would have been worth the scramble round the cliff path. I had never seen anything like it before, a crescent of dazzling white, where a million pearly shells had been pounded and smashed by the Atlantic swells into fine sand, marked only by the tides, and above the tide-marks by the myriad criss-crossing prints of sea-birds.

It was not to be resisted. I sat down and took off my shoes and socks – I was wearing slacks and trainers – and then walked across the bay, luxuriating in the feel of the fine warm sand under my bare feet. I went right down to the sea's edge, but the water was too cold for pleasure, so I retreated to the dry level and sat down to brush the sand off my feet and put on my shoes again.

This done, I stood for a moment looking across at the broch islet. Directly across the channel was another, bigger bay, a long curving stretch of lovely white sand, with above it a sweep of green turf and bracken rising as far as the dark circle of the broch. The whole place was alive with the wings and calls of sea-birds. It was very tempting, but it would be stupid to go across now, until I knew more about the tides. I wondered where John Parsons was; looking for his garnet-studded 'intrusion', whatever that was, on the other side of the island? I could see the tent from here, pitched in a hollow not far from the broch wall. The entrance flaps were shut.

I trod up through the seaweed at the edge of the beach, then followed the path to the gate in the garden wall. I peered through the bars. Inside the grounds the path continued, curving up between the overgrown rhodo-dendrons in the direction of the house. I hesitated. There would presumably be a driveway of sorts leading from the back of the house to the road and my easiest way home. To try and get to it by going round outside the garden wall meant ploughing through waist-high nettles and clumps of bramble. So ...? So I opened the gate and went through.

There had never been much of a garden, only the rhododendrons flowering red and pink and lilac, where bees droned happily. Beyond the wild tangle of flowers I could just see the upper storey of the house, grey stone with tall sashed windows and a roof of grey slate with its unsmoking chimney stacks. There were curtains in the windows. The place must still be furnished, then. I tried to remember when Mrs McDougall had said the old lady had died. February? And Archie McLaren had told me that the house would probably have to be sold, so it was to be supposed that at any time now people might be coming to look at it.

It was the subconscious mind taking over again. I found myself half-way up the path between the rhododendrons before the conscious mind caught up with the fact that, though there had been a padlock on the garden gate, the gate had been unlocked. So, surely there could be no objection to someone taking a look at a place that would soon be up for sale anyway? I crossed a lawn that badly needed cutting, and started on a cautious tour of the Hamilton house.

I doubt if there are many normal women who can resist looking at houses. I believe, in fact, that when a house is up for sale more than half the people who look over it are not prospective buyers, but merely ladies who cannot resist exploring someone else's house. I had never done that, but I was not immune. I trod carefully up to the most important-looking window, and peered in.

The drawing-room. A rather lovely fireplace, with a hideous overmantel. Faded carpet and curtains. Typical family paintings of dim-looking, not-quite-Raeburns, and improbable horses and dogs. Round tables with skirts, their surfaces smothered with photographs. Sagging armchairs with faded covers, not too clean. A quite awful vase in one corner, full of dried pampas grass.

The dining-room. More portraits, if possible duller still, and lightened by a couple of horrendous still-lifes, dead hares and poultry, staring eyes and blood congealing from beaks and nostrils; just the thing to give one an appetite for meals.

The gun-room ... But enough of that. It was a very ordinary, rather pleasant, Highland country house; originally a shooting-lodge and of no great size or importance for the day when it was built. And meant only for summer and early autumn; no heating apparatus except the open fires, and a kitchen rather on a par for mod cons with my cottage at Otters' Bay.

The only thing that was quite extraordinary was what I found when I got as far as the back premises.

The back door was standing open.

*

My excuse, a thin one, is still the subconscious mind. I did knock at the door, then, when there was no response, took a couple of steps through into a passage floored with stone slabs and containing nothing but some buckets of coal and a rack of ancient clothes, gardening clobber by the look of it. In spite of the open door, the place smelled of damp and disuse.

The kitchen door was on my right. I pushed it open. Emptiness again; somehow a kitchen, which is the warm heart of any house, is the worst place of all when it is disused. The house is dead without the warmth and the smells of cooking and the pulse of daily living. In the stuffy silence the sound of the cold tap slowly dripping was almost cosy; a substitute heart-beat. Even so, my presence felt like an intrusion. But as I turned to go something caught at my attention. A key-rack just beside the doorway, with keys hanging there, labelled. One hook was empty; the hook labelled 'C. na Dobhrain.' Otters' Bay.

For no good reason, that settled it, by which I mean that what conscience I had was put to sleep by sheer, raging curiosity. Could my night-time visitor have called in here to pick up the key he had shown me, and left the back door open at the same time? Had he put into this bay first, then come up past the house and, finding it open, taken the key? But why should he trouble? If he had really only been looking for shelter and a place to doss down for the night, why look further than this? Why make the wet and stormy trek to Otters' Bay? Even if he had thought that his parents were still there – which I found hard to believe – he could have visited them in the morning.

Somehow, this seemed to justify what I had done. If there was indeed any mystery about Ewen Mackay's visit to my cottage, the clue to it might well be here, in the house he had claimed to be familiar with. More, he had hinted, unless I had misread him, at a connection with the family. Perhaps he even considered himself to have some kind of claim to the place? At least, then, the note that had been left for me ('See you around?') gave me some excuse for trespassing now.

I went on down the passage, towards the green baize door that closed the back premises off from the gentry's quarters, pushed the door open, and trod tentatively into the front hall.

This was darkish, lighted only by the stained glass fan-window over the shut front door. To one side stood a heavy oak table piled with the usual clutter – magazines, newspapers, a couple of heavy electric torches, some anonymous boxes. Opposite this another, smaller table held gloves, a sou'wester, and a gardening-basket crammed with implements. There was a brass stand holding walking-sticks, and a dark oak settle where someone had thrown down a Barbour coat and an old anorak. Some pairs of boots and wellingtons were lined up beside it, and on the wall, above a crude, oil landscape that seemed meant to depict the moor where the diver nested, was a long rack, presumably meant for fishing-rods.

The impression of a house where the occupants had just walked out for a stroll in the garden was very strong. My presence there seemed, suddenly, an intrusion; my curiosity, if not an outrage, at any rate no excuse for going any further.

I turned to go out the way I had come. But even as I turned, I heard something. A sound from upstairs. The creak of a door.

My heart gave a jump, then resumed something like its normal beat as I registered the fact that even in an empty house there were draughts, and doors moved and creaked with no one to push them. But I did make for the baize door a little more quickly than on my way in, and in the semi-darkness stumbled over one of the wellingtons, kicking it half-way across the floor. I only saved myself from falling by clutching at the arm of the oak settle.

Something came down the stairs like an avalanche. A pair of powerful arms seized me from behind, jerking me upright and off my feet. Clutched tightly to the breast of a Shetland sweater I took breath and screamed.

The arms, suddenly nerveless, dropped me, and the Shetland sweater retreated smartly. I fell onto the settle, hit my elbow on the carved arm-rest, and drew in my breath to scream again.

'Don't!' said John Parsons hastily. 'Please don't! I'm terribly sorry. I thought it was – I didn't realise it was a girl. I wouldn't dream of – Oh, it's you.'

I abandoned the scream. I rubbed my elbow, regarding him thoughtfully. He towered over me, looking anxious, rather flustered, and not in the least dangerous. I said: 'Well, who says it first?'

'Says what?'

'"What are you doing here?" So what *are* you doing here? I know you found your tent, but perhaps you thought this might be a more comfortable bivouac than my cottage? Is that it?'

'Not quite. I – actually, the tent was never lost, but – '

'Where's Ewen Mackay? Is he sleeping here too?'

'No. Why should he be? Then he isn't with you?'

'No, he is not.' Because I felt both guilty and embarrassed, I reacted sharply. 'For goodness' sake, surely you didn't fall for all that nonsense of his the other night? I'd never seen him before in my life! I think he must have taken the key for my cottage from the board by the kitchen door. It seems to be true that the cottage used to be his home, but you don't carry a big old-fashioned key like that around in your pocket for years, so I don't see how else he got it. If he broke in – but then why come to the cottage at all? And why should you? Did you break in here, too, or has the back door been unlocked the whole time?'

He answered only one question out of this barrage, and it was enough. 'Neither,' he said. 'I had a key.'

'You had a key?' The repetition sounded stupid. But the situation was itself a repetition of Wednesday night's adventure. 'You, too?' I took a breath. 'But perhaps – did you have an order to view, or something?'

'Not quite. The house is mine.'

'Oh, no! Not again!' I must have sounded, if possible, more stupid than ever. 'Yours?'

He smiled suddenly. 'Yes, mine. I'm not sure how long wills take to prove, but I was Aunt Emily's only living relative, and it's always been understood that the place would come to me. In any case, someone had to come and try to sort things out. I'm Neil Hamilton.'

I managed to stop myself from repeating that, too. 'I see. Well, thank you for telling me, Mr Parsons.'

He said, apologetically: 'I'm sorry about that, but there were reasons. Why don't we go somewhere more comfortable and discuss them? I do owe you that. In here?'

He opened the drawing-room door and ushered me through.

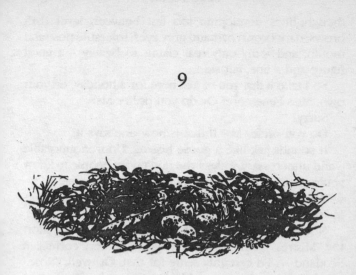

9

He crossed to the french window and pushed it open. Seen in this light, and in the light of what he had now told me, I studied him afresh.

He was tall, and looked sunburned, as if he had spent time recently in a climate far from the Hebrides. Not handsome, but nice-looking in a way I had usually rather deprecated, if not despised: not the lean and craggy looks that I had always admired, but a blunt-featured face with a wide mouth, dark eyes tilted slightly down at the outer corners, and an untidy thatch of brown hair of which a couple of locks fell over a broad forehead, and were from time to time irritably brushed back. I saw that he was, in his turn, studying me. He would be seeing, I thought, an unremarkable young woman, rather too solemn, with thought-lines developing too fast between level dark brows; dark-brown hair and grey eyes; tolerable nose and mouth, and – my only real claims to beauty – a good figure and a fine, fair skin.

'So I take it that you're just here for a holiday, on your own, Miss Fenemore? Or do you prefer Ms?'

'Sorry?'

'Do you prefer Ms? If that is how one says it?'

'It sounds just like a goose hissing. Unpronounceable – and unnecessary, unless you don't want people to know you're not married. Which I'm not, but I still hate it.'

'You sound a bit fierce. I wasn't sure. Some ladies insist.'

'Not this one. Actually, if you could say it was short for "Mistress", which is rather nice, and very correct in Scotland ... I'd certainly settle for that. Or, well, "Rose" would be the easiest, wouldn't it? Sorry, don't tell me, I know. I'm being priggish. But I like words, and that's a non-word if ever there was one.'

'Well, it's a good hobby-horse.'

'Hobby-horse nothing. It's my job. I teach English at Cambridge. Haworth College. And yes, this is just a holiday. My brother was to have come with me; he's a doctor working in Petersfield, and he's a dedicated bird-watcher and photographer. He was to have joined me this week, but his train met with an accident, so he's been detained for a few days with an injured ankle. He's coming over as soon as he can. Monday, I hope. That's all about me. Your turn, Mr Hamilton-Parsons.'

'Oh, well. The Parsons bit was a not very inspired lie. You saw it, didn't you, when you got up to go upstairs? The postcard on the mantelpiece?'

'Yes. But the point is, why?'

'I couldn't give my own name, till I found out what that

fellow was up to. I should have thought up something better on the way over, but no one could think in that wind. It was all I could do to keep my feet.'

'So you knew he was "up to" something? You mean you knew from the start that he had no connection with me?'

'No, no. I did take you for a couple staying there together, and normally I would have retreated smartly and come back here again, but for what had already happened. Look, why don't you sit down and make yourself comfortable? I'd better start at the beginning, and it's a long story.'

I did as he suggested. He stayed on his feet by the window.

'I'm Neil Hamilton, as I told you, and Mrs Hamilton was my great-aunt. I'm a geologist – that bit was true – and until recently I've been working in Sydney. Then I heard about Aunt Emily's death. The end came rather suddenly, so I couldn't have got back in time to see her, but I flew over as soon as I was free, to see what had to be done. There's no one else. I was very fond of her when I was a child, and used to spend most of my holidays up here with her – my father was in the Consular Service, so my parents spent a lot of their time abroad. But latterly I've been here very little; in fact it must be at least fifteen years since I stayed here for any length of time ... Yes, I had my fourteenth birthday here. Uncle Fergus gave me a gun, I remember. He still had hopes of me, but I'm afraid I never enjoyed killing things. Still don't.' He smiled. 'He'd have been ashamed of me. Not the ideal Scottish laird at all.'

As he spoke, he had been wandering round the room, picking up photographs, looking at books, standing in front of the pictures; a sort of half-abstracted and apparently unemotional tour down Memory Lane. I brought him back to the matter in hand.

'And what brought you to my cottage in the middle of the night, with that story about your tent blowing away? In fact, why a tent at all? All those lies for Ewen Mackay before you'd even met him?'

He turned back to me. 'Yes, we come to that. They were lies, but as it happens I had met him before. Many years ago, when we were boys. If you remember, he half-recognised me. I had already recognised him, but fifteen years or so, boy to man, is a big change, and I doubt if he got it. In fact I'm sure he didn't. We talked late that night, and he would surely have said something.'

'I see. Or rather, I don't, yet. Are you telling me that because you recognised him you had to put on that charade? That you had some reason to distrust him?'

He nodded. 'As a boy he was – well, shall we just say undependable? But it wasn't that. I had my lies ready before I ever recognised him. I'd seen him earlier that night, here at the house, behaving in a way that made me very anxious to find out what he was doing here on Moila.'

'Here? You were here then? Everyone said the place was empty.'

'It was. I'd just arrived, and I hadn't been up to the village yet, or seen anyone. Still haven't, if it comes to that.'

'How did you get here?'

'I have a boat. Hired. Aunt Emily sold the one that was here; she had no use for it latterly. I came across from Oban – made a run for it, with the weather worsening all the time, but got here safely and made straight for our bay. Put the boat into the boat-house and made the doors fast, then came up to the house. I'd been to see my great-aunt's solicitors in Glasgow and they gave me the keys. I'd bought all I needed in Oban, so I just came up here and got myself settled in. It was pretty late and I was tired, so I found my old room and went straight to bed. It was well after midnight, getting on for one o'clock, when I went to open the bedroom window, and saw someone coming up through the garden from the bay.'

He stopped prowling at last, and dropped into one of the easy chairs facing me.

'Of course at first I just thought it was someone from a boat that had been driven in by the weather. You remember that night was pretty dark, so I couldn't have seen if there was a boat tied up at the jetty. The chap had a torch. Coming to ask for shelter, I thought, though why he couldn't sleep in his boat . . . As I said, it's quiet down there in the channel, even in a storm. That made me wonder what he wanted, so I stood and watched. He got as far as the lawn, just out there, and then he stopped and stood, seemingly just staring at the house. That seemed odd, too, in all that rain. Anyway, I came downstairs. The front door was still locked and bolted – I'd only used the back one since I'd got here – and the keys were out the back, so I came in here to open these french windows. I didn't put any lights on, and when I got into this room I was thankful I hadn't. I found him trying the window.'

'Well,' I said reasonably, 'in that storm, and if he thought the house was empty –'

'I know. I thought so, too. But he didn't just try the handle. He had some kind of tool, and he was trying to lever the window open. I stood there like a fool, watching him. Somehow one isn't prepared for that kind of situation . . . Then I thought, well, I'll have to tackle him somehow, so the best way, rain or no rain, was to go out the back way and take him from behind.'

'He had a gun,' I said.

That startled him. 'Had he indeed?'

'I think so. But go on, please!'

'I'm not exactly a man of action – that kind of action. Who is, except in television series? There used to be guns in the house, of course, but it never occurred to me to look if they were still there. But I must have felt the need for some support, because I found I'd grabbed hold of one of my hammers – a geologist is always armed with a hammer – and when I got through to the back of the house he was there already, at the kitchen window.'

'Good heavens! So?'

'I'm not quite sure what might have happened then, but for some reason he gave up. He could have forced the window in time, anyone could, but he seemed suddenly to think better of it. One moment he was there on the sill, and then suddenly he was gone. I ran upstairs to see what I could, and there he was, torch and all, running down the garden and then dodging his way up to the cliff path, and fast, as if he knew exactly where he was going. Of course I knew the path led to the Camus na Dobhrain, and the lawyers had told me that the cottage was let to a girl, so I wondered why he was headed there. I mean, there was nowhere else he could have been going. So I decided to follow along and see what was going on.'

'But you had a duffel bag ... Was that just scene-painting to go with your story about the tent?'

'More or less. I have got a tent here, as it happens, because I want to work on Eilean na Roin – that's Seal Island, where the broch is – and the tides are awkward, so

I need a base there. I took the tent across next morning.'

'I know. I saw it. But surely you weren't really here as a student? If you'd met Ewen Mackay then –'

'He'd have recognised me now, of course. Yes, that was a lie, too. Not the igneous intrusion – that's there all right; a colleague of mine told me about it – and I did intend to work there while I was here in Moila. Something to do while the estate business is being settled.'

'And did you bring the hammer, too, when you came chasing over to my cottage?'

'Er – I hardly remember. I don't suppose I did. And then, of course, when he opened the door to me, I recognised him. And since he obviously hadn't recognised me, I didn't want to connect myself with the house, until I'd found out what his game was.'

'And mine?'

'Well, yes. And yours.'

I smiled. 'Fair enough. But whatever your motives for coming over, I'm glad you did. If he was really up to no good the situation might have turned awkward – though as it happens he was perfectly civil, and I wasn't nervous.'

'I could see that. And that made me wonder if you were in it, too, and he'd had a rendezvous at the cottage. I found out next morning that his boat was in Halfway House, but when I first saw him I had no idea he was a Moila man, and it didn't occur to me that he would know the mooring there. I just assumed he was making for Otters' Bay.' A pause, while he seemed to be studying the pattern of the carpet. Then he looked up at me. 'What reason did he give you for coming all the way over to Otters' Bay when he could perfectly well have slept in his boat?'

'Oh, that the cottage had been his home, and he said

– or pretended – that he didn't know his people had moved away. I'm sure it was true that he didn't know the place was let to me.'

He was silent for a while, frowning at the prospect, from the window, of the neglected garden. 'Well, I still can't imagine what his game is, and I can't say that I like it.'

'When the pair of you went off to find your tent, what happened?'

'Nothing much. We made a token search for it on the way back to the bay, but then he went straight to his boat, and it's gone, and I've no idea where to. No sign of him anywhere near you since then?'

'None. So what happens now?'

'Nothing, let's hope. I honestly don't see what's to be done except wait and keep our eyes open. Nothing's happened to justify reporting to the police. The man did nothing, after all, except shoot a line to you, and if it's a crime to wander round an empty house on a wild night, trying the windows, well . . .'

'I take your point. Nobody's going to listen. Just one other detail; the key of my cottage. I don't believe he's been carrying a huge old-fashioned thing like that around ever since he left. I see there's a place on your key-rack by the back door for the cottage key, and it's missing. Unless you took it –?' He shook his head. 'Then if Ewen Mackay took it, that wasn't his first visit to this house. He'd been here before, and –'

'– And left the french windows open so that he could get in again! You're right! I did find the window open, and locked it myself because of the way it was rattling in the wind. I thought nothing of it, just that whoever closed the house up had overlooked it. So that could be it. He came back, and when he found the place locked up again, he got a scare, or he just decided to play it safe, and made off.'

'He did tell me he'd been to the house,' I said. 'He made out that he'd gone to take a nostalgic look at it, and of course he never said he'd tried to get in, or that he'd been before . . . I must say I thought at the time that it was a pretty rough night to choose for a sentimental journey . . . He did throw out a hint – ' I stopped.

'Yes? About what?'

'No. It was – well, personal. Nothing to do with this.'

'Till we know what "this" is,' he said reasonably, 'everything may be to do with it.'

'I suppose so.'

'So go on, please. What did he hint at?'

'Honestly I doubt if it matters, and I don't want . . . Oh, all right. He hinted that he might actually be connected with your family. At least that's what I thought he was trying to convey.'

To my relief, he laughed. 'That figures. Great-Uncle Fergus's love-child, adopted, presumably for a consideration, by the gardener? Don't worry, I've heard that one before. And a few others even wilder. He lived in a fantasy world of his own, even as a small boy. He used to lie for no reason at all, as if he enjoyed it. I was only a couple of years older myself, but I knew enough never to believe a word he said. Did he shoot any more lines to you? Tell you where he's been since he left Moila?'

'Only that he'd been abroad. I gathered that he'd been around in some pretty exciting – oh, do you mean he might have made that up, too? He didn't actually sail round the Horn?'

'I'll believe that when I've seen the boat's log,' said Neil drily, 'and only then after it's been checked by an expert. And talking of checking, I'd better have a look through the house to see if anything's missing. The lawyers gave me an inventory. Blast. I had hoped to take my time over sorting out the house contents, but I'd better take a look straight away – at any rate for the movable stuff. Tell me, how sure were you that he had a gun?'

'Not sure at all. It was just the way his hand flew to his pocket when you hammered at the door.'

'Hm. Then let's hope that was window-dressing, too. Well . . .' He set his hands to the chair arms, as if about to rise. 'He's gone, so perhaps that's the end of the mystery. When did you say your brother was coming?'

'Monday, I hope.'

'Then all we can do is keep our eyes open for the next couple of days, and you see that your doors are locked and bolted at night.'

'I certainly will. And you?'

'As you saw, I've got my tent set up now on the island. I'll work there, and I'll come back and sleep in the house. If Ewen does come back, he'll see the tent, and if he thinks that "Parsons" is safely out of the way, then whatever his interest is in the house, he'll no doubt show it. And I'll be here to tackle him, hammer and all.'

'And I?'

'Stay safe at Otters' Bay, and wait for your brother. Forget all this,' he said, with decision.

'I could try,' I said.

He got to his feet then, and I followed suit. The sun, slanting in through the window, showed up the faded shabbiness of the room, but outside the treetops were golden and the bees were loud in the roses. The scents of the garden, blowing in through the open window, had removed the last trace of stuffiness from the room. It smelt fresh and warm. He moved to open the door to the hall.

'So before I see you safely home, would you like a cup of tea?'

'I'd love it. But there's not the slightest need for you to see me home.'

'Probably not. But I'm going to,' he said cheerfully. His spirits seemed suddenly to have cleared. The sun, perhaps. 'This way, then, Mistress Fenemore. But I forgot, you've already explored my kitchen, haven't you? After you.'

10

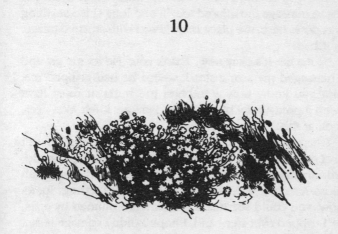

After tea we walked down through the remains of the garden. The path was ankle-deep in weeds, and to either side the overgrown rhododendrons, heavy with flowers, crowded in over the mosses and ferns of a mild damp climate. Wild honeysuckle clambered everywhere, and the air was sweet with it.

'We'll take a short cut. The grass is quite dry,' said Neil, and led the way through a gap in the rhododendrons into a broad, grassed walk leading directly down towards the sea. At the end was an opening, now almost closed by the crowding trees and bushes, through which one could see the glimmer of the sea and the northernmost hill of the broch islet.

I was looking at this, and not at where I was putting

my feet. I stubbed my toe, swore, tripped, and almost fell, to be saved by a robust grip above the elbow.

'Are you all right?' He held me while I stood on one leg to massage the injured toe. 'It's so long since anything was done here, the place is cluttered with storm damage. Is it bad?'

'Not a bit. It's okay now. Thank you.' He let me go, and I massaged my arm instead, where he had gripped me. 'But you know how a stubbed toe hurts. It must have been a pretty hefty bit of storm damage. It felt like – yes, look at this!'

Deep in the grass, embedded like a sleeper in soft green, lay a naked figure. Perhaps four feet high, a girl, daintily made, her body stained and streaked green with moss. A marble girl, once white, blind eyes staring. Somehow, you could see that the eyes were blinded by tears.

'I tripped over her hand. I hope I didn't damage it. No, it looks all right. Who is she?'

'I think she's meant to be Echo.' He stooped to push the grass and ferns back. 'She stood there, can you see where the plinth is? And there was water in a stone basin, but yes, that's broken, too. I remember when she arrived, and was set up. My great-uncle brought them from Italy; he was terribly proud of them.' He laughed suddenly. 'I'm no judge, but I believe they're quite good. Dear old Uncle Fergus's one successful venture into the art world. His taste in pictures was pretty awful. You may have noticed.'

'I wouldn't have said a word, but yes, I noticed.' I was still looking down at the girl in the grass. The breeze stirred the shadows over her, as if she breathed. 'I'm not an expert, either, but I love Echo. You said "them". Are there more?'

'There were four. There should be another across from

this, on the other side. Yes, here it is, and still standing.'

He crossed the ride, pushing some of the strangling boughs aside, to show the other figure, which was in fact kneeling. The stone basin was intact, and half-filled with black, dirty rain-water. A marble boy, a youth, knelt over the water, gazing down.

'Narcissus?'

'I suppose so,' he said. 'I don't remember. The others are along there, at the end of this walk. My great-uncle made a little belvedere there, with that view of the sea and the Eilean na Roin. I can't see them, though. The trees grow at such a rate here that you can hardly even see the sea.'

He turned and stood looking back at the house. In this sunlight the dilapidation showed up clearly, and the mess of the garden.

There was something in his face which made me say, gently: '*"But beauty vanishes, beauty passes, However rare, rare it be."*'

'What's that?'

'Walter de la Mare. *"And when I crumble, who shall remember That lady of the West Country?"* And heaven knows, there's beauty here and to spare, without anything men have built.'

He was silent, still looking at the house. Eventually he said, as if to himself: 'I'm glad I came back.' Then, briskly, to me: 'I sometimes think it's a mistake to have been happy when one was a child. One should always want to go on, not back. Poor old Echo. Maybe whoever buys the house will set her up again where she can see Narcissus – and much good did that ever do the poor girl.'

'Will you really sell?'

'What else can I do? I can't live here.'

'I suppose as a holiday house it is a bit far from Sydney.'

'Not Sydney. I was going to tell you earlier, but somehow Ewen's misdeeds threw us off track – I'll be in Cambridge next term. Living at Emma.'

'Well, that's great! Congratulations. You'll be looking forward to it.'

'Sure. And more than ever now.' He did not explain what he meant, but went on rather quickly to tell me about the appointment, and for a while we talked about Cambridge, and places and people that we both knew well. He would be living in college at first – Emmanuel was his own college – but he would like, he said, to find a place of his own, preferably outside the town.

This brought us back rather abruptly to the present, and the house he already possessed. It appeared that although Taigh na Tuir had not been formally put on the market, there had already been some interest shown. A London agent, apparently acting for someone anxious for an island property, had made a good offer 'sight unseen', and Neil's solicitors (who knew the place and the difficulties involved) had strongly advised him to accept it. Neil had taken their advice, and there had been the exchange of missives which, I gathered, served in Scotland as a binding contract.

'Binding on me, that is,' said Neil, 'though the buyer, once he sees the property, may still withdraw.'

'So there's still a chance you could keep it?'

He shook his head. 'Not really. How could I? Even if I didn't have a job that keeps me at the other end of the country for most of the year, this sort of place couldn't provide a living. Originally the family owned the whole island, which holds about four farms, but those have all been sold off now, and there's no land except the stretch from Otters' Bay to the other end of the machair. And Eilean na Roin, of course.' He shrugged, a gesture at once apologetic and dismissive. 'But even if the estate was still intact, there's hardly a living in farming nowadays. Or so I understand. There certainly wouldn't be for me. I don't know a tup from a gimmer. Shall we go?'

When we reached the jetty we paused for a few moments to look across at the islet. Gulls were wheeling over it, and the noise was incessant. A different noise made itself heard, and there among the circling gulls, high up, a fighter plane among the domestic craft, tore a peregrine falcon.

'She nests on the mainland cliffs,' said Neil. 'Ever since I remember there's been a peregrine on that cliff. I tried to climb down to the nest once. I was about eleven years old. They caught me at it, luckily, before I'd gone over the edge. Over there, see? The white streaks high on the cliff.' He was pointing northwards, to the cliffs towering beyond the machair. I could just make out the spot he indicated.

I said, with reverence: 'My God.'

He laughed. 'Makes your blood run cold to think what small boys will do without a second thought.'

'I don't suppose my brother will have any hope of a picture there, even from a boat and with a telephoto lens ... But if he can manage it, may I please take him over to the island to look at the birds there? What is its name again?'

'Eilean na Roin. It means Island of the Seals. They come ashore there to breed. Go over by all means, but do watch the tides. The crossing's only really safe for about two hours to either side of low tide. You see that rock there, shaped a bit like a shoe?' He pointed at a rock near the causeway. 'When the sea gets to the base of that, the tide's already too high, and it comes in like a horse trotting, as they say. You don't need my permission to go over there anyway. Didn't you know there's no law of trespass in Scotland?'

'Not even in your house?'

He smiled. 'That was a pleasure. The whole visit has been a pleasure. I'd have liked to prolong it by asking you to supper, but . . .' A gesture finished it for him: the empty house, the deserted kitchen.

'That was very nicely done,' I said appreciatively. 'Aren't you taking a risk, though? I mean, I'm a don. What makes you think I can cook as well as get stroppy about words?'

'The fact that you came to Moila and took that godforsaken cottage – and that your brother agreed to come with you,' said Neil cheerfully. 'Besides, I saw eggs and cheese and all sorts of stuff in the cupboard when I spent the night there. Do I take it that I'm invited, Mistress Fenemore?'

'Well, of course, and for pity's sake stop reminding me about that. My name's Rose. Just tell me, though – failing our meeting this afternoon, what were you planning to do? Suck gulls' eggs?'

'Come over to Otters' Bay again and beg for shelter. What else?'

'Considering you told me that you'd taken supplies on in Oban and that you managed perfectly well all of yesterday, and that your boat is probably stiff with tins and even bottles –'

'Bottles! Now, that's a thought. We'll collect a couple here and now . . . And you might be right about the supplies. Will you dine with me tomorrow, please? And if your brother should happen to make it, bring him, too, of course.'

'At the house? Lights on, chimney smoking, and your lovely alibi wasted? Had you forgotten your plan, Mr Parsons?'

'Do you know, I had. And how right you are.' He sounded, suddenly, irritated. 'And how absurd to think that there's any need for all this cloak and dagger stuff ... Yes, I'd forgotten. All right, we'll give it another day or two, but I'm seeing you back home now, and don't try to talk me out of it. I'm starving. And for pity's sake call me Neil.'

'All right.' It was extraordinary, but suddenly we seemed to be on quite different terms. 'All right, I'll feed you. But only if you do get those bottles, and quickly. I'm starving, too.'

'Red or white? And is it gin or sherry?' He was at the boat-house door, taking a key from his pocket. 'No, never mind. I'll bring the lot. And I promise to help with the washing up.'

11

Saturday morning, and once again a fair and breezy day, so fair that I decided to give myself a holiday from writing, and go straight after breakfast to pick up the supplies I would need for the weekend. Mrs McDougall had promised to have milk and bread for me, and there might possibly be mail, brought over by the morning's ferry.

Neil had told me to try and forget about the 'mystery', and this proved surprisingly easy to do. On such a morning, with the sky full of larks, and the banks beside the road stiff with foxgloves and wild roses, the odd events of Wednesday night seemed remote, and indeed little more than odd. So I busied myself, as I walked, with plans for supper on Monday night, when I hoped that my brother would be here, and I had invited Neil to join us.

When I drew near the village I could see two girls sitting on the parapet of the little bridge. They seemed to be watching me, and then one of them waved, and I saw that they were Megan Lloyd and Ann Tracy.

Ann, Megan's constant companion, was a complete contrast to the dark, rather intense Welsh girl. She was a land agent's daughter from somewhere in Norfolk, tall and fair, with heavy gilt hair curling down over her shoulders, and a long, slim, slightly drooping body that had a certain elegance. Her oval face, with its thick fair eyebrows, blue eyes, and high colour, and the small mouth with the slight droop there, too, looked deceptively gentle. In fact I knew her for a tough-minded young woman with feminist leanings and rather more interest in student politics than would be helpful in her academic work. At present, Ann led and Megan followed, but that would sort itself out in the long run. Ann had a good brain, but Megan had it in her to be brilliant.

When the greetings and exclamations were over, they told me that they had been staying on Mull for a few days, and had just arrived on Moila, and were putting up at the post office with Mrs McDougall.

'She told us where your cottage was, and we've got a map. Not that you really need one on Moila. We were planning to come down today and see you.' That was Ann. Megan put in quickly: 'We knew you were on your own. Mrs McDougall told us about your brother. We're terribly sorry. Is he badly hurt?'

'No, no. He says it's nothing, and he should know. He's a doctor. I've talked with him on the telephone and with any luck he should be over here on Monday. I don't know how well he'll be able to get about, but we'll manage somehow. I'd love you to see the cottage. Were you thinking of visiting me this morning?'

'Yes,' said Ann, 'and then Mrs McDougall said you'd be coming up here for your shopping, so we waited.'

'And don't worry,' said Megan, patting a haversack that lay beside her on the parapet. 'We've got masses of food for a picnic, so you don't have to feed us. We were going to say hullo to you, and then walk round to that little island – it's called Seal Island – I can't say the Gaelic name but Mrs McDougall told me that's what it means. It's the one with the broch on it. It looks as if there's a path over from your cottage, so perhaps we could walk round there and then come back to you for tea?'

'Well, of course you may, but did you ask about the tides? That's not a bridge that's marked on the map, it's a causeway that's covered most of the time. I was down there yesterday, and I doubt if you'll be able to cross much before two o'clock. Why not make sure? I think I saw tide tables in the post office.'

While the girls studied the tide tables I bought my groceries. There were no letters, and to my relief no messages either. No news being good news, that meant Crispin on Monday. I told Morag (Mrs McDougall was busy over the tide tables with Ann and Megan) then went out to wait for them.

It appeared that my guess about the tide had been near enough.

'Low tide at 4.04,' said Ann, 'and we've been warned to leave not one second later than six, or be marooned all night. Oh well, we'll just have to have our picnic on the mainland. Did you say you were down there yesterday, Dr Fenemore? What's it like? There's a house marked, right beside the bridge – the causeway, I mean – so will there be people about?'

'The house is empty, and the place is quite lovely. I

103

was just too late yesterday to go across, but the islet looked marvellous. There's quite a lot of the broch showing, too, almost the complete circle, with one very high bit where I'm told there are steps going up to what's left of the top level, with a view.'

'It sounds terrific,' said Megan.

Ann made a face. 'You can have it.' Then, to me: 'We went to Orkney last summer, and she made me crawl in through a ghastly tunnel into some underground charnel-house. Never again! It's bad enough now, but it must have been really something when it was occupied. Apparently they ate nothing but shellfish, and just dropped the shells on the floor when they'd finished. You can imagine.'

'Unfair to Celts,' said Megan. 'Racist. We had middens, and –'

'Yes, just outside the front door. We saw those, too . . .' Ann turned a laughing face to me. 'Dr Fenemore, would you like to come with us? We'd love you to, and you can tell Megan all about her wretched broch. She's been reading them up for days.'

'Yes, do!' Megan joined her plea to Ann's, with such eager sincerity that I laughed and agreed.

'I'd love to. But Megan can do the lecturing. I don't know the first thing about brochs. Look, why not come down to my cottage now, and we'll have lunch there – I never have much more than just a picnic myself – then we can go across this afternoon, and maybe take tea to have on the island? But on one condition, that you stop calling me "Dr Fenemore". We're a long way from Cambridge now, and my name is Rose.'

We shared our resources for lunch – the girls' picnic sandwiches and a cold pie and some fruit I had bought that morning – and ate it comfortably in the cottage kitchen, with its grandstand view of the bay. To our delight we also got a grandstand view of the original owners of the bay – the otters. An adult, presumably the female, came close inshore, followed by two young ones, and she seemed to be teaching them to fish, but after a few splashing sallies with no success she gave up, and dived away. The pups slithered out onto the weedy boulders, not forty feet from the cottage window, and waited expectantly until she reappeared carrying a sizeable fish, which the two of them ate together, wrestling over it among the sea-tangle. Then the three of them swam away into the deeper water under the headland.

'They'll come back,' I said comfortingly to the girls, who were lamenting that they had forgotten to bring a camera. 'Surely they will. This isn't called Otters' Bay for nothing. And if they come when my brother's here, he'll get some marvellous shots of them, I promise you, telephoto lens, the lot, and I think he's got a video camera now, too. He'll make prints for you. Now, anyone for coffee?'

*

'It is thought by some,' said Megan, in a smooth lecturer's voice from which all trace of her faint Welsh lilt had vanished, 'that the Scottish brochs may be an extension of the southern round-house culture, as exemplified in some sites of south-western England, but this seems unlikely, in view of –'

'The Scots'll be pleased to hear that,' said Ann. 'But I'm not just enthralled, and I'm sure Dr – I'm sure Rose isn't either.'

'Do I really sound like that?' I asked.

Megan gasped and went scarlet. 'It wasn't – I didn't –'

Then she saw me laughing and flopped her hands forward in a gesture of relief. 'Of course you don't! I was quoting, anyway. I've been reading up on brochs, but when you're actually there it's really just the setting that's so marvellous, and trying to imagine the sort of life they lived.'

'Raw shellfish for breakfast,' muttered Ann.

She was ignored. 'Weren't they really forts?' I asked. 'Defensive places?'

'Yes. They must have been the Iron Age equivalent of the mediæval castle with the village and everything clustered round. You can see where there could have been some buildings outside the main ring wall. Hey, Ann, be careful! Where d'you think you're going?'

Ann was already half-way up the primitive stairway, a series of flat stones jutting out from the inner surface of the highest section of wall. 'To look at the view. It's quite safe. They're solid. Come on up.' And Megan went, as she always went where Ann led.

As she had said, there was really nothing left here but the view, and the girls were exclaiming over it now, talking eagerly, and pointing. I left them to it and made my way along the inner side of the curving wall towards the doorway. This high western section was remarkably well preserved, the stone slabs tightly laid, and the primitive stairway safe and solid. But apart from this the broch wall showed only as a circle of raised turf, with a tumble of stones here and there. Outside the circle a few mounds and stones were all that remained of the huddle of huts that had once crowded under the broch's protection. Nettles grew everywhere, and ragwort, and the wall itself was thick with plants growing in every available gap. I saw saxifrages and wild thyme and others that were unfamiliar to me. There was a lot of some sort of stonecrop, which was pretty enough, but smelled at close quarters rather like cleaning fluid.

The girls were still on their perch. I called out: 'I'm going over to look at the birds,' and left them to it.

From what Neil had told me over supper last night, I knew that the main bird colonies were on the western side of the island, where the cliffy coastline was cut into deep gullies, some of them sheer, and some filled with tumbles of massed boulders. I walked across that way, over the crest of the island, easy walking on wind-swept turf which in a short distance sloped gently down towards the head of the cliffs, where clouds of sea-birds were already wheeling and screaming at my approach.

There was a long promontory thrusting out to sea, with a deep inlet to either side where the tide sucked and swirled among fallen rocks. Above the water the cliffs rose sheer, but seamed with ledges and tufted with sea-pink and white campion. The birds were there.

I had never seen a big sea-bird colony before. The noise was horrendous, and the depths in front of me, filled with whirling wings, were frightening. I backed a step or two and sat down. Automatically – the writer's habit – I was trying to find the right word to describe the scene. The one I came up with eventually was 'indescribable'.

I gave it up and sat still, content to watch.

No rare birds; just the incredible numbers, and the variety. Every niche of the craggy cliff held a nest, every hollow of the turfy ledge just below me had eggs or young gulls nestling there. Further down I saw kittiwakes, with their gentle dark eyes and neat nests; below them, in deeper crevices, the ugly shags with their uglier young, showing the brilliant apricot gape of their beaks as they craned for food. Here and there, unperturbed, solitary among the crowd, the fulmars; and out there in the air, huge and unmistakable among the teeming thousands, those unpleasant predators the great black-backed gulls, with their cruel beaks and dead eyes like sharks' eyes, and their ineffable grace of flight.

The girls arrived then, breathless and laughing, and making sounds of disgust at the pervading smell and slime of birds' droppings.

'And to think the stuff's valuable!' That was Ann. 'Guano at how many thousand pounds a ton ... What a job! I wonder what they pay the chaps that shovel it up? Why don't they make an industry of it here? I'm sure there's just as much on these islands as there is in Peru or wherever ... No, don't tell me. It's a bit vertical, isn't it? Do you mind if we move back a bit? I don't normally mind heights, but this is different.'

We retreated to the crest of the island, and sat down where the turf was clean and dry. Megan unpacked the picnic tea and handed me a plastic cup.

'Would you like a biscuit? We've got ginger snaps and shortbread.' Her eyes were shining. 'What a wonderful place! You'd think that with all those wings the island itself would start to fly!'

'Like that one in *Gulliver*,' said Ann, and this started a discussion as to whether Scotland could engineer the flight of its islands to hover over England and starve her of sunlight and rain, like Laputa in *Gulliver's Travels*. And this, in spite of some effort on my part to prevent it, led to the subject of science fiction, and where it had gone since the original efforts of Swift and Verne and H. G. Wells. But fortunately there would be no embarrassment: when Megan did eventually mention Hugh Templar, it was in passing, and with respect, along with John Wyndham and Arthur C. Clarke and Ursula le Guin.

Ann had never heard of any of them, and refused to be interested in a genre which she dismissed contemptuously as 'fairy tales'.

'But fairy tales were topical and highly moral,' began Megan.

I had to intervene there. '*Puss in Boots? Jack the Giant Killer?* All those murderous little thugs in Grimm who cheated and stole and lied their way to the princess and half the kingdom? No, no, I know what you mean, and on the whole yes, you're right; your modern fairy-tale – I don't just mean what's miscalled "science fiction", but all the stories that feed the modern hunger for the supernatural – they do tend to be more or less moral now. Surprisingly enough, considering the norm of fiction.'

This steered them away, as I had meant it to, and they talked for a while longer, then fell silent, enjoying the warmth and the view.

Away to the west was the enormous glitter of the sea, where the small islands floated, weightless in the gently moving water. Even Mull, with its mountains, looked insubstantial. I could just make out Tobermory, looking like an Anne Redpath painting, cubes of white and blue and primrose and Venetian red, the houses and shops strung out along the bay, tiny in the distance.

'Can't see your cottage from here,' said Ann. She had binoculars out and was looking the other way. 'Can't really see that house, either; too many trees.' She focussed nearer. 'I wonder whose that tent is? No sign of them. Rather an odd place to camp, having to keep your eye on the tides the whole time.'

'He's a geologist,' I said. 'I've met him. And he has a boat.'

She lowered the glasses and glanced at her wrist. 'And talking of watching the tides, it's nearly half past four, and

Mrs McD does a high tea at half six. If we're to go home through the fields by the shore – what did you call them, Meg?'

'The machair. Yes, we ought to go. Can we get there along the shore from the causeway? Can you see? It looks as if there's a wall sticking right out over the shingle.'

'That's the belvedere at the end of the House gardens,' I said. 'But there's a path round under the wall, and the machair starts just beyond the trees.'

'Yes. You're right.' Megan had the glasses now. 'That's fine, then, we'll go that way ... These are good glasses, Ann. I can just about see that B & B we had in Tobermory, and – hang on a minute ... I wonder? Yes, it could be ...'

'What?' Ann and I spoke together.

'The *Stormy Petrel*. I'm sure it is.'

'*What?*' My voice went high with excitement. 'A stormy petrel? Where?'

'There. You see? That boat just out of Tobermory. You take a look, Ann.' She handed the binoculars over. 'Is it?'

'Wait a mo.' Ann stood up and focussed. 'I don't think – I can't quite – I honestly can't tell one boat from another, but it looks different. I think it's just a fishing boat.'

I subsided on to the turf. 'A boat ... I thought you were talking about a bird, though how you'd spot one of those little things ... Ah, well, skip it. What boat did you think it was? What's this *Stormy Petrel?*'

'Oh, it belongs to a terribly nice chap we met on Mull.' Ann lowered the glasses. 'No, he's not coming this way, so I can't get a close look, but I'm sure it's not him.'

'Probably just as well, from what Mrs McDougall told us,' said Megan.

'Just what are you two talking about? What has Mrs McDougall got to do with it?' I asked.

'It's nothing, really. We met a chap the other day when we were staying near Dervaig, over the other side of Mull. We found a tiny B & B in a heavenly spot, a lovely bay and hardly any people. He had this boat called *Stormy Petrel* and he was living on it. Well, we sort of got together a couple of times – he was an interesting sort of man – done a lot of sailing, single-handed stuff. He'd even been round the Horn –'

'Had he indeed?' I sat up again, all interest now. 'Sorry, go on, Ann.'

'He did have some really good stories,' said Ann, 'and the way he told them – well, he was fun, and we both liked him. He took us out in his boat a couple of times, and he offered to take us over to the Treshnish Isles, but the forecast wasn't too good, so we never made it. He said he was coming to Moila later on, on business. He really was terribly nice, wasn't he, Megan?'

'Well, we thought so.'

I looked from one to the other. 'And Mrs McDougall told you something about him that changed your minds?'

Ann said, judicially: 'What she told us doesn't alter the fact that he had bags of charm, but it seems that it's his – well, his stock-in-trade ... She knew him. She said he was from Moila, and ever since he was a boy he'd been a sort of con artist, and could get away with anything –'

'A pathological liar and a thief.' Generations of Welsh Methodists spoke in Megan's direct voice. 'What she told us meant just that, even though he was only a boy when she knew him. And as for sailing single-handed round the Horn –'

'We'd have been lucky to get as far as the Treshnish Isles,' said Ann. 'And Mrs McD was a bit staggered when we told her he was in Mull. Apparently everyone was hoping that he wouldn't come back here, because his people moved out after he went to prison, and asked Mrs McD not to let him know their address.'

'*He went to prison?*' I caught Megan's quick glance, but Ann seemed to take my sharp interest for granted.

'Yes. She says he must have been released early, and, she's dreading him coming to see her and demanding his parents' address. His name's Mackay, so if you should come across him –'

'Did she tell you what he'd been in prison for?'

'No. She rather skated away from the subject after a while.'

'After she learned that you knew me and were coming down to see me?'

They were gathering their things together, ready to go. They stopped and stared at me.

'Well, ye-es, I suppose it could have been? Ann?'

'I think so. Why, Rose? What's it got to do with you?'

I got to my feet. 'Nothing, I hope,' I said cheerfully. 'Only that the Mackays used to live in my cottage. They moved away two years ago. That's all Mrs McDougall told me. Perhaps she didn't want me to worry about it. In any case, she must have thought he was still safely locked away.'

'Now that you know he's out – and around – will you mind being alone down there till Monday?'

'No. Now, don't worry about me. If you want to get back for your high tea, you'd better go.'

'Aren't you coming over now?'

'Not straight away. There's time yet. Come and see me again, won't you, and thanks for the tea.'

'Thank *you* for the lunch,' they said. 'It's been a lovely day. Be seeing you!'

I watched them down to the causeway. Once across, they turned and waved, then were soon out of sight beyond the belvedere.

12

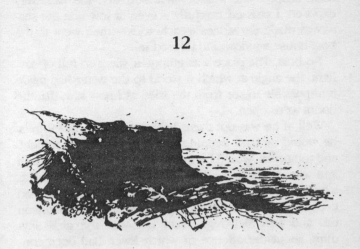

After the girls had gone I sat for a little time, thinking.

What they had told me put quite a different complexion on the 'mystery'. I would have to seek Neil out and tell him that his old acquaintance was now, if not necessarily dangerous, at the least some kind of villain, who needed careful watching.

Neil had told me that he might spend the daytime hours between tides over here on Seal Island. He was working at present on the rocks at the north-west point, which were only accessible at low tide, or from a boat. I thought that, in spite of the noise of the birds, I would have heard a hammer going down there along the cliffs. In any case, there was not enough time left for me to go that way to look for him.

I made my way down towards the causeway. Neil's rock, shaped like a shoe, was still dry, the causeway exposed. I crossed carefully – even at low tide the sea-weeds made the stones treacherous – then went to the boat-house window and peered in.

No boat. The place was empty. It was also full of day-light: the angle at which it stood to the water had made it impossible to see from the islet, as I now saw, that the doors were open.

Well, if he was out there hammering the cliffs to bits, he would be back keeping watch on the house tonight, and tomorrow would be time enough, surely, to see him and warn him? After all, he had known Ewen Mackay as a boy, and was aware of the reputation the latter had had even then. The only new thing I could add was the prison bit, and Mrs McDougall had not told the girls any-thing about the offence of which Ewen had been con-victed. I thought about it as I walked up through the weedy garden. Even if I had had pencil and paper on me, I would not have cared to leave a note where someone else might see it first. So tomorrow would have to do, and the obvious move now was to see Mrs McDougall myself and get what might be called hard evidence from her. She might be willing to give me, as the tenant of the former Mackay home, the details she had kept back from Ann and Megan. For my part I would have to decide how much I could tell her without giving away Neil's presence on Moila. I did not see how he could keep it secret for much longer, but that was his business.

However, after that visit to my cottage, Ewen Mackay was mine.

For form's sake, when I reached the house, I tried the french windows, then, round at the back, the door. All locked. I went home to the cottage, had an early supper, then set off on the walk to the post office.

*

The shop was shut, but the house door stood open. There was no sign of the girls, so I supposed they must have gone out again after their high tea. I met Morag on the step. She had been a message, she told me, and was it the telephone? Her auntie was in, but I was to go at any time for the telephone . . . Well, but her auntie would be pleased to see me. Any time. Please to come in . . .

Mrs McDougall was in her kitchen, not baking this time, though a pleasant after-smell of cooking pervaded the room. She was sitting beside the Rayburn, knitting. She made me welcome, and nodded me to a chair on the other side of the stove. Morag unpacked her 'message', which was a large cauliflower from someone's garden, and a couple of pounds of tomatoes which had obviously, from the scent, been freshly picked, then, after we had admired them, left us.

'Tomatoes already?' I was actually fairly ignorant about the timing of tomatoes, or indeed, of any home-grown vegetables. But in view of the admiration that had obviously been expected, it was the right thing to say.

'My sister,' said Mrs McDougall. 'Duncan – that's her man – spends near all his time on the garden when he's not fishing. They have a greenhouse, and he keeps adding to that – he's a handy man, is Duncan – and they are always earlier than anyone else around here.' She reached the end of a row, paused for a moment to count, then turned her knitting and started again. 'He comes from Achiltibuie, and worked for a bit at the hydroponics there. So now he's trying the same way here. Have you been there? I have not, but my sister worked in a hotel there for a time – that is where they met – and she says it is very remarkable.'

I said no, I hadn't, and what were hydroponics? She told me, while the kettle sang gently on the top of the Rayburn, and the creamy Aran knitting grew perceptibly on her lap. What she told me about vegetable growing meant very little to me, so I can barely recall now what was said, except that she would let me have some strawberries on Monday for my brother's supper, but I remember how easily the talk went, my unexpected visit serenely taken for granted, with no query as to why I had come. Just a pleased acceptance of the company, and a chat while the kettle sang its way to the boil.

It boiled, and she laid the knitting aside and made tea. From a tin in the cupboard scones were produced, and spread with butter and honey. I accepted plate and cup, thanked her, and wondered how on earth, into a conversation which had ranged from hydroponics to knitting to the situation in the smaller countries of the Warsaw Pact to the best breed of wool for spinning tweed to the honey and the siting of the hives – how on earth I could decently introduce my queries about Ewen Mackay.

I need not have worried. What I was experiencing was an islander's version of the tea-ceremony and its ritual. As she took her own cup and settled herself again in her chair, Mrs McDougall looked at me over her spectacles and said comfortably: 'The girls will have told you about Ewen Mackay.'

'Yes, they did.'

'And I think that Archie told you that your cottage used to be where his family lived. So perhaps you are worried

118

in case he comes home, now that he is back in these parts.' It was a statement, not a question.

I hesitated, then shook my head. 'Not really. But I did feel I'd like to know a bit more about him. Why he went to gaol, for instance. Was it for something he did up here – in the islands?'

'No. It was in London.'

'But his parents still lived here then?'

'They did. And of course everyone knew all about it, just as they knew that the Mackays, poor souls, had done everything they could for the boy ever since they took him in for adoption.' She sipped tea. 'You know that they left Moila. It was partly for shame after all the talk and the things that the papers said, but as well as that they wanted to cut him off for good.' A little smile. ' "For good." That is exactly what it was. He was bad all through, that one, and they were good folk. They wanted rid of him for good, and I think they were a bit afraid he might come back, and then how could they turn him out?'

'Afraid of him? Of violence, you mean?'

'I do not know. I did hear once that he had threatened his father, but I do not know if this is true, and they, poor souls, never said a word against him.'

'Mrs McDougall,' I said flatly, 'what was he sent down for?'

She set her cup aside and picked up her knitting again. 'Miss Fenemore, they do say that if a man has done wrong, and has been punished for it, that should be the end of it. Do you not agree? It is true the man is bad, but he has done two years, almost, in prison. It might be better to forget it.' The needles clicked. 'No, do not look like that, lassie. I'm not calling shame on you. I blame myself for talking to those other lassies. I would have done better to have held my tongue.'

'You did hold your tongue. You said nothing to me. You only let it out to the girls because you got a shock when they said they'd seen him, and you were afraid yourself that he might come here and demand his parents' address from you. Isn't that true?'

'Aye, it's true. Not "afraid", though. There's no harm could come to me here, with good neighbours round and about all the while. And he'd not offer harm to me, I think. But you, lassie –' once more I was promoted from 'Miss Fenemore' – 'there's no need for you to fear him coming to the cottage, even though he has a boat and could get into the bay without anyone seeing him. He'll have been told, for sure, that his folks are gone, and the place is let.'

'Yes. Well . . . Thank you for the tea, Mrs McDougall. It's been lovely talking with you, but if I'm to get home . . .' I rose. 'Since I'm here, may I use the telephone, please, before I go?'

'You may.' The knitting was in her lap and she was regarding me steadily over the spectacles. 'Just sit you down again for a minute, lassie. It wasn't just for idleness that you came to ask about that rapscallion, was it? Are you afraid to sleep in that cottage? Because if you are –'

'No, it's all right. It's not that.'

She nodded. 'I thought so. It is something else.' Silence for a minute. She seemed to be deciding something about the knitting in her lap. Then she said, with apparent irrelevance: 'Those two lassies, they think the world of you.'

I could think of nothing to say to that, so I said nothing.

She nodded again, as if I had answered her. 'Very well, I will tell you what you ask me, and I do not want to know why you ask it.' She picked up her knitting again, and the needles clicked. 'It came out in the court that he had been robbing old ladies . . . confidence trickster was the word. He would watch the notices in the papers, and when someone died and the widow was left alone, he would go there and think up some sort of lie – he lied always, as a boy, even when there was no need, and he looked so clean and innocent that if you did not know him you would believe him, every time. And sometimes even though you did know him ... So he would use the charm and the lies on the old lady in her grief, and cheat her out of everything he could get. The one they took him for in the end, she was eighty-five years old, and ailing, and he robbed her of her life-savings, and that was less than three hundred pounds. He would spend that much, they said, in a week. He pleaded guilty to three other offences. Do you see what I mean about shame?'

'Yes, I see.' I was thinking hard. Should I tell her here and now that Ewen Mackay had already been to the cottage? It was possible that his return to Moila had been sparked by the notice in the papers of Mrs Hamilton's death. He had been in gaol when that occurred. On his release he had come straight up to Moila, and by last weekend – it was possibly true enough – had not heard of his parents' departure, but had thought he could go straight home. And then what? There was no elderly widow to con, but there was an empty house, and one he knew well. He must know, at least casually, what there was of value there. So, no con-tricks needed here, just a simple robbery? But his luck was out, in that the new owner, who was no old lady, but a sufficiently able-bodied young man, was here before him. And knew him.

And Neil, for his part, knew that if anyone on Moila heard of his, Neil Hamilton's, return, the news would fly around and certainly reach Ewen Mackay. So, since for the present Neil preferred to lie low and find out just what Ewen was up to, I could not tell Mrs McDougall of

121

Ewen's night-time visit. If I could not reassure her by telling her Neil was there, and watching, it was possible, more, probable, that she would insist either on my moving into a lodging in the village, or that some of the men from the village would keep watch on Otters' Bay and the empty house.

I would have to talk to Neil first. Tomorrow. Tonight all I could do was make sure of Crispin. I thanked Mrs McDougall again and went to the telephone.

The hospital answered, with cheering news. It seemed that my brother would soon be on his way. He had left that morning, to stay with his Glasgow friends; and yes, he had left the Glasgow number in case I should call.

I called, and Crispin answered, so cheerfully that I knew all was well.

'Yes, I'm all set to come up tomorrow. We'll be at the Columba Hotel, and on the ferry first thing Monday.'

' "We?" '

'Yes, there was someone else heading for Oban, and we were in the crash together. He'll be getting the same train. To tell you the truth, I'm quite glad of his help. I'm what they laughingly call mobile, but carrying a suitcase, as well as all my camera junk, is a little beyond me as yet.'

'But the foot really is mending?'

'It's fine. Another day or two and I'll be skipping like a ram on the high hills. Depending, of course, on what you've got laid on for me. Anything new?'

'Only several hundred thousand gulls and shags and things. But I did see black guillemots swimming down in the bay, and a gully full of boulders where they probably nest.'

'Sounds great. Accessible?'

122

'From the sea. And there's a boat handy. Don't forget the binocs.'

'Is it likely? Anything else you need me to bring? The local supermarket's open on Sundays now, and Laura's going there in the morning, she tells me.'

'Nothing I can think of, unless you want something fancy in the way of cheeses. Can't get those here. Oh, and some cream, too. You're getting strawberries for supper on Monday.'

'Good heavens. The only ones I've seen here are from California, and they don't taste like the real thing at all. What are the Hebrides coming to? Greenhouse effect?'

'No. We've got hydroponics. I must go now. I've got a long lonely road home in front of me. Good night, Cris.'

'Good night. Take care, and *hasta la vista*.'

We rang off.

*

Nearly ten o'clock, and still light. I saw no one on the long lonely road home, and the only enemy that attacked me was the midges.

13

I slept later than usual next morning, and woke to see half past nine on my bedside clock, and a cascade of raindrops chasing each other down the window. By the time I had had breakfast and done the morning's chores it was after eleven and, though the rain was letting up, it was still wet enough to keep anyone indoors who didn't have to go out.

I decided that I didn't have to go out. It was not a hard decision to take. Rationalised, it meant that Neil already knew enough about Ewen Mackay's record, and of course he was already on the watch for any more suspicious moves. If he, Neil, was content to leave the house unwatched by day, and to spend his time looking at rocks on the broch island, then I could stay indoors with a clear conscience, and wait for the rainstorm to pass.

I got back to work, by which I mean that I got my papers and notes out, and then sat looking at them for what seemed like a dreary lifetime, and was really probably only twenty minutes. The words I had written – and had almost, in the interval, forgotten – mocked me and were meaningless. My notes told me what was to happen next, but my brain no longer knew how to move plot and people forward. Block. Complete block. I sat and stared at the paper in front of me and tried to blank out the present and get back into my story – forward, that is, into my invented future, and out of the world of queries and vague apprehensions.

From experience, I knew what to do. Write. Write anything. Bad sentences, meaningless sentences, anything to get the mind fixed again to that sheet of paper and oblivious of the 'real' world. Write until the words begin to make sense, the cogs mesh, the wheels start to turn, the creaking movement quickens and becomes a smooth, oiled run, and then, with luck, exhaustion will be forgotten, and the real writing will begin. But look up once from that paper, get up from the table to make coffee or stir the fire, even just raise your head to look at the view outside the window, and you may as well give up until tomorrow. Or for ever.

It was the rain that saved me. I could not have looked out of the window if I had tried, the chores were all done, and there was nothing whatever to do except sit at that table and write.

I wrote. A year or so later, or it may have been an hour, I crumpled up four sheets of paper and threw them to the floor, and started another, and I was there. And in another light-year or two I was through the word-barrier, and the book had suddenly reached the stage – the wonderful moment to get to – where I could walk right into my imaginary country and see things that I had not consciously created, and listen to people talking and watch them moving, all apparently independent of me.

I came out of it and saw the window clear and the sun shining and the heavy clouds rolled back to leave a blue, washed sky. I could hear gulls crying, and the soft, flattened whispering of the sea. My watch said twenty past one.

Scrambled eggs again, and coffee, then I made a thermos of tea, pushed that, with a packet of biscuits, into the pocket of my anorak, and set off along the cliff path.

*

It was half past two by my watch when I reached the Hamilton house. I went to the back door – still fast shut – and knocked. The sound echoed through the silence with that hollow, unmistakably empty noise. Perhaps he was working on the island again. I made my way round the house and crossed the mossy terrace to look in through the drawing-room window. Nobody there, of course. It looked just the same. If he was really living in the house he must be taking pains to leave no signs of his occupancy. Somehow the knowledge irked me. He had been right, I thought; in spite of what the girls and Mrs McDougall had told me, the whole idea of a 'mystery' was, in this place, wrong and irritating. Whatever Ewen Mackay was up to, it could really hardly matter. Must not be allowed to matter. He no longer belonged here. Had never belonged. He was the changeling of the classic tale, thrust on good people, who was to repay good with evil.

127

The hints he had thrown out, that he was connected in some illegitimate way with the Hamilton family, could be dismissed as a typical lie told to impress, another Cape Horn. I wondered what his real origins were, and if there really was such a thing as original sin, people born evil. It was fashionable not to think so, but there were people of whom it had to be believed. For instance –

I checked the train of thought. This was no place for it. Moila was too lovely, and my ivory tower was still solid. This was my holiday, and my brother would be here tomorrow, and all would be normal once more.

The boat-house was empty again, its sea-doors fastened back. I walked to the end of the pier and looked across at the island. There was no sign of life except the birds, and Neil's tent was again fastened shut. I glanced at my watch. The tide was still falling, and should be safe for another three hours or so. I went across.

*

I climbed the slope to the hollow where Neil's tent was pitched. There was no sign of him there. I stood still, listening. No sound of a hammer. There were gulls flying and calling, but I had not disturbed the main colony, and I thought that I would have heard if he had been working below the cliffs at the north-west point. I gave it a couple of minutes, then made for the broch and the steps up to the landing where the girls had gone yesterday.

The steps looked fragile; transverse slabs of stone with one end built into the dry-stone structure of the curving wall, and jutting into the air with no other support. But they were solid, and led safely up to the ruined top of the wall where another, larger slab made a good viewpoint. From here I found, as I had hoped, that I could see down to the shore at the point where Neil had told me he wanted to work. If he had been close to the cliff I would not have been able to see him, but I could see the whole section of shoreline, and there was no boat there. Short of clambering down there myself I could be no surer, and there was no real need for that. More rationalisation. I made my way carefully down the staircase, intending to sit in the sun at the foot of the wall and drink my tea, but the breeze could find no way there, and the strange, musky smell from the wall where those plants grew was stronger than ever. Besides, the midges were out. I left the broch and walked uphill as far as I could without disturbing the bird colony, then made my way towards the southern end of the island, where the land sloped gradually down to the sea in long, flat terraces of rock. I found a niche where a small landslide had left a level lawn with a backing of turf, and where the breeze still moved enough to allay the midges, and sat down to my picnic.

The silence – for the sound of birds and sea adds up to silence as beautifully as we ever know it in the noisy world of today – together with the sweetly moving air, and the scents of thyme and bell heather and sun-warmed bracken, all combined to distil something very potent. It was the sort of time and place where one might have expected an idea, the spring of a poem to well up from the quiet and the beauty. But sheer sensation – the warmth of the sun, the scent of the air, the mundane pleasure of tea and biscuits – simple well-being possessed me so that I could only feel, not think. A look at the sea below me told me that the tide was still low, though presumably it had begun to turn. A glance at my watch showed that it was still only ten past five. I leaned back again, shut my eyes, and let the sun have its way.

Gradually, as the breeze moved and eddied, I became conscious of a strange, soft sound that was filling the air. It was like the sound of the sea, but it was not the sea. It was like the wind, but was not the wind. It was as if sea and wind together were singing a lament, mourning with a not quite human voice, the voice of water echoing in a sea-cave, weird, unearthly.

I opened my eyes and sat up to listen, with the skin furring up on my arms.

Teach me to hear mermaids singing ...

The wonderful thing about literature is that great poetry can chime in on any thought or experience. As Donne's line rang in my head I placed the sound. Something Neil had told me about the island. This was Eilean na Roin, the Island of the Seals, and the grey seals came ashore here to breed and to bask. And now, perhaps, with the evening tide coming in, the seals had come with it, and were singing.

It is no wonder that, hearing that uncanny sound coming out of the mist, the old sailors ascribed it to mermaids or sirens or strange creatures of the deep. It is almost music, almost a human sound, but never quite. It is as if a wind instrument, soulless in itself, were being played through warm and breathing tissues instead of through wood or metal. And it is magical, compelling wonder. For me, it was the peak of a perfect day. I had done some good writing, and I had heard mermaids singing.

Very slowly, and keeping down below the seals' horizon, I crept forward towards the sound of singing. At last I gained the crest of a rise, and there below me stretched the sloping flat rocks, and yes, the mermaids were there, their fur dry in the sun, their bodies slack and contented, their eyes closed, enjoying the afternoon, exactly as I had done myself. A fat, grey mermaid, waving her flippers gently, turned on her back to show a pale, spotted stomach. Another came heaving out of the sea and flopped to where her calf lay, and, delightfully, the baby nuzzled in to suck. Not very far from me another baby lay, apparently full fed and contented. It saw me, and the big eyes stared with mild curiosity, but without fear. This was Eilean na Roin, and I was only a passer-by.

It was time to go. Reluctantly, I inched backwards without disturbing the sleeping nursery, and stood up. I took another glance at my watch. Ten past five.

Ten past five?

It had been ten past five when I had last checked on the time.

I held the watch to my ear – it was battery-run, but a faint tick could normally be heard. No sound. And now that I thought about it, I had vaguely wondered at the 'good time' I had made on my walk from the cottage, and at the leisurely stretch of time I had had on the island. Had I even left my cottage at two o'clock? My watch must have been gradually slowing to a stop all day.

I ran.

I could still see the causeway. I could also see the rock that Neil had pointed out to me, still half out of water. It was all downhill to the causeway, and the turf was smooth. I would make it.

I had forgotten the other thing that Neil had told me. 'The tide,' he had said, 'comes in like a horse trotting.'

And it did. Though the marker stone had been half out of water when I started to run, the whole barrage of banked stones, with the causeway atop, was suddenly aswirl and, as I raced for the crossing, the level seemed to rise a foot or more.

I stood hesitating. I could probably still have got across, but as I have said, the stones of the causeway were thick with seaweed, and treacherous even when exposed. And though I can swim pretty well, the swirl of the tide was fierce, and looked dangerous; and besides, I had no desire to swim.

And of course the moments of dismay and indecision were moments lost. The next wave came round the point, and the marker vanished. So that was that. And the tide would be high at what? Midnight?

I had a few moments of fury, a fury compounded of shame at my own stupidity, the triteness of the situation, the thought of my cottage and supper and the cosy fireside. Then the fury faded. Other pictures took the place of these; Neil's tent, not far up the brae, and the possibility not only, at worst, of having its shelter for the night, but of my seeing from that vantage point when Neil came back with his boat. If so, and if I could attract his attention, he would surely bring the boat over for me.

I trudged up to the camp-site again, to find that there was no need even to look for driftwood for a fire. Inside that stout little tent was a very efficient camping-gas burner, complete with kettle, billycan, matches, tea bags and powdered milk. And investigating Neil's stores I found baked beans, sardines, a couple of small tins of ham, and some crispbread. Like the Swiss Family Robinson, I had very little to complain about. There was also, of course, a good sleeping-bag. I only hoped, as the sun sank lower and the breeze grew cool, that I was not going to be obliged to use it.

The seals sang until sunset, and then fell silent.

As dusk drew in, the air emptied of birds, and gradually

they, too, fell silent. Only the tide, full and flowing, filled the half-light of the Highland night with its cold sound. I could no longer distinguish the house, and even the boat-house, much nearer, was lost in the shadows. But no boat came in.

Long before the sky dimmed enough to let the stars through, I lit the gas burner and ate baked beans off a paper plate and finished off with tea and biscuits. Then I got into the sleeping-bag.

14

I had gone to sleep with the sound of the sea filling the
night with subdued song. What woke me was the land
singing.

At first it was part of a dream, which vanished as soon
as I woke and knew that I was alone on the broch island,
lying on the turf in a sleeping-bag, with my head pillowed
on my rolled-up sweater, but seemingly connected with
the earth itself, from which, apparently right below my
head, came a sound every bit as strange as the mermaids'
song of the seals.

It was a soft, slow moaning, punctuated with sharp little
sounds like cries; the earth grieving in a whisper, but in
some weird way with a purpose as if this were a language,
a communication. Crooning would be the better word

for it, and as the word suggested itself I had a swift and vivid mental picture of the colony of birds on the west of the island, birds aggressive, protective, maternal, tender.

Weird, perhaps, but not frightening. I sat up. The sound retreated, but still it was there, somewhere in the night, as if thrumming along some wire sunk in the ground. I slid out of the sleeping-bag and unzipped the tent opening. I stuck my head out and looked around me.

Twilight still, no more than that. The sky was clear, greyed over, with stars. The moon, a half moon polished thin at the edges, swam low and gave a little light. My world, the island, was drained of colour, but every shape was clear. Nothing stirred, no bird cried. But still, faint now but persistent, came that crooning subterraneous song. Then all at once, so subtly that I could hardly be sure when I first saw it, I realised that the sky was full of movement, small shadowy shapes skimming low over the ground, silently, as if bats or night-time swallows were criss-crossing my line of vision, swarming between the broch and the sea.

The stormy petrels. Mother Carey's chickens. The fragile, tiny black birds, nocturnal and solitary, that come ashore to nest, but spend most of their lives flying close above the sea-waves, come storm or shine. They must be nesting in the rabbit-holes beneath the turf where the tent was pitched, and in the broch, where the queer chemical smell I had noticed came, not from the plants, but from the holes where the birds sat on their eggs.

If anything had been needed to crown my day, this would have been it. To be here, alone in the Highland night, and to witness the flight of these marvellous creatures, so shy, so rarely seen . . . I found I was outside the tent, standing up with my jacket clutched to me, the better to see them. They took no notice of me; they were

136

creatures of the night, the air and the ocean, and I was only a piece of the land, meaningless, to be flown round like a boulder or a stump of wood.

I was brought back to the mundane present by the shiver of chill that ran over me. Pulling my coat more closely round me, I turned my attention from the dark shape of the broch and its flitting ghosts to my own situation. I looked across to where the Hamilton house must stand in its shadows. No light there. But that, of course, meant nothing. Even if Neil had returned while I had been asleep, he would take care not to show a light.

More importantly, somewhere in the early morning hours the tide was due to turn. I had no way of telling what time it was, but surely it might soon be possible for me to escape from my desert island and make my way back to the cottage and a warm bed.

I was not familiar enough, yet, with the light nights of the Highlands to be able to guess at the time, but the sky was paler, and the stars were fading. I took a few cautious steps forward to where, by craning, I could just make out the ghostly crescent of the beach opposite the pier. I could not see the state of the causeway.

Then suddenly, I heard it. A boat's engine, throttled back and purring softly, somewhere beyond the headland to the east. Neil, coming back to keep the promised watch on his house. And from where? Fishing?

At that moment, all that this suggested to me was the possibility of fresh mackerel for breakfast . . .

I dived back into the tent and scrambled into my sweater and shoes. I did zip the tent flap shut, but wasted no other time on housekeeping; I would come back in daylight to tidy up and replace the stores I had used. It was not possible to hurry downhill in that half-light, so I made myself go slowly, and at last reached the beach and the end of the causeway.

It was almost uncovered. Almost – but I could just make out a narrow stretch half-way over where the water flowed smooth and fast with each swell. As I craned to see, the next wave broke and swirled, luminous with foam. Even if I failed to attract Neil's attention, I would probably be able to cross quite soon.

I found that I could no longer hear the boat's engine. I knew very little about boats, and had hated what little experience of sailing I had had, but it seemed unlikely that any boat would shut down its engine until it was safely round into the bay, or even then. I strained to hear, and had just decided that it would be difficult to hear an idling motor over the lap and rush of the sea in the channel, when I saw the light.

Not a boat's riding light; this was the small, dodging light of an electric torch coming round the path that skirted the headland. It was the path from my cottage, and I remembered the little cove called Halfway House, a cove where in any weather a boat might tie up safely and its owner make his way round to Taigh na Tuir. Its owner who did not want, or did not dare, to bring his boat round to the jetty? Not Neil, then. Someone else who did not want his visit known. Ewen Mackay.

The mackerel disappeared from the breakfast table, and the mystery came back with a rush. It was certainly Ewen Mackay. I could see him now, outlined fairly clearly against the light background of the beach, as the torch-beam cleared the path and he came fast along the shore towards the boat-house.

I sat down on the sand, in the darkness cast by a large boulder. He would never see me unless I moved. He was at the boat-house. A flash of the torch again, as if to check that no boat was there, then he turned to face the causeway, took something from a pocket and raised what were apparently night-glasses to his eyes. I froze in the shelter of my rock, but the glasses were aimed higher, at the tent. I had a momentary qualm; what would he read into the carefully closed flaps? That Neil was not sleeping there after all, or merely that he shut the flaps at night against the midges or the weather? I supposed, since to him Neil was only 'John Parsons', it did not matter either way, and if Ewen saw the little pile of debris – tins and used paper plates and my thermos – that I had left outside the tent, it would surely go to persuade him that Neil was safely ensconced on the island.

But, unfortunately, Neil was not even safely ensconced in the house, as he should have been, so Ewen Mackay was free to resume whatever his business had been there on Wednesday night. And with no witness but me.

I sat very still. He turned away, apparently satisfied, then pushed the glasses back into his pocket, flashed the torch briefly down at the rough stones of the pier, and went away with long strides in the direction of the house.

The next wave broke with a crash and a swirl and a dangerous-looking suck of water back into the channel. Not this time. Nor next. Nor the time after, I thought, even if the causeway came clear. There was no way I was going across to follow Ewen Mackay to spy on his activities at the house. If he really had left his boat in the cove round the point, he would have to come this way again, and I would certainly be able to see if he brought anything with him. I hugged my jacket close round me, and waited.

*

It seemed a very long time before he came back. The tide had cleared the causeway, and it was perceptibly lighter, when he came out through the stone arch of the garden gate. He carried what looked like a bag, bulging with something, over one shoulder. He made his way rapidly to the boat-house – there was no need, now, for the torch – and disappeared behind it. Almost at once he reappeared, without the bag, and set off again, walking fast, for the house.

I stood up, the better to see the state of the causeway, and made some rapid calculations. Though it was now possible to cross, the central stones were still wet, and in that poor light would be treacherous. It was an easy decision to make. Sensibly, I decided to wait and see.

Which was just as well, as this time he came back after a very few minutes. He was carrying a flat, square object which looked heavy. When he had left that, too, behind the boat-house, he emerged stretching his arms as if in relief, as he stood once more scanning the bay and the shadowy slopes of the broch island.

And that seemed to be it for the night. He vanished again behind the boat-house, and when I saw him again he was aiming fast for the cliff path, with the bag once again slung over his shoulder. I watched him round the end of the point, and out of sight, then ran for the causeway.

I got across without mishap, and was at the back of the boat-house within seconds. The square object was there, leaning against the wall. It looked, in that half-light, like a big framed picture, propped up with its face to the wall.

It *was* a picture. I tilted it to see. A portrait, unglazed, in oils, with a heavy, ornate frame. The portrait of a man, not young, in country tweeds, with a gun over his shoulder and a spaniel at heel. I did not know enough about painting to recognise it, or even guess at its value, but in the present-day crazy art market even a relatively modern painting might well be very valuable, and this one was apparently worth the trouble and risk that Ewen Mackay had taken. I toyed with the idea of taking it myself, and hiding it somewhere, but it was almost too heavy for me to carry, and there was nowhere much nearer than the house itself where it could be hidden. The boat-house was too obvious, and anywhere in the woods or garden was still wet with the night's dew. Besides, the move would hardly help, only alert him and start him searching, not just for the picture, but for whoever had moved it.

In any case, no need. I took a quick breath of relief as I heard it; the engine of another boat, throttling down to a murmur as she crept into the bay.

This time I waited to make sure before I ventured out on the jetty, but it was Neil's boat, and Neil himself standing ready to step out of it as it nosed in alongside the landing-place.

15

I ran to him, stumbling and nearly falling on the rough stones of the jetty. He jumped out of his boat and caught my arm to steady me.

'*Rose?* Rose! What on earth are you doing here?'

'Sh! Keep your voice down! He's been here again. I saw him go up to the house –'

'Hang on. Take it easy. You're shaking . . . Why, you're cold –'

'I'm not cold. I'm all right. Neil, it's Ewen Mackay. I saw him – never mind how, I'll tell you later, but the point is, he's been up to the house and taken things. Brought them down here and then gone off along the cliff path with them. He'll be coming back, because he left something here –'

'Along the cliff path? Did you hear a boat?'

'Yes. I thought he must have left it in that place round the point, Halfway House. Did you see anything as you came in?'

'No, but you can't see into that cove from the way I came. But what are you doing here? No, that can wait. You say you saw him go up to the house and take something? You mean you actually saw him breaking in?'

'No. I was over on the island. I saw him take a look at the boat-house first, then, when I suppose he saw you weren't home, he went up towards the house, and after a bit he came back with a bag, you know, like Santa Claus, slung over his shoulder. It looked like that duffel bag of yours, and it was heavy. He dumped it down behind the boat-house and went back towards the house, then after a bit he came down again with a picture, and dumped that, then he took the bag and made off up the path with it.'

'Hold on a minute. A *picture?*'

'Yes. A big one. It's behind the boat-house, there. I took a look at it.'

'There's no picture in the house worth stealing.' He moved quickly to knot the boat's rope through a ring sunk in the jetty. 'Let's have a look. Maybe there was one I didn't know about ... Good God!'

'Do you know it?'

'I should. It's Great-Uncle Fergus.'

'Valuable?'

'Good heavens, no. Not even good, apparently, though it's very like him, and dear old Sam – the dog – and Aunt Emily loved it. She used to say it was the best thing in the house. It was in her bedroom.' He was looking around him as he spoke. 'This was all? This and the duffel bag?'

144

'All I saw. I heard the boat, and then I saw him. He only made the two trips to the house.'

'The duffel bag. Could he have been carrying guns – shotguns – in it?'

'I don't think so. Guns? You don't mean –?'

'Yes.' His voice was grim. 'I told you I was going to check the house. Uncle Fergus's guns have gone missing. I've been to the mainland to report it. So if he did take them, it must have been when he was here before.'

'And they could be in his boat, couldn't they? Neil,' I said, urgently, 'he did take this picture tonight, and whatever he took it for, it's got to mean he'll be coming back for it, and soon. Look, if you put your boat into the boathouse now, he wouldn't see it till he got right down here again, and then perhaps –'

I stopped. Clear in the silence we heard an engine start.

Neil grabbed my arm again. 'Quick. Get in. He's not coming back, he's running for it. He must have heard me. Come on!'

Somehow I was in the boat, and Neil had cast off and was edging her out from the jetty. She backed in a gentle arc to face the open sea, and as Neil gunned the engine she jumped forward and then settled to a smooth, fast pace.

'There he is. No, there! You're too far out!' I had to shout it above the noise of the engine. I pointed to where, just visible against the dark background of the cliffs, the grey boat raced, the foam white under her bows and in her long wake.

Neil shook his head and made some gesture which I could not interpret, but as it was obvious that he, too, had seen *Stormy Petrel* and knew what he was about,

145

I let it be. There were a hundred questions still to be asked and answered, but at this speed and in this noise speech was impossible. I hung on, keeping one eye on Neil in case I could help him, and the other on *Stormy Petrel*.

Now I thought I could see what Neil was trying to do. The two boats were running along the coastline on almost parallel courses, Ewen close in, perforce following the jagged line of the shore, and our boat (I found later that she was called *Sea Otter*) on a straight course some way out. When on two occasions Ewen turned to make for the open sea, Neil, increasing our speed slightly, held on to what looked like a collision course. Even though it must have been obvious that he would not hold to it at the last, the threat was enough to make *Stormy Petrel* veer again to her original course, and though she was trying to increase speed, and was perhaps a little more powerful than *Sea Otter*, we, on our straight line, could hold her comfortably.

We were almost round to Otters' Bay now. The headland looming ahead of us out of the growing daylight would be the one immediately to the west of the cottage. *Stormy Petrel* wheeled again towards us, and this time Neil gave her sea-room. In a moment I could see why. From the tip of the headland and for some way out to sea the waves were breaking white against half-submerged fangs and stacks of rock that had in time past broken away from the main cliffs. They were no real danger to anyone who knew the coast, and all the time the light was growing stronger. Ewen obviously knew his way, but although Neil gave him room he made no further attempt to break free, or even to reach open water. He slowed down to pick his way among the patches of white water quite close inshore, at one point even vanishing between a towering sea-stack and the main cliff, then, once past the headland, he throttled right back and motored tamely into Otters' Bay, making for the jetty there.

I turned in surprise to Neil, to see him pointing away from the bay towards where, in a cloud of spray, a power-ful-looking launch was heading fast towards us. I had never seen a police launch, but this one had an unmistak-ably official look about it, and in size and speed would be more than a match for either *Stormy Petrel* or *Sea Otter*.

Ewen Mackay was still tying up when we nosed gently in to rub shoulders with *Stormy Petrel*, and Neil jumped ashore and turned to hand me out.

'Why, Miss Fenemore! You were out with Mr Parsons, then?' Ewen straightened with a look of surprise and pleasure. With dark hair rumpled by the wind, flushed face and those brilliantly blue eyes, he looked very handsome. His expression was one of uncomplicated welcome, which altered as he turned to Neil. 'Or is it Mr Hamilton? Oh, yes, it took me a bit of time to recognise you, but I got there in the end. Did you have a good night's fishing? I've been out myself, and I didn't get a thing. Not a thing.' Another glance at me, apparently quite free of guile. 'Well, I'm glad he got you home safely ... It seems you've forgotten how to handle a boat, Neil, all those years in Dismal Swamp with canoes and muggers and billabongs, whatever they may be. Just what the hell were you doing? A game's a game, but you could have piled me up back there, and then you'd have had a few questions to answer!'

'I have one to ask.' Neil made no attempt at a normal

tone. His was grim and totally unfriendly. 'Where are the guns?'

*

'Guns?' asked Ewen blankly. 'What guns?'

It was some time later, and the scene had shifted to the cottage sitting-room which, with myself and the two men, and two large detectives, was rather crowded.

Ewen had shown surprise, which of course looked genuine, when the launch, on coming alongside the jetty, turned out to belong, not to the police, but to Customs and Excise, who announced their intention of searching the *Stormy Petrel*, while the detectives had 'a few questions to ask.' He did make the inevitable protest of the recently released prisoner: was he to be hounded wherever he went, just because of the recent trip 'abroad', and surely that debt was paid in full and he could be allowed to start again in, of all places, his old home, which he was only visiting in the hope of finding where his parents had moved to; to lose touch with his dear mother was not to be borne; he needed to talk with his parents, to explain things to them, and ask for their forgiveness. And why the Customs men anyway, and what on earth did they hope to find . . . ? And so on, still in that pleasant, reasonable voice, with eyes that were just guileless enough, appealing for sense and clemency from his audience.

The official section of that audience was attentive but impartial. Far from hounding him gratuitously, they said, they were acting on information received. They would like to search his boat. No, they had no warrant, but they could take him and the boat back to Oban, where a warrant could be obtained. No objection? Then, sir, they were much obliged, and we'll leave it to you chaps while you, Jimmy, come with me to the cottage and talk with Mr Mackay there.

Then, to me: 'If we may? I understand that you have rented the cottage, miss. Miss Fenemore, isn't it?'

I said that it was, and they were welcome to come in. He thanked me, and introduced himself as Detective-Sergeant Fraser, and his companion as Detective-Constable Campbell.

I unlocked the door and led the way in. Ewen came, with a shrug and a smile and a lifted eyebrow, and the two detectives close behind him. Neil followed them in and shut the door. He was rather pale, and tended to watch the policemen rather than Ewen. I noticed that Ewen did not look in his direction.

'"On information received?"' he said, looking from one detective to the other. 'From whom, and about what? It must be serious, to have brought you out on that TV-type chase? And why the Customs people? Just what is this all about?'

The sergeant consulted a notebook. 'You hired the boat *Stormy Petrel* on June fifteenth from one Hector McGillivray of Uig on the island of Faarsay?'

'Yes. At least, I suppose it was the fifteenth ... It was three days after – Yes, the fifteenth. So what? I paid him, didn't I?'

'We have reason to believe,' said the sergeant, taking no notice of the question, 'that this boat has recently been involved in illegal traffic, and that the said operation was centred on the island of Faarsay.'

'Illegal traffic?' Ewen looked taken aback, then he laughed. 'Faarsay? Do you mean that old Hector's been poaching salmon again? But how does that affect me? I've only had the boat since the fifteenth, and before that I was –' A quick glance at me. 'I don't need to tell you where I was, do I?'

Once again the sergeant ignored the question. He watched Ewen steadily, while the constable, who had seated himself at the kitchen table, was taking notes. I thought that Neil, still over by the door, had a puzzled look. He glanced from time to time out of the window, as if to see what was happening down at the jetty.

'Not salmon,' said the sergeant. 'No. That would not bring the Customs here. They are looking for drugs.'

'*Drugs?*' This time, unmistakably, the shock was genuine. Ewen went as white as paper, and jerked upright in his chair. 'Drugs? What are you talking about? What's it got to do with me? Do you mean that that bloody fool Hector McGillivray fobbed me off with a boat that's – that's been –?' He stopped abruptly, biting his lip. The two detectives watched him, unmoved. Ewen sat back in the chair, and managed, very creditably I thought, a wry little smile. 'No wonder I got the damned boat cheaply,' he said. 'That comes of trusting chaps you've known all your life. Like Neil here. Well? Just when did all this so-called traffic take place? While I was safely locked away, I hope? As far as I'm concerned, I went to Hector because I knew him and I knew he'd let me have a boat cheaply, and I've used it since then – since the fifteenth – for pleasure, and now to come over and look my people up. So the Customs can search all they like; they won't find a thing.' And he included Neil, and then me, in the smile.

'Thank you, sir.' The sergeant glanced across at his colleague, saw him busily writing, then turned back to Ewen. 'You must understand that the boat's history is the affair of the Customs officers. They will talk to you later. We have our own inquiries to make. The launch gave us a lift over, to save us waiting for the ferry in the morning, that is all. But their search of your boat will save us time, as well. We have been lucky there.'

'Haven't you just?' said Ewen. 'Search for what, since you're not after all the heroin, or whatever I'm supposed to have been ferrying around the islands for a week?'

'We have reason to believe that you recently broke into Taigh na Tuir, the house belonging to Mr Hamilton here, and that you know something of the whereabouts of two valuable guns.'

'Guns?' repeated Ewen blankly. 'What guns? And who gave you reason to believe – ?'

'I did,' said Neil.

The surprise and shock registered yet again on Ewen's face were so real that even I, if this time I had not known better, would have thought them genuine. He turned to face Neil, and their eyes met. Ewen's were wide, injured, unbelieving; Neil's stony, but I could see the effort that kept them level. He was hating this. So, as a matter of fact, was I. I took the woman's way out. I retreated to the scullery to fill the kettle for a cup of tea.

'All right,' said Ewen to Neil. 'So supposing *you* explain. When am I supposed to have broken into the house, and why on earth should you think I know anything about any of the guns?' He sat back, apparently at his ease now, and crossed his legs. He was sitting in the same chair he had had before, on that late-night chat. 'Go on, Mr Parsons. Explain.'

There was a slight flush on Neil's cheekbones, and he seemed to be avoiding Ewen's eye. In view of the latter's steady, incredulous gaze, I could not blame him. He spoke to the hearthrug.

'I have already told Sergeant Fraser what happened. I was in the house the night you came back, and I watched you try the french windows, and then go round to the back to find the kitchen window locked, too. Possibly this made you uneasy, or possibly, with the storm blowing up, you did not want to take your boat across to the mainland again, so you decided to let things alone, and not risk taking any stolen goods on board. I watched you make off along the cliff path, as if you were making for Otters' Bay. The lawyers had told me that the cottage was let to a girl, who was here alone. For all I knew she was with you, but if she was just a visitor, I had to make sure she would be all right. So I followed you over, and found you here in the cottage. You had told Dr Fenemore that you thought your parents still lived here. That may have been true, but for the moment it's irrelevant.'

'That's wonderful!' Ewen was letting anger show now through the hurt. 'Anything that "may be true" is irrelevant! I'll tell you what is irrelevant, all that breaking and entering bit. You've just said yourself that all I did was try the windows. And why not? I'd been welcome in that house for as long as you had – longer, because you were away and I just about lived there. So go right ahead. What's all this about stolen goods and, for God's sake, guns?'

'Only that it wasn't your first visit since my great-aunt's death,' said Neil. 'You heard me say you "came back". I don't know when the first visit was, but it must have been very recent, possibly within a few days of your, er, release.' He paused, and looked across at Fraser.

The sergeant nodded. 'We know you hired a boat,' he said, 'straight away after you came out of prison, and came up to Oban. It was possible that you would come over to Moila, and of course there was nothing suspicious about that. And of course, to start with, we knew nothing about the boat's history. That, if you will allow the word, is also, for the moment, irrelevant.' An explosive sound from Ewen, which was ignored. The sergeant continued: 'But then Mr Hamilton found the valuable guns missing from Taigh na Tuir, and he reported that, with the story of your attempt to get into the house last Wednesday night. So our enquiries – and possibly the search of your boat – '

'Will get you nowhere. In fact,' said Ewen, and was there just a shade of genuine relief in his tone? 'you don't know anything at all. And as for the guns that are supposed to be missing from Taigh na Tuir, I can tell you all you want to know about that. When the Colonel was alive, he always took me shooting with him, and I helped look after his guns. He had quite a few, half a dozen there in the gunroom, with the light one he got for Neil as a boy, and I used to use. Mrs Hamilton hated guns, and never shot.' He looked up at Neil. 'Nor did you, when you could get out of it. And I was here when the Colonel died. You were in Australia, but even if you didn't know, the police here should have known ... The guns were sold. There were some that were quite valuable, a Churchill, I think, and a Boss, but they were sent to his gunsmith in Glasgow, Peterson and Briggs, and they were sold. As far as I know, the gunroom's been empty ever since. You should know, inspector. Don't you have to check them all nowadays, ever since the Hungerford affair?'

It was Neil who answered. 'You haven't mentioned the Purdeys.'

'Purdeys?'

'Don't pretend you didn't know about them. His favourite guns, the "specials" that were made for his father, my grand-uncle, in 1906, in the great days of shooting-parties. He shot once with King Edward. You knew all that, it was one of his favourite stories, and you must have known all about the guns. If they were valuable when Uncle Fergus died, they're astronomical now.'

'Well, and so what about them? Of course I remember them. He would never let me touch them, always cleaned them himself. They were sold with the rest, weren't they?'

'No. They were never sold, though the lawyers thought they had gone with the others. My great-aunt may even have deceived them deliberately; I don't know. I know she would never have parted with them. Her husband had asked her to keep them for me – keep them in the family, that is, but she didn't want to be troubled with all the precautions and inspections since the Firearms Acts. In fact I'm not sure that she even attempted to understand them. She merely packed the pair of Purdeys away in a trunk in the attic, locked the trunk, and told no one, and it must have been assumed that they were sold with the rest of his things. She left a letter for me, and she did include the Purdeys in her Will, and told us where to look. I looked, yesterday, and found the trunk empty. So I went to the mainland to report it, and we have been in touch with the lawyers, the gunsmiths, and the salerooms. No trace, but from our description one saleroom – it was Christie's – quoted us about thirty thousand pounds.'

'So?' Ewen's air was still jaunty, but the syllable came tightly.

'So it occurred to me that you, as my great-uncle's ghillie, might even have known what his plans were for his "specials". And putting that together with your visits to the house, and the guns' disappearance –'

Ewen had himself in hand again. He appealed to the sergeant. 'Do you hear that? And you call this grounds – *grounds* for suspicion? Isn't it time you either made a charge and got it over with, or you damned well got out of here, and Mister Bloody Hamilton with you?'

The sergeant did not answer. His head was turned towards the door, where we could hear footsteps approaching. I glanced at Ewen, relaxed once more in his chair, as the door opened and one of the Customs men came in.

His eyes sought the sergeant's, and he shook his head. 'Nothing. Of course it's only a rummage-search, but as far as we've gone, there's nothing in that boat at all that hasn't a right to be there.'

It seemed as good a moment as any for a change of scene. I carried a tray across and set it down on the table in the window. Outside it was full daylight. Soon the sun would break through the mist. I sat down by the table and lifted the pot.

'Would anyone like a cup of tea?'

16

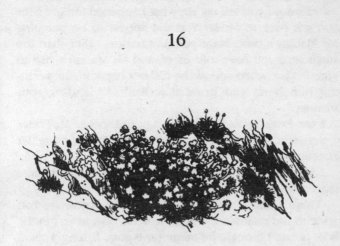

It seemed that the cliché of the detective story – that a policeman drinks nothing when on duty – did not apply in the islands. After that sea-trip through the damp mists of early morning, I didn't blame them. The sergeant accepted a cup of tea, then gave a nod to the detective-constable which the latter seemed to understand. He took the cup I gave him over to Ewen, who accepted it politely, shook his head to the sugar-bowl, and then sat sipping, for all the world as if this were a normal tea-party and he was waiting for someone to start the conversation.

As, of course, he was. For him, so far so good. Plenty of talk, but no proof of anything but a misdemeanour, so keep quiet and let the opposition make the running...

I poured tea for the four of them, then went to refill

the pot. When I had filled my own cup and sat down again by the table, the sergeant was speaking to Neil.

'So would you tell us, sir, what happened tonight after you got back to Moila? You did appear to be pursuing Mr Mackay's boat. Have you any reason, other than the suspicions you have told us of, and Mr Mackay's visit to your house, when you say he did *not* break in, for pursuing him here, and in what looked like a dangerous manner?'

I saw Ewen smile into his teacup, and spoke. 'Mr Fraser – Sergeant – may I tell you what happened before Mr Hamilton got back here to Moila tonight?'

He looked surprised. 'Then you were not on the mainland with Mr Hamilton?'

'That's right. I was not. I didn't even know he had gone to the mainland. When I saw his boat wasn't in the boat-house I thought he might have gone fishing. I spent the night on the island where the broch is.' I set my cup down. 'I can't pronounce its name. The one opposite Mr Hamilton's house. In English it's Seal Island.'

'I know the one. Eilean na Roin. Yes, Miss Fenemore?'

The constable, Jimmy, was writing busily. I did not look at Ewen, but was conscious that he had gone very still. I cleared my throat. 'I won't make a long story of it, but I went across there after lunch, to the House. I thought I might see Mr Hamilton there. He has told you about his first visit here; we have met since that day, and he asked me to go over whenever I wanted to. Well, I wanted to visit the island – Seal Island – because Mr Hamilton had told me there really were seals there at low tide. I went to the house first, and he wasn't there. Then I found that the boat-house was empty, so I assumed he was away with it, perhaps on the island, looking at the rocks on the far side – you know he's a geologist, I suppose? – or else out fishing. Well, I went across and the seals were there and I watched them. A bit later I found that my watch had stopped, and I had misjudged the tide. When I found that I couldn't cross by the causeway I went up to Mr Hamilton's tent and made myself some supper.' I looked at Neil. 'I didn't think you'd mind.'

'Of course I don't. You're welcome.'

'And just where is all this getting us?' asked Ewen. He set his empty cup down with a thump on the floor beside his chair, and gripped the chair-arms as if about to rise. 'Sergeant Fraser, do I have to say it again? Either you will show grounds for holding me, or you will please let me go, always providing that my boat is undamaged by your pals out there, or by my friend Neil's lousy seamanship.'

The sergeant ignored him. 'Go on, please, Miss Fenemore.'

'I was hoping that Mr Hamilton might bring his boat in, and take me off the island, but he didn't come, so I went into the tent and went to sleep. I woke a bit later, and thought by the light that enough time might have passed for the tide to have turned. I went outside the tent, and then I heard a boat's engine. Of course I thought it might be Mr Hamilton, so I put my jacket and shoes and things on again, and went down to the causeway. Then I saw Mr Mackay. He must have berthed his boat in Halfway House and then come round the cliff path and down to the pier.'

Dead silence. I had never had a more attentive class. The sergeant sat back in his chair. As if at a signal, the constable took over. 'You're sure it was Mr Mackay?'

'Certain. If you know the island you'll know that the channel isn't wide, and I was at the end of the causeway and he came right down to look in the boat-house. I suppose to check that it was empty.'

Ewen said sharply: 'Guesswork or lies, what does it matter? Sergeant, can't you see that there's nothing here? Low tide was between quarter and half past four this morning. She was stuck on the other side till three o'clock or near it. Could you identify anyone at that hour, and in that light?'

'If I was you I'd keep quiet, sir, and let the lady finish,' said the sergeant. 'Go on, please, miss. Never mind what you supposed. Just tell us what you saw.'

I took a deep breath. Somehow, telling my story in that charged atmosphere was like swimming against a strong current. 'I saw Mr Mackay get out some binoculars and look at the tent. I had closed it. He must have thought – sorry, skip that. Then he turned and went in through the garden gate. That path leads to the house.'

'Could you see the house from where you were?' That was the sergeant.

When I said 'No,' he nodded, and I realised that of course he knew the house, too. I ploughed on. 'I waited, and after a while – I put it at about half an hour – he came back, and he was carrying a bag over his shoulder. It was about the size – it could have been a duffel bag. It seemed to be quite heavy. He left it behind the boat-house and went back to the – that is, through the garden gate again.'

'Ah,' said Ewen, 'we have stopped supposing, have we?' The words were mocking, but when, caught off guard by the interruption, I met his eye, there was no mockery there. Anxiety, appeal, the knowledge that here, at last, was coming something that could be verified. That picture, that totally irrelevant portrait of Great-Uncle Fergus Hamilton, was still propped behind the boat-house, waiting to bear my story out, and to set the police searching for the duffel bag, which he must have dumped somewhere during the chase along the coast-line. I remembered suddenly how *Stormy Petrel* had crept out of view behind the big rock stack, close inshore, presumably after Ewen had seen the Customs launch approaching. Had he dumped the bag there somewhere, to be called for later?

They say that a computer works a problem out, from given data, in milliseconds. It still has nothing on the human brain. In the micromoment when I reluctantly met Ewen Mackay's gaze, I had gone back through all I knew of his story. The adopted boy, the good parents and their efforts to combat the bad heredity; the boredom of life on the quiet, remote island for an active, wild and clever boy with the added qualities of looks and charm. A boy who shared, with every other normal human child, the desire to be noticed, to be someone, to be important. And to the old gentleman at the big house, the Colonel, he did become important. Neil – presumably to damp Ewen's pretensions – had used the word 'ghillie'; Ewen himself had put it differently; he had been the old man's 'companion' whenever he went shooting. It was possible that the boy had really liked the old man, and the Colonel seemed to have trusted him. Then the Colonel died, and the widow (could one, wise after the event, ascribe it to that legendary feminine instinct?) had found no place for him. So the boy, with possible dreams of a better 'adoption' dashed, had left Moila, and, in the congenial bustle and anonymity of a big city, had learned to use the cleverness and charm and the middle-class manners he had learned, and had done well by them until some mistake was made, and he paid for it. Paid for it: and here Mrs McDougall's words flashed up on the computer screen, to be immediately blanked out and replaced by all I had seen and heard of Ewen myself since that Wednesday night. This was exactly what he had counted on before; other people's kindness and pity were, to him, weapons to his hand. Great-Aunt Emily Hamilton was just another widow to be robbed. And for the moment it was up to me to see that he did not get away with it.

'When he came back to the boat-house,' I said, 'he was carrying a large picture. An oil painting. He put that in the same place, behind the boat-house. Then he grabbed the duffel bag and set off up the cliff path with it. Neil's boat came in soon after, and when we heard Ewen's engine start we went after him. The duffel bag – well, never mind, that's supposition. But the picture is still there.' I drew a breath and said, not happily: 'That's all.'

'Well,' said Ewen, 'I should hope it is.' He got to his feet and held out his wrists in a consciously theatrical gesture. 'I give up. I did go up to the Hamilton house this morning in the small hours, and I did take down a picture. I admit it. But it was not theft. It was Colonel Hamilton's portrait, and I reckoned it was due to me. The Colonel always said I was like a son to him, the only son he had ever had, and Mrs Hamilton said that when she had gone I might have it to remember him by.'

'She would never have done that. She disliked and distrusted you,' said Neil, angrily.

'And what would you know about that? You were never there, only on holiday from school, so what would you know about the way they felt about me?'

'Plenty.' Suddenly, between the two men, a real spurt of antagonism had sprung up. 'And what you felt about them, too. Oh, yes, you got on fine with my great-uncle, but you and Aunt Emily never hit it off, and there are plenty of folk in Moila who know that and will swear to it.'

'Then will you tell me why I should go to the trouble

and the risk, yes, because I'm admitting I went into the house, and I did it while you were out because I knew fine that this was the line you'd take – why should I want the picture, if it wasn't promised, and if it wasn't that he'd been like a father to me, more than the one I'd had to call my own?'

There it was again, the indefinable but clear emphasis on the word 'father'. It was clear to me because of Ewen's earlier hint at a possible connection between himself and Neil's family, the suggestion that the adopted son of the gardener might in fact be a Hamilton love-child, and hated therefore by the Colonel's wife.

'Probably,' said Neil, in a tone nastier than I would have thought him capable of, 'because you heard my great-aunt say that it was the most valuable thing in the house, and you're too damned ignorant to know better.'

'And was it?' asked the sergeant, who, ignoring Ewen's theatrical gesture, had seemed quite content to watch and listen.

'Valuable? Heavens, no, it's very ordinary. But it was like him, and so she valued it.'

Quite suddenly, I had had enough. I got to my feet.

'Sergeant Fraser, if you'll excuse me. It's been a long night, and I want a bath and a change and some breakfast. The first two right this minute. Of course you're welcome to stay as long as you have to, and if you're still here when I come down I'll see what I can manage for breakfast.'

He was beginning some sort of protest about that, but I did not stay to listen. I went upstairs and into my bedroom and shut the door.

*

I have not yet got it straight with my subconscious. It is possible, I admit, that I deliberately wasted time in the hope that it would be all over and the police, preferably along with Ewen Mackay, would be gone before I went downstairs again. I did not know whether in fact any charge could be brought; that would surely depend on whether the duffel bag could be found, and what its contents were. The picture, except in so far as it bore my story out, could be ignored. It was even possible, I thought, as I stripped off my slept-in clothes and reached for a dressing-gown, that the whole situation would collapse into a mere incident of petty theft; it was the alleged theft of the guns that had brought the police across so quickly, and there seemed to be no way of knowing if Ewen had ever touched them. Was it, as he had bitterly pointed out, a case of 'give a dog a bad name'? It was an uncomfortable thought, but there was nothing to be done except tell the truth and leave it to the professionals. I could hear them still at it, question and answer, when I crossed the little landing to the bathroom and shut the door. Then nothing could be heard above the gushing of the taps.

Back in my bedroom, still not hurrying, I dressed. As I was brushing my hair, a sound from outside took me over to the window, to see Archie's Land-Rover starting on its careful way downhill towards the cottage. There was someone with him – two people, I thought.

I whirled to look at the bedside clock. Surely the ferry was not in yet? It was not due for another half hour at least. My brother could not get here much before nine or half past, and I had been counting on this unpleasant situation's resolving itself before that.

The Land-Rover bumped down the last curve of the track, and came to a halt. Ann Tracy jumped out, with

Megan behind her. Someone must have opened the cottage door, because I heard them come right in, and then a babel of voices and questions.

It could not be put off further. I went downstairs.

17

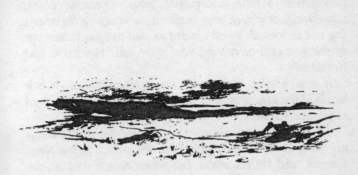

'Here she is!'

'Oh, Rose!'

Megan and Ann spoke together. They were both sitting at the table in the window. Just inside the door, which was shut, stood Archie McLaren. Seeing the boats at the jetty, he must have come with the girls to the cottage to see what was happening, and now, presumably, he would stay to see the drama out, and the ferry passengers would have to take care of themselves.

The scene in my sitting-room was certainly set for drama. Ewen still sat in the chair by the hearth, with Sergeant Fraser across from him, but the detective-constable had moved his chair to block the doorway to the scullery, and Neil was beside the fireplace, standing

167

with an elbow on the mantelshelf. Someone had pushed the Calor gas poker into the dead logs in the fireplace, and added the rest of the peat from the hearth. The fire had caught, and was burning cheerfully.

'Hullo, there. Good morning, Archie.' I greeted the newcomers a little uncertainly, then – because doing something, anything, was better than standing there trying not to look at Ewen – went to pull the gas poker out of the fire and turn it off. 'An early call? Have you had breakfast?'

It was a silly remark in the circumstances, but it bridged the moment. Ann spoke breathlessly. She looked tense and excited.

'Rose, we had to come . . . Of course we didn't know anything like this had happened, the police being here, I mean, and Mr Hamilton, but when Archie told us, we knew we'd have to come and tell you what happened yesterday.'

I went across to the sofa and sat down, looking enquiringly at Sergeant Fraser.

He nodded. 'Yes, it does have to do with this. It seems that while you were away on the island yesterday, the young ladies came down here. What they have told us may be important, but since you are the owner, the lessee, rather, of this cottage, we waited for you. Perhaps Miss Tracy or Miss Lloyd would repeat their story for you?'

I raised my brows at them. Megan, looking flushed and unhappy, shook her head. Ann leaned forward.

'Yes. We came down here in the evening. Yesterday evening. We wouldn't have disturbed you if you'd been busy, but we wanted to watch for the otters again. You weren't at home, so we went up there – ' she gestured vaguely – 'behind the cottage, and found a place we could watch from without being seen. You know, a hide.'

'Ann.' It was Megan, her voice low. 'Not all that. Just finish.'

Ann took a breath. She seemed to have no difficulty in looking at Ewen. 'All right. He came. Ewen Mackay there. His boat came in to the jetty. He got out and went to the cottage door and knocked. Because of what we had heard about him, we stayed where we were and didn't say anything. He knocked again, but of course there was no answer. Then he went in. He had a key. We didn't know what to do, so we stayed put and watched. He didn't stay long – just went in and called out, as if he was checking to see that the place was empty. Then he went back to his boat.' She paused. 'Megan?'

'No. You.'

'He took something out of the boat, a bundle. It was wrapped in what looked like cloth, thick, but it was long, and stiff, not just cloths, I mean. He went round the back to that shed, not the loo, the tool-shed, and of course that was just below us and we saw it all. He was hurrying. He went into the shed. He wasn't there long. When he came out he didn't have the bundle. He went to the boat and then away.'

She stopped. Silence for a moment. Megan said, miserably: 'We waited, but you didn't come, so after a bit we went down and had a look in the shed, but there wasn't anything to see. Nothing that seemed to matter, I mean. So we went home. We thought of telling Mrs McDougall, but we decided you ought to know first. Anyway, she'd gone to bed. She leaves the door for us – actually I don't think it's ever locked. Then this morning Archie came in at breakfast-time and said the police were here, and the Customs, so we knew there must be something really wrong, and he said he'd bring us down.'

The sergeant got to his feet. 'You did right, miss. And now, Miss Fenemore, with your permission, we would like to take a look at that shed ourselves.' A look down at Ewen. 'Unless Mr Mackay would like to save us the trouble?'

Ewen smiled at him. He had abandoned any pretence of indignation, and was merely patient and interested. 'Look and be damned,' he said, and leaned back in his chair.

'Very well. Jimmy, you stay here, but give a shout for Sandy or Calum to come in here, will you? . . . No, not you, Archie. There's the ferry now, did you not hear her? You'd better go. You'll hear soon enough what happens – but till you do, see you keep your mouth shut, do you mind me?'

'I mind you.' Archie sketched a farewell gesture to me and the girls, and went, so quickly and willingly that I was surprised, till I remembered that of course he would be back here very soon with Crispin, and possibly in time to see the result of the search.

'Just a minute.' Neil put a hand out as the detective, with one of the Customs men, made for the door in Archie's wake. 'If I come with you – '

'No. You'll stay here, please, Mr Hamilton.' The sergeant did not add that three women would be no help if Jimmy should have any trouble with Ewen, but his meaning was plain enough. I expected to see Ewen smile, but saw, with a queer, unpleasant little thrill, that he was staring up at Neil, with something new in his face. He had lost colour again, and over the prison pallor shone a faint sheen of sweat, and I saw him swallow a couple of times, as if his throat hurt him.

Neil said: 'I doubt if they would find anything, sergeant, short of taking the shed to pieces, but if you let me go, I

know where to look. I suppose there'd better be someone with me, as witness –'

'All right,' said Ewen abruptly. 'All right.' He sat up,
flexing his shoulders, and slanted a look up at Neil. I saw
nothing there now but a sourly humorous acceptance.
'I'd forgotten. Stupid of me.'

'Forgotten what?' demanded the sergeant. He looked
alert and vigorous, not like a man who had lost a night's
sleep. At his gesture, the other men stayed where they
were.

It was Neil who answered him. 'Only that he stole my
trout rod once, when we were boys, and I saw him fishing
with it later, and followed him back home – here – and
watched him hide it in a place he'd made in the garden
shed. There were a few other things there that I knew
had gone missing from people's boats and gardens and
so on. I didn't give him away – boys of that age don't –
so his parents never knew. I waited till I saw him using
the rod again, and, well, I took it back.' He looked at
Ewen, and for the first time there was something like
sympathy there. 'Eventually.'

'It was quite a fight,' agreed Ewen. 'Well, go on. Go
and get them.'

'The Purdeys?'

'The Purdeys. And I hope you get well and truly done
for all the years of illegal possession.'

The sergeant nodded at Jimmy, and he, with Neil and
one of the Customs officers went out of the cottage.

✦

I caught Megan's eye, and what I saw there made me get
to my feet.

'Sergeant Fraser, my brother is due to arrive on this ferry, so Archie will be down here again soon. Will you want Miss Lloyd and Miss Tracy again, or may they go back with him?'

'Surely. I know where they are staying, and we will be in touch again before they leave. Wednesday, you said, Miss Tracy?'

'Yes, that's right.' Ann was on her feet, reluctantly, I thought. Megan was already making for the door.

'Then will it be all right if we wait outside?' I asked.

'Surely,' he said again. He had risen from his chair when the other men went out of the room, and now he moved to open the door for us.

Megan paused on the threshold and looked back to where Ewen sat, with every appearance of ease, in the armchair by the fire. She cleared her throat, but the words came hoarsely, in a rush. 'I'm sorry. I truly am. But it was the truth.' She looked and sounded like an awkward and unhappy schoolgirl.

Ewen raised his head and smiled at her, a smile full of his own powerful brand of charm. He lifted one hand, and turned it over, palm up. 'Of course it was. Don't give it a thought. I never had a hope anyway, did I? Dogs with bad names ... Goodbye, then. Enjoy your holiday.'

I saw the tears start to her eyes, and said savagely under my breath: 'Damn you, Ewen Mackay!' then, with an arm round her shoulders, urged her through the doorway and down the path to the beach.

Ann spoke quickly, fiercely. 'Look, Meg, don't upset yourself. What could we do? We had to tell the police, and it's not as if there was any doubt about it, because he admitted it himself, so it's nonsense to talk about dogs with bad names. The man's a thief and a liar, we knew that from Mrs McDougall, and you said so yourself,

172

remember? He had it coming to him, so don't talk such balls!'

'It was a Judas thing to do. I know Mrs McDougall told us about him, but he was nice to us, and we didn't have a thing against him ourselves. I know we had to tell the police, but it still feels like a Judas thing to do.'

I sat down on the edge of the jetty, where it jutted from the sand above the high tide mark, and pulled her down beside me.

'Megan.' I was still angry, but not with her. 'This is nonsense, and you've got to snap out of it here and now. Listen to me. I had a talk with Mrs McDougall myself last night – no, Saturday night. She told me more than she told you. Ewen Mackay is not a man to be pitied, except in that he was born without scruple, yes, literally without a scruple of conscience. He had every chance, loving parents, an indulgent patron, brains, looks, charm. All assets. The only thing he didn't have was money, and to get that he set out in cold blood to rob people – some of them as poor as himself, but who had spent their lives working, and had saved something for their old age. He robbed them, without a second thought, of everything they had. Think about *them*. The last one – the one he went to prison for – was an invalid of eighty-five, and he robbed her of something less than three hundred pounds. All she had. Not even as much as it would cost him to hire that boat of his.'

' "The smiler with the knife under the cloak," ' quoted Ann.

'It doesn't matter a damn about the guns, or whatever he had in that duffel bag,' I said. 'But you see what this dog with a bad name is like ... He comes out of the slammer, having seen the notice of Mrs Hamilton's death, hires a boat and comes straight up here to rob the dead,

173

and perhaps – though we don't know if that bit was true – to settle again on the parents who left their home to get away from him.'

Megan nodded. 'Yes, I'm sorry. I do see. It was only seeing all those police, and all they wanted was to catch him, and all he could do was sit there, and it was four to one, eight to one counting us –'

'I know. It was beastly. But there was no Judas about it. Stick to that. It's over now, anyway. There they go. And it looks as if they've found the guns.'

The three men were coming round the corner of the cottage. Their search in the shed had apparently been successful. The detective-constable was carrying a slim, wrapped object, and under Neil's arm was the long, gleaming shape of a shotgun.

'They have indeed,' said Ann. She did not trouble to keep the satisfaction out of her voice. 'And let's hope that those so-special Purdeys do the trick, and put our friend Ewen straight back where he belongs.'

Megan sent her a look where a shadow of trouble still showed, but all she said was: 'I suppose it was because it was guns that the police came roaring over like that?'

'I don't think so,' I said. 'You heard what the sergeant said – no, that was before you came down here. Once Neil reported the guns missing they would certainly come over, but normally it would be by ferry; it wouldn't be so very urgent, and anyway I doubt if there's a police boat in Oban. But Ewen made the mistake of hiring a boat cheaply from a pal on one of the outer isles, and it was a boat that was suspected of running drugs in the islands. There've been cases, but I don't know much about them. Anyway, that's what brought the Customs men roaring over, to see if Ewen Mackay was into that racket, and I suppose the police thumbed a lift with them.'

'Drugs?' Megan looked horrified.

'I don't think he had anything to do with that. He was quite genuinely shocked and scared when he knew – and furious with the pal who'd flogged him the boat. His error.'

'Greed,' said Ann flatly. 'Tried to get a boat cheaply, so brought the sheriff's posse straight in. Serve him right. If he'd had till morning he might just have made it, and he could have come back for the loot later on.'

'I still can't see why he should have gone for those guns,' said Megan. 'With an empty house to choose from ... What's so special about "Purdeys"? If he'd just gone for the silver or whatever, he might have got away with it.'

'Twenty or thirty thousand pounds, and going up each year,' said Ann, who knew about such things. 'That's how special. I'm talking about honest prices, auction prices – if you call them honest ... He'd get less, of course, but it still made the trip worth while.'

'Good heavens!' said Megan, wide-eyed. The thought, unspoken, came to me again, that Megan's assets, as the daughter of a farm worker, were much the same as Ewen Mackay's. But they had got her to Cambridge on a good scholarship, and would get her very much further.

'That's what brought him back to Moila, to pick up the guns,' said Ann. 'And I suppose he thought that he might as well swipe some other stuff, whatever he had in that bag. But why the portrait?'

'Yes. Why?' Megan was, I was glad to see, back to her normal self. 'You can't tell me he went to all that trouble for auld lang syne?'

'You heard what Neil said,' I said drily. 'He'd been told

that it was the most valuable thing in the house, and because he knew nothing about pictures he believed it. Pictures are going even madder than guns at auction, aren't they, Ann?'

'I don't know much more about them than Ewen Mackay does, but I wouldn't give twenty-five pounds, let alone twenty-five million, for a daub of greenery yallery flowers,' said Ann, and Megan laughed. It was apparently something they had argued about before. But whatever she had been going to say was never said. Two things happened almost simultaneously.

The cottage door opened, and Ewen Mackay came out, with the two detectives, and Neil behind them. Ewen wore handcuffs.

And from the curve of the track came the note of the Land-Rover, as Archie McLaren returned to the scene of the crime, bringing my brother with him.

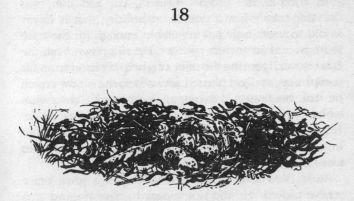

18

He brought another man as well. Climbing carefully out of the Land-Rover came a man apparently somewhere in his fifties, dressed, incongruously for the Western Isles, in a dark business suit two sizes too big for him, complete with waistcoat and a tie of such subdued and dreary colours that it had to be regimental or public school. His face, like his figure, looked as if it was meant to be fat and good-natured, but had been reduced by a very effective slimming diet, so that his cheeks looked flabby and his neck showed folds below the chin. His hair had thinned and receded, and showed a pepper-and-salt powdering of grey. With his pointed nose, smallish mouth, and twinkling eyes of some shade between grey and green, he looked like a good-tempered gnome. Of the Zürich, rather than the Disney variety: the suit was expensive, and his wrist-watch and cufflinks had the rich and unmistakable glint of gold.

In contrast my brother Crispin, tall and thin, was dressed exactly like a doctor on holiday, that is to say in old trousers only just reputable enough for the train journey, and an ancient sweater. He slid down from the Land-Rover, ignoring the offer of a helping hand from his companion, and got himself adjusted to the elbow crutch he had mentioned, a strong affair of tubular chromium which supported wrist and elbow on the injured side. His movements were careful, and he limped slightly, but he walked well enough to meet me, and leaned down to kiss my cheek.

'Rose. You look wonderful, and what a great place you've picked.' He did not appear to have noticed anything strange, yet, about the group of men further down the beach at the boats. 'This is Hartley Bagshaw, who travelled up with me.'

'Mr Bagshaw,' I said, and shook hands, murmuring the usual things about hoping the journey had been comfortable, and had they had breakfast, while wondering madly why Crispin had brought him along, and was I going to have to put him up and feed him, and at the same time trying not to miss what was going on down at the jetty's end. 'Are you on holiday, too?'

But Mr Bagshaw's gaze had gone past me, and he certainly had not missed what was going on. 'What the hell?' he said, explosively. 'That's a police boat, isn't it?'

'No, Customs, but –'

'And those men – they've got to be policemen. They *are* policemen! What goes on?' And then, fortissimo, 'Ewen Mackay? *Ewen Mackay?*'

The police had looked our way as the Land-Rover stopped, then had made some sort of tactful haste to get their man away before my visitors arrived. But now the whole group froze as Ewen, in the act of stepping, escorted, into the launch, stopped and turned, with the handcuffs clearly visible.

Mr Bagshaw froze, too, for two long seconds, then, starting forward, he exploded again into speech, and I learned three new words in the next three seconds, and then several interesting ways of using well-known and respectable words that would never have occurred to me in a lifetime. I caught a glimpse of Archie's face of startled horror, of Ann's mouth dropping open, of Megan's flushed cheeks, then Sergeant Fraser barked something, Ewen held up his cuffed wrists and laughed, and Mr Bagshaw shut his mouth with a snap, said: 'I beg your pardon, ladies. I got a shock. The police seem to have arrested a friend of mine. It must be a mistake. Excuse me.' And he darted down the beach towards the group there. In spite of the apology, he was still flushed, and all the good nature had vanished from his eyes, which were bright with fury and what might have been fear. Crispin said 'Steady on!' and moved to hold him back, but his injury checked him, and he stumbled, saved himself by grabbing at me, said 'Damn and blast,' and stood still, rubbing his leg. Archie, still looking outraged, called out: 'Hey, there!' and started down the beach after Mr Bagshaw.

It was reaction, I suppose, from the sleepless night, the unpleasant tensions of the recent interview in the cottage, and now this totally unexpected irruption into the scene. I wanted to laugh, and saw, suddenly, that the girls, clinging together on the jetty, were about to succumb to the same near-hysteria. I beckoned to them, controlling myself sharply, and when they came, introduced my brother.

'Ann, Megan, this is my brother. Crispin, meet Ann Tracy and Megan Lloyd.'

That did it. If I had hoped that the semi-formal introduction would sober us up, I had not reckoned on my voice sounding exactly like the lecturer's voice Megan had so wickedly imitated on the broch island; and now it was accompanied, in a cruel counterpoint, by another spate of angry and idiomatic speech from Mr Bagshaw, every word of which carried clearly up the beach to where we stood. The girls did manage to take Crispin's hand and say something, then they both went off, helplessly, into peals of laughter.

'His friend, he said...' That was Ann, wiping her eyes. 'What d'you suppose he calls people he doesn't like?'

'If we stay a bit longer,' quavered Megan, 'we might learn.'

'I would like,' said Crispin, 'to know just what has been going on here? If you three idiots will stop laughing for a moment and tell me –'

'Idiots, he called us,' wailed Ann. 'So rude. And we've only just met. Oh, R-Rose –'

I took a hold of myself, and of Crispin's arm. 'Come on, let's go in and get ourselves some coffee. Cris, I suppose you had breakfast on the boat? Well, I haven't had mine, and I don't suppose the girls have either. I haven't a clue what's going on now, but we can talk in the house. Come on.'

*

'They're coming back,' said Megan.

She was at the window, opposite me where I sat at the table finishing my coffee. All four of us – myself, Crispin and the girls – had started by declaring that we could not possibly eat any breakfast, and we had all ended up at the table with mugs of coffee and a stack of toast and marmalade, with a jar of local honey on the side. Crispin had even produced a bag of fresh doughnuts which he had bought on the ferry, but we did jib at those, and put them aside 'for afters'. No one said 'After what?' but we all knew. There would be no peace on this peaceful island until its storm centre had been removed.

Which might be at any moment now. *Sea Otter* was still at the jetty, rubbing shoulders with *Stormy Petrel*, but the Customs launch had gone, not back to the mainland, but along the coast towards Halfway House and the broch island. The detective-constable had gone with it, and Neil, along with Ewen and the Customs officers. It was to be assumed that they had gone to look for the dumped duffel bag: I wondered if, having admitted to the major theft of the guns, and with the picture sitting behind the boat-house as witness of my story, Ewen would settle for co-operation as the most sensible course.

If so, they might not be gone long. It seemed that Mr Bagshaw was nursing the same hope; he was down at the jetty, talking volubly to an impassive Sergeant Fraser, with Archie McLaren as an apparently fascinated listener. I had hoped that the latter was waiting to take Hartley Bagshaw back with him, but from what Crispin had told us, it seemed that he was here on business, and had come to see Neil.

Over our non-breakfast we had exchanged news and stories. First of all, Crispin's injury: this was still pain-ful, but mending normally, and though it would inconvenience him for some time, would not stop him getting around reasonably well, and the elbow crutch would allow him, he said, to use both hands for his camera. That being disposed of, we all – the girls and I – clamoured for an account of Mr Bagshaw, but Crispin refused to speak until we had filled him in on what Ann called the Great Moila Mystery, and the girls, who of course knew very little of what had been going on, supported him, so I told my story, and afterwards answered the questions they asked, while we drank coffee and munched toast, and watched the window for the return of the launch.

'More coffee?' asked Ann, when question and answer ran at length to a standstill.

We all refused, and Megan, picking the pot up, looked a question at me. 'What about Archie and Mr Bagshaw? Shall I make some more for them?'

'Not until we've heard my brother's side of it. Cris, who is Mr Bagshaw, what is he? And did he tell you what he wanted with Neil Hamilton?'

'And there did seem to be some connection between him and Ewen Mackay,' said Megan, reaching absently for a doughnut. 'Wouldn't you say?'

'They were friends, he said so,' said Ann, on a little bubble of laughter. 'But somehow not very likely ones. I wonder where they met?'

'I can guess,' I said, and Crispin cocked an eye at me. 'Am I right? Prison? Or didn't he confide in you that far?'

'Yes, it was, and oddly enough he did. There's something about coming through a disaster together that seems to lower the barriers, and he knew I was a doctor, of course. People get used to talking to us. He made no secret of the prison bit, in fact he seemed to want to go public on what had happened to him, so I'm not betraying a confidence. We travelled up together, and he did quite a lot of talking. He had just come out after doing two years, though he'd been innocent, he said, of any part in the fraud.'

'Of course. But – fraud? Do you mean he was in Ewen Mackay's beastly racket, watching the obit columns and robbing lonely old women?'

'No, no. He was one of the men caught up in the Prescott take-over scandal. You remember it? Three or four years ago.'

'I can't say I do. I don't take much interest in City goings-on. Do you remember it?' This to the girls, who shook their heads.

'It doesn't matter,' said Crispin. 'Actually, I may say, I believe him. He told me a good deal about the Prescott affair, and when I said he was "caught up" in it I meant just that. He's a tough little chap, self-made, from a rough background – you can ignore the Guards tie – but I'm sure he's relatively honest, and it was partly bad luck and partly a rotten partner that landed him with a conviction. However. The point is – the reason he's here – he's a property developer, and when Ewen Mackay, who was due out at about the same time, told him that he knew Moila, and that an old lady had died there recently, and there might be a good property for sale, Bagshaw was interested, and apparently Mackay promised, for a cut, of course, to help him negotiate with the family. Made out that he was practically one of them himself.' He raised a brow at me.

I shook my head. 'No connection,' I said, 'and there's no family to negotiate with, apart from Neil, who doesn't need any persuading anyway. But it figures. Ewen had plans of his own, didn't he? Go on.'

'Well, from what you've just told me, I gather that poor

little Bagshaw was lined up as a victim even before Mackay got out of gaol. Bagshaw arranged for Mackay to have funds to hire a boat and get up here to start things moving with the family . . . Which he certainly seems to have done.'

Megan said, forcibly for her: 'You were right, Rose. Not Judas stuff at all . . . Do you see? It means that even when he was in gaol he was watching the papers for someone else to cheat!'

'Leopards,' said Ann, 'probably wouldn't change their spots even if they could.'

'I wonder how much Mr Bagshaw gave him for the boat hire?' said Megan. 'And he even tried to make something out of that by taking the poor old *Stormy Petrel*.'

'His mistake,' said Ann. 'Go on, Crispin. So that's Mr Bagshaw's business with Neil Hamilton? He's going to buy the house?'

'And Seal Island?' asked Megan, and looked distressed when my brother nodded.

'He's already made an offer,' I told them. 'At least, I suppose it was he. Through an agent. He must have set it in motion on Ewen's say-so while he was still in gaol.' I told them what Neil had said.

Crispin nodded again. 'Yes, it was Bagshaw. He's very keen. Apparently Mackay really sold him on it. I doubt if the house matters; he'd want something a good deal bigger, but of course there's plenty of room to build. It's the beaches and the island that are the attractions; you know the sort of thing, a marina and what he calls a big "leisure centre", and a "luxury apartment block" with a golf course –'

'Along the machair?' asked Megan, almost in a whisper.

'If that's what it's called. The strip along the west coast.

He showed me the map when we talked in the train. I did try to say something about the beauty of the islands and what this kind of development does to it, but it was no use. I know. It's grim. But what can one do?'

'Surely, there must be something?' I said. 'I know Neil's thinking of selling, and in fact he's granted the option, but I doubt if he'd want to see that kind of development here, and there might just be some way to stop it, and wait for a different offer?'

'From what you've told us, I doubt it,' said my brother. 'Bagshaw told me about the option, and I gather he's paying a very good price – more than this sort of property usually fetches nowadays. I've no idea how binding the agreement is, or what the details are, but as I said, he's still very keen. That's all I know.'

'But if Mr Bagshaw's fury at Ewen Mackay was because Ewen had come up here on his own and couldn't resist a spot of easy pillage, perhaps he – Mr Bagshaw – is afraid that may have queered his pitch? It sounds as if it may not be all that binding,' I said hopefully. 'I mean, if Ewen's a crook, and he's had something to do with the offer Mr Bagshaw made – '

'We'll soon know,' said Megan, at the window. 'They're coming back.'

*

I am not sure what I had expected to happen when the launch returned, but it was a relief to find that we were not to be confronted again with Ewen Mackay. He did not, in fact, reappear, but must have been below with the detective-constable. The launch came round neatly and reversed in beside *Sea Otter*, stern to the jetty, and

Neil got out, then he and the sergeant made for the cottage.

Not before, predictably, they had been ambushed by Mr Bagshaw, who still apparently had a great deal to say, but the sergeant forged placidly through it, and came on up, with Bagshaw close beside and still talking. Neil stopped for a few moments' chat with Archie, then he, too, came up.

The sergeant was brief. The duffel bag had been recovered, he told us, and found to be full of small stuff, mostly silver, but with a few pieces of china and other objects of virtu wrapped in towels and various kitchen cloths, and the clock from the drawing-room mantelpiece. Apart from one vase, which was cracked, and the clock, which would never be the same again, nothing was damaged. The bag had been dumped into shallow water when Ewen's boat had slipped out of sight behind the rock stack, and had sunk gently to lie on a sandy bottom. And yes, they had found the portrait of Great-Uncle Fergus, propped just as I had said behind the boat-house, and yes, Mr Mackay had been helpful in the recovery of the duffel bag, and would now go back to the mainland to assist the police with their inquiries ... And no, there was no need for any further search of *Stormy Petrel*. They were satisfied that Mr Mackay had nothing to do with any Customs offence, so the boat could remain here. He understood that Mr Bagshaw had in fact provided the money for the hire, so if he wished to use the boat he was free to do so.

Meanwhile, said Sergeant Fraser, suddenly human, he was sorry to have had to intrude on Miss Fenemore's holiday, and he hoped there would be no further trouble. Of course Mr – or was it Professor? – Hamilton would have to be called upon later, and statements would be taken from Miss Fenemore and the young ladies, but in the meantime he hoped that we would forget all about it and enjoy our holiday, and now he really must go . . .

I shook hands with him and murmured something, conscious again of that missed night's sleep, and of quite a lot of talking to get through before peace came back to the ivory tower. But, mercifully, Mr Bagshaw seemed content to keep quiet and let the sergeant go. From the fragments of speech I had overheard as the men came up to the cottage, I thought that he, Mr Bagshaw, had been eagerly trying to dissociate himself from Ewen Mackay's latest exploits, except as the innocent provider of *Stormy Petrel*, and was now only anxious to be allowed to sink into the background and see the Customs launch safely on its way.

Finally the sergeant took himself off. Neil went with him down to the jetty, stood for a few moments more talking, then the two men shook hands, and the policeman jumped aboard. The launch moved off, took a gentle curve out of the little bay, then, with a suddenly white wake, headed fast for open water and was lost to sight beyond the headland.

It was as if its disappearance had been a signal, as definite as the dropping of the curtain in a play. Drama and mystery were finished with; here was only a group of ordinary people who wanted to get on with their ordinary lives; who had been touched for a moment with the end of a live wire and shocked into unaccustomed and unpleasant action, then left to recover themselves and hope for the burns to heal.

Archie, with a muttered word, went down to the Land-Rover and lugged Crispin's cases out of the back. Crispin, limping after him, lifted out the precious camera equipment himself. They took the things upstairs and into the bedroom I showed them. Megan was busily clearing the table, and Ann had vanished into the scullery, from which presently came the sound of washing-up and the smell of fresh coffee brewing. Mr Bagshaw, silent now and looking exhausted, had sunk into the chair recently vacated by Ewen Mackay, and was staring at the ashes of the fire. In the wrinkled clothes that had fitted him before the years in prison, he looked deflated and absurd, and, somehow, suddenly vulnerable.

I said gently: 'Mr Bagshaw, you must be tired. There'll be some coffee in a minute, and then perhaps you'll let Archie McLaren take you back to the village. Why not leave your business with Mr Hamilton till after you've rested? I'm sorry we haven't room to put you up here, but I'm sure Mrs McDougall at the post office will be able to help you, or tell you where to go.'

He raised his head, but did not take his eyes from the fireplace. It was as if he was speaking to the dying fire. 'I had no idea he had this in mind. No idea at all. They have got to believe me.'

'They do. I'm sure they do. If they hadn't believed you, they wouldn't have gone away without you, would they? They don't even think Ewen Mackay was involved in the drug thing, either, or they'd have taken the boat for a detailed search. You heard them say so. What's been happening here isn't anything to do with you at all.'

His eyes came to me then. 'I couldn't go back there, Miss Fenemore. I told your brother about it. We came up together in the train. I told him about it then.'

'Yes, I know.'

'He saved me, you know. We were in that train accident together, the one that came off the rails near Kendal. When the engine went off the line, and the crash came, I was caught under something, I couldn't see what, it was so dark, but he pulled me out. Your brother pulled me out.'

'Did he? I didn't know that. It must have been awful. Were you hurt?'

'No, no. Bruises and shock, that's all. But if he hadn't pulled me out ... Just after he did it, the whole thing slid down the bank and I might have been killed. That's when his foot was hurt, but even after that he was trying to help some of the people.'

'Yes, well, he's a doctor. They do.'

'Then when we were taken to hospital we found we were both coming up here to Moila, so I said I'd wait a couple of days, to be in the train with him, you see, in case he needed looking after. Carrying luggage and all that. So when they let him out of hospital he took me with him to stay with his friends in Glasgow. They were very kind. Both doctors, he's a heart surgeon and she – Laura – she's a paediatrician. But I forgot, you probably know them. Anyway, I stayed there, and then came up with him. It was the least I could do.'

'It was good of you. I'm sure it was a help.'

'But don't you see –' He sat up as he spoke, and with the bitter spice in his voice, the life had come back to it. The dull eyes began to brighten. 'But don't you see, if I had come straight up here – and I could have got the Saturday's boat – I could have stopped that f—, pardon, I'm sure, that stupid, bloody, sorry, Mackay from taking all that stuff and bringing the police down on our necks when all this is above-board and a perfectly straight transaction, because whatever was said at the time, and your brother knows all about this because we talked it over as I told you, I did not know what was going on, or I do assure you I'd have been out from under, because I didn't get much out of it all except a couple of years that I'd sooner forget, and don't intend ever to repeat, and if I had known what that Mackay intended, do you suppose I'd have left him up here on his own to queer my pitch and make a – a mess like this?'

'Coffee?' said Ann, from the doorway. She came in with a tray, and crossed to the table. 'Milk and sugar, Mr Bagshaw?'

'Yes. Thanks. Both, thanks.'

'And a doughnut?' asked Megan, coming in with a plate. 'They're terrific. If I wasn't a student of Dr Fenemore's and a fan of Hugh Templar's I'd say *fantastic*.' She met my eye. 'Yes, I'm sorry, Rose, but you did leave your papers there on the window-sill, and I honestly couldn't help seeing. I say it again. Lit. and met., fantastic.'

'What are you talking about?' Ann, spooning out sugar for Mr Bagshaw, did not sound interested. 'Oh, Archie, there you are. Coffee?'

'Thanks, I don't mind.' Archie came down the stairs and took a mug. 'Just a half, though. I'd best be getting away again. Thanks. You'll be coming with me, ladies? And you?' This to Mr Bagshaw, who gave me a glance and then nodded.

'I guess so. I guess you're right, my dear. I'll not impose on you any longer. You look tired, and I reckon nothing good will come of this day until we've all rested and got ourselves back to normal. Mr Hamilton's still out there, is he? I'll get a time fixed with him, and maybe we'll meet again later. You've been very kind, and I'll call on your brother again before I go back to London.' He heaved himself to his feet and put his mug down on the table. 'And when I get the place going here – and your brother will tell you the plans I've got – you and he will always be welcome, and I'll personally see you get the best of everything Moila has to offer.'

'Thank you very much.'

He held out a hand and I took it. 'Give my best to your brother, and I hope that foot will soon be better.' In the doorway a thought seemed to strike him, and he paused. 'That boat, now. It looks as if I'm stuck with that boat, and I wouldn't know how to handle it, not in this sort of place. If you and your brother would like the use of it – nothing to pay, of course, it's all seen to – you're very welcome, and when you're finished with it, just leave it, I can find some way of getting it picked up and taken back where it came from. With your brother lame as he is, a boat might be a good way of getting around to see places.'

'Well, how very good of you.' It would have seemed ungracious to say that I was counting on the use of Neil's boat, with Neil to manage it, so I merely thanked Mr Bagshaw again and watched while he made his way down to where Neil, in *Sea Otter*, was busy with the engine hatch open. The two of them spoke briefly, and I saw Neil pointing in the direction of Taigh na Tuir, and then Mr Bagshaw shook hands with him, too, and climbed into the Land-Rover. It moved off up the hill.

The girls came out of the scullery.

'Don't worry,' said Ann, 'we're going. Let you and your brother say hello to each other and have a bit of peace. You look as if a long sleep wouldn't come amiss, either. Come on, Meg.'

'But Archie's just gone,' I said.

'I know. We told him we'd walk back. Believe it or not, the day's yet young, and we've got a picnic here. We thought we'd go back along the machair.'

'While it's still there,' said Megan. 'Before the golf balls start to fly. Do you think it would be safe to have a swim?'

'I don't know. Ask Neil.'

'I didn't mean currents and things. I meant swim raw. We haven't got swimsuits.'

'Oh. I still don't know, but good luck to it. It's a gorgeous day for it. Well, thanks for all your help. Come back, won't you, whenever you want to.'

'Love to,' they said. 'Goodbye.'

As they set off Megan looked back over her shoulder, and said, under her breath: 'Fantastic!'

'What?' asked Ann.

'Nothing,' said Megan. 'A rose by any other name. Come on.'

They picked their way down to where Neil still stooped over *Sea Otter*. There was a brief conversation, then Neil jumped out onto the pier and came up to the cottage, while the girls waited.

He looked in at the cottage door. 'Rose. Are you all right? It's been a grim morning for you.'

'For us all. Yes, thank you, I'm fine. What happens now?'

'Now, today, nothing. They'll let me know. So try to forget it, and have a rest. I'm going back to Taigh na Tuir, and I'm taking the girls round in the boat; it'll give them a short cut to the machair. So I'll be off now.'

'You are coming over for supper tonight, aren't you? Love to have you.'

'I'd like that very much. If you're sure –'

'Of course. I'll do nothing all day, and Crispin's brought some goodies, so the meal's no problem. And there's still a lot I want to ask you before I can really start to forget it all.'

'Then I'll come with pleasure. About seven?'

'Yes. And – Neil.'

'Yes?'

'It's none of my business, but has Mr Bagshaw said anything yet about the House? The sale, I mean?'

'No. We've arranged to meet there tomorrow, and I'll show him round. But let's forget that, too, for the present, shall we? Tonight at seven, then. Goodbye.'

19

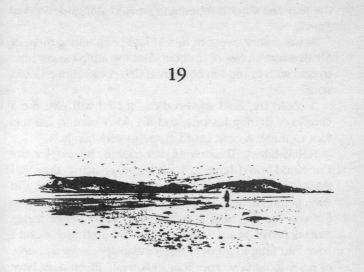

It was after supper that evening. After its explosive start, the day had been peaceful. No one had called at the cottage. I had caught up on some of the sleep I had missed, and then through a long day of sunshine and soft breezes Crispin and I had talked, and lazed, and talked again, till we had caught up on our personal news, and I had told him all I knew about the recent happenings on Moila. Supper was easy, cold chicken and ham with salad, followed by the promised strawberries, and some cheese brought that morning by my brother, and afterwards Neil brought out some camp chairs he had seen that morning in the shed, and set them in the grass by the cottage door. We took coffee cups out and sat there, while below us the sea creamed up over the stones of the beach, and at the jetty *Sea Otter* bobbed and swayed alongside *Stormy Petrel*.

'It was rather sweet of him.' I had been telling them of Mr Bagshaw's offer of his boat. 'But I wouldn't know how to deal with it, and I'm not sure if Cris could either. Could you?'

'I could try,' said my brother. 'If Neil will give me a couple of driving lessons, and if I don't have to use this foot of mine. A boat could come in very handy.'

Neil laughed. 'The driving part couldn't be simpler, but I'm afraid you'd have to be a bit more active than you think. There's a lot of clambering about to be done, and even getting in and out of the dinghy could be a problem for you for the next few days. No, you'd better forget *Stormy Petrel*, at any rate for now, and until Archie and I have had time to go over her for damage. I saw a couple of nasty-looking scrapes that look fresh. Ewen must have squeezed it a bit, to get right into the shallows behind that stack. Meantime there's my boat, and I'll be very happy to take you both wherever you want to go.'

'Well, thank you,' said Crispin. 'That sounds to me an altogether better idea.'

'Once I've got tomorrow over, that is.' Neil set his cup down on the grass beside his chair. 'I told Rose, I've arranged to see Bagshaw at the house. I'm not sure how long he plans to stay in Moila, but naturally he wants to see all there is. And as far as I'm concerned, if it has to be done, the sooner the better.'

'"If it has to be done?" Does that mean that you're changing your mind about it?'

'I don't know,' said Neil heavily. He sounded tired and despondent. I had put it down to the recent happenings, which of course had been a good deal more unpleasant for Neil than for me, but now I could see that it went

196

deeper. He looked at Crispin. 'After what you've told us about his plans, he's certainly not the buyer I would have wanted, but it looks now as if that's up to him. We can only hope the place doesn't meet his standards.'

'It's a problem,' agreed my brother. 'You might have considered handing the house to an agent for winter lets, and using it yourself in summer, but if you're teaching in Australia that's hardly feasible. I don't really see what else you can do but sell.'

'My job in Sydney is finished. I'll be in Cambridge next year. So your solution, Crispin, might be possible, if only this option business can be got round.'

'What changed your mind?' I asked him.

There was a silence, which all at once seemed charged, and stretched itself almost to breaking before he spoke.

'You,' he said.

I stared at him.

'The way you talked at supper. The things you said about the place, the broch, the machair, this little cove with the otters. And Eilean na Roin ... I've known all my life about the seals and the birds, and I believe I knew about the storm petrels, though I never saw one, but you talked about them –' he hesitated – 'well, you talked as if the place belonged to them, and when you come to think about it, I suppose it does. I was only a boy when I was here before, and I'd forgotten ... Then, coming back, and going round the place with you ...' He paused again, then added, almost as if it were something he was ashamed of admitting· 'When you told us about your night on the island, and the petrels, I could see that they had really got to you. It was like, well, I suppose poets must feel that way.'

I said nothing. I saw Crispin smile.

'So when I heard what Crispin had to tell us about

Bagshaw's plans – Bagshaw was pretty specific, wasn't he, during that night in the train? – I knew I had to get out of the sale if I could. But how?'

'Hope that he finds the house depressing,' said Crispin. 'Hope that it pours tomorrow and the roof leaks and then tell him that one can never get workmen to do anything in the West Highlands. Everything's *mañana*, or whatever that is in Gaelic.'

Neil laughed. 'There's no such word in Gaelic. It conveys too much urgency. Any other ideas?'

'Invite him to stay,' I offered, 'and give him a horrible supper, and tell him that you simply cannot get supplies here in Moila, and that the electricity fails almost every night.'

'The absurd thing is,' said my brother, slowly, 'that I rather like him. I know he's brash and full of ideas that we might find hideous, but he's not a bad sort of chap, and he's had a horrific couple of years in gaol, and I honestly believe him when he says he got in too deep before he quite knew what was happening. I'm talking about the Prescott fraud case. It's just possible – no, no, I'm talking nonsense.'

'You're not. I like him myself. Go on,' said Neil.

'In the first place – I know nothing about Scots law, but it's possible that this option business is not binding on you, in which case you have no problem, except what to do with the place in the long run. But it does occur to me that if you show Mr Bagshaw everything – I mean the beauties of the place just as it is, with the birds and seals and the machair flowers – and try to show him how the holiday crowds would destroy the very things that they thought they were paying for ... Isn't it just possible that he might decide to go somewhere a little more suitable?'

'It's possible, but I wouldn't bet on it,' said Neil. 'I have a feeling that the whole set-up is too tempting. We'll just have to trust that the option won't hold water, and let me worry about the future once Bagshaw has given up and gone home. I won't pretend it isn't a worry. That house won't be easy to get rid of reasonably, even letting it as you suggested. Of course, the setting's lovely. That's what will do it, if anything does . . . You sound as if you know it. Have you been here before?'

'No. Rose has told me about it. She was, well, poetic on the subject. I can hardly wait to see the petrels. I suppose that must wait till tomorrow night, and then, if their fate is sealed, it will be a sad sort of pilgrimage.'

'It needn't wait,' said Neil. 'We could go now, if you're not tired? You spent last night on the train, after all. And don't worry about the leg. We'll take the boat; the tide's wrong for the crossing, and in any case I'm sure you couldn't manage the causeway. You'd really like to go? What about you, Rose?'

'I've rested today. I'm fine. I'd love to go.'

'Then let's do it at once,' said Neil, rising. 'And I doubt if there's a word in Gaelic for that, either.'

*

They were there. There was no sound from the seals' rocks, and from the seabirds only the occasional muted cry, sounding distant and sleepy. But the petrels were there, waiting for night. Dusk fell slowly, the veils of evening. For some time, as we sat in silence outside Neil's tent, we heard nothing but the slow hush of the sea below us, and the faint stirring of the long grasses in the dying breeze. Then at last the song began.

In that long, quiet twilight the sound was still as weird,

as romantic, as spirit-stirring as anything I had ever known. We sat quite still. Nobody spoke. And then the flight began. The motes of shadow whirled and dipped, and now and again a bird went by so closely, and in such a silence of small velvet wings, that it was as if a flake of the very darkness had broken away to be blown, weightless, out to sea.

All at once, the spell was broken. Neil got to his feet suddenly, as if impelled by springs, said 'Hell!' and started rubbing a hand violently over his face and hair. Then he turned and dived back into the tent, and we could hear him rummaging there.

I came back from Cloud Nine to feel my face and hands stinging and my hair itching as if I had been beaten with nettles. As the breeze had died, the midges had come out, and in force. The bracken near us would be full of them, and possibly, even, the petrels as they crept from their burrows had disturbed them and sent them to fill the air like stinging dust.

My brother, moving more clumsily and rather more slowly, was on his feet propped by the elbow crutch, and he, too, was rubbing and slapping furiously. Neil crawled out of the tent with a small plastic bottle clutched in his hand.

'Here. *Shoo* them,' he said.

'I'm trying, but they don't take a damned bit of notice,' said Crispin testily.

I laughed. 'It's the name of the midge-repellent, you nit. Quick. Put it on.'

'After you. Look, Rose, Neil – this has been very wonderful, and I wouldn't have missed it for worlds, but do you mind very much if we go away now, this moment, and come back another day when there's a Force Five gale?'

I handed him the bottle. 'Suits me. I should have warned you. This time of year, whenever the breeze drops, the Defenders of the Highlands are out in force. Neil? You ready to go?'

'Not quite,' said Neil. He finished shutting the tent, and turned to take three long paces over to where I stood waiting to help my brother down the slope.

'Excuse me,' he said, and pulled me into his arms and planted a kiss on each cheek. 'There. That's by way of a "thank you". You've just shown me what to do tomorrow. And now let's just get the hell out of this infested isle, and leave the petrels in peace.'

20

'I'll be frank with you,' said Mr Bagshaw, sounding very frank indeed, 'there'll be a lot of work involved, and you say it's difficult to get construction work done here?'

'Almost impossible,' said Neil.

'But given the time and the capital, it can be done? A good team in from Glasgow, get a supply chain going, they live in the house while they get set up, then the Portakabins on that flat field by the beach ... It could be done.'

'The weather can be a problem,' said Neil.

We were standing in the belvedere, which commanded a view to northward of the machair, and straight across the channel to the island where, in the sunlight, the out-lines of the broch showed sharply. Down to our left Neil's boat lay by the jetty, with Crispin sitting in the stern, fishing.

It had been a long day. Neil had brought *Sea Otter* round soon after breakfast, and taken Crispin and me to the house. Not long after that Archie's Land-Rover brought Mr Bagshaw down, and the tour of inspection began. At Neil's request I had stayed with the two men while they looked over the house, and then had – this at my own suggestion – given them lunch of a kind in the kitchen. I had made sandwiches earlier with the rest of the cold chicken and some ham, and brought some cheese and fruit to finish with. Crispin had taken his share earlier, and had gone off on his own to look at the machair; he had insisted that he could manage perfectly well with the elbow crutch, and since he could obviously look after himself we had let him go, and turned our attention to a hopeful discouragement of Mr Bagshaw.

It did not appear to be working. On that lovely sunny day the house failed to look depressing, or even very neglected, though I drew Neil's attention twice to damp-marks on the ceilings, and Neil responded with a rueful remark about the state of the roof, then checked himself with a quick, worried look at Mr Bagshaw. The rather awful back premises of the house drew nothing more from the latter than pursed lips and a reference to the excellent architect who was, apparently, living only to make Mr Bagshaw's dreams come true. And the weedy garden was no problem at all: with those bushes, whatever they were called, said Mr Bagshaw, eyeing the rhododendrons with enthusiasm, all you needed do was keep the grass cut, and who needed a garden when you had a view like this?

And of course the machair decided it. It looked, to Neil's and my fury, exactly like the most idyllic picture postcard of an island view. There was the long, gentle curve of milk-white sand, backed by a sea of turquoise and pale jade and indigo. There were the far cliffs, violet-shadowed as any classical landscape. And for the four miles of the flat coastline, between the white beach and the green slope of the moor, stretched the wild-flower meadow that in Gaelic is the machair. The turf is barely visible, starred with the tiny yellow and white flowers of tormentil and daisy and silver-weed. Then comes the next layer, at a few inches high, eyebright and bugle and yel-low rattle, and over these, in soft motion always in the breezes, the dog-daisies and ragwort and knapweed and brilliant hawkears and the lace of pignut and wild chervil, and the sweet delicate harebells that are the bluebells of Scotland.

They may not all have been flowering at once, but that is the impression the machair gives you, and the scent, mingled somehow with the smell of the sea and the tan-gle at the tide's edge, is the unforgettable, unforgotten smell of the summer isles.

Mr Bagshaw, predictably, was in ecstasies. The bathing, the sun-beaches, the pictures in the brochures, the water-sports, and yes, he supposed there were wet days, but he had been assured in the village that the television recep-tion was OK, and in fact had watched it last night, and of course there would be the night-life, the leisure centre, discos ...

So at length we came back to the garden and the bel-vedere. Mr Bagshaw did not notice Echo and Narcissus watching us sadly from their weedy beds, or I am sure they would have inspired him to new plans, but he kept his eyes fixed on the bright prospect framed by the trees at the end of the belvedere.

'That's the remains of a broch you can see,' said Neil.

He sounded tired and dispirited. 'An Iron Age stronghold. You wouldn't be allowed to touch that, of course.'

'Of course not. But it would make another attraction. Culture,' said Mr Bagshaw. 'And that's another good beach on the other side. There's something romantic about an island, I always think. Don't you?'

'Oh, yes. But the tides are difficult, and the channel can be very dangerous.'

Mr Bagshaw was silent for a minute, then turned those bright, shrewd little eyes on him. 'I get the impression that you're not all that willing to sell. Am I right?'

Neil hesitated. 'I suppose so. I realise that I may have to, but it's – well, it's not easy to envisage such, er, changes to a place one has known and loved. And what you propose, Mr Bagshaw, would change the whole island. I wouldn't want to feel responsible – I mean, I did try to explain –'

'Yes, you did. But the whole world changes, every day,' said Mr Bagshaw, with truth, 'and this sort of place has to change with the times. People have leisure, and they want clean air and the sea, and to have fun, and if we can provide it here in this country, it keeps their cash here, doesn't it?'

'So you really want to take up the option?'

'I can see nothing against it.'

'Well, that's it, then,' Neil got up from where he had been sitting on the wall. 'But would you like to see the little island, too? I'll take you right round it, to the bird cliffs, and then if you like we can land you to look at that beach, and the broch.'

Mr Bagshaw would be delighted. And presently he was in *Sea Otter* with the three of us and we were cruising round the outside of Eilean na Roin. The birds rose in screaming clouds, to the pleasure, different in either case, of Crispin and Mr Bagshaw, as Neil took the boat gently on and along the machair as far as the peregrine cliffs. Then, slowly, back again. It was difficult to talk above the noise of the engine, and Mr Bagshaw seemed deep in his own thoughts. I handed round plastic mugs of thermos tea, and then sat enjoying the colours of the advancing twilight, and the pleasure in my brother's face.

Some time around half past six the wind died, and with it the last brightness fell from the day. The evening was still far from dark, but all through the afternoon the slow clouds had been building up in the west, and as the sun sank lower behind them, twilight dimmed the outlines of the land and greyed the sea.

I saw Neil looking around him with satisfaction, and then the engine's noise sank to a mutter, and he brought the boat softly in to the inner shore of Eilean na Roin, and let her drift alongside the causeway. He jumped out and handed Mr Bagshaw ashore.

I made ready to get out, but he shook his head at me. 'Wait a bit, do you mind?' Then, to Mr Bagshaw: 'Why don't you go ahead and take a look around before it gets too dark? Take your time. I'm going over to the boat-house for a few minutes to fix something. OK?'

Mr Bagshaw was understood to say OK, and *Sea Otter* drifted back into mid-channel. We saw Mr Bagshaw making his way rapidly uphill towards the broch, then Neil turned the boat and headed, not for the boat-house, but for the headland beyond which lay the cove called Halfway House.

It was a narrow cove, with a wedge of stony beach, and to either side sheer-sided rocks where a boat could lie as if at a jetty. Landing was simple. We tied up to a ring that he himself, said Neil, had driven into a crevice in the rock many years ago, and silence came back as the engine died.

'Am I to understand,' said Crispin, 'that you are leaving the Defenders of the Highlands to do the job for you?'

'To make a suggestion merely,' said Neil.

'They're making it here,' I said, slapping. 'Where's the stuff?'

'Some in the cabin. I never move without it.'

'One sees why.' Crispin was slapping, too. 'But this surely won't be enough? I don't mean the *Shoo*, I mean the suggestion.'

'I thought it might give him time to think. And give me time to think as well. It'll probably just make him mad at me, but even that might be helpful.'

'If he did withdraw?' I asked, smearing midge-repellent.

'I simply don't know. All we can do is wait and see.'

We waited.

*

When at length we went back to Eilean na Roin we got a bit of a fright, which, I suppose, served us right. As the dusk had deepened, a merciful little wind had got up and begun to stir the bracken, but we fully expected to find a furious and agitated Mr Bagshaw waiting at the causeway rubbing at his midge-bites and ready to agree to anything as long as he need never see the island again. But there was no sign of him, and when we called, there was no reply.

'They've driven him over the cliff and into the sea,' said Crispin, but nobody laughed. To someone like Mr Bagshaw, not used to the Highlands, and moreover, only just freed from a rather restricted form of life, the rocky island could hold, in the half-light, some very real dangers.

'I've been a double-dyed fool,' said Neil, explosively. 'Come on, let's find him. Crispin, you'd better stay put. Tie the boat up will you, please? Come on, Rose.'

He led the way uphill at a fast pace, and I followed. We paused, but without much hope, at the tent.

'If he'd been in here, he'd have heard us,' said Neil. 'Are you there? Mr Bagshaw?'

No reply. He pulled the flaps open to show an empty tent.

'I can hear the gulls at the cliff,' I said, with misgiving.

'Only a few. Don't worry, nothing's happened, I'm sure. He struck me as having a lot of sense. I'll go over there, I know the ground better than you. You go the other way, downhill, towards the seal rocks, and take care ... Mr Bagshaw! Are you there?' He strode away and was soon lost to sight in the growing dusk.

On the seaward side of the island the rising breeze was stronger, and waves boomed and echoed against the rocks. Some of the birds, disturbed, were out and calling. My eyes were used to the half-light, but even so the going was uneven, and needed care. I heard Neil call out a couple of times, but then the wind noises and the sea noises and the lie of the land blotted his voice out. I did not pause to listen for the enchanted sounds of the other island nights. I hurried, trying not to feel the older, stronger enchantment of the lonely Highland places, where the ghosts walk of all the dead, and the following shadows thicken your blood with cold.

I was almost at the seal rocks when I found him. I heard him first. Not the moan or cry for help that by now I was half expecting, but a soft, impatient shushing noise that came from a small figure kneeling, hunched, over something on the ground.

'Mr Bagshaw! Oh, thank goodness! I was so afraid . . . Are you all right?'

'Hush up, lass! Keep your voice down! Of course I'm all right, but there's a bird here with a broken wing or something, and you'll frighten it if you shout . . . Careful now, slowly . . . Here, see.'

I saw. Below him, barely visible in the deep shadow of a fallen-in rabbit's scrape, a small black bird lay, half hidden by dust and pieces of broken turf. One wing, curved and narrow, protruded from the debris, moving feebly. The small body quivered and shifted, as if its feet, under the weight of dust, were still trying for take-off. But it was trapped. Behind it was the rabbit-hole, and to either side the turf bank rose sharply, where the recent fall of sandy stuff had half buried it, shutting it in like a golf ball in a bunker.

Mr Bagshaw was making no attempt to touch it. He backed off a pace. 'If it's got a wing broken –' he began.

I knelt down, and began very gently to scrape away some of the fallen stuff. It was sandy, light and friable, and moved easily. 'Look,' I said, 'the other wing's out now, and it's moving it. Not damaged, then . . . I don't think it's hurt at all. It must have just been coming out of the burrow when that bit of the bank came down and trapped it. It looks recent.'

'It is. I did it. I thought I heard something funny from under ground, and then I stepped too near the edge of the rabbit-hole. Could have broken my ankle in the dark.'

'I know. I'm sorry. It was stupid of us, really, to go off like that, but you see, we were hoping . . .' I stopped. I could hardly tell him what we had been hoping.

'Never mind,' said Mr Bagshaw. 'But how about getting

this little bird out of here? If we scrape the stuff away gently ... yes, that's fine. What's it doing in a rabbit-hole anyway? There, now, there, now ... I'm used to birds. I like them. We kept pigeons when I was a boy, and my grandfather used to breed canaries. That was in the days when they bred them at the pithead to find the firedamp. I used to help him. He kept them in the engine-shed, and you should have heard them all singing whenever the engine was running to lift the cage in the shaft...' He was speaking almost in a whisper, while he gently shuffled the dust and fragments of turf aside, and I scattered them away. 'I think you're right, the wings are OK. But – oh, here's your brother coming. He wants to watch himself in this light.'

'What is it?' asked Crispin, limping up. Neil must have heard our voices, too. I saw him coming downhill towards us.

'A bird, here on the ground. A house martin, I think. It can't fly. I thought it might be hurt, but your sis says not.'

'A house martin? Here?' And indeed, with the sickle wings spread, and the white rump now clearly visible in the dusk, Mr Bagshaw's guess was fair enough.

'It's a stormy petrel,' I said. 'I've never seen one before, close to, but that's what it's got to be. And it's grounded. At least I hope that's all that's wrong.'

My brother laid the crutch aside and knelt down. Neil joined us, with a question, and I said quickly: 'It's OK. He's here. One of your petrels in trouble, that's all.'

Crispin was saying quietly, to Mr Bagshaw, 'Rose is right. I don't think it's hurt. Why don't we just lift it out of there and give it a start?'

He reached down, but I caught at his arm. 'Mr Bagshaw's used to birds. Let him do it.'

My brother glanced up. I saw him hesitate, then he moved back and got to his feet.

'Go on, then, Mr Bagshaw. Your bird, I think?'

'Sure.' I felt Crispin relax beside me as Mr Bagshaw slid gentle palms under the petrel's breast, folding the wings in and cradling the little creature firmly and expertly. It made no attempt to struggle. It looked very small and fragile in his hands, like a tiny bat with velvet wings. I smelled again the sharp, chemical smell that pervaded the broch wall.

'Well, what do you know about that?' said Mr Bagshaw admiringly. 'The little bugger spat at me.'

Crispin laughed. 'If it got on your clothes, you may as well put them on the bonfire. You'll never get the smell out. Now, if we just take it somewhere near the edge of the cliffs . . .' He led the way across the turf. At this end of the island the cliffs were lowish, with stacks jutting from the swell and wash of white water.

We stopped a few feet from the edge. 'This will do,' said Crispin. 'Throw it over now, into the sea.'

Mr Bagshaw turned to stare at him, his face a pale blur in the dimness. I could see his mouth opening to protest.

'Go on,' said my brother. 'Quickly. That's where it was going. It's a storm petrel. Except when they're nesting, they live at sea. Really. They follow ships, and they can swim if they have to. That little thing can fly anywhere – anywhere, as long as it's at sea. Go on, throw it.'

'You're the boss, doctor,' said Mr Bagshaw, and threw. The tiny bird made a curve up into the air, turned over, flapping a couple of times, like a moth caught in a draught, and then fell in a great sweeping dive to the sea. For a few moments we could see it, a scudding speck, black against the luminous white of the breakers, then it was gone, beating strongly out towards the open Atlantic.

Mr Bagshaw was looking down at his hands, curved as if they still held the warm shape of the bird. 'Well, I never did. I wouldn't have believed that if you'd told me. A pigeon, yes, maybe, but that little spelk of a thing ... What did you say it was?'

'A stormy petrel. They call them Mother Carey's Chickens. The storm birds. Very small, very strong, very tough. I told you, they spend all their lives at sea, except when they come ashore to nest.'

'And they nest on this island?'

'Yes.' It was Neil who replied, and I added: 'That was what you heard, Mr Bagshaw. It must have a nest in that burrow, and what you heard under the ground was the bird crooning on its egg. They only have one. They sing every night. Its mate may just have come in from the sea to change over on the nest. Usually they wait till it's darker than this.'

'You don't say?' He looked out for a few moments towards the deepening darkness to the west, filled with the sounds of the sea. He spoke to Neil. 'You didn't tell me.'

'No. We try to keep quiet about them because they're so rare, and so vulnerable when they do come in to land.'

'I see. And you didn't tell me about the seals, either. Did you know there were a lot of seals at the end there, on the rocks? Some of them with young ones, too.'

'Yes. I knew. The island's called Eilean na Roin, which means Seal Island. They've been here since – well, since long before the broch. Long before men came here in the Iron Age.'

'I see,' said Mr Bagshaw again. 'Well, I don't know that I can actually ... That is – ' He did not finish what he had been going to say, but asked instead: 'Did you get your boat fixed?'

'Yes, thank you. And I think we ought to get back to it and I'll get everyone home before the wind gets any stronger. Shall we go? Can you see your way, sir?'

'Sure I can. You give a hand to the doctor here. And don't call me sir, my name's Hartley, but I get Hart as a rule. Now look . . .' This as we started back towards the boat. 'I don't know if there's anywhere back in the village where I can ask you to come and have supper with me, but if there is, I'd be glad if you'd all join me there.'

'I doubt if there is,' I said. 'No hotel, of course, and I don't think you could take three extra to wherever you're staying, without giving notice. But why don't we all go to the cottage? I can manage. Let's all go back there, and I'll fix something.'

'And I'll run you home afterwards in the boat,' said Neil.

We had reached the causeway. Mr Bagshaw stopped and turned back to face the three of us. 'I won't say no. I'd like that very much. And here and now I'd like to say thank you for this day. I've enjoyed it all, and that island there has been a rare privilege, and something more than I expected.'

There was a silence that could be felt. Then Neil stepped forward and put out a hand to help Mr Bagshaw into the boat. 'It's been rather more than any of us expected, I think,' he said. 'Can you see, Hart? Then let's go.'

21

It was a good supper. Since everyone in Moila knows everything, and Archie McLaren would certainly have broadcast yesterday's proceedings, and of course Mr Bagshaw had seen no reason to make a secret of his plans, Mrs McDougall had assumed that he might stay to supper at the big house, and be taken back to his lodgings by boat, so she had helped me out by sending down with Archie that morning a bag of freshly picked – presumably hydroponic – french beans, an apple pie of her own baking, and half a dozen rolls. Neil handed them over to me, and I made that most delicious of standbys, a macaroni cheese, which we ate with bacon and beans, with the apple pie to follow.

Mr Bagshaw, remarking that this was the best food he

had tasted in a very long time, ate with great enjoyment. The burning subject of the house sale was not even touched on. Neil, who still looked tired, said little, and the bulk of the conversation was between Mr Bagshaw and Crispin. The former obviously regarded my brother as an expert on birds, and asked more questions about the petrels, and in his turn Crispin asked about the vanishing art of canary breeding. This led naturally to reminiscences of Mr Bagshaw's childhood in some remote mining village near Durham, and so the meal passed pleasantly enough, and more easily than I had anticipated.

Neil helped me with the clearing and the coffee. As we waited for the kettle to boil he said, softly: 'I can't thank you enough. I couldn't have coped on my own.'

'That's all right. Did you gather from what he said that he's planning to leave tomorrow?'

'Yes. I did make a sort of offer of a bed, as I thought there would still be a lot to talk about, but he said he wanted to be back in the village to get the ferry in the morning. So your guess is as good as mine. But –' He stopped.

'But?'

He lifted his shoulders in a tired shrug. 'But whatever comes in the near future, I do most passionately want to see this place left in peace. Aunt Emily used to call it her ivory tower.' He gave a little half-laugh. 'Something everyone should have. They're getting rare.'

'And expensive.'

'That's the trouble. Well, we'll try and pay the price, if he'll only let us. Here, let me take that tray.'

'I can manage. Neil, Crispin brought some brandy. It's in that cupboard, and you know where the glasses are. How about that?'

'Wonderful.'

216

I carried the tray through and handed cups of coffee round. 'Only instant, I'm afraid. How do you like yours, Mr Bagshaw?'

'Milk and sugar, please. Thanks.'

'And thanks to Crispin, brandy,' said Neil, coming across with the glasses.

'Just what the doctor ordered,' said Mr Bagshaw, and laughed heartily at his own joke. 'Thank you. That's plenty. And now –' He took a sip, raised his glass to me, and said, across it: 'I'm not going to make a speech, folks, I wouldn't know how, but there's something I've got to say. And the first thing is, how much I've enjoyed this little trip, and getting to know you folks. I can't say that yesterday was anything great, and I'm sorry for what happened with Neil and that little rat Ewen Mackay, but it wasn't any doing of mine, and you've all been good enough to treat it as such, and not hold things against me that weren't all my fault neither – either. So here's to you, and thank you, all of you, and specially you, Miss Rose, for this.' A gesture took in the table.

'You're welcome,' I said, smiling. 'I thought you said you wouldn't know how to make a speech? That was a pretty nice one.'

'I haven't done yet.' He was looking at Neil now. 'You all know what I came for, and about my plans for opening the island up. I like the place, and it could be done. Boy, could it be done! Except for two things.'

'Which are?' This from Neil.

'You don't want to sell,' said Mr Bagshaw flatly, 'and don't think I didn't get all the things you let drop about the weather and the roof leaking and the light failing and no one coming to do the plumbing when the toilet seized up, excuse me, Miss Rose ... No, Neil, let me finish. Whatever you've been told about this option business, there's no way I could make you sell if you didn't want to, and after today, there's no way I would make you, either. Because of the second thing.'

This time no one spoke. He took a sip of brandy.

'That island, the seal island, you called it. There's a romantic little spot if there ever was one, history, nature, good beach, nice harbour, the lot. But it would take a rhinoceros to want to sunbathe on those beaches, and you can't tell me you didn't know it. What the hell are they?'

'Midges,' said Neil. 'Argyll variety.' He set his glass down. The colour had begun to come back into his face. He spoke soberly. 'Mr Bagshaw – Hart – I owe you an apology. We all do. I feel ashamed about today, and I've no right to be thanked for it. It was a – well, it was a conspiracy to make you hate the place. It was also stupid of us to think you wouldn't see it. And to leave you deliberately – yes, of course it was deliberate – on the island at the time when the midges are worst ... That was childish, a rotten thing to do. The only excuse is that you ... you seemed so keen, and I honestly did think I would be held to it. And you took it all so well. You make me feel ashamed, and I beg your pardon. I hope you'll forgive me.'

'And me,' I said. 'You've been sweet, Mr Bagshaw, and I'm sorry.'

'For what? Giving me my favourite supper? Forget it. You –' this to Neil – 'are a very lucky man.'

Neil looked blank. I felt myself go scarlet. Crispin smiled into his brandy glass.

Mr Bagshaw pushed his chair back. 'And now I'd better be going. Neil, you and I can talk on the way back in the boat. And don't feel bad about it. As far as I'm concerned, there's plenty of good fish in the sea still, and I'll find some place where I won't be doing Mother Whosit's chickens out of a roost, and where I can get the john mended the same day. I'll say goodnight, then, Miss Rose, and thanks again and no hard feelings. Crispin –'

My brother was on his feet. 'I'll see you to the boat. Leave the dishes till I get back, Rose.'

He went out with Mr Bagshaw, the latter waiting to help him carefully down the steps to the path. Neil smiled at me. The tired look had dropped away.

'I ought to make a speech, too. Thank you for today, and I really mean that. It's been quite a day, and I don't know where I'd have been without you. Shall I see you again soon?'

'I'll be here. The ivory tower is mine for another six days.'

'For as long as you like, and rent-free at that,' said my landlord. 'Crispin's missed a whole week as it is, so why not stay over and make it up? I'll fix it for you with the agents. Now I really must go. I'm just hoping that the lawyers or the police won't drag me straight back to Glasgow, but I'll be round with the boat just as soon as I can make it. So – see you soon. And in any case –'

'Yes?'

'See you next term,' he said, and went.

*

The sound of the boat's engine died. Crispin came back to help with the dishes, and then he went up to bed while I set the place tidy for the night. Before I locked the door I went outside, and down the steps to the edge of the beach. Crispin's light was out already. My own tiredness had gone, but I welcomed the silence and the solitude.

It closed me round, the blessed silence, made up of all the peaceful sounds of night; the whisper of sea on the shingle, the breeze in the bracken, the rustle of some creature in the grass, a splash from the tide's edge, and a movement among the rise and fall of the sea-tangle, dark in the dark.

'Good night,' I whispered, and went indoors to bed.

I was just falling asleep when, from somewhere just outside the bay, I heard a boat's engine mutter softly past.

'See you next term,' I said, and smiled into my pillow. I believe I was still smiling when I fell asleep.

THORNYHOLD

To the memory of
my mother and father
with love and
gratitude

Enter these enchanted woods
    You who dare.
Nothing harms beneath the leaves
More than waves a swimmer cleaves.
Toss your heart up with the lark,
Foot at peace with mouse and worm,
    Fair you fare.
Only at a dread of dark
Quaver, and they quiet their form:
  Thousand eyeballs under hoods
    Have you by the hair.
Enter these enchanted woods,
    You who dare.

George Meredith,
'The Woods of Westermain'

1

I suppose that my mother could have been a witch if she had chosen to. But she met my father, who was a rather saintly clergyman, and he cancelled her out. She dwindled from a potential Morgan le Fay into an English vicar's wife, and ran the parish, as one could in those days – more than half a century ago – with an iron hand disguised by no glove at all. She retained her dominance, her vivid personality, a hint of cruelty in her complete lack of sympathy for weakness or incompetence. I had, I think, a hard upbringing. And so, I believe, must she have had. I remember a photograph of my grandmother, her mother, whom I never met, but whose picture terrified me through my childhood; scraped-back hair, piercing eyes and a lipless mouth. She had lived in the wilds of New Zealand and had shown all the tough virtues of the pioneers of her day; she was a notable nurse and healer, who would have been classed in an earlier day as a wise woman or even a witch. She looked it. My mother, a handsomer version of her, had the same abilities. Merciless to the healthy, disliking all other women as a matter of principle, indifferent to children and animals, she was nevertheless endlessly patient with small babies, and was a splendid nurse to the sick. A couple of generations earlier she would have been carrying jellies and soups to the ailing and deserving poor in the parish, but those times were past, and instead she presided over village working-parties and made jams and jellies which she sold ("We need the money, and besides, they don't value anything they get for nothing") and when there was an accident at the pit she was there, along with my father and the doctor, and as useful as either.

We lived in a bleak, ugly colliery village in the north of England. Our house was well built, but hideous, far too big, and very cold. The water was limestone-hard, and always icy; my mother had never in her youth known hot water laid on, and she saw no reason to waste money by using the damper at the back of the vast, extravagant Eagle range. If we needed hot water for washing, we boiled it in pans on top of the range. Baths were allowed once a week, two inches of warmish, hard water. Coal was expensive at a pound a ton, but the vicarage and church got their electricity free, so in my small, arctic room at the top of the house I was sometimes allowed a single-bar electric fire to keep the

cold at bay. I never remember having hands or feet free
from chilblains; this did not count as an ailment, but merely
as weakness, and was ignored.

The vicarage lay at one end of the village, isolated beyond
the church in its own large garden, where my father, aided
by the old sexton ("I'm a powerful digger; I has to be")
spent every hour he could spare from his parish duties. On
one side of our grounds ran the main road; on the other
three sides were graveyards. "Quiet neighbours," we used
to say, and they were. I never remember being troubled by
the thought of all the bodies buried so near at hand, and
our normal short cut to the village lay through the oldest
field of graves. But it was a grim place for a solitary child,
and I suppose my childhood was as bleak, as comfortless,
and even lonelier than the Brontës' cold upbringing at
Haworth. It had not always been so. I had my own small
Golden Age to look back on; my brief span of dream days
that made the real days of childhood bearable.

Until I was seven years old we had lived in a small village
of two hundred souls or thereabouts. It was an unimportant
little parish, and we were very poor, but the place was lovely,
my father's work was easy, and the house was compact and
comfortable. That vicarage was ancient, low and white, with
a white rose rambling over the porch, and ivied walls with
beds of sweet violets beneath. There was a summer-house
set in a lilac grove, and a tennis-court carefully kept by my
father, where occasionally neighbours would come to play.
The parish consisted mainly of farmland, farms scattered
through a few square miles, with only one 'main' road
through it. Cars were rare; one walked, or went by pony-trap.
There were no buses, and the railway station was two miles
away.

Only seven years. But even now, after a lifetime ten times
as long, some memories are printed, still vivid and exact
through the overall smudging of times gone by and best
forgotten.

The village green with its grazing goats and donkeys, and

the grey church at its centre. Huge trees everywhere, on the green, in the cottage gardens, studding the circling meadows, shading the dusty road. The road itself, with the deep triple ruts made by wheels and hoofs, winding between its thick borders of hedgerow flowers. Sunshine hot on the paving-stones of our back-yard, where hens strutted and the cat lay dozing. The ringing of the smith's hammer from the forge next door, and the sharp smell of singeing hoofs as he shod the farmers' horses. The vicarage garden with its paeonies and violas and the columbines like doves roosting. The clouds of lilac, the hops climbing over the door of the schoolhouse at the foot of the garden, and the double yellow roses by the steps that led to the tennis-lawn.

But no people. Those golden memories, I suppose significantly, hold no single person. Except one. There is no smudging of the picture on the day when I first met my mother's cousin Geillis.

She was my godmother, so presumably I had encountered her at the font, but the first time that I recall talking with her was on a summer's day when I was six years old.

It cannot have been my birthday, because that is in September, but it was some sort of special day, an occasion to which I had looked forward with all the starved longing of a lonely childhood, and which, when it came, was just like any other day. Which meant that I spent it alone, because my father was out on his parish visits, my mother was too busy to bother with me, and of course I was not allowed to play with the village children.

I doubt if I was allowed to leave the garden, either, but I had done so. At the bottom of our vegetable garden, behind the schoolhouse, was my own private gap in the fence. Beyond it stretched a long slope of meadow-land, studded like a park with groups of great trees, and at the foot of the slope, backed by a little wood, lay a pond. For no reason, except that its bright mirror made a point to aim for, I wandered downhill to the water's edge, and sat down in the grass.

I believe that I remember every moment of that afternoon, though at first it was only a blur, a richness of colour like something in an impressionist painting. There was a confusion of sound, birdsong from the wood beyond the hedgerow and grasshoppers fiddling in the long grass near at hand. It was hot, and the smell of the earth, of the crushed grasses, of the slightly stagnant pond-water drugged the sleepy day. I sat dreaming, eyes wide open, focused on the glimmer of the pool where the lazy stream fed it.

Something happened. Did the sun move? What I seem to remember is a sudden flash from the pool as if a fish had leaped and scattered the light. The dreamy haze of colour sharpened. Everything, suddenly, seemed outlined in light. The dog-daisies, white and gold, and taller than I was, stirred and swayed above my head as if combed through by a strong breeze. In its wake the air stilled again, thick with scents. The birds had stopped singing, the grasshoppers were silent. I sat there, as still as a snail on the stem, in the middle of a full and living world, and saw it for the first time, and for the first time knew myself to be a part of it.

I looked up, and Cousin Geillis was standing there.

She cannot have been much more than forty, but to me, of course, she seemed old, as my parents, in their thirties, were old. She had something of my mother's look, the proud mouth and nose, the piercing grey-green eyes, the erect carriage. But where my mother's hair was golden-red, Cousin Geillis's was dark, clouds of it, swirled and swathed up with tortoiseshell pins. I don't remember what she wore, except that it was dark and voluminous.

She sank down beside me on the grass. She seemed to manage it without disturbing the dog-daisies. She ran a forefinger up the stem of one daisy, and a ladybird came off it onto the finger and clung there.

"Look," she said. "Quickly. Count the spots."

Young children take the strangest things for granted, a double-edged innocence that can be totally misunderstood

11

by the adult using the guidelines of maturity. I saw nothing odd about Cousin Geillis's sudden appearance, or her greeting. It was part of the child's world of magical appearances and vanishings, timed inevitably as they are for the child's need.

I counted. "Seven."

"Seven-spot *Coccinella*," agreed Cousin Geillis. "Now, hadn't you better warn her?"

Instantly, the need seemed urgent. I sang obediently:

"Ladybird, ladybird, fly away home,
Your house is on fire, your children all gone,
All but one, and her name is Jill,
And she's quite safe on the window-sill."

The ladybird flew. I said, anxiously: "It's only a song, isn't it?"

"Yes. She's a very clever little beetle, and she lives in the meadows, and gets all her babies out and flying before anyone can burn the stubble or cut the hay. Do you know who I am, Jilly?"

"You're Mummy's cousin Jilly. She has a photo of you."

"So she has. What were you doing down here?"

I must have looked apprehensive. Quite apart from the forbidden adventure outside the garden, I was not supposed to waste time dreaming. But, fixed by Cousin Geillis's straight gaze, I told the truth. "Just thinking."

"What about?" Miraculously, she sounded not only unruffled, but interested.

I looked round me. The illuminated missal of grass and flowers was dissolving again into a formless, impressionist blur.

"I don't know. Things."

It was the kind of answer that usually brought a sharp rebuke. Cousin Geillis nodded as if she had just taken in every word of my detailed explanation. "Whether there are tadpoles in the pond, for instance?"

"Yes. Oh, yes! Are there?"

"Probably. Why don't we look?"

12

We looked, and there were. Minnows, too, and a couple of sticklebacks; and then Cousin Geillis pointed to where, at the foot of a tall reed, the surface of the water bulged suddenly, rounded to a bubble, then broke to let a brown, grub-like creature emerge. Slowly, laboriously, testing the strange element, the ugly creature inched its way up the stem till, parting with its reflection, it clung clear of the water, exposed to the drying sun.

"What is it?"

"It's called a nymph. Watch now, Jilly. Just watch."

The creature moved. The ugly head went back, as if in pain. I did not see what happened, but all at once there were two bodies there on the stem, the split shell that had been the nymph, and, climbing from the empty helmet of the head, another body, newly born, supple and alive, a slimmer, bigger version of the first. It clung there, above the wrinkled discard of its muddy skin, while the sunlight stroked it, plumped it with liquid life, drew the crumpled silk of the wings out of its humped shoulders and slowly pulled them straight, taut and shining and webbed with veins as delicate as hairs, while from somewhere, it seemed from the air itself, colour pulsed into the drab body till it glimmered blue as a splinter of sky. The wings stretched, feeling the air. The insect's body lifted, straightened. Then into the light, like light, it was gone.

"It was a dragonfly, wasn't it?" I found myself whispering.

"It was. *Aeshna Caerulea*. Say it."

"*Aeshna Caerulea*. But how? You said it was an imp, but was there a dragonfly inside?"

"Yes. The nymph – not 'imp' – lives at the bottom of the pond in the dark, and feeds on whatever it can get, till one day it finds it can climb out into the light, and grow its wings, and fly. What you've just watched," finished Cousin Geillis cheerfully, "is a perfectly ordinary miracle."

"You mean magic? Did you make it happen?"

"Not that, no. Some things I can make happen, but not that, apt though it was. Some day, if I'm right, something

13

very like that miracle will be needed. Another nymph, another way, another day." A quick, bright glance. "Do you understand me?"

"No. But you can make things happen? Are you really a witch, then, Cousin Jilly?"

"What makes you ask that? Have they said anything at home?"

"No. Mummy just said you might be coming to stay and Daddy said you weren't very desirable."

She laughed, rose, and pulled me up after her. "Spiritually, I hope, rather than physically? No, never mind, child, we'd better get you home, hadn't we? Come."

But the afternoon was not over yet. We went slowly back through the meadow, and it seemed natural that we should come across a hedgehog with her four young ones, rustling busily through the grass, rootling with long, shining snouts. "Mrs Tiggywinkle," I breathed, and this time Cousin Geillis laughed, and did not correct me. One of them found a snail, and ate it with a cheerful crunching. They went close by us, totally without fear, then moved off. Afterwards, on the way back, Cousin Geillis picked one flower after another, and told me about them, so that by the time we reached the vicarage I knew the names and habits of some twenty plants. And somehow, though I should have been punished for climbing out of the garden, my mother said nothing, and all was well.

Cousin Geillis stayed for a few days. Most of them, I believe, she spent with me. It was halcyon weather, as always in those far-away summers, and we were out all day. And during our day-long picnic walks, as I see now, the foundation of my life was laid. When she left, the light went out of the fields and woods, but what she had kindled in me remained.

It was the last of the lovely summers. The following spring my father was moved by his bishop to a new parish, a big ugly mining parish, where the pit-heap and the smoke and the blaze of the coke-ovens and the noise of shunting engines filled the days and nights, and we settled into the cold discomfort of the house among the graveyards.

———————— ◆—●—● ————————

There were no dragonflies, no wild-flower meadows, and no hedgehogs. I begged for a pet, an animal of any kind, even a white mouse, but although, like all vicarages of that date, the place boasted a stable with stall and loose box and outhouses in plenty, I was allowed nothing. Occasionally, when the cat caught a bird, or even a mouse, I tried to nurse the victim back to health, but without success. The cat herself resisted all overtures, preferring a semi-wild life in the outhouses. Then one day I was given a rabbit by the curate, who bred them. It was an unresponsive pet, but I loved it dearly, until within weeks my mother insisted that it be given back. Next morning, when the curate called, as he did daily to talk with my father, he brought my rabbit back, skinned and jointed, and ready for the pot. I ran upstairs and was sick, while my father tried gently to explain to the astonished and offended curate, and my mother, for once warmly sympathetic, followed me and mopped up. By the time grief and horror had subsided the curate, rabbit and all, had gone. The incident was never mentioned again.

They say that the mind makes its own defences. Looking back now down the years, I can recall very little about this part of my childhood. The occasional treat – trips by bus with my father, walking with him round the parish, the kindness of some of the miners' wives who called me 'Jilly' and treated me with the same sort of fond respect they accorded my father, and then looked sideways and asked, with a different kind of respect, after my mother. And the hours spent alone in my cold bedroom, drawing and painting – always animals or flowers – or standing looking out of the window over the graveyards and the sycamore trees, at the red dusty sunset beyond the pit-heap, and wishing – wishing what? I never knew.

15

Then one day, without warning, she came again. Cousin Geillis, paying what she called a farewell visit, before leaving on a trip to see her and my mother's family in New Zealand. She would, she said, take messages or gifts, and she would be gone for some time. In those days, before air travel, such a journey took months, and a year was hardly too long to reckon on for a trip which would take the traveller right round the world. There were so many places, she said, that she wanted to see. The names went by over my head; Angkor Wat, Cairo, Delhi, the Philippines, Peru . . . She would come back when she had seen them all, and meanwhile . . .

Meanwhile she had brought a dog for me to keep.

It was a collie, black and white, thin and eager and loving. A lost dog that she had taken in, and would not leave to chance and man's unkindness.

"Here is the licence. It is Geillis's dog. She needs –" I thought she was going to say "something to love", and went cold, but she finished merely, "companionship. Someone to go walks with."

"What's his name?" I was down on the cold flags of the kitchen floor with the dog. It was too good to be true. I dared not look at my mother.

"That's for you to give him. He's yours."

"I shall call him Rover," I said, into the dog's fur. He licked my face.

"*Un peu banal*," said my cousin Geillis, "but he's not proud. Goodbye."

She did not kiss me when she went. I never saw her kiss anyone. She walked out of the house, and a moment later the bus came along and she climbed aboard.

"That's strange," said my father, "it must be an extra. The regular bus went ten minutes ago. I saw it."

My mother smiled. Then the smile vanished as her eye fell on the dog, and on me, down beside him with both arms round him. "Get up at once. And if you are going to keep that dog, he will have to be tied up. What on earth Geillis was thinking of, saddling us with a dog when there

16

will be nobody here to look after him I do not know."

"I'll look after him! I can easily –"

"You won't be here."

I gaped at her. I waited. One did not question my mother. What she wanted to tell, she told.

She set her mouth till it looked very like the one in my grandmother's portrait.

"You are to go away to school. Cousin Geillis is right. You need companionship, and to be brought out of yourself and made less of a dreamer. And since she –"

"Don't look so stricken, darling." This was my father, gently. "You'll like it. You will, really. And you do need companionship and friends. It's such a chance for us, we couldn't possibly afford it ourselves, but Cousin Geillis has offered to pay the major part of your fees. As your godmother –"

"She prefers to be called a sponsor," said my mother, a little sharply.

My father looked grieved. "Yes, I know. Poor Geillis. But since she is so kindly helping us, we must seize the chance. You do see, don't you, Jill?"

The dog was standing very close against me. I stooped and put my arms around him again. Suddenly the bleak lonely vicarage seemed very desirable, the meagre fields and the walks over the starved countryside lovely and beckoning places.

"Please," I said, "oh, please, need I go, Mummy?"

She was already turning away, no doubt with clothes-lists and school trunks in her mind. And also, as I think I knew even then, the delectable prospect of eight months of the year free of the presence of a daughter. She did not reply.

"Daddy, do I have to?"

"Your mother thinks it best." He let it slide, uneasy, but always kind. A hand went to his pocket, and came out with half-a-crown. "Here, Jilly. Get him a feeding-bowl of his own. Wood's shop has some with DOG on them. I noticed yesterday. And keep the change."

The dog licked my face. It seemed he liked the taste of tears, because he licked it again.

2

The school that was chosen eventually was an Anglican convent, of which Cousin Geillis, safely out of reach on the Atlantic, would have violently disapproved. My mother, indeed, made her protest. Leaning out of my bedroom

18

window one summer evening, I overheard my parents talking beside the open window of my father's study just below me.

"My daughter to be brought up by nuns? Absurd!" That was my mother.

"She is my daughter too."

"That's what you think," said my mother, so softly that I barely caught it.

I heard him laugh. I said he was a saint, and he adored her, always. It never occurred to him to interpret what she said as another man might have done. "I know, my dear. She has your brains, and one day she may have a little of your beauty, but I have some claim to her, too. Remember what the old sexton used to say?"

My mother knew when she had gone too far, and never fought a rearguard action. I heard the smile in her voice. " 'Thee cannat deny thysel' o' that one, Vicar . . .' And neither you can, dear Harry. She's lucky there – to have got your dark hair, and those grey eyes that I always said were far too beautiful to be wasted on a man . . . Very well. The convent does seem good enough, if the prospectus is anything to go by. But there's this other one – where's the booklet got to? This sounds just as good, and not much dearer."

"But much further away. Devonshire? Think of the train fares. Don't worry, my dear. I know these places are not renowned for scholarship, but –"

"That's what I meant. They may try to turn her out religious."

My father sounded amused. "That's hardly something you can expect me to condemn."

She laughed. "I'm sorry, I put it badly. But you know what I mean. One hears so much about religious teaching being emphasised at the expense of other subjects, especially sciences, and I think that's where Jilly's interests will lie. She's quick, and she's got a good brain. She needs good teaching and hard work and competition. I should know. That's the part of her that's like me."

Her voice grew fainter as she turned away from the window. I heard him murmur something in reply, and then a snatch or two that, craning from my window, I just managed to catch. Something from my father about "the county school" and "only two stations down the line", and an emphatic speech from my mother which I could not hear, but which I had heard so often that I could supply every word. *Her* daughter to go to school with the village children? Bad enough that she had to attend the primary, but to go to the local county school till she was seventeen or eighteen, to end up with all the wrong friends, and an accent like the miners' children? Never!

It was the protest of a lonely woman sealed tightly in her own narrow social sphere, an attitude which for those days was not outrageous, and was indeed common enough, fostered in my mother's case by the isolated Colonial upbringing with its dreams of 'home' still coloured by the standards of Victoria. It was also, as I knew even then, the voice of frustrated ambition. My mother's daughter (never my father's on these occasions) must have the chances which had been withheld from her own generation; her daughter must have independence, the freedom, that only education could give her, to choose her own line of life. The higher education, at that; a University degree, and a good one . . . A First? Why not? Of that, and how much more, would her daughter be capable.

And so on. I could guess at it all, and with it my father's invariable protest (he was as Victorian in his way as she) that a daughter, a beautiful daughter, would surely get married, and find in that way the greatest happiness, the only happiness and true fulfilment a woman could know. If Jilly had been a boy, then a public school and University by all means, but for a daughter, surely quite unnecessary?

My mother was back at the window again, her voice clear and sharp. Too sharp. This was no longer theory; the hope was about to be realised, and in the heat of actual decision, she was less than tactful.

"And if she doesn't qualify to earn her own living, and get out of here, who will she ever meet that's *fit* for her to marry? Do you really want her to stay at home and become just 'the vicar's daughter', the parish drudge?"

"Like the vicar's wife?" asked my father, very sadly.

Looking back now, after a lifetime, I can see past my own unhappiness, to what must have been my mother's. Ambitious, beautiful, clever, and with that spark of manipulative magic that we call witchcraft dormant in her, she must have been worn down, bit by bit, by poverty and hard work and the loneliness induced by my father's absorption in parish affairs, and by the whole world of distance between herself and her own people in New Zealand. By disappointment, too. My father, contented in his work, even in his poverty, would never push his way into the higher clerical spheres which she would have delighted in, and adorned. I did not think about it then; I just knew that some unhappiness, unexpressed, lay between my parents, in spite of their deep affection for one another.

After a pause she said, in a voice I hardly recognised: "I have all I want, Harry. All I have ever wanted. You know that." A short silence, then she went on, but gently now: "I hope Geillis will have it too, some day. But we have to face the fact that she may never marry, and that we can leave her nothing."

"Not even a home. I know. You are right, as usual. This offer of Geillis's is a godsend – yes, whatever she might want to call it, a godsend. Well, what about it? Can you reconcile yourself to the convent? Your fears may have no foundation. The entrance examination did look a pretty stiff one to me."

"I suppose so. Yes, all right. But oh, dear, a convent!"

"It's the cheapest," said my father simply.

And that seemingly clinched it, for to the convent I was sent.

It was a gaunt place, near the sea cliffs on the east coast, and my mother hardly need have worried that the good nuns would have any undue influence over me. The good nuns, indeed, believed in what they called 'self-government' in the school, which meant merely that a form leader was selected, the biggest and toughest and most popular girl in the form, and that all discipline, including punishment, was in her control, and that of her 'second', usually her closest friend and crony. As a system to save trouble for the nuns it may have had something to recommend it; from the point of view of a shy and studious child, it was the stuff of a lifetime's nightmares.

I arrived at school with a reputation for being clever, fostered by that 'stiff' entrance examination which I passed with ease, and was put by the good sisters into a class of girls at least two years older than I was. Scholarship not being a forte of the convent, I was soon head of that class, and, longing for approbation, and therefore working harder than ever, I no doubt richly deserved the jealous dislike which was presently meted out to me. I was eight years old, with no defences; school became a place of torment and misery. The days were awful enough; the nights in the dormitories were a hell of teasing and torture. We, the bullied and tormented children, certainly never dreamed of complaining. The punishment for that, in the unsupervised classrooms and dormitories, would have been too horrific. Each evening, after compline, the silent file of nuns would pass through the junior dormitory, heads bent, veils hiding their faces, arms in their sleeves, looking neither to right nor left at the beds where, still and apparently asleep, lay torturers and tortured, waiting till the door closed before the nightmare began again.

Even at home, I told no one. Least of all, at home. My childhood had conditioned me to unhappiness, to not believing I was wanted; to fear. So I lived through term after wretched term, my only resort being books, and the security of the working classroom where of course I went even further ahead of the bigger girls who bullied me. The only gleam of light and love was the thought of the holidays. Not the bleak boredom of the vicarage, or even the gentle companionship of my father, but the single-minded love of my dog Rover.

Too single-minded. He loved, obeyed and followed no one but me. My mother put up with our joyous partnership for something over a year. While I was away he stayed tied up; she would not walk him, so when she released him at all he vanished into fields and village, looking for me. She was, she said once, afraid he might become a sheep-worrier. So at the end of one term I came home from school to be told that he had 'gone'.

That was all. It may be hard now for modern children to understand that I did not dare even ask how, or when. I said nothing. I did not even dare let her see me crying. This time no one blotted my tears.

The birds and mice, the rabbit, the beloved dog. I did not try again. I stayed within myself and endured, as silently as I could, until, again, help came. It came in a strange and roundabout way. It was discovered (foolish and innocent as I was, I had confided in someone) that I believed in magic. I was young for my years – still barely ten years old – and the myths and legends of the classics and the Norsemen, the stories of Andrew Lang and Hans Andersen and Grimm still trailed their clouds of glory through my imagination. And it must be admitted, also, that the church-haunted life I led, with its miracles and legends, and its choirs of angels, conspired with fairyland to make an Otherworld both real and probable.

So it was rumoured that little Jilly Ramsey believed in fairies. It was the senior girls, kinder than my own contemporaries, who hatched a plot. Rather sweet, they said, and wrote tiny notes for me from the Fairy Queen, then they hid and watched me steal out and pick these up from a sundial which stood in a neglected part of the school garden. I do not remember now how it started, nor how much I believed, but it was a happy secret and seemed to mean me no harm. I would take the little letter, then run off into the wood (there was no privacy anywhere within doors) to read it, and write my reply.

The last time it happened was in early June, about the middle of my second summer term. There was the note, tucked into the mossy stone. The minute writing said merely: *"Dear Jilly, In your last letter you were wishing you had a fairy godmother. I am sure you will be hearing from one soon. Your Queen, Titania."*

What they had planned for me I was never to know. Something, a sound, a movement, made me look up. Behind the bushes I saw the crouching forms of the girls who had perpetrated the hoax.

I got to my feet. I cannot now remember what I felt, or what I intended to do. But at that moment the voice of one of my form mates called my name from the edge of the garden.

"Jilly! Jilly Ramsey!"

"I'm here."

"There's a letter for you!"

The stocky figure of Alice Bundle, one of my fellow sufferers, and as such, something approximating to a friend, came running down the path, waving a letter.

I did not look towards the bushes. I said, very clearly: "Thanks a lot, Alice. Oh, yes, I know the writing. It's from my godmother. I was expecting it. She's going to take me away from here."

I crumpled the Fairy Queen's note, threw it to the ground and ran back into school. The senior girls straightened as I passed them. One of them called out something, but I took no notice. I was buoyed up by the first defiance of my childhood, the first deliberate lie, the first don't-care attitude I had dared to take. I left the older girls staring after me. They must have thought that their false magic had somehow worked for me.

It had. The letter, as I had expected, was from my mother. It was the day when her weekly letter invariably arrived. It started with the name she used for me when she was pleased about something.

Dear Gillyflower,

Your Cousin Geillis is home now, and came to see us on Friday. She was not at all pleased when she found out what school you had been sent to. Since she is putting up most of the money for your board we have to give in to her wishes, and she wants you taken away from the convent. You will have to sit for another entrance scholarship, but I have no doubt you will get it. See that you do. The new school is in the Lake District and I hope its record for scholarship is better than your convent, since, as you know, you will have to earn your own living, every penny of it . . .

Blessed Cousin Geillis. Or rather, since she would have spurned that adjective, beloved Cousin Geillis. I could, and would, start again.

3

Life could not be anything but better at the new school. I was still too clever for comfort and not clever enough to hide it, but I had learned to free-wheel a little, and to be content with second or third place in class. I was fairly good

26

at games, too, and my talent for drawing, an acceptable one, was admired. So, though I remember little in the way of positive happiness, the years went by smoothly enough.

The school itself was beautiful, a big eighteenth-century house surrounded by park and woodland, where we were allowed to wander at will in our free time. This only in theory; in practice we got little free time, but I believe I was, in fact, the only one who really coveted the privilege. Accustomed to solitude all my young life, I now craved it, and whenever I could escape my schoolmates I found my way into the woods where stood an abandoned summer-house which I thought of as my own. It was dilapidated and dirty, and on damp days the rain dripped through the roof, but near by was the lime walk smelling of honey, and if one sat still enough in the shelter of the summer-house the red squirrels would come right in through the doorway, and the birds fly to their nests under the eaves.

And there, once again, it happened; the one memorable encounter of those green and growing years.

It was half-term, in the summer of my fourteenth year. Almost everyone had gone out with parents, so I was free for the day. My parents of course never came. I sat alone in the summer-house, drawing. I had found globe flowers and herb Paris, and lesser twayblade, and these were in a jar on the rickety wooden table in front of me.

A footstep sounded on the mossy path outside. Cousin Geillis said cheerfully: "I thought I might find you here. Have you had tea?"

"Oh, Cousin Geillis! No, I haven't."

"Then come along. We'll go down to the river. I've brought a picnic with me. Leave those flowers, you can get them when we come back."

I don't remember that I ever asked her how she had come, or how she had found me. I suppose I still took her kind of magic for granted. She even knew, without telling, that we were not allowed to go to the river in the normal way. Nobody saw us. We crossed the hockey pitches and walked along the banks of the river under the oak trees. Beyond their shadow was a long, sunny curve of water-meadow where, once, a bank or causeway had been built to keep the river back in flood-time. We sat there, while below us, as if it were a matter of course, a kingfisher flashed down from a dead branch, caught a fish, and vanished with it into his hole in the sandy bank.

"Do you remember the ladybird," asked Cousin Geillis, "and Mrs Tiggywinkle?"

"*Coccinella*," I said demurely, "and *Erinaceus europæus*? Of course I do."

She laughed. "Poor child. But you were a quick study. And I gather you've been a quick study ever since. Those drawings you were doing were quite beautiful. How old are you now?"

"Nearly fourteen. I do School Cert. next year."

"And then? What are you planning to do with yourself, Gilly?" (I should say here that when I reached my teens I discarded the childish spelling of Jilly, though my name was pronounced in the same way.) "Do you know yet?" asked my cousin.

"Not really. University, Mummy says, and then teach, but –"

"But?"

"I'm not sure that I want to. What I'd really like is to be an artist."

I believe that for me at that age 'being an artist' meant a kind of picturesque independence in a well-lighted garret, with a dash of Paris and Burlington House thrown in. Most importantly, it meant having my own place, garret or otherwise, and being alone when I wanted to. I longed to go to an art school, but there was no way my parents could have afforded it, and since Cousin Geillis was already paying for most of my schooling, I could hardly tell her so. Nor, even if she had paid for me, or (as my teacher seemed to think was possible) I had secured a scholarship, would my mother have let me go. She had made that clear. So I knew I would have to go with the tide, earn a University place, teach if I had to, perhaps some day meet someone . . .

"If that's what you really want to do, then what's to stop you?" asked Cousin Geillis briskly. "You have the talent. No need to be modest. You must know it."

"Well, yes, but you see –" I bit my lip and stopped.

She read my thoughts unerringly. "And don't give me any nonsense about 'not having the chance' or the 'luck'! Let me tell you something. The only luck you have in this life is the talent you're born with. The rest is up to you."

"Yes, Cousin Geillis."

Her eyes twinkled. "All right. End of sermon. Have a sandwich, and let's talk of something else, shall we?"

"Yes, please." I accepted both offers with relief. The sandwich was a new roll, bulging with scrambled egg and cress, a wonderful change from school meals. "Tell me about the places you've been to. Have you really been right round the world?"

So while we ate the picnic she had brought she told me about the places she had seen, so vividly that now, when I remember that day, I can see some of those exotic landscapes as clearly as the river bank with the Eden flowing below us, and the kingfisher flashing to and from his bough.

The chime of the church clock, striking five, floated across the hockey pitches. Soon it would be time to go. We gathered up the picnic debris and stuffed it back into Cousin Geillis's holdall. Interlude over. Back to school. Back, in fact, to earth.

"It's a bit like that other time, isn't it?" I said. "You just coming out of nowhere, and a lovely afternoon, and then ordinary things again. Like a fairy godmother. Once when I was little, at the convent, I pretended you *were* a fairy godmother, and as a matter of fact, I still think you are. It's such a nice thing to have! And you did say one thing that I've always remembered. When the dragonfly climbed out of the pond and flew away. Do you remember that?"

"I do indeed. What about it?"

"I asked you if you were a witch, and you said you could

sometimes make things happen. What did you mean? Was it true?"

She was silent. Then she reached into the holdall and brought out something about the size of a tennis ball, wrapped in black velvet. Holding it in her palm, she unwrapped it, letting the velvet fall away until the object lay exposed, a ball certainly, but not a tennis ball or indeed like any ball I had ever seen. It looked like glass, but not ordinary glass, and I knew straight away what it was. A crystal ball. A small reflecting world of misty green and gold, where the breeze in the boughs threw shadow and shine, and the sun on the water made sparks that dazzled the eyes.

My cousin was speaking. "Whether I can make things happen or not I do not know. But I do sometimes see what is going to happen, and then whatever one does appears as its cause." She smiled faintly. "A prerequisite for prophetic power?"

I did not understand her. I ploughed on. "You mean you see things in that crystal?"

"In that, and in other ways."

"Then it's true it can be done?"

"Oh, yes, it's true."

I stared, fascinated, at the globe in her hand. "Cousin Geillis, could you – *could* you look now, and see what's going to happen?"

A direct look, grave and gentle. "You mean to you, don't you? That's what everyone means when they talk of 'the future'. It's a very narrow channel, the future."

"I'm sorry. It was only – you did ask me what I was going to do when I grow up, and I wasn't sure –"

"Don't be sorry." She smiled suddenly. "We're all alike. I've peered down my own channel already."

"*Have* you?" I suppose I was naïvely surprised that anyone so advanced in years should have any future worth longing for. Life, for anyone of Cousin Geillis's age, was all in the past.

She had read me with ease. She was laughing. "Well?

Wouldn't you want to know when it was all going to end for you?"

"N – no. No!"

"You can't choose, you know. When you look, you may see what's near at hand, or you may see right to the very end. Would you want to do that?"

"I don't really know. Would you?"

"I have done. That's enough of mine, would you like to look for yours?"

The globe in her hand was flickering with light and dark from the flow of the river. I hesitated. "How? Just look, do you mean?"

"That's all. Don't be scared, you'll probably see nothing except what's there of the world right round us now. Here, take it." She put the crystal, still lying in its velvet, into my cupped palms. "Now empty your mind as best you can, and look. Without hope, without fear, without memory, and without guile. Just look."

I looked.

My own face, small and distorted. The running light of the river. A flash of blue, the kingfisher. A shoal of black streaks, like tadpoles, but I knew from the screaming in the sky that they were swifts, skimming the treetops. Another shoal, white, sailing, tilting, silent as a snow-storm: a flight of doves or pigeons, wheeling and dipping, like a cloud of snow in an old-fashioned paperweight. Then crystal, grey as mist, reflecting my eyes and the crimson of my school blazer and the tiny trees behind me.

I looked up, blinking. The sky was empty.

"Well?" she asked.

"Nothing. Only what you said, the world that's here, the trees and the river and the swifts and that flock of pigeons." I looked about me. "Where did they go? Where are they?"

"In the crystal."

I sat up straight, and pushed the hair back from my forehead. "Are you saying they weren't real? But they were!

Look, there they are again!" as the swifts tore past above us, shrilling like bosuns' whistles.

"Oh, they're real enough. But not the pigeons," said Cousin Geillis, reaching to take the crystal from me.

"Do you honestly mean there wasn't a flock of them flying over? White ones and grey, quite low?"

"That's what I mean."

"Then," I drew a breath, "I *did* see something?"

"It seems so."

I took another, longer breath, and let it go on a sigh. "But why? And what does it mean?"

She was wrapping the crystal and tucking it carefully away into the holdall. She took her time over the answer. "Only that you have just told me what I wanted to know. That you are your mother's daughter, and, for want of a better term, my godchild."

And that, in spite of my eager questions, was all that she would say.

I gave up at length, and went back to something she had said earlier. "You said you had looked at your own future. Did you see it?"

"I didn't need to see that in the crystal." We were walking back now, skirting the edge of the hockey field. She paused and looked up, but I got the impression that she was looking clear through the branches of the trees to something way beyond, and shining. "A little more travelling here and there, and learning a little more, I hope. Did you know I was a herbalist? I collect when I travel, and there's always something new to learn in the out-of-the-way places. Then home." She looked down at me. "I have a home now. I saw the house, and it seemed made for me, so I took it on. Some day you will see it."

Not "you must", but "you will".

"What's it like?" I asked.

"A good house, deep in the woods, with a garden all around it and a river flowing past it. Fruit trees, and flowers planted for the bees. A place to grow my herbs. Silence in winter, and in summer nothing but the birds. Lonely as the grave, and every bit as restful."

To me, at that age, rest was not something I wanted, and the grave was so far off as to be unimaginable. But there was one essential for any worldly heaven. I asked eagerly: "Will you keep animals?"

She gave me a sidelong look. "Still? You poor child. Well, I'll tell you one thing I did see in the crystal, Geillis my dear."

"What's that?"

"You and I," said Cousin Geillis, "and for all I know the doves and the hedgehogs and the tadpoles and your poor lost dog and all, will live there together one day."

We had reached the door that led through a high wall into the school grounds. With my hand on the knob I said, without looking at her: "I didn't think such things ever really happened. The 'happy ever after' things, I mean."

"They don't," she said gently. "Not for ever. Happiness changes as you change. It's in yourself. But I will be there just as long as you need me, which won't be for ever, or even, perhaps, for very long." She reached over my shoulder and pushed the door open. "Go along now, and don't forget your things in the summer-house. I won't come in. I'm going to Langwathby to get a train. Goodbye."

The door shut between us.

4

I did not after all get a degree, but my mother never knew it. At the end of my first year at Durham University she died. My father was with me; he had travelled by bus into Durham to attend a meeting in the Chapter House, and afterwards we went home together, to find the local policeman at the door and a few people in the road, watching.

It transpired that my mother had gone with the car to visit an old lady at the far side of the Deanery. On the way back she met with an accident. Another car came fast out of a side road, and smashed head on into her offside door. She was a good driver, but she cannot have had a chance. The side road was no more than a farm track, and traffic would hardly be expected on it. The driver of the other car was the farmer's young son, who had only recently passed his driving test, and was going far too fast. It was thought that he pressed the throttle instead of the brake, but that was only a guess. He was killed instantly.

Through all that followed, the inquests, the visits to the bereaved farmer and his wife (my father saw their comfort as his first duty), the funerals, both taken by my father, with a brief talk for the bereaved, he moved with an air of sweet and gentle abstraction. He ate what I put before him, went into his study, from which no sound of his typewriter came, went across to the church, came back, sat in his study alone, went to bed.

The morning after the funeral he did not appear. I found him still in bed and, for the first time that I remembered, disinclined to get up. Delayed shock, said the doctor, when I sent for him, but I knew that it was more than that. My mother had been the spring that drove him. Now it had snapped.

Of course it meant the end for me of any thought of a degree and training for a job away from home. Even if my father could have afforded to pay a housekeeper, nothing of the sort could be thought of until he was well again. I wrote straight away to the University authorities, conscious only of a shamefaced feeling of thankfulness that it was my father I was called upon to care for, though to tell the truth I doubt if my mother, similarly bereaved, would have needed or even wanted me to stay at home with her.

But now at home I had to stay. The green years had gone,

it seemed in a flash, and sometimes, in moments of weary frustration, it seemed for ever. The Cumberland hills and lakes, still in those days lapped in Wordsworthian calm, the glories of Durham, with its islanded towers and trees, and the precious solitude in which one could shut oneself away and study, these I could have now only for memory. I was back in the wilderness, trapped by the ugly brick houses, the towering, smoking black of the pit-heap; and beyond those, almost to the edge of the county, and right down to the sea, the starved and meagre landscapes of the coalfield.

If I fretted, it was briefly. I was young, I loved my father dearly, and truth to tell the relief of my mother's death was so intense as to make a new kind of happiness. I was surprised to find how much genuine satisfaction there was in the management of the house and the parish affairs that had been her domain. The only real worry was my father's failing health, and sometimes – not often, because youth cannot see an end to vigour and life – sometimes in the night a misgiving about my own future when he died. He must have had the same thought; he never spoke of it, but he must have known the nagging fear at the back of the clergyman's mind; no home after the work is done. What I think he still clung to was the belief of his generation, that in time I would marry, and so be provided with a home, and what used to be called 'an establishment'. Man-like, he never paused to wonder how, in our isolated life, any such opportunity was to occur.

There had, of course, been friendships made in my senior days at school, but it is rare that such friendships go on into adult life, and besides, though I had once or twice spent part of a school holiday at a friend's house, the return visit to our grim and isolated vicarage was never a success. So also during my brief year at Durham: friendships, not carried over into home life, could not persist. The same went for any young men I met; they soon gave me up as too serious and too shy; "wrapped up in her work" was the kindest comment; so at the end of that university year I went home heart-whole, and hardly even knowing what I had missed.

And so for a few more years. The war came, and its privations and fears and exhaustions served to drive other fears for the future from our lives. We had long since lost touch with Cousin Geillis; or rather, she had lost touch with us. I had not seen her since that strange interlude by the River Eden, and though I had written to her at intervals, she had never answered. There had been no sign from her even when my mother died, and when I wrote to the only address I knew, that of her solicitors in Salisbury, there was no reply. She might be living abroad, having been caught on one of her travels by the outbreak of war, she might even be dead. We had no way of knowing, and she gradually became one with the fading memory of the green years.

Some three years after the end of the war my father died. He died as he had lived, quietly and with more thought for others than for himself.

After the funeral was over, and everyone had gone, I went across to the church again to lock the vestry after the officiating clergy, then walked back alone through the grave-yard to the vicarage. It was August, and the path between the graves was matted with fallen grass-seeds and petals. The trees hung heavy and still in the dead air.

Some of the village women, who had helped with the funeral arrangements, were still in the vicarage kitchen making a cup of tea for themselves when the washing-up was finished. I joined them, then they finished clearing up, and went.

The house was empty, echoing, no longer mine. I sat down in the rocking-chair beside the grate where the fire slowly died from flame to ash, and for the first time realised that I was alone, that the night-time fears had materialised, that I had nothing, nowhere even to go after the new appointment had been made and the vicarage handed to its next incumbent. Before that happened I would have to sell the furniture, realise everything I could, then take myself off and start looking around for work.

Where? And what work? I was qualified, as my mother would have said crisply, to do nothing. A year at University doing botany, chemistry, geology – not enough of anything to justify even the most elementary of teaching jobs, and in the '40s jobs of any kind were hard to get. I straightened wearily in my chair, stilling the rockers. In the morning, perhaps, I would be able to think more clearly, gather a small residue of courage. Meanwhile, before the fire died right out, I must get myself some supper. The ashes fell in the grate. Even that small sound had its echo in the emptiness.

The doorbell rang.

At the back door one of the women was waiting. She had a long envelope in her hand.

"Oh, Miss Gilly, I forgot this. I'm that sorry. It came this morning, and what with one thing and another I clean forgot to give it to you. It's a letter."

I took it and thanked her. She hesitated, her eyes on my face.

"Are you sure there's nothing I could do? Doesn't seem right for you to be all alone, not with your dad gone like that. Why don't you come over the road and take a bite of supper with us?"

"It's very kind of you, Mrs Green, but I'll be all right, I will really. Thank you for bringing the letter. You shouldn't have troubled. Tomorrow would have done."

"That's all right. Well, if you're sure ... I'll be up in the morning to help you with the house. Good night, Miss Gilly."

"Good night."

I went back to the cooling fireside, turning the envelope over in my hand ... Thick, good paper, typed. The crest of some firm, vaguely familiar to me. I opened it. It held a folded document with an official look to it; another, smaller envelope; and a covering letter bearing the same crest. I read it.

Sat down slowly. Read it again.

It was from Martin and Martin, the solicitors in Salisbury.

They were forwarding a letter, they wrote, from my cousin Miss Geillis Saxon, who, they regretted to inform me, had died suddenly a month ago on July 16th, of pneumonia following influenza. With Miss Saxon's letter they were enclosing a copy of her will, in which I would see that she had named me as her sole beneficiary, leaving me her house in Wiltshire "with its entire contents". The accompanying letter had been lodged with them when the will was signed, and Miss Saxon had instructed them to forward it, together with a copy of the will, to reach me on August 12th, 1948. She had presumably meant the copy of the will "for information only", but by a sad coincidence (they wrote) her death had occurred shortly before the specified date. They were sorry to be the bearers of such sad news, but they hoped to be of service to me in the future. If I would let them know when I would like to travel down . . .

My fingers seemed stiff. I opened the other envelope. I had never seen Cousin Geillis's handwriting, but somehow, characteristically, it spoke of her.

My dear Geillis,

I have never given you my address, because I live very much to myself these days. But if you like to come now to Wiltshire, the house is called Thornyhold, and is on the edge of Westermain Forest. The train stops at St Thorn and the taxi knows the way.

There is no such thing as coincidence. The house is yours whenever you need it, and when you read this letter that is now. Don't leave it too long before you come down. You will find everything here that you have most wanted. Take it and be welcome, my child. Look after Hodge. He will miss me.

Your Cousin Geillis.

The last of the ashes fell in with a soft puff of grey smoke. I was staring at the date of Cousin Geillis's letter. It had been written more than six months ago, on December 9th, 1947.

5

I can hardly remember now what I had imagined Cousin Geillis's home to be like. The reality is always very different from a mental forecast, and inevitably wipes out the false image. I believe I had envisaged something of the picture-

40

postcard variety, something romantic, rustic and picturesque, an ancient thatched cottage cosily nestling in flowery
woodland, with briar roses thick in the garden hedge, and
lilacs crowding beyond the chimney pots. Something, in
fact, conjured up from the country memories of childhood.

The name itself should have suggested that Thornyhold
was not in the least like that. It had, as I discovered, once
been the agent's house on a big estate long since broken up
into several farms. A timber village had been built some
miles away, where the Forestry Commission had bought
its acres and planted its regimented softwoods. Two long
driveways ran through ancient woodlands, to meet at their
centre in a space where once the great house had stood.
Here, there was now only a pile of huge sandstone blocks,
with balustraded steps rising to an empty doorway, and one
wall still standing with its window frames rustling with the
boughs of trees. The balusters, the carving over the windows,
and beyond, the ruined archway and weedblanketed cobbles
of the stableyard, told of a once-stately Georgian mansion.
But everything, including the last scion of the family, had
long since gone. Apart from the foresters' village, which
went by the name of Westermain, all that remained was the
gatehouse, a tiny structure split in two by the main gates,
and the former estate agent's house, deep in the woods,
where Cousin Geillis had lived.

I saw it first on a dampish day of September, almost a
month after my father's death. All was settled, his simple will
read, the main part of the vicarage furniture either sold, or
left in place: some of the larger pieces had gone with the
house for the last two or three incumbents, and I left others,
knowing that Thornyhold still held all Cousin Geillis's furniture. I had saved the few pieces that my father had treasured,
and these were in store and waiting till I saw what room
there was in my new home.

I went down by train. Our old car had long since begun
to cost too much in repairs, and besides, I would no longer
be entitled to the petrol allowance my father had claimed.

So it was sold with the rest. For all I knew, Cousin Geillis had had a car, and this would be mine along with Thornyhold itself. But that could wait. All I wanted now was to get away. The sale of my effects had gone through more quickly than I had expected, so, laden only with a couple of suitcases, and the ring of keys I had asked the Salisbury solicitors to send me, I set off for St Thorn and that taxi that knew the way.

It did. When I gave the driver the address he paused with one of my cases half lifted into the boot.

"Thornyhold, is it? Miss Saxon's house? The old lady that died a few weeks back?"

"Yes."

He shut the boot on the cases, and opened the back door for me. "A relation of yours? I'm sorry about that."

"A cousin. My mother's cousin, actually. You knew her, then? May I sit in front beside you, please?"

"Sure. You'll be more comfortable there anyway." He saw me seated, shut me in, and took his own place. "No, I wouldn't say I knew her. But she always took my taxi when she came home from travelling. A great traveller she was till the last year or so. Used to tell me about it. All over the world she'd been." A sideways glance, carefully incurious. "Nice for them that can do it. But she never did look all that comfortably off, even."

"I wouldn't know," I said.

I would, though. Cousin Geillis had by no means left a fortune, but she had left me what would, along with my father's few hundred pounds, keep me modestly for some time. Very modestly. All I wanted, wealth abounding. I looked out of the taxi window as the houses dwindled back and the road began to wind between high, banked hedges full of ivy and holly glistening with recent rain, and the red berries of honeysuckle twining through pillowfight drifts of traveller's joy. I hesitated. But I was going to live in this part of the world, and people might as well know what, in any case, they would soon find out. "I haven't seen Miss Saxon since I was a child, but I was her only relative in this country, so she left the house to me. I'm going to live there."

"Well," said the driver, and I could hear the reservations in his voice, "it's a nice part of the world. A bit lonesome, perhaps, down there in Westermain. You got a car, I suppose?"

"Not at the moment. Did Miss Saxon have one?"

"Never saw one, but I wouldn't know. Only ever saw the old lady when she came home by train. Folks from that side of the forest do their shopping at Arnside. But if you should be looking round for something, I might be able to put you in the way of a good second-hand car. Hannaker's garage, other side of the cinema, next to the White Hart."

"Well, thank you. It depends a bit on whether I can get petrol coupons."

"You ought to get those easy enough, living right out there, and I'd see you all right, no problem."

"Well, thank you," I said again. "My name's Ramsey, by the way. You're Mr Hannaker?"

"Yes. Call me Ted."

I sat back. "You spoke of the forest. That's Westermain?"

"Yes. We're coming into it now."

I knew, of course, that 'forest' did not necessarily mean woodland, but some tract of unfenced land, a wild uncultivated space which had formerly been wooded. The road now left the hedges and farms of the tilled countryside and ran, narrow and white, across moorland where rusting bracken competed with straggly heather and wide patches of reedy green where cattle grazed. Clumps of fir trees, with their rooks circling like smoke, stood up against the sky. The driver pointed. On the horizon half a mile away I saw the delicate, trotting shapes of deer. Rabbits scuttled for cover into the thickets of gorse. There were copses of birch, with their leaves round and golden as sequins. Not a house in sight. Then the road dipped gently, to thread a hump-backed bridge over a smooth river.

"That's the Arn," said Mr Hannaker.

"And is that Arnside beyond those trees? I thought I saw a building of some sort."

"No. Arnside's a few miles yet, right beyond Westermain. What you saw was just the old abbey, St Thorn. It's a ruin, nothing left now but a few pillars and some broken walls, and maybe a couple of fallen arches." He laughed briefly at his own joke. "Nothing worth keeping up, but it must have been pretty once. Here we are now. Westermain woods."

The road curled upwards from the bridge to run between ranks of trees. These were huge and seemed very old, standing back from the road among the tall autumn bracken. They were mainly oaks, with beech and elm and smaller trees like holly interspersed. Where trees had fallen they had not been cleared, and lay in thick tangles of creeper and fern. Fifty yards or so in from the road's edge the forest looked as impenetrable as a jungle. So for perhaps another mile. Then we were running alongside a high, crumbling wall, built of stone in more expansive days, with broken gaps where the great trees had grown through them and where encroaching ivy, eating the mortar from the joints, had pulled them down.

"Thornyhold," said the driver.

He slowed, and the taxi turned in through the massive ruinous pillars of the main gate.

To either side of this crouched a tiny house. The eighteenth- century passion for symmetry had split the gate-house into two. The pieces were twins, mirror images. There were lace curtains in the windows, a suburban touch which looked oddly out of place in the country.

In the window to our left, as we passed, the curtain twitched slightly, then fell back into place. In its twin window on the right the lace hung still, but behind it, vaguely, could be seen a movement, as of someone rocking to and fro, to and fro.

Then the taxi was past, and gathering speed up the long winding avenue.

"Funny sort of house that, I've always thought,' said

Mr Hannaker. "Looks as if there's only one room on each side. Some old-time landlord's idea of a joke. Do you suppose they live on one side and sleep on the other?"

"Goodness knows. Do you know who lives there?"

"Name's Trapp. She's a widow woman. All the old lady ever told me. Keep themselves to themselves, the folks over this way."

"It's a long driveway, isn't it? Is it far now?"

"Another quarter mile, maybe. There's a road off soon, but you won't see it till you're right on it . . . Here we are."

He swung the wheel as he spoke, and we turned left into a narrower driveway. "There's the gate. You expected?"

"Not that I know of."

The car stopped. He came round to open my door, and jerked his head sideways.

"Reason I asked, there's smoke from the chimney."

"*Is* there?" I straightened and looked.

The driveway here came to a dead end, with a smallish turning circle for the car. The surface of the drive was pitted and green with disuse; the marks made by the taxi were the only signs that a vehicle had ever been this way. On either side the woods crowded in, to meet where a hugely tall thorn hedge barred the way. Set deep in this hedge was a small wicket gate that had once been white. The quickthorn met over it, and had been cut and trained to form a thick green archway. Beyond the hedge nothing could be seen of the house but a roof of grey slabs patched golden-green with lichen, and rosy with thick tufts of houseleek huddled below the tall chimney-pots.

From a chimney on the left a faint veil, of heat rather than smoke, slowly climbed towards the boughs of the beeches that towered beyond.

"The lawyers must have arranged for someone to come down and open up for me," I said.

"Well then, that's all right," said Mr Hannaker, "I'll just see you in, though. Your heavy stuff coming later, I reckon?"

"Yes. That's very kind of you. Thank you."

He pushed open the wicket gate for me, picked up my cases and followed me up the path.

The path was straight, brick-paved, and only about ten yards long. This was the north side of the house, and the strip of garden between hedge and house wall would get very little sun. Even so, the garden was something of a shock. Though I had learned from the lawyers that Cousin Geillis had been poorly for some weeks before her death two months ago, I had somehow still expected the place to be as she had described it to me, but at that time of year a few weeks' neglect can soon transform a richly flowering garden into a mass of weeds and seed-heads, and the tidiest brick path into a slippery ribbon of moss and algae. To my dismay the house, which should have held up longer against the lack of care, had something of the same dilapidated look. There must have been a storm not long ago, for the windows were hazed with leaf-blow from the encircling trees, a roof gutter sagged under a tangle of fallen twigs, and from that and other places dripped the water of a recent shower. Everywhere were the damp drifts of autumn's first leaf-fall. At the windows the curtains hung crookedly, as if pulled back by a careless hand, and on the sill of what was presumably the kitchen window – to the left below that smoking chimney – I could see pots full of dead and dying plants.

Small things. Inevitable things, soon to be put right by an owner's care. The air of depression and neglect that hung over the place could not hide the fact that the house was handsome. It was stone-built, and, though not large, was well proportioned, with an attractive door and long-sashed windows. No doubt the south face would be better still, and certainly more cheerful, with the 'best' rooms overlooking the main garden, where the trees stood back to let the sunlight in.

There was a knocker on the door, a lion's head mouthing a ring. It should have been bright brass, but now showed a dull olive-green. I had the key in my hand, but that smoking chimney made me hesitate. I put a hand to the door-knob.

Before I could turn it, the door opened. A woman stood there. About ten years older than I was, I guessed. (I was twenty-seven.) Not so tall; fresh-faced, blue-eyed and brown-haired, with smooth rosy cheeks, and the wrong red too thick on a small mouth. In spite of a stocky figure and thick ankles she was pretty, with dimples at the corners of a mouth very ready to smile.

She did not smile now. Her gaze went straight past me, with scarcely a pause, to the driver, and the cases which he had dumped beside me on the step, then to the open wicket beyond which the taxi waited.

"Good afternoon," I began.

"Good afternoon, miss." Her voice, with its country accent, was soft and breathless. "It's Miss Ramsey, is it?"

"Yes. And you are –?"

"I'm Agnes Trapp, from the gatehouse. I was cleaning up. I wasn't expecting anyone today." She sounded flustered, and all the time she was speaking her eyes flickered from me to the driver, to the taxi by the gate, to the two heavy suitcases, then back to me again. "They said – the lawyers said she'd be coming soon, but they never told me the day, and they never said there'd be two ladies. She's in the car, is she, the old lady? I've only readied one of the rooms, but if you're staying just now I can easily sort another one for you. If they'd told me – But you'd better bring her in now, and not keep her waiting in the car."

"Look, don't worry," I said quickly, "it's all right. There is only me. No one else. I'm Miss Saxon's cousin, Geillis Ramsey."

"But I thought – they never said – I just thought –" She stopped, and swallowed. Her hands plucked at the apron she wore, and she flushed vividly. The red began at the neck of her blouse, then rose, smooth and swift as the first wave of the tide, right up to the hairline.

"I'm sorry if I startled you," I said uncomfortably. "The solicitors didn't say anything about getting someone in to open the house for me, and I wasn't sure which day I could get away, or I'd have let them know, and they might have got things clearer. They did send me the keys, so of course I just came down as soon as I could." Embarrassed, I was talking too much and too quickly. As if, I thought with acute discomfort, I had caught the woman out in some dishonest act, and was myself feeling guilty in consequence, as one does. As I had always done. The feeling was familiar, and so was the placating note in my voice: "So please don't worry, Mrs Trapp. I'm sure everything will be lovely, and I'm so grateful to you for coming along."

"Well," and now she smiled, a charming smile full of relief and pleasure. The flush had gone, as quickly as it had risen. "How silly of me. But when they said her cousin, I was looking for an old – an older lady, that is. You're very welcome, miss, and it's good you were able to come so soon. It's been kind of lonely with no neighbour here in Thornyhold. We've been looking forward to you coming. I'll take the cases in for you now, shall I?"

She lifted them and stood waiting while I paid Mr Hannaker. He thanked me, repeated his promise about a car, nodded at Mrs Trapp and took himself off.

6

I followed Mrs Trapp into the house. It must have been built at the same time as the great house; there were the graceful proportions of the eighteenth century, scaled down to the humbler requirements of the squire's agent. The hall was

49

square, with doors opening off it to left and right, and beyond the left-hand door a staircase with wide shallow treads leading up to a broad landing. At the rear of the hall was a shallow archway through which a kind of minor hallway could be seen, with a tall window showing a glimpse of trees and sky, and to the right of this another door which led, presumably, to a drawing-room. The floor was tiled, and felt gritty underfoot, and the rugs were clearly in need of a good shaking.

So much I saw before Mrs Trapp set my cases down and hurried ahead of me towards a door covered with faded baize which was set back under the rise of the staircase.

"This way. Wait a minute while I put the light on. The passage is a bit dark if you don't know the way. Mind that rug, it's a bit torn. It'll be cosier in the kitchen. If I'd 'a known you were coming today I could have got the sitting-room done out, but first things first, so the bedroom's all done, and I must say it needed it, with your aunty being in bed there for a bit before she went to hospital."

"It's very good of you –" I was beginning again, but she cut me short.

"As if we could let you come all this way, and to a strange house, and not have a fire lit and the bed aired! As soon as we heard there was a Miss Ramsey coming to live, I said to Jessamy, he's my son, we'd better get straight up there and get things sorted out a bit for her, poor soul, or she won't sleep easy, the way things have been left. I mean, Miss Ramsey, the place is clean enough, that goes without saying, but it's been neglected lately, and you can see it. Here we are, the kettle's just nicely on the boil."

The kettle looked, indeed, as if it had been on the boil for some time, but whatever the tea was like, I would be grateful for it. They say that to travel hopefully is better than to arrive: on the way down in the train I had been drifting in a dream, or rather, towards the fulfilment of a dream. A house of my own, a garden, a wood to the very door; the picture Cousin Geillis had drawn for me years ago, lighted by sunshine, and filled with flowers. I had not paused to consider that the reality, on this sunless September day, would be very different. I was only thankful that the solicitors' forethought had sent Mrs Trapp to make some kind of preparation for my coming.

She was busying herself with pot and kettle. There seemed to be supplies; she lifted an old-fashioned caddy down from the mantelpiece and spooned out the tea. A milk bottle, half-empty, stood on the table.

"Soon be brewed," she was saying. "Would you like a biscuit, or a bit of toast, maybe? No? Then you won't mind if I have one myself? I brought a packet in."

Beside the milk bottle was a quarter-pound of butter, still in its wrapping, but partly used. A bowl full of sugar, a loaf, also half-used, and a packet of biscuits, lay beside them. She took a biscuit, and, munching, began to pour tea.

"There now, if I didn't forget what I should have said straight away, how sorry I was about your poor aunty . . ."

"My cousin."

"What?"

"She wasn't my aunt. Miss Saxon was my mother's cousin. I always called her Cousin Geillis."

"Oh. Well, yes. There now. A very nice lady she was, and always very good to me. I did what I could looking after her. They say you need good neighbours in the country." A smile, as if I should understand her readily. She had very pretty teeth. She chatted on, munching biscuits. She took three spoonsful of sugar in her tea. I drank mine, and looked around me.

It was a big kitchen, old-fashioned but well enough planned, and, after the vicarage kitchen, a delight. Instead of our vast black Eagle range there was a cream-coloured Aga, nestling under the old mantelpiece as if it had been built with the house. This would not, I guessed, be the original kitchen; no eighteenth-century servants would have been pampered with this light and pleasant room. One window – the one with the dead plants – faced north.

Another gave on the woodland beside the house; I could see little beyond a tangle of elderberry and rowan overhanging what looked liked a shed roof and a tall chimney. The old wash-house, perhaps? Possibly the original kitchen lay that way, concealed by bushes, and functioning now as scullery and outbuildings.

Opposite the fireplace was a tall dresser with rows of pretty plates in white and powder-blue, with cups to match hanging along the front of the shelves. The new fashion for built-in kitchen units and 'worktops' had not reached so far into the wilds, it appeared. The big table in the middle of the room gave all the working space necessary, and there was another long table under the window, cluttered, now, with various boxes and jars, and a pile of books which had presumably been lifted down from a hanging shelf beside the window.

"I was just cleaning some of the bookshelves down. It's funny, isn't it, how they do collect the dirt?" Mrs Trapp set her cup down and got to her feet. "And now you'll want to see your room."

With all the air of a hostess, she ushered me out of the kitchen and back along the passage to the baize door. She swung my two cases up as if they weighed nothing, talked down my protest, waited while I gathered up handbag and coat, then led the way upstairs. She trod – curiously lightfooted on those thick legs – along the wide landing that ran the width of the hall. To either side of the landing, at the head of a shallow rise of three steps, was a door. She opened the one on the right. Beyond it lay a small, square lobby, with a window facing us, and doors to left and right. She opened the door on the left, and showed me into a bedroom.

After what I had seen downstairs, the bedroom was a surprise. It was a big room with two tall windows giving on the back, or south side of the house. In each was a wide window seat, set in the depth of the wall. The fireplace was delicate, with pretty flowered tiles. A bow-fronted chest did duty as a dressing-table, and a deep cupboard beside the fireplace stood open, showing the hanging-room of a big wardrobe. The bed was double, and high. The carpet was a soft green, linking the room, as it were, with the woods outside. By one of the windows was an easy chair.

A lovely room. True, the carpet was faded near the windows, the curtains had shrunk a little, and the fabric had begun to go rotten where the sun had caught it. There was a patch of damp in one corner, just below the cornice, and the faded wallpaper had begun to peel there. But the room was clean. It smelt fresh, and one of the windows was open at the top.

"The bathroom's next door," said Mrs Trapp.

She crossed to the nearest window and gave the curtain a twitch. I was reminded of the lace curtain at the lodge, and wondered who was there in her absence. But she was eyeing me, so I gave her what she was waiting for.

"It's lovely," I said, warmly. "I know I shall love being here. Thank you very much for getting it so nice for me, Mrs Trapp."

"I told you, we couldn't let you come in, the way it was. Not much done downstairs, there wasn't time. But the bed's well aired and the bathroom's done, too. Want to see it?"

"Later, thank you." I was wondering – and wondering how to ask – what payment she expected for the work she had done. Possibly, if they had asked her to clean for me, the solicitors might have seen to it.

I put a harmless question.

"If you live at the lodge it's an awfully long way to come up, isn't it? Do you have a car?"

"I've a bicycle, but there's a short cut through the woods. I come that way, usually."

"I gather you've been keeping an eye on the place since my cousin was taken ill? Did you work for Miss Saxon?"

"Off and on. She liked her lonesomeness. But come spring I usually gave her a hand with the cleaning. Do you want to see the rest now?"

"I'll unpack first, I think. But perhaps, before you go, you'll show me where all the kitchen things are, and how to cope with the stove?"

"All right, miss. But you don't need to bother about the stove. That's all set for the night, and I'll be up in the morning. And you don't need to worry about your supper, neither. There's something cooking in the oven, and I'll leave the bread and that for you, no bother, no need to worry about the rationing, there's always plenty to be got hereabouts, when you've known the folks as long as I have, and your aunty wasn't one for letting her cupboards go empty."

"It's terribly good of you. I did bring as much as I could, but until I get to know about shops and registering for rations and so on –"

"I can tell you where to go, and you can be sure you'll get treated right, when they know you've got Miss Saxon's place." She followed me down the stairs. "That's it, then, miss, I'll let you get yourself sorted out now, but I'll be up first thing tomorrow, and I'll fetch the milk, and something for your dinner, too, so just you rest easy, and we'll soon get the house readied up between us."

"You're very kind." I hesitated. But it had to be said. I neither wanted, nor could afford, daily help in the house. "Mrs Trapp, it's terribly good of you, but you really mustn't bother about me. I know I'll need all the advice I can get, about shops and rations and things, till I get myself organised. But as for helping with the house, I – well, I plan to look after things myself. I'm quite used to it, and in fact, honestly, I prefer it. Like my cousin, I like my lonesomeness." I gave her a smile. "But I'm really very grateful for what you've done, and of course I'll be very glad if you'll help me out from time to time, the way you did Miss Saxon."

It happened again, the scarlet flush rising swiftly up her neck and right over her face. And this time, with a curious inner lurch of nerves, I recognised it, and knew why it had so disconcerted me, and why my dealings with her so far had been timid to the point of misgiving. I had seen someone blush like that before. My chief tormentor at the convent, in anger, or in contempt when she had managed to make me cry, had looked like that. And the blue eyes, fixed like a doll's eyes in the suffused face, had looked just the same.

Through it she smiled, the white teeth flashing. "Well, of course, it's just as you like, Miss Ramsey. But almost the last thing your aunty said to me before they took her to hospital was, 'Agnes dear, this being such a big, roomy house and all, wouldn't it be great if you'd move in with me, and look after me right here.'" The flush receded. She smiled again, charmingly. "And that's just what we was planning to do, Jessamy and me, when she took ill and died. But it's all different now, isn't it?"

I was not, repeat not, eight years old, and this was not the Führer of the third form. I was the owner of Thornyhold, standing in her own front hall talking to the hired help. But I had to clear my throat before I could say, cheerfully and I hoped firmly: "Yes. It's all different now. Thank you again, Mrs Trapp, and goodbye."

7

Back in my bedroom, and alone, I heaved a case on to one of the window seats, and started to take out the things. I was thinking hard, and not very comfortably. The first thing I must do, I thought, was get in touch with Martin and Martin,

Cousin Geillis's firm of solicitors, and find out if – and how much – I owed Mrs Trapp. At least, with the firm's backing, there could be no trouble there . . .

Trouble? I took a pull at myself. In the face of an angry flush, a passing resemblance, I must not regress to the fearful, bullied child I had once been. And why should there be trouble? I was not an elderly, sick lady who needed a housekeeper. I was young and strong, and had kept house myself for years. Kept it successfully in a much less attractive and convenient house. I was quite capable of telling Agnes Trapp, thank you for past services, and here's the money, and I'll let you know when I want you again. As for her preposterous suggestion that she should move in with me . . .

And there was the reason, surely, for the dismay and anger she had shown? It had been a shock, and a dash to her hopes of a comfortable future, to find a young and vigorous 'cousin' on the doorstep. She had expected an elderly woman, Cousin Geillis's contemporary, who would possibly welcome the offer of a live-in housekeeper and a man-about-the-place. Cousin Geillis, who "liked her lonesomeness", must have felt pretty ill before she could have made such a suggestion. If, indeed, she ever had.

That was ridiculous, too. Of course she had. What need was there for the woman to lie? Agnes Trapp was a good neighbour, country-style, which meant that she was used to letting herself in and out of her neighbour's house at will, and giving a hand if and when it was needed. One didn't lock one's door in those days in the country.

And that was another thing. Surely, after Cousin Geillis had been taken to hospital, the house would be locked up. So presumably Mrs Trapp had a key. Something else I would have to be firm about. It seemed, I thought, as I heaved the first armful of clothing from my case to the bed, as if it was going to be more difficult than I had imagined to have my own house, and to have it to myself.

I did not hurry over my unpacking. Perhaps subconsciously I was hoping that Mrs Trapp would have gone before I went downstairs again, and that anything else that needed to be said could be said tomorrow. And it might well be, I thought to myself, as I folded my clothes or hung them away, that I would be very glad of her help with the rest of the house. She had done this room quite beautifully. There were clean papers in the drawers, and on the base of the wardrobe cupboard. The sheets were linen, immaculately ironed, and smelling of lavender, and a couple of bulges showed where the hot water bottles, now almost cold, had been put to air the bed. (For the old, sick lady to take to?) There was a candlestick beside the bed, with matches laid near. I smiled as I saw it; the feeling that I had stepped back in time was very strong. But the bed-head light worked when I tried it. The candle was a precaution, no more.

The bathroom, next to the bedroom, took me straight back into the twentieth century. It, too, was spotless, white and gleaming, and outside the window the clouds had packed away to show a clear sky of evening beyond the trees. I opened it and leaned out, but before I could do more than get an impression of colour in a flood of green, and the remote glimmer of water, I heard from below me and to one side the sound of a door closing. I craned further. Away to the left I caught a movement. There was a path skirting the house, leading presumably from the back door to a side gate that gave on Mrs Trapp's path through the woods. Mrs Trapp herself came into view. In each hand was a bulging carrier bag. She hurried down the path and out of sight.

Peace had come back and with it pleasure. I went lightly downstairs to the kitchen. Any more exploring could wait till morning. It had been a long day. I would have supper early, and go to bed in that lovely room. I looked, but briefly, into the kitchen drawers and cupboards, located enough in the way of crockery and cutlery for my evening meal, then lifted Mrs Trapp's casserole from the oven and raised the lid. It smelled very good. I took a spoon and tasted

it. Delicious. Beside it on the oven shelf was a large
potato wrapped in foil. Yes, a good neighbour. We should
see.

"Well, Cousin Geillis, thank you for everything," I said,
and sat down to my first meal in my own house.

Afterwards, country or no country, I locked up.

I found I had been right about the old kitchen. The back
door opened straight out of it, through a small porch where
coats hung, and sticks and umbrellas stood with a row of
shoes and gumboots. The old kitchen was a square, flagged
room, dismal in the weak light of an unshaded electric bulb.
Two small windows, blurred with cobwebs, would even by
day give very little light. One wall was almost filled by a vast,
rusting range. No furniture beyond a couple of tall built-in
cupboards and a deal table covered with peeling oilcloth
and laden with piles of old newspapers and cardboard boxes
and other forgotten debris. An earthenware sink under one
window. A couple of buckets and a chipped enamel jug. A
watering-can and a stiff garden broom.

There was no key in the lock of the back door. Presumably
this was the one that Mrs Trapp held. But the door had a
couple of very adequate bolts. I shot them home firmly, and
went to bed.

The silence woke me. At first, when I opened my eyes on
blackness, I thought I must still be asleep, so used had I
become to nights lit by the dirty orange glow of sodium
lamps and the intermittent snarling glare of the pit's traffic.
Now even the wind had died. There was no sound of rain,
no movement of the trees. Slowly, as I lay with open eyes,
the darkness dissolved into shapes of varying blackness; the
room was a cave of blackness with the faint oblongs of the
uncurtained windows showing indigo. I could see no stars.
A long way away a train whistled, emphasising the emptiness
of the night. From somewhere nearer, but still far enough,

came the whining bark of a dog; not the steady bark of the chained watch-dog, but some dog, I thought, urgently asking for something; to be let in, to be let out, to be fed, to be freed. It stopped abruptly and the silence returned.

To be broken by a much nearer, much fainter, and more disturbing sound even than the dog's misery. Just above my head I could hear a scratching, scrabbling, tapping noise that must mean some small inhabitant of the roof. I lay quite still, listening. Bats? I knew nothing about them, but imagined them as silent creatures, hanging in their shelter. In any case, surely they would be out in the night, and flying. If swifts or starlings or other birds nested in the roof, they would be gone long ago. Mice? Too spasmodic, too faint. It could not, I told myself firmly, be rats. It could not. I loved animals with all my soul, but I did not desire a close acquaintance with rats.

It was not busy enough for rats. In fact, it was an oddly comfortable sound. It was company. I slept.

8

I went exploring next morning, as soon as I had finished breakfast.

It was a strange experience. Nothing in the house yet, apart from the few things disposed in the bedroom, seemed

61

to belong to me. I felt as if I ought to knock on the doors.

As I had guessed, the door at the rear of the hall led to the drawing-room, which was large enough and well enough proportioned to deserve the name. Mrs Trapp had done no cleaning here, and it was apparent that Cousin Geillis had not used the room for some time; dust lay everywhere, and the cretonnes of the armchairs were crumpled. The room was comfortably furnished, with easy chairs and sofa, a couple of occasional tables, a big breakfront bookcase and a baby grand piano. There were pretty china ornaments on the mantelpiece, and in a shelved alcove beside the fireplace. The pictures were water-colours, rather faded, since the room faced south and on good days the light would be brilliant. French windows opened on the garden, and another window faced west. The room was directly below my bedroom, and slightly larger; I guessed that my bathroom had been taken off the recess below which Cousin Geillis's piano stood.

Next to this, at the front of the house, was a dining-room, apparently little used. It held a longish pedestal table with chairs for eight people, a sideboard, a couple of side tables and a tall plant-stand with a sick-looking fern. In the drawers, a glimpse of silver in need of cleaning, and linen yellowing with time and disuse. A severely functional room which had outlasted its function. I shut the door on it and crossed the hall to the room near the foot of the staircase.

This had been lived in. It showed the comfortable clutter of a den; a big roll-top desk, a couple of deep leather armchairs, shelves with more books, a wireless set. This room had been used recently; the desk was not dusty, and stood open. There were papers in some of the pigeon-holes, and in the drawers. Well, they could wait; they were presumably neither private nor important. What was important was the telephone. I looked for it, but it was not in this room. I went back to the kitchen to look for it there.

There was no telephone in the kitchen. I gave it up, and went upstairs to finish exploring.

I went first to the side of the house opposite my bedroom. Here the lobby, with its end windows and its doors, was the mirror-image of mine. The south-facing bedroom, too, was almost a twin of my own, and was obviously the main spare room. It smelled stuffy, as if long disused, and there was dust on all the polished surfaces. There were twin beds, and the white coverlets laid over them were creased and not quite clean.

Opposite, and set over the den, was another, smaller bedroom, with a single bed, a chest of drawers and a narrow cupboard for clothes. A secondary spare room, or possibly a bedroom for the 'help', in the days when one was kept? A simple, pretty room, with white painted furniture, a couple of bent-wood chairs, sprigged curtains and a frilled window-seat. I walked over to look out of the window.

My foot struck a soft object, which lay half hidden under the window-seat. A slipper. I picked it up. Downtrodden heel, dirty orange quilting torn at the toe and sides. As clearly as if it had been labelled in marking ink, I knew whose it was. Agnes Trapp's.

I drew the coverlet back from the bed. There were no sheets, but the blankets were crumpled, as if the bed had been hastily stripped. I pulled open a couple of drawers in the chest. The linings were crooked, and on the chest surfaces there were a few hairs from brush or comb, and a sprinkling of powder.

It brought things clearer, and with a kind of relief. I knew now why Mrs Trapp had left so promptly, and without protest last night, and what she was carrying in those bulging bags. She had not been making off with any of Cousin Geillis's – my – property, but hurriedly concealing the evidence that she had been sleeping in the house.

For how long? I knew that the solicitors would have sent people to the house after Cousin Geillis's death, to make or check the inventory and attend to such things as electric meters, water and so on, before asking anyone to come in and clean up.

If, as she had implied, they had asked Mrs Trapp to come in, they surely would not have asked her to stay? If they had done so, they would have told me. So, indeed, would she, who had seemed so set on 'living-in' that, when she reacted so sharply to my rejection of regular service, she would surely have quoted Messrs Martin and Martin at me.

And why should she want to stay? If she had been living in the house for more than a day, or two at the most, she had certainly done very little in the way of cleaning. The bedroom and bathroom that Cousin Geillis had vacated, that was all. She must have known, she had admitted knowing, that I was due to come, so she had prepared for me, but even so my coming had taken her by surprise. Her staying in the house accounted for the lived-in look of the kitchen, and the warmth everywhere from the Aga which must have been lighted some days ago.

Well, she had gone. And since I would almost certainly be needing her help and goodwill in the future, I would let well alone. I dropped the slipper back on the floor, kicked it under the window-seat, where I might have missed seeing it, and went on with my tour.

Broom cupboard, another bathroom, linen cupboard. A view from the window over the low roof of the old kitchen, where I could see the side gate and the path into the woods. The sun was high, and a light breeze had set the boughs dancing. I would hurry through the rest of my tour and then go out.

One final thing I had to investigate, and perhaps the most intriguing. The third of the spare rooms, the one opposite my own bedroom, was locked. I had tried the door this morning. Above the old keyhole was a new, brass mortice lock, and there was no sign of a key. My handbag was in my bedroom, with Cousin Geillis's ring of keys in it. As I picked it up from the window-seat I heard the squeak of the side gate and, a few seconds later, the opening and shutting of the back door.

I went quickly downstairs, to find Mrs Trapp in the kitchen.

"It's the milk. Here. He's stopped coming up here, but I told him you'd be wanting some, and he'll bring it till you get your milk coupons. And you needn't bother too much about them, either. Any time you want a bit more you've only to ask."

"Oh? It sounds too good to be true. Actually, half a pint's quite enough for me, normally, but –" I hesitated. "Mrs Trapp, are there mice or something in the roof? I heard something in the night. Or bats, perhaps?"

"That I don't know. I never –" She stopped. I thought she had been going to say, "I never heard it myself when I slept here," and had understandably thought better of it. She added: "The food she used to put out – there was always birds and such, and anything could get in. I used to say to her –"

"Didn't she keep a cat?"

"A cat?" She looked blank.

"Isn't Hodge a cat? When I heard the sounds in the night I thought of mice, or even rats, and this morning I remembered Hodge. It's a cat's name, and she particularly asked me to look after him. And in the big spare room, it looked as if a cat had been sleeping on the beds. Do you know where he is?"

"I really couldn't say. I dare say he'll be about somewhere. Did you enjoy your supper?"

"I certainly did. It was delicious. Thank you."

"Don't mention it. Well, I must be off. Shall I tell the milk, then?"

"Yes, please, and if Hodge does come back I might be glad of a bit extra when he has it to spare. If he doesn't come back, I think I'll get a kitten. Do you know anyone who's got kittens, Mrs Trapp?"

"No, I can't say I do. And call me Agnes, do."

"All right. Thanks. Look, then, Agnes, I wondered . . . What with you doing all that work here, cleaning my bedroom, and cooking, and everything, how much do I owe you?"

"Oh, nothing. Call it neighbourly. I'll ask for pay next time."

"Well, thank you. Thank you very much. But the supplies you've left here, and anyway, the milk —"

"That'll be on his bill at the end of the week." A gesture brushed the rest aside. "And I'll bring the sheets back as soon as they're washed. I stopped the night in the little bedroom, you see. I meant to stay till I got the house cleaned right through, but then you came back." That pretty smile, showing a smear of fresh lipstick on a front tooth. "If you want the truth, the casserole was for me. Didn't you wonder?"

"Do you know, I never thought about it? I guess I was a bit tired, and just thankful to find the house so warm and welcoming. I can't say I'm sorry I ate your supper, because it was delicious, but what did you have yourself?"

"Oh, there's always plenty, and you were welcome. Did you finish it? I'll take the dish, then, shall I?"

"Yes, of course. I hadn't realised it was yours. I put it away in the cupboard. Here."

"Thanks." She dropped it into her carrier bag. "Well, I'll really have to be off now, and let you get on looking around the place. I reckon you'll be dying to. Don't let the dust get you down. There's nothing a bit of elbow-grease won't cure. If you'll just let me know when you want me to come and help . . ."

As easy as that. She had succeeded in making me feel thoroughly ashamed of my suspicions and distrust. I said, genuinely, warmly: "You're very good. Of course I'll let you know. Just one thing . . . The locked door on the landing upstairs. Where does it go?"

"Oh, that one. What she called her still-room. A kind of pantry, I reckon. She dried her herbs and made wines and medicines and that, and I reckon some of them might be poisons, so she kept the door locked. I've never been in, myself. I did look for the key, to give it a clean along with the rest of that landing, but I couldn't find it. Maybe it's on that bunch you had in your hand when you got here."

"Oh. Yes. Well, I'll have a look later on. One other thing – I can't find the telephone. Is it in a cupboard somewhere that I've not noticed?"

"There isn't one. Never would have it put in. Very old-fashioned in some ways, was Miss Saxon. Never had a car, neither. Used a bike, same as me. Well, I'll be off. Let me know if there's anything more you want."

"Do you have to go? Won't you have some coffee?"

But she declined, and took herself off. I made coffee for myself, then, looking round at the clutter in the kitchen, decided that first things came first. I would go on finding exactly what had come my way before I began to do anything about it. The garden was calling, and it was a lovely day. I had noticed, in the back porch, a pair of wellingtons that looked my size. I tried them, and they were. And above them hung a padded waistcoat of forest green, the sort worn by every countrywoman from Cape Wrath southward. It fitted, too. I zipped it up and went out to see what there was to see.

9

I have said that the house lay at the end of a branch of the driveway. Around it the woodland had been cut back many years ago, to make a clearing where the sun could get in, and grass grow. This sunny enclave was shaped like a blunt wedge, or better, a half-opened fan, with the house at its narrow point, and the garden stretching down to the bank of a river which here wound its way through the forest to form Thornyhold's southern boundary. The property, open to the river, was otherwise completely enclosed by its high hedges of thorn, backed by the crowding woods. At the widest part of the garden could be seen the curve of a wall that protected the vegetable plot, and opposite this, planted as if to preserve the symmetry of the place, stood a grove of fruit trees, in effect a miniature orchard. No fruit was visible, but the leaves of cherry and apple trees were already showing the reds and golds of autumn.

The garden must once have been carefully cultivated, but it was apparent that Cousin Geillis, through time, had adapted it to the kind of care she could give it. Now it consisted mainly of grass – not shaven lawn, but mossy turf kept short and pleasant to walk on – with a few trees and bushes islanded here and there, and to either side a wide flower border, backed with roses that climbed and fountained up the hedges. All that remained of the original plan was the broad flagged walk that ran straight from the house, bisecting the lawn, to a belvedere at the river's edge. This was a paved half-moon, edged with a low balustrade, holding a pair of curved stone benches. Between these a shallow flight of steps led down to the water where just below the surface could be seen a row of stepping-stones that would, in summer or at low water, be uncovered. On the opposite bank willows trailed their hair in the shallows, and golden flakes of fallen leaves turned idly on the current before floating downstream. Coppices of hazel framed the entrance to an overgrown forest ride stretching up through the trees.

There was a wrought-iron gate set in the wall of the vegetable garden. I pushed it open and went through to find a smallish enclosure surrounded by a high old wall thickly covered with ivy and bristling with self-sown saplings of ash and rowan. The vegetable beds ran right round the perimeter under the wall, and were already beginning to succumb to the autumn squalor of weeds and rotting haulms of cabbage and potato, but the centre of the garden was still neat, and was, indeed, something beyond my expectation.

It had a mediæval look, like the jewelled, out-of-perspective illuminations in a tale like *The Romance of the Rose*. Within the irregular circle of walls and vegetable plot someone, a long time ago, had made a garden within a garden. At its centre stood a well, ancient and canopied, and knee deep in bushes of lavender and sage and lad's-love. The broken paving that made a ten-foot ring round it was almost hidden by creeping plants, some of them, in that sheltered spot, still flowering, campanula and wild thyme and the rose-purple of sedum, with saxifrage and wild strawberry and late gentians; the plants of garden and woodland at home together. Raying out from this carpeted pavement, in regular sectors edged with clipped box some nine inches high, were the flower beds. Few flowers there, but the autumn sun falling warmly after yesterday's rain on leaves of green, of grey, of silver and rusty gold, sent up a cloud of scent which told me at once what sort of place this was. A herb garden, planned and planted as some Elizabethan gardener might have made it, in the days when herbs and spices were as essential in the kitchen as flour and salt.

Between the sections ran narrow pathways. I walked up one of these to the well-head. The coping, in spite of its arras of greenery, looked as if it had been pointed fairly recently, and was safe. I approached cautiously, and peered over the edge. Not very deep; I saw the flat gleam of water at about six feet. And certainly safe; a grille covered the shaft, a foot or so below the coping. And over the grille was stretched some small-mesh wire netting. It had been put there the day after a foolish blackbird, deceived by the gleam of water, had perched on the grille to reach for a drink and had fallen through and drowned.

It was like a flash photograph taken on a grey day. For a split moment everything was outlined with light, then, the lightning gone, the trees, sky, bushes and shrubs were normal once more. Like a dream that is recalled, still vivid and moving in one's waking moments, but as one tries to remember further, it is gone, and further gone with every effort made.

It was not even a dream, certainly not a memory. Trivial, in any case, not worth remembering.

But I knew it was the truth. Even stranger than the flash of knowledge sent to me out of nowhere, was my calm acceptance of it. Because, with it, came a memory that was completely my own; the moment beside the pond in the vicarage meadow, when my Cousin Geillis first came to me. And with that, another moment beside the River Eden, and my cousin making me a promise, which, at the time, I had misunderstood. *"You and I will live there together ... for as long as you need me, which won't be for ever..."* I looked up across the ivied wall at the chimneys of her house, my house, and I thought I understood it now.

I let myself out of the herb garden, and, moving in a kind of dreamy contentment, started back up the flagged walk. Half way along it, I paused to look at the house again.

It was beautiful. Even the prisoning hedges were beautiful, protective with their rusty thorns, their bastions of holly and juniper, and at the corners, like towers, their thick columns of yew.

Yes, it was beautiful. Still floating, euphoric, I walked on. Nearer, I could see how the sun showed up the shabbiness of the paint and the stains where water had spilled from blocked gutters, but nothing could detract from the elegance of the long windows and the roof with its tufts of rosy houseleek and the spreading gilt of the lichens, and the charm of the three gabled windows peered out below the tall chimneys.

I stopped short. Gabled windows? There had been none on the north side of the house, so I had not known, till now, that there must be a third floor. Attics? So those night-time sounds had come, not from the roof spaces, but from an attic which, I could see now, lay directly above my bedroom.

Back now, myself, on ground level, I thought rapidly. My first thought was Hodge. Could he have been locked up there? With relief, I dismissed the idea. The window above my room was open. If a cat had been shut and starving there since Cousin Geillis had left the house, he would have scrambled out somehow, down the roses and clematis that reached almost to the roof. Or he would be sitting outside on the attic sill, making his troubles known.

Not urgent, then. But I would certainly like to find the way up there as soon as possible. Since I had seen no sign of an attic stair, it was to be assumed that the way up lay through the locked still-room. If I could not find the key to that room today, then when I went into town to register for supplies and to do my shopping, I must call on Martin and Martin's agent there, and ask about it. About Mrs Trapp's pay, too. And about getting the telephone put in . . . And the priority for all these plans was to find Cousin Geillis's bicycle and see if it was roadworthy.

There was a toolshed near the side gate, and the bicycle was there. I wheeled it out into the daylight and examined it. It looked sound enough, but the tyres were soft. It was years since I had been on a bicycle; was it true, I wondered, that one never really forgot how to ride? At least I could practise on the driveway before I reached the main road. Any humiliating moments would, with luck, be private ones.

There was no pump on the bicycle. I went back into the shed to look for it. There were the garden tools, spades, forks, rake, hoe, a scythe and sickle and (I was thankful to see) a motor mower. Plant-pots on the shelves, along with a stock of empty jam-jars, an oil-can, some tattered packs of bone meal and potash and other garden preparations. Sacks of peat and sand and charcoal. But no bicycle pump.

It had to be somewhere. The porch? The old kitchen? It might take days to find it, and meanwhile I was marooned. Now, I thought, was a convenient moment for that flash to light my mind again. If I could remember a bird that had drowned itself under Cousin Geillis's eyes, surely I could remember where she had last put her bicycle pump?

Where *the hell* would she put the bicycle pump?

"Miss Geillis?" said a voice just behind me, in a kind of startled squeak.

I spun round.

It was a boy of perhaps ten or eleven years old. He wore shorts and a tattered sweater, and dirty sand-shoes with holes in the toes. He had dark hair and eyes, and he was as thin as a garden rake. He was holding a fawn-coloured ferret in his arms.

He hadn't much colour at the best of times, I guessed, but now he was quite spectacularly white. His mouth was a round O of shock, and his eyes were twice too big for his face. The ferret, perceiving a lack of attention, gave a quick wriggle which brought the boy back to his senses.

"You're wearing her clothes."

He spoke abruptly, almost accusingly, and it made things plain. Seen from behind, and stooping over the bicycle, in the old green wellingtons and jerkin I must have looked very much like the Miss Geillis he had known.

"Only the gardening things," I said apologetically. "Miss Saxon was my cousin and I've come to live here now. I'm sorry it gave you such a shock seeing me here like this. My name is Geillis, too. Geillis Ramsey. What's yours?"

"William. William Dryden." A pause. Another wriggle from the ferret. The colour slowly crept back into the boy's face. "You did look just like her from the back. And I – I was at the funeral, you see. I didn't expect anyone to be here at all."

"I see." I considered him. "Then – forgive me for asking, but Thornyhold is so far from anywhere – if you didn't expect anyone to be here, why did you come?"

A half lift of the ferret in his arms. "Him. She used to look at them for me."

"My cousin looked after your pets, you mean?"

"Not pets. They're working ferrets."

"Sorry. You mean she used to doctor them for you?"

"Cured them. I'm not so worried about Silkworm, because I know what to give him, but if anything else goes wrong, with the others, or with the rabbits . . . You aren't a witch, too?" Wistfully.

"A *what*?"

"A witch. Curing things. It's what –"

"I heard you. I was a bit shocked. She was not a witch. Just because she was a herbalist, and used plants and so on to heal with –"

"I know. I'm sorry. It was only a joke. She used to laugh, and say it was a bit less arro – arrogant than calling herself a wise woman."

The last words were spoken, muffled, into the back of the ferret's head.

I spoke gently. "It's all right, William. I was joking, too. Miss Saxon was certainly wise, and she did have a kind of magic. I've met it myself. I'm sorry if you miss her so much. And I do hope you'll still come and visit here whenever you like. But I'm afraid I'm neither wise nor magical myself. I wouldn't know what to give to Silkworm. Isn't there a vet in the town?"

"Not enough pocket money," said the boy shortly. "My father says I can only keep what I can look after myself, and it doesn't stretch to vets. Miss Geillis would have done it for nothing, because she loved them all, but my father said I had to earn it, so I used to come and help in the garden, and cut wood and clean things. I could do that for you if you like?"

"I'll probably be very glad of your help, once I've found my way about. But I'll have to pay you in other ways, William. All I know about medicine is a kind of elementary first aid."

"But I do!" He said it eagerly. "I know which medicine she gave Firefly, and this one's just the same. It's just a tonic. Couldn't we give him some, just to try?"

"I don't know where it's kept. I only came yesterday evening. I haven't really explored yet."

"That doesn't matter." My mild objection was swept aside. "I'll show you. I know where everything is."

"Do you? Well, there's a door upstairs, over the dining-room. Mrs Trapp called it the still-room. Is that where the medicines are kept?"

"That's right. Opposite Miss Geillis's bedroom."

"Then I'm afraid it's locked, and I don't know whether the key's on the house ring. I haven't had time to try yet. Perhaps –"

"Oh, she always kept that one locked. I expect," said William cheerfully, "that it's chock full of poisons. But it's all right. The key's not with the others, but I know where she kept it."

"Do you indeed? And the back door key, too, or has Mrs Trapp got that one?"

"I don't think she has a key, but she'll know where it's kept. It's usually hanging on a nail under the jasmine beside the back door."

"I see. And you intended to go in, otherwise you wouldn't have brought Silkworm over, since you didn't know I would be here. Did you really intend to go into the house, William?"

"She would have let me." He added, a little stiffly: "I don't think she thought of me as a child. Of course I know where the keys are. She told me."

"I see. Well, then, lead on. You can show me, and we'll see if we can find something for Silkworm."

10

I disposed of my wellingtons by the back door, then the boy led me, not upstairs as I had expected, but into the den. I thought he would make for the desk, and perhaps even disclose some secret drawer, but he crossed the room to the fireplace.

This had not seen a fire for a very long time. The pretty mantelpiece framed a chimney that must have been blocked off from above. It was dusty, but there was no sign of soot. On the wide hearth stood an electric fire.

Before I realised what he was doing William had put the ferret into my arms and was reaching forward and up into the chimney. I had never handled a ferret before, and if I had been given the choice, would have refused to touch it. Something about the pink eyes and nose, the ferocious reputation, the whiplash strength of the hot little body, inspired wariness. But the little beast nestled comfortably into my hands, and without thinking I cradled it close to me. Its skin was like smooth silk, its body all slender muscle, and very warm. It lay still as a sleeping kitten and watched with me as William turned from the fireplace with a key in his hand.

"There it is."

"Why on earth did she keep it there?"

"I expect she didn't think anyone would look there. I mean, if Mrs — if anyone wanted to hunt for a key, they'd look in the desk, or the drawers, or something like that. She didn't want anyone going into the still-room when she wasn't there."

"Except you."

A sideways look. "I told you, I helped a lot. I helped pick them and dry them, too. The herbs and things. I even helped make some of the medicines."

"It's all right, William. I'm only teasing you. I can see that I'm going to rely on you a lot. Perhaps you can even teach me something about the herbs. Let's go upstairs now, shall we?"

The still-room was the same size as the dining-room below, but was much lighter. The furniture was simple. There was a big table in the centre of the room, and another under the window. They were plainly made, like kitchen tables, and were obviously working benches. In the alcoves to each side of the boarded-up fireplace were shelves full of books. Against the inner wall, alongside the door, stood a big, ancient dresser, with a locked cupboard below, and on its shelves, instead of plates, rows of jars and bottles. In a corner, where possibly a washbasin had once stood, was a small sink with an electric water-heater above it.

"Here," I said, "take Silkworm, will you?"

William, who was already looking along the rows of bottles, turned quickly. "I say, I quite forgot! I'm terribly sorry. You don't mind ferrets? A lot of ladies don't like them. I never thought, because of course Miss Geillis could do anything."

"I've never met one before, to tell you the truth. Here. He's certainly got very nice manners – or perhaps he isn't well enough to bite?"

"That might be it. But he likes you, anyway. I say, should I run down and get his basket? It's strapped on to my bike."

"I think that's a good idea."

He ran off with his ferret, and I looked about me.

The room was very clean and very tidy. The books were all in place, and looked, from one or two titles, to be in order. The wood of the tables was scrubbed white, and nothing stood on them, except, on the long table by the window, a pair of scales and a biggish mortar and pestle. From the absence of all the things I had expected – bunches of herbs, sacks of roots, and so on – it looked very much as if the room had been scoured and everything put away. As if Cousin Geillis had tidied it all away at the end of her life to leave it ready for me. Apart from the orderly rows of bottles and jars the only sign of herbs was a big bowl of pot-pourri which stood on the end of the dresser nearest the door. It was mostly of rose petals and lavender, with geranium leaves and wild heartsease scattered over, but there was some strange fragrance about it that I couldn't place. I stooped to sniff, just as William came running back into the room, with the ferret now in its carrying-cage.

'Trefoil, John's-wort, Vervain, Dill,

Hinder witches of their will," he chanted.

I straightened. "What do you mean?"

He pointed to the pot-pourri. "They're all in there. I helped her make it. She told me about it. It's an old charm, or something."

"Goodness. Well, now, what about Silkworm?"

He set the cage down on the table and reached for a bottle from the dresser shelves. The label, in my cousin's neat writing, was in Latin and meant nothing to me.

"Are you sure?"

"Yes, quite sure. Anyway, it can't do any harm. I'm allowed to touch any of the bottles except the ones with red labels, and all those are locked in the bottom cupboard. This is the one. Look at the instructions."

He handed me the bottle. Underneath the Latin inscription were the words: *"Small a. one p.d. for 3 d."*

"That's small animal. It was one a day for Firefly."

I opened the bottle. In it were some small, blackish pills. "Well, it's your ferret. If you're really sure –"

He nodded.

"Then I suppose we'd better have a go. Do you know how to do it?"

"Just open his mouth and pop it down." For the first time, he looked uncertain. He eyed me. "It looked awfully easy when Miss Geillis did it."

"I'm sure it did. Well, we'd better start by getting him out of the basket. We can't get at him like that. Put him on the table and hold him. That's right."

I tipped a pill into my hand and looked dubiously at the ferret.

William swallowed. "Would you – would you like me to try? It's my ferret, after all, and if anyone has to get bitten it ought to be me."

I laughed. "I never heard a braver word. No, I'll have a go. I've got to start some day, that's for sure, and you did say it was easy . . . If you'll just stop him squirming like that . . . Aah!"

The 'aah' was one of sheer surprise. It *was* easy. I had done it a hundred times. Swiftly, expertly, I cupped my left hand over the ferret's head, squeezed the cheeks gently till the pink mouth gaped, then dropped the pill in, far back, and held the jaws shut till it swallowed. As I lifted the little animal and settled it back into William's arms, I got the sharp impression that if it had been a cat it would have purred.

I went across to the sink to wash my hands while William put the ferret back into its cage. When I turned, it was to see the boy regarding me with what looked like awe.

"What is it?"

"You said you'd never touched a ferret before. You did it just the way she did. How did you know?"

The brush of gooseflesh along the skin. The moment of suddenly clear sight. There stood the bottle whose label I had not understood. There, all at once wide awake, and weaving to and fro in its cage with whickering sounds and tiny sharp teeth showing, was the ferret which, now, I would not dare to touch.

"I'm not sure," I said. "I wasn't thinking about anything but getting the pill into him. William, where does – where did Miss Saxon keep her bicycle pump?"

"What?"

"Her bicycle pump. Something reminded me. I can't find it, and the tyres are flat. I wanted to go into town fairly soon."

"It's usually on the bicycle."

"Well, it isn't now."

"I don't know, then. Sorry. I expect it'll turn up. I'll tell you what, shall I blow them up with mine before I go?"

"Oh, great, if you would. Thanks very much."

"I say," he exclaimed, "look at Silkworm! That's good stuff, isn't it?"

"It does seem to have done the trick. Look, William, it says the pills have to be taken for three days. Can you come back, or would you like to take a couple home and try it yourself? Could you manage? He really did take it very easily."

"For you he did." He hesitated, then flashed a sudden smile. "Well, I could try. Dad would probably hold him for me if he had his driving gloves on. There's some empty pill-boxes in that drawer. Here."

"Thank you." I dropped the pills into the box, capped it, and gave it to him. "Do you know what's in them?"

"No, not really. There's gentian, and honey, but I don't know what else, or how they were made up. She had a machine for doing pills; I think it's in that other drawer –"

"Never mind now. I'll look later." I glanced at the book-shelves. "I dare say it's all there somewhere. It does look as if I've got an awful lot to learn."

"She used to say it was all there, magic and all. And –" lovingly regarding the ferret – "it *is* magic, isn't it? Look at him! Thank you ever so much for letting me bring him in, and for giving him the dose. It's – I'm glad you're here. You love them too, don't you? I can tell. So could Silkworm. Actually, ferrets are good as pets. Even working ferrets," he added hastily. "You never had one, then?"

"I was never allowed any pets."

"How awful. None? Not even a dog?"

"No."

"Why not?"

"No one to look after him when I was away at school. Who looks after Silkworm and co? You told me your father would only let you keep them if you did it all yourself. What happens in term time?"

"I have to feed them before I go, and clean them out at night, or at weekends."

"Oh, you're at day school?"

"Yes, I'm a day boy at Arnside. I think my parents had always fancied a boarding school, but I didn't, and then my father said okay, it probably wouldn't have suited me anyway. He always hated his. He said they weren't a good idea for loners."

"And you're a loner?"

"Well," said William, sounding all at once about twenty

years older, in what must have been an unconscious mimicry of his father, "let's say that my hobbies aren't popular ones. Reading, gardening, collecting flowers and watching birds and animals, and I'm not terribly good at games. So I can do all that at home, and if I look after the animals properly I can have them. If not, not. It's fair enough, isn't it?"

"More than fair. In fact, you're lucky."

"I know. How awful not to have any animals. Not a cat, either?"

"There was a cat, but she was an outdoor cat mostly, and I never got to know her. Which reminds me, do you know where Hodge is?"

He looked troubled. "No, sorry, I don't. I've been awfully worried, as a matter of fact. Miss Geillis was sure he'd be all right. He's got a bed in the shed, and there's a cat door, and when she knew she'd have to go into hospital she fixed with Mrs Trapp to feed him, and I said I'd come over whenever I could. I did see she'd put saucers out for him, but the food wasn't touched – except where it looked as if mice or birds or something had been at it."

"Do you mean you haven't seen him since Miss Saxon went into hospital?"

"I did think I saw him once. It was last Saturday, when I was clipping the box borders in the herb garden, and I thought I saw him on top of the wall and I called to him, but he – if it was him – just slipped down the other side and disappeared."

"Then it does look as if he might still be somewhere about. Was the house empty then?"

"Yes, of course. Oh, I see what you mean. Well, Mrs Trapp was here when I came over on Saturday. When I went in to wash my hands she had the kitchen upside down, and I thought she was looking for something, but she said no, she was just cleaning up, because the old lady was expected some day soon." A bright glance up at me. "Was that you?"

"It was. I was quite a surprise to her."

82

"Was she here when you came, then?"

"Yes. I did ask her about Hodge, and that surprised her, too. All she said was that he'd be about somewhere. She was in a hurry, and she didn't seem much interested. But if she did put saucers out ... I'll ask her again when she comes back."

He followed me out of the still-room, and watched while I locked the door again. We started down the stairs.

"How *did* you know about Hodge?"

"My cousin left me a letter, asking me to look after him. Don't look so worried, William. Cats are pretty competent. And so was Miss Saxon. She obviously expected him to stick around till I came, and –" I hesitated – "she knew I'd be coming soon. If you saw him on Saturday, that's probably just what he's doing."

But he still looked troubled. He paused on the landing, holding the ferret's cage close in to his chest, his head bent as if to study the animal inside. "If anyone –" He stopped, undecided, then tried again. "That is, if someone wanted to harm him –"

"Oh, William, who would? Anyway, they'd have to catch him first, and have you ever tried to catch a cat that didn't want to be caught?"

"Well, but poison or something?" The words, muttered into Silkworm's cage, could hardly be heard.

I drew a sharp breath, decided not to ask the question that instantly suggested itself, and instead said firmly: "That's even more difficult than catching him. A vet once told me that it's next to impossible to poison a cat. A dog, yes, but cats are far too fussy. You'll see, he'll be waiting to find out what happens here, and he'll turn up just when he wants to."

"You bet he will, once he knows you're home," said William, suddenly cheerful. He started down the stairs again. "They really *are* competent, aren't they? And of course if Hodge was a witch's cat as well – Oh, golly!" This as he caught sight of the clock in the hall. "Look at the time! I'll have to rush! Thanks a million, Miss – I'm terribly sorry, but I've forgotten your name."

"It's Ramsey, but won't you call me Geillis?"

"I – well," said William, not committing himself, "thanks, anyway. I've got to go, but please may I come over, and help you, the way I used to?"

"Of course you may." I would not have dreamed of querying his use of words. "But just a minute, I forgot to ask, where's the key to the poisons cupboard?"

"Under the pot-pourri."

"And the attics?" I had to raise my voice. He was ahead of me, and already at the baize door. "How do you get to the attics?"

"Through here. From the kitchen."

"The kitchen? But I didn't see a door there."

"The back kitchen. A door in the corner. Looks just like a cupboard. I won't forget the bike! Goodbye!"

The baize door shut behind him with a soft puff of dust.

Trefoil, John's-wort, Vervain, Dill,
Hinder witches of their will.

The scented leaves rustled, and gave up the key. I knelt and opened the cupboard door.

It was as William had described it, full of bottles with detailed labels printed in red, with the POISON warning on each one. Boxes, too, similarly marked, and full, when I investigated a couple of them, of what looked like the raw ingredients of the distillates and decoctions; dried leaves, stems, roots, to me unrecognisable.

I sat back on my heels, regarding them, and wondering again why, since Cousin Geillis had apparently foreseen, and so carefully prepared for her end, she had not taken more pains to leave detailed instructions for her successor. Though the actual end had come suddenly, nothing, surely, had been left to chance. The essentials had been taken care of, and long before the event; the will, the letter, the consigning of Hodge to my care, the hiding of the still-room keys until the transparently trustworthy William could show them to me. So I could take it that the lack of direction about the precious still-room contents was deliberate, too.

And where did that leave me? Did she mean me to assume her mantle – herbalist, wise woman, witch? – as today I had assumed her actual clothes? Circumstances seemed to be pushing me that way. Perhaps, I thought, but not seriously, her knowledge and skill would come to me with the ease and brilliance of today's fragmented vision . . .

What did come was a memory of that long-ago day beside the River Eden, and Cousin Geillis's sharp comment: *"The only luck you have in this life is the talent you're born with. The rest is up to you."*

Well, I knew all about hard work. Just give me time, Cousin Geillis, as you have given me your calm refuge, your tools, your precious solitude. Give me time to be myself, know myself, become a little used to happiness. The rest will be up to me.

I locked the cupboard, buried the key back among its protective petals, and went downstairs.

I made myself cook and eat lunch before I attempted to look for the attic door. I even washed up and then sat, carefully leisurely, over a cup of coffee, before at last making my way through to the back kitchen.

Now that I knew, of course it was obvious. In the days when maids had been kept here, the back staircase to the garret bedrooms would open from the kitchen. The first of the two cupboard doors was, as I had guessed earlier, a broom closet. The second gave on a flight of narrow wooden stairs which led steeply up between boarded walls. There were no banisters, and the treads were bare.

A step sounded on the flagged path outside. I turned,

expecting to see Agnes, but it was a young man, a youth of perhaps sixteen. He wore stained trousers and a ragged sweater, and had a carrier bag in one hand. He did not pause in the doorway, but walked straight into the house and dumped the bag on the table. There was no need to ask who he was. Brown hair, blue eyes, fresh complexion, thickset body. At a guess that was a certainty, Jessamy Trapp, Agnes Trapp's son.

"I'd take care how you go up there, I would surely," he said. "There be a main of strange things in the roof, I reckon."

11

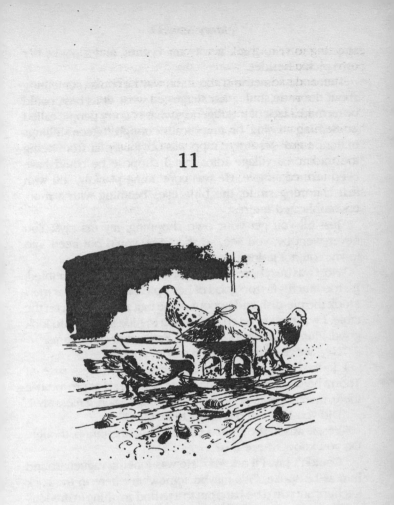

"You must be Mrs Trapp's son?" I asked him.

"Aye. Jessamy's my name. She sent me over with a pie for your supper, and to say she was baking today so she made two, one for you and a bigger one for her and me and Gran, so you wasn't to think it was any bother, and a pot of her own pickle besides."

There was something about the way he spoke, something about the wide smile, that suggested what, at its best, could be termed a lack of intelligence, what country people called 'something missing' or, graphically enough, 'fifteen shillings in the pound'. Jessamy Trapp was obviously far from being the traditional village idiot, but I suppose he could have been termed simple. He was continuing placidly, still with that charming smile, the blue eyes beaming with a mild, uncomplicated interest.

"Just till you get your own shopping, my ma says. You never went by, you see, so she knew you'd not been into town. You not going this day?"

"No. I was busy here. But she really shouldn't have troubled. It's too much – far too good of her – please thank her for me." I took the pie-dish and pot out of the bag and set them on the table. I was embarrassed, and trying to hide it. "They do look good! Plum chutney, too! I love it. From your own plums?"

"Nay, we've none o' they. It's from your'n."

I looked up quickly, remembering the fruitless state of Thornyhold's orchard, but there was nothing sly or provocative there, merely a statement of fact. He smiled again, guilelessly.

"Did you find the old lady's bike, then?"

"Yes, it was in the shed. I couldn't find the pump, though. Do you know where it is?"

"Couldn't say. I'll ask Ma." He was looking vaguely round him as he spoke. "It's maybe somewhere here in the back kitchen, but you'd be hard put to it to find anything in this lot."

"Have you a bike yourself?"

"Aye, but mostly I walk. There's a short cut through the woods that saves near half a mile. I'll show you if you like."

"Thank you. Some time. Well, thank your mother for me, will you, Jessamy, and tell her I will try to get some shopping done for myself tomorrow. Goodbye, then."

I turned to mount the attic stairs, and found that, far from going, Jessamy Trapp was just behind me.

"Dunno what you'll find up there, miss. Must be a main long time since anyone took a broom to it," he said, and because there seemed no civil way of stopping him from escorting me, I went on, and he followed.

There was dust on the stairs, scuffed as if there had been some recent traffic that way. At the first-floor level was a small square landing, and there the stairs took a bend towards the back of the house. At the top of the next flight, and lighted by a roof-light, was a door. It was shut, and, when I tried it, locked. But beside it, hanging on a nail, was a Yale key.

With Jessamy on my heels, I opened the door and went into the attic.

There was only one attic, a long room running the length of the house, lit by the three dormer windows I had seen. On that sunny afternoon it was full of light and air, but extremely dirty. Against the wall opposite the windows was a double rank of boxes, standing on their ends, each one containing a slanting wooden block covered with bird droppings. Some of the boxes also held large earthenware bowls, and in them were what looked like old nests. In the centre of the floor stood a covered feeder, like a lantern with a roof to keep dirt out of the food, and several spaces through which birds might feed themselves. Beside this stood a metal water-trough. There was no food, and no water. Everywhere was dirt, feathers, dust, droppings.

The attic was, in fact, a disused pigeon-loft.

Not quite disused. With a clap and whistle of wings a pigeon flew down from its perch in one of the boxes, and strutted hopefully, head jerking, towards the feeder in the middle of the room.

———— ◆ ◆ ————

"Well, now," said Jessamy's voice behind me, "there's one of them back."

"Back? Back from where?"

"Dunno. Left the window open always, she did, let them fly free, she said. But pigeons always comes home."

"How many did she have?"

"Dunno. Used to see them, quite a flock, flying their ring over the woods there. Nice birds, pigeons. Friendly, like."

"Well I'm sure they haven't been here for quite some time. That bowl's dry as a bone, and there's no food to come for. When Miss Saxon was first taken ill, I'm sure she would make certain that someone –"

"Food's over there." He pointed. Between the windows stood a crock of the kind my mother had used for 'putting down' the eggs in waterglass for the winter. It was covered with a heavy wooden lid. Jessamy lifted this, scooped out a handful of mixed grain, and threw it to the pigeon on the floor. The bird stopped its strutting and began, eagerly, to peck.

"Water's downstairs," said Jessamy. "She used to bring it up in a jug. Well, now, if Ma didn't always be telling her to watch that dratted cat of hers."

"Cat? What do you –?"

I stopped. It was clear what he meant. There was a dead pigeon lying on the floor just behind the door.

"Told her, my ma did," said Jessamy, stooping to pick it up. Its wings fell open, trailing, in a light flurry of dust. The neck hung loosely, the head dangling.

"Hodge?" I spoke doubtfully, eyeing the dead bird. "But the door was shut and locked. How could Hodge have got in?"

"Window," said Jessamy, simply. "Told you, that was always open for the birds. You know about Hodge, then?"

"I know he lived here, and that she was very fond of him. He's gone, too, hasn't he, Jessamy?"

"Aye. Good thing she'd never know what he'd been up to. Went the day after she was took away. Pigeons gone, and cat gone, too. Seemed like nothing could stay when she'd gone herself. And likely, you won't want to be bothered, neither. Don't you fret about this. I'll take it away for you."

He lifted the hand holding the dead bird. As it moved, the living bird, which had been greedily eyeing us the while with one anxious ruby eye, fled upwards with loud wings fanning a plume of dust into the air. It landed back into the box from which it had come.

With a smooth movement, quick as any cat, Jessamy reached into the box and, before the flustered bird could turn to fly again, caught and lifted it, turning with it cradled in his hand.

"Like I said, you don't want to bother yourself with these birds, miss. I'll take she as well, and I reckon she'll go to a good home."

"Well, if you're sure you know someone –"

This time there was no flare of light, no touch from the air. But a vivid blink of memory, as if someone had flicked open the shutter of a lantern. Jessamy stood in front of me, smiling, with the living bird cupped between his palms and below it the dead one, dangling. It was black, and looked like a crow hung up to scare its fellows.

I did not consciously notice this. What I was seeing, in that extraordinary shutter-flash of memory, was my father's curate taking my rabbit away to fill a rabbit pie.

I said quickly: "No. No. I'd like to keep it, for now anyway. I'll be glad if you'll take the dead one away and bury it, please, but let's put the other one back, shall we?"

"All right, miss," he said agreeably, and handed the bird to me. "Do you want me to fetch some water up?"

"No, thank you. It's all right. I'll bring it up later. The window's open, anyway. Thanks very much for coming, Jessamy, and thank your mother for me, will you?"

To my relief he accepted the dismissal, and went. I crossed to a window with the pigeon nestling in my hand, and watched him go. As the wicket gate clicked shut behind him I turned back to survey the pathetic pigeon-loft.

It certainly smelt very strongly of pigeons, and the air was full of the feather dust that they must shed all the time. But there were signs, which I had not mentioned to Jessamy, that many other birds must use the place. The rafters – for the attic was right under the roof – held abandoned swallows' nests, and in the dust near the feeder, and on the deep sills of the windows were dozens of prints of smaller birds' feet. More interesting than all, perhaps, was a small grey object, the size of a peanut shell, which lay beneath a beam in the dimmest corner. An owl's pellet. I regarded it thoughtfully. It was to be supposed that, however welcome the wild birds were, no owl would be *persona grata* in a loft where pigeons bred. It must have come in to roost since the loft was deserted by the tame birds and their caretaker. Since Cousin Geillis's departure, in fact. The pellet was fresh, dark grey and still moist. Searching, I found two others, only one of them beginning to dry to paler grey.

So the birds had all gone. Nothing strange about that. Only that William had never mentioned them.

I opened my hands, and the pigeon, released, flew straight down to the floor at my feet and began to feed again. I left the attic, closing the door behind me. I locked it, and this time pocketed the key and took it with me. Then I went downstairs, and out once more into the garden.

❖

The bicycle had been wheeled back into the toolshed, presumably by William, who had pumped up the tyres as he had promised me. It would not have surprised me if I had found the missing pump quietly restored to its clamps on the bar, but it was not there. I looked for, and found, what must be Hodge's 'bed in the shed' – a deep pile of sacks, old carpet, and newspapers in a corner behind a tea-chest which acted as umbrella-stand for garden canes and a birch broom. No sign of a cat, and the sacks and paper were cold. I walked down the flagged path as far as the herb garden, calling his name, but without hope. Then back to the house. Now that supper was provided for, I no longer wanted to make the trip to town. I would do a bit of cleaning, I decided, and leave the store cupboard till morning.

Possibly the most surprising thing about that day was the discovery that I enjoyed housework. My parents' house, the vicarage, had of course not belonged to us, but in any case 'helping mother' is not the same as working for oneself in one's own house. I had certainly been mistress of the house after her death, and tasted some satisfaction then, but never with this heady knowledge that the place, and all about it, was my own. It was, in fact, the first thing that I had ever really owned. Throughout my youth nothing had been mine; even my childhood's toys and books, the pictures and small ornaments from my bedroom, had been quietly removed and given away when I was from home, like the rabbit and the dog and all else I had thought to own. That the trivia of today are the treasures of tomorrow would not have occurred either to me or to my mother; I only knew that all the small things that make the landmarks of growing up had disappeared. I had come to Thornyhold almost empty-handed, the most dowerless of brides. And now this . . .

Cousin Geillis must have seen it, and understood how, along with everything else, it would help to develop the strong sense of property that I had, the two-way need of belonging, and the almost fierce sense of responsibility that went with it. Thornyhold, with all it contained, would be safe with me.

So for the rest of that day I cleaned my kitchen out, every cupboard, every shelf. Every pan was scoured, every piece of china washed. The curtains went into a tub to soak, and the mats went into the sunshine.

By the time I was feeling really tired, and most things were back in place, it looked quite different. So good, in fact, that I went out and gathered a big bunch of asters and snapdragons from the tangled garden at the front of the house and put a vase of them on the windowsill. There was a clean cloth on the table, the cushion-covers from the Windsor chair and the old rocker were in the tub along with the curtains. They could go out tomorrow, and let us pray for a fair wind to dry them.

Then it was dusk, and time for supper. I put Agnes's pie into the oven to heat, then went upstairs and ran a deep, hot bath. By the time I was dry again, and had put on housecoat and slippers it was quite dark outside. As I drew my bedroom curtains I heard an owl hoot close by. Tomorrow, I thought, the town and my shopping list, bank, food, telephone. The rest of the cleaning could wait. Till I expected company? With an odd lifting of the spirits, I realised that I did not need company. I had never been so happy in my life.

As I opened the baize door on my way to the kitchen I thought I heard a sound from the back premises. A soft thud, like something falling. I went through. Nothing. The back door stood open still, and I went outside, to stand for a few moments, listening. The night was warm, and smelled fresh and sweet. I looked up through the trees at a sky full of stars and faintly moving tides of shifting cloud. The owl called again. I wondered if he was on his way to the attic roost, but nothing stirred in the still night. As I turned to go back into the house the scented strands of mint brushed my long skirt and I smelled rosemary.

Happiness, driven out momentarily by the faint worry of that unexplained sound, came back with a rush. I reached up under the jasmine and took the key down from its nail. Then I went into the warm and welcoming house, my house, and shut the door behind me. I locked it, and drove home the bolts. Now for a glass of sherry, and supper . . .

I went into the bright kitchen.

There, on the mat beside the Aga, sat a cat. Thin, matted, eyes large, their distended pupils hard and very bright, staring at me, sat a big black cat with white shirt and paws, the hair along his back still ridged and stiff from fear or hatred.

But not of me. He stood up, stretched, spoke, and began to purr.

12

"And was it you who killed that pigeon?" I asked.

It was some time later. First things first, and the first was
that the cat was starving. I warmed some milk and put it
down, then unearthed a tin of cat food I had seen in one of

the cupboards and gave him as much as I dared. He took both, ravenously but with perfect manners, then stretched again, jumped straight into the Windsor chair, and began to wash. While I had my sherry he washed; while I dished up my supper he washed; while I ate an apple he washed; only as I finished a cup of coffee did he consider himself fit for the fireside, and curl up, purring loudly, but still staring, wide awake, at me.

"Don't bother to answer," I told him. "It was a silly question anyway. If you had, you'd have eaten it. But you wouldn't, would you? Because of course you're Hodge?"

A movement of the head, a glint of those magnificent eyes, confirmed it.

I poured myself another cup of coffee, sat down in the rocker opposite him, and considered.

Hodge. Cousin Geillis's cat. Who had disappeared when she left Thornyhold. Who had come back the moment I was here, with the house to myself. Who, incidentally, must have made the sound that had disturbed me as I came down from the bath.

I was very glad to see him. Now that he was here, and safe. I realised how much I had been worrying over his disappearance and possible death. *Look after Hodge. He will miss me.* The only specific request Cousin Geillis had made, and I had not been able to carry it out. Moreover, though I had thought myself beyond wanting company I was glad of this, the ideal companion. Hodge, the cat of the house.

The witch's cat.

That was what William had said, wasn't it? The witch's cat. And he had vanished, to starve or worse, when she had gone. And now that I was here, he had come back.

"Are you a witch, too?" William had asked.

I laughed, and set down my empty cup. "Am I?" I asked Hodge. "Well, I dare say we'll find out somehow, soon enough. I'm going to bed. Where do you sleep? Oh, I see. I might have known."

As I rose, the cat jumped down from his chair to lead the

way, tail high, for the stairs. By the time I was ready to get into bed he was there before me, curled by the pillow, purring.

He must have been tired as well as hungry. Before I slept myself the purring had stopped, abruptly, and the witch's cat was silently, profoundly, asleep.

———◆———

I awoke, it seemed immediately. It was still quite dark, but I knew that I must have slept already, soundly, for I felt wide awake, and refreshed. More, eager to be out of bed. A feeling of breathlessness made me long for the air.

Trying not to disturb the cat, I slid out of bed and padded to the window.

Behind the upper branches a few stars pulsed, and a cloud-held moon. Their pale light served only to show the black tracery of the boughs. But my own night-sight seemed strangely accurate: I could have sworn that I could see, quite clearly, a pair of owls sitting high in a beech beyond the toolshed. They sat huddled near the trunk of the tree, and as I watched, one of them elongated itself till it was tall and stiff as a billet of wood, its head swivelled round in the extraordinary way of its kind. It was watching something beyond, behind the trees.

A light. Low down and dancing, a yellow light. And with it, though from much further away, a sound. Incredibly, people were singing. It was no song that I had ever heard, a low, almost dirge-like chant, with little tune to it, but with a strong and steady rhythm which coincided with, or gradually overtook, the heartbeat that I could, now, strongly feel as I leaned out over the windowsill.

It was like looking down from a height into a swirling sea; the rhythmic beat, the little whirls of wind in the branches, the shifting and beckoning light; all conspiring to draw the dreamer out towards the dark, into the night.

But I was not dreaming. I was not asleep. The room, the

garden, all was familiar, and from somewhere, as if in reply to the music, a dog began to bark, distressfully. The same dog, I was sure, that I had heard last night. And now, beside me on the windowsill, was Hodge, wild-furred and wideeyed, teeth and tongue showing as he spat and hissed at the darkness.

The witch's cat. And what I could hear, what the light betrayed, beckoning into the deep wood, was a meeting of witches. The sabbath of the local coven. I knew it, as if the knowledge had come in one of those edged flashes of illumination, certainty held in spell-light. So it was true that there were witches still. And true, perhaps, that Cousin Geillis had been one of them? And was this proof that I, the second Geillis of Thornyhold, was one of the elect? The thought was heady, a flow of power going through body and brain, strong and cool and sweet.

Here Hodge, the cat, leaped out from the windowsill into the darkness. And I, reaching to catch him, for the leap was too high even for a cat, overbalanced and fell.

I never reached the ground. Nor was it truly a fall. The wind, the sweep of the night air, sucked me out of the window and carried me up, up above the trees, as easily as if I had been a bird or a dead leaf. Round me the air felt as buoyant and resistant as water. I could control my passage, almost as if swimming. I shook my head and my hair flew out in the race of air. I opened my lips and drank the flood of my own passing. Ecstasy was in every pore, every hair. This was power and glory. Whatever was required, it was worth it for this.

Below me, as motionless as if there were no wind at all, the forest stretched black and still. The airstream that carried me flowed high between the black boughs and the stars. It flowed between the very stars, above the moon. The moon had sunk low, and presently the trees were gone, and in front of me a hill rose from the darkness, lifting a black curve to cut across the moon's face. There were stones on the hill, massive menhirs, some fallen, some upright, set apparently at random in the turf. The light that had drawn me out through the window was circling among them, and presently it alighted.

I sank down towards it, landing effortlessly, as lightly as a gull on water, and there, a few yards away, was the fallen shape of a vast stone, and on it a bowl where the yellow flame floated in a pool of sweet-smelling oil. Beside the bowl a heap of something; feathers? a trailing wing? A black pigeon with its neck wrung.

Shadows were moving round among the stones. People. They were barely visible, but from all around came that same rhythmic, meaningless chant that the wind had brought to me at Thornyhold.

Hesitantly, not afraid, but full of awe and a strong, tingling excitement, I approached the lighted stone. The grass beneath my bare feet felt ice-cold. I welcomed it. My body burned still, as if it had been drenched with very hot water. The dizzy euphoria of the flight was fading. My eyes ached. The light, gentle though it was, hurt them; there was grit inside the lids. I stretched a hand towards the fallen stone. I was conscious of the shadow-people crowding nearer, of the chant growing and swelling among the standing stones. The moon had almost gone. She filled only a copper rim, and a cloud scarred her face.

Someone stood between me and the stone, a woman, tall, dressed in a long cloak that blew about her. She looked familiar, like a memory from the pond in the meadow when I was six years old.

"Cousin Geillis?" I shouted it, but made no sound. The woman never moved, but there was a rustle at my feet, and I paused and looked down. A hedgehog, whining and snuffling, nudged about amongst the grass. A bird flew across at waist height, a flash of deep kingfisher blue even in the dead light of the moon. And after it leaped Hodge the cat, a small shadow among the other shadows. He shot hissing between my feet, tripping me. I fell on my face. The turf was surprisingly soft, and not cold any more.

Hands took me, gently, and turned me over on my back. In the yellow light, swimming against the blackness, I saw faces. Most were strange, misty and changing as I looked, like faces in a dream. But foremost and unchanging, were two that I knew.

"Be she all right?" asked Jessamy Trapp. His voice was anxious.

"Oh, yes, she's all right." Agnes smiled down at me, triumphant, smug. "I knew it all along, didn't I? You're fine, my lady . . . and next time it'll be better still. Now shut your eyes again, and we'll see you back where you belong."

Before she had finished speaking, my eyes had shut fast, like the eyes of a doll that has no will of its own. There was the faintest sensation of floating once again, or being lifted, then nothing. As if Agnes's order had blacked out my conscious brain, I either fainted, or fell into another deep sleep, for when I opened my eyes again I was in bed at Thornyhold, and the window was shut, and Hodge the cat was asleep at my feet, and it was morning.

And I awoke, and behold it was a dream.

It took me a long time, through clinging mists of that deep sleep, to shake off the effects of the dream. For dream it had to be. Now in the sweet daylight the beckonings of witchcraft were impossible and wrong.

It had to be. I drew myself up against the pillows and thought about it. I felt, it was true, much more as if I had spent the night flying to meet a coven than resting, even dreaming violently, in my own bed. My head ached; the gritty sensation behind the eyelids was still there; the faintest residue of heat remained in my skin. The bedclothes smelled of sweat, and though I knew that one sweated with a vivid nightmare, this smelled somehow different.

But did this mean that, my God, I had been flying – *flying* – over the forest tops, had been watching a coven dancing among Druid stones, and had tried to reach what was probably their altar light? An altar where Jessamy and Agnes Trapp moved among the crowd, where a tall shadow like my dead Cousin Geillis was standing, and where the corpse of the dead pigeon from the Thornyhold attic had been brought as an offering?

All the indications, I told myself, were that I had had a bad nightmare. The dream was made up of the elements of yesterday, and of the further past – the hedgehog, the kingfisher, Cousin Geillis herself. And supposing, impossibly, that it had been true, how had the Trapps brought me home? How had they got in? Both doors downstairs were locked and bolted. And now, in this morning daylight, with a wren singing in the bushes outside, I refused to believe that they had flown with me through the bedroom window. And shut and latched it, I supposed, by magic, after they had flown out?

Here Hodge the cat opened his eyes, put out a paw, and stretched.

"Were you out flying last night?" I asked him.

And got no answer, or only a negative one. The cat had certainly moved during the night, for where he had gone to sleep curled close against me, he was lying now near the foot of the bed, on top of the dressing-gown I had left there.

Which proved nothing. But common sense (so easy to assume in daylight) insisted that Hodge had merely been part of a nightmare which had been brought on, probably, by the stuffiness of the room. Since I had forgotten to open the window –

I had not forgotten to open the window. I had done it, as I now clearly remembered, just before I got into bed; and now it was shut.

I sat there staring at the shut window, while common sense fought a losing battle with imagination. Perhaps, I told myself, the aged sash-cords had given way, and the heavy window had fallen shut of its own accord (without waking me?), and in the warmth of the room I had slept too deeply, and had had a bad dream. A dream vivid enough to tire me, and to leave a hangover. But I was awake now, and it was a brilliant day, a normal day, and Hodge was home, and there was work to do. Work, the answer to every kind of nightmare. And to begin with, I would clean this room myself, and change the bedding all over again.

I threw back the bedclothes, swung my feet over the side of the bed, and reached for the dressing-gown.

"Come on," I said to Hodge. "You'll have to –"

I stopped short. The cat had moved when I did, and now jumped to the floor, yawning and stretching. Where he had been lying, on the folds of my dressing-gown, was a wisp of dry grass, pressed flat by his sleeping weight. And halfway between the bed and the window, yellow against the green of the carpet, lay a dead leaf.

There is a passage somewhere in Coleridge's writings which, once read, had stayed in my memory. I could not then have quoted it accurately, but the gist of it, as I sat there on the edge of the bed, with one arm arrested as I reached for the dressing-gown, came flooding to drown the weak struggles of common sense. *If a man could pass through Paradise in a dream, and have a flower presented to him as a pledge that his soul had really been there, and if he found the flower in his hand when he awoke – Aye, and what then?*

What then, indeed?

No answer there, either, for a woman who had passed through some shadowy annexe to the Otherworld, and found dead plants for proof when she awoke . . .

From overhead came a patter, a scratching and the scrabble of claws. Hodge looked up sharply, yellow eyes narrow and concentrated.

"I forgot to take water up," I said aloud, and had to clear my throat to say it. Then I grabbed the dressing-gown, banished Coleridge back to his opium-clouds, and went to have a bath.

By the time I had bathed and dressed the dream had receded, as dreams do, and the ideas it had engendered had faded even further. Before I made my breakfast I let Hodge out of the back door (still locked fast) and then filled the enamel jug with water and carried it up to the attic.

I opened the door gently, and went in. There were two pigeons in the attic. One, my friend of yesterday, was pecking round on the floor, but on a windowsill, regarding me with an eye the colour of a Mexican opal, was a new one, a blue-grey pigeon, with white barred wings. It made a soft sound in its throat, shifting from foot to foot as if nervous. I scattered a handful of grain, and bent to fill the trough with water. The blue-grey pigeon flew straight down and stooped to drink.

Then I saw the ring on its leg.

Gently, carefully, I took hold of the bird. It made no attempt to escape. I managed to detach the tiny ring. Then I put the bird down again, and let it feed.

Over by the window, I unfolded the flimsy paper. There was a message printed very small, in capitals.

WELCOME MY DEAR FROM YOUR COUSIN GEILLIS.

13

When I left for Arnside soon after lunch, I took care to lock
both doors.

Arnside was a pleasant, small market town, with a few
good shops, a cobbled market place, and a church rather

too big for its present needs. The choice of shops was not great, and I soon made my selection and registered for groceries and meat, did what shopping I could, then visited the bank and made myself known to the manager, a pleasant man, Thorpe by name, who spoke warmly of my Cousin Geillis, and expressed himself very willing to help me in whatever way he could. I handed over the letters from Martin and Martin, signed papers opening my new bank account, and was shown a very cheering balance. On my asking Mr Thorpe's advice about installing a telephone, he made the call for me there and then. It was still not easy, he told me, to get a new line put in, but as Thornyhold was so isolated he thought he could press my case, and the telephone would surely be installed before winter came. And yes, he said, he knew Hannaker's Garage at St Thorn, and when I did see my way clear to buying a car, I would be in safe hands there.

Finally, on my mentioning Mrs Trapp, he put a call through for me to Martin and Martin and then left his office while I took it. What I heard from them did something to set my mind at rest; they had certainly informed Mrs Trapp of Miss Ramsey's impending arrival some time in September, and, Miss Saxon having employed her from time to time, Mrs Trapp had her own key, or rather, knew where one was kept. By the same token, the solicitors had judged her to be the best person to get the house ready for me. They did hope that all was well? I was quite satisfied with the way I had found things? I assured them that I was, thanked them, thanked Mr Thorpe, and then, on the strength of that bank balance, went into the ironmonger's next door and managed to buy, with a feeling of quite absurd pleasure, the first gift for my new home, a pair of tea-towels and three yellow dusters.

Then I set off for home. After only a mile or so on the main highway, my way branched off into empty country roads, which curled along in the shade of deep banks clad with ivy and crowned with trees. Here and there along the roadside were quarries, long disused, where road metal had been dug. They were filled now with thickets of sloe and bramble, and I could see the sunlight glinting on fruit reddening to ripeness. I remembered the empty jars in the toolshed, ready for the bramble jelly I intended to make . . .

Of such small things is happiness made. I pedalled home to the sound of tins clinking in the basket, and presently turned in through the drive gates towards Thornyhold.

As I passed the lodge I saw Agnes, out in the tiny yard at the side, pegging out some towels and a couple of checked shirts which must belong to Jessamy.

She hung the peg bag on the line and waved, taking a step towards me. I stopped, and she approached, smiling.

"You been to town?"

"Yes. I enjoyed it, too. It's a lovely ride, isn't it? It's years since I've been on a bike, but it's true that you don't forget how! By the time I got to the end of the drive I felt fine, and there was very little traffic on the main road."

"It can be bad market days, when the farmers go in. Nice town, though, isn't it?"

"Very. I didn't really explore, because I wanted to get back, but there seemed to be lots to see. The church looks lovely, almost a cathedral. Is the music good?"

"Music?" She looked blank. "I don't know much about music. Never been in there, anyway. You a churchgoer, then?"

I laughed. "Brought up to be as regular as clockwork."

A quick look. "More than your aunty was."

"Not my aunt, my cousin. You don't surprise me. I seem to remember that she wasn't exactly a believer."

"Hm." A nod, as if I had confirmed something. Then another speculative look at me. "Is everything all right at the house? You look as if you haven't slept. Was them birds in the roof disturbing you? Jessamy told me about that pigeon. All sorts used to go in there after the food. Dirty things. Vermin, I call them, but fond of them all, she was, for all she was such a real lady. Kept you awake, did they?"

"No. Actually, there was only one, and I didn't hear it at all."

"You should ha' let Jessamy bring it away with the dead one. Then keep that window shut."

"I'll think about it. But I did sleep pretty well, thank you."

"That's all right, then. I just thought you looked a bit peaky. You don't mind me asking?"

"Of course not." The questions, surely too many for casual interest, made me decide to probe a little on my own account. "As a matter of fact, I did have a bad dream."

"That's nasty, when you're alone in the house. What was it about, then?"

Certainly not casual. "I've forgotten," I said indifferently. "No – there was something in it about music. But you know how it is with dreams. They seem terribly vivid, but as soon as you wake up, they've gone."

"I thought maybe it was about me, seeing as it was a bad dream." She laughed merrily, looking at me sideways.

"Do you know," I said slowly, "I think you did come into it somewhere . . . But that sounds rude, doesn't it? Oh, yes, there's something I've been meaning to ask you about. There's a dog barking at night – it seems quite near. Do you know whose it is, and where? It sounds – well, I wondered if it was all right."

"I couldn't say, I'm sure. You get used to the noise after a bit, in the country. I've never noticed."

"Well, never mind. I must get back now. Oh, Mrs Trapp –"

"Agnes. Do call me Agnes."

"Agnes, then. When will the brambles be ripe enough for jam?"

"If this sun goes on, another week and you might find plenty. They grow down this way, along the road you came."

"I know, I saw them."

"You make your own, then?"

"Oh, yes. That is, if I can find the recipe. Miss Saxon seems to have left quite a stock of sugar. I'd rather make jelly than jam with the brambles, but I never can remember quantities, and my own books haven't come yet. Have you got a good one?"

"I have, but you use Miss Saxon's. She has lots of books, you'll find a recipe somewhere. She was always trying things, and if they came out well, she'd write them down herself. Her jams and such were real lovely, better than anyone else's."

"Oh? I will, then, if I can find it. Didn't she give it to you?"

"She never gave her recipes to no one. But if you do find her book, and *you* don't mind, I'd be right pleased to see it. I did look in the kitchen when I had the books down to clean, but it wasn't there. I reckon it would be in the still-room, along with the concoctions she made up there. Wine and such she would make, cordials she called them, and very good they were. But the last year or so she didn't bother so much. You ever made wines yourself?"

"No, but I'd like to learn. I'll look out for the recipes, and we might have a go."

"I'd take that kindly. You do your own baking as well?" Eyeing the bread flour in my basket. "You got your rations all right, then? And that's a nice chicken, Bolter's, was it? You've been lucky there, and I see he let you have two eggs. Like gold they are these days, so watch those tins don't break them. I can let you have a box for them if you like."

"Thanks, but it's not worth it. I'm nearly home, and I'm being careful. I'll only get one a week after this; I had two weeks' rations to pick up today."

"Well," said Agnes, "when you get to know folks better . . ." She let it hang, then added, meaningly: "I never knew your aunty go short."

"It looks like it. Her store-cupboard's a sight for sore eyes. Well, goodbye, Agnes. It's a lovely drying day, isn't it? I've got some washing out, and it'll be ready for ironing by now, I expect."

When I got home I wheeled the cycle straight round to the shed, and was startled to see that the back door stood open. William appeared on the step.

"William! How did you get in?"

He ignored the question. He was bright with excitement. "Oh, Miss Geillis! Did you know Hodge was back?"

"Yes. He came back last night. But William, how did you get into the house? It's all right, I don't mind, seeing it's you, but I was so sure I'd locked the doors, and I know the back door was bolted. I went out by the front."

"Oh, there's a broken sneck on the back kitchen window. It's been bust for ages, but Miss Geillis never bothered. When I got here Hodge was sitting on the sill, and I thought he'd just come home and was hungry, so I climbed in and got him some milk. You really don't mind?"

"No."

"You said he would come back! How did you find him? Where was he?"

"He came back himself, late last night. He was dreadfully hungry, and he looked as if he'd had a bad fright. William, did you know Miss Geillis kept pigeons?"

"Yes, of course. In the attic. All the birds used to come in. I used to help her feed them. But just before she went to hospital someone came with a big basket and took them away. Let me carry yours for you. Gosh, it's heavy. Oh, you got two tins of cat food, and doesn't the fish smell! I needn't have asked if you knew Hodge was back! It looks as if he's the only one going to eat."

I laughed as I followed him into the house. "I got a chicken, and two whole eggs, so I won't starve yet awhile unless Hodge helps me with that, too."

"He probably will. But I brought you some eggs. My dad sent them. That's why I came over. There's a dozen, all brown ones. I put them on the kitchen table."

"Why, how lovely! Thank you very much. Please thank your father for me. Where do you live, William?"

"Over towards Tidworth. It's called Boscobel. At least, it used to be called Taggs Farm, but Dad changed the name."

"Boscobel's nicer than Taggs Farm. Is your father a farmer, then?"

"No. It's not a farm now, it's just a house. Dad writes."

"Writes what?"

"Books. I've never read one, not right through, that is. I tried once, but it was a bit dry. He's pretty famous, I think, but it's not his real name."

"What is it?"

"Peter Vaughan. Have you read them?"

"I'm afraid not. But I do know the name. I'll have to look for his books, now that I've met you. Is he writing just now?"

"Yes, and it puts him in an awful temper most of the time. So I come out," said William, simply. "He can't do with me around the house at such times."

It sounded like an echo of something often said. I smiled. "And your mother? Does she hide away from him, too?"

"She does better than that. She left us." His tone was quite indifferent. "Has Hodge had his dinner?"

"Yes. He had it before I went out. But you can give him some of the fish, if you like, while I get my things off."

When I came back into the kitchen Hodge was under the table with his chin in a saucer, with William kneeling beside him. The boy's face was rapt, loving. I thought of my own childhood, so rich in practical care, so starved of the real needs of the lonely and imaginative child. I had wondered why a lively boy seemed happy to spend so much time, first with my cousin, who was old enough to be his grandmother, and now apparently with me. Much was now explained, the self-absorbed father, the absent mother, the long days of the school holiday. There was no need to feel pangs of conscience about letting him stay and help; presumably his father knew where he was; but one day soon I would have to find my way to Boscobel and make myself known there, and find out if the child was needed at his own home or not.

William looked up. "What are you thinking about? You look kind of sad."

"Not sad," I said, "and nothing much."

The first was true, the second a lie. I was thinking three

111

things. The first was that Agnes Trapp had examined the contents of my basket, and had not seen fit to remark on the couple of tins of cat food, and the damp, smelly parcel of fish scraps that cushioned the eggs from them. She who remarked on everything.

Hence, she knew that Hodge was home.

She had also asked, with some interest, how I had slept last night.

And thirdly, there had been a way into the house last night, for someone who knew the sneck on the back window was broken. If William could climb in and unfasten the door, so could Jessamy.

It was crazy, it was in itself a nightmare, but was it possible that Agnes and her son Jessamy had really been in my bedroom last night, and that they had carried in the grass and the dead leaf? That in the moment between sleeping and waking they had been in very fact bending over my bed, and had seen Hodge then – even a glimpse of him as, presumably, he had jumped off my pillow and fled into hiding?

But why? William had told me that Agnes had had the place upside down "looking for something," and I had certainly arrived too soon for her. I had declined her help in my cleaning, and since then had kept the doors locked. But it really was absurd. If she had wanted to search the house she would do far better to wait till I was out, like today, than break in at night, with the risk of waking me . . . Unless, of course, she could have drugged my sleep. More and more absurd. And how and when? While I was upstairs in the bathroom? The sound I had heard? Easier still, the pie she had given me for supper? Some drug dropped in it to make me sleep heavily, which had induced that incredible nightmare of flight and fantasy? Forget it, Gilly, and don't pretend the woman is anything but perfectly friendly and helpful, or that there's anything weird about this place or anything to do with it, because Thornyhold is heaven and you love it.

"William," I said suddenly, "what time did you come along here – to the house, I mean?"

"About two o'clock. You can't have been gone long, because Mrs Trapp came up just after, and said she'd seen you go out the main gate."

"She was here?"

Something in my tone caught at him. He eyed me. "Yes."

"Why did she come?"

"She didn't say. She just said how funny that you'd washed the sheets again when they were just fresh on, and were the eggs for you and she would put them in the pantry and take the sheets in because they were dry. So I said she couldn't because the doors were locked and you'd taken the back door key and I was going to do some gardening and wait for you myself."

I was silent.

"I'd locked the door again, you see. When I'd given Hodge his milk I came out again to get the eggs – I couldn't carry them when I climbed in – and then I saw her coming through the wood and so I just shut the door and put the key in my pocket."

I took a breath. "She'll think I don't trust her," I said uncertainly.

"Miss Geillis didn't. She told me so."

"Oh?" Some relic of my Victorian upbringing made me feel how unsuitable it was to let a child talk so, but William was more sensible than a lot of adults I had known. Besides, I needed to know. "Did you tell her Hodge was back? Or did she see him?"

"No. He went upstairs after he'd had the milk. I didn't tell her because she hates Hodge, and he hates her. That's why he went. After Miss Geillis died, Mrs Trapp was going to drown him."

"William!"

"It's true. I heard her say so."

"Who to?"

"Jessamy. He's all right, actually, but he's a bit simple, and he is scared of her, and does what she tells him."

"I see." A lot was beginning to explain itself. I decided to treat his fears as rational. "So that's why you were so worried about Hodge's disappearance?" He nodded. "And about the saucers that weren't touched?"

"Yes. I didn't tell you for fear of upsetting you, too."

"You know, the saucers were probably quite all right. You didn't find the place strewn with dead birds and voles, did you?"

"No." He smiled then, relieved, I thought, at not being laughed at.

I was, indeed, far from laughing. I said slowly, after a pause: "Well, look, William, this may all be true, but one needs to be on good terms with one's neighbours, so just go easy with Mrs Trapp, will you, even if you don't like her? Or even if, much more important, Hodge doesn't like her? So far she's been very good to me, and I want it to stay that way. Okay?"

"Okay," said William the sensible. "She was good to Dad and me, too. Made cakes and things for us, and she's a smashing cook. But she used to stay around and talk, and Dad couldn't take it. I told you, I get chased out myself when he's busy. I don't mind her really. It's only because of Hodge."

"She was probably joking about Hodge. It can't be easy to drown a full-grown cat, even if he would have let her catch him. Anyway, he's all right now."

"We all are," said William, half to himself, half to Hodge, who was sitting back from the saucer and starting to wash his face. "I'll go on with some weeding now, if you like?" He paused in the doorway. "By the way, did you notice that your bicycle pump had come back? It's on the shelf in the shed. Flew, I expect."

14

The year drew on into a lovely autumn. The days went by, bright and still, or with a breeze that lifted a few leaves from the trees. The horse-chestnuts turned first, a rich golden yellow, then the cherries, to scarlet and saffron and jade. No frosts as yet. In the garden asters and chrysanthemums smelled rich and sweet. I found autumn crocus one morning just beside the front door, and on the Garrya against the north wall the grape-bloomed catkins were beginning to lengthen for winter.

I had never worked so hard, physically, in my life, and had certainly never been so happy. My luggage came, and with it the furniture and household effects that I had kept from the vicarage, so, before these could be arranged, I started on the promised turnout of the house. Drawing-room, den, dining-room, hallway – I swept, scrubbed, polished. One day Jessamy Trapp came up with his mother, and offered to climb up and clear the roof gutters. Agnes came two or three times, with renewed offers, insistent ones, of help, so that I began to wonder if she needed the money, and in the end set her to scrub out the old kitchen and back premises, and then, I am afraid with intent, to do the same for the pigeon-loft. To do her justice, she did the jobs well, but it seemed that the pigeon-loft was enough, for, after I had thanked her and paid her, she did not come back, and I was left in peace.

At length the house, scoured, polished and smelling of autumn flowers, was as clean as it would ever be. I spent two or three satisfying days rearranging the rooms to accommodate my own things, leaving the picture-hanging – always a slow job – till last. I had rehung most of the pictures from the hall and drawing-room after cleaning them, but had kept one or two aside to make way for my own – flower studies I had done some time ago, which my father had thought good enough to frame. These, I thought, might go well enough with Cousin Geillis's pictures, which were all water-colours, pretty things, the sort you can live with. Her taste had been conventional and gentle: all her spirit and energy, it seemed, had gone into her care for garden and still-room.

One of her pictures intrigued me. It was a tinted drawing, very much faded, of Thornyhold seen from the belvedere, its south front, bare of creepers and climbing plants, looking vaguely unfamiliar. The garden, too, was different, with paths cutting curved lines through close-mown grass, and flower beds crowding between. The enclosing hedges were barely breast high.

There was nothing surprising about finding a 'view' of the house done many years ago, but what aroused my curiosity was the signature, a monogram of a G and an S entwined. Geillis Saxon? She had surely never seen Thornyhold when it looked like that? She could not even have been alive at the time. Then who? Not another Geillis, that was too fanciful . . . But the very fancy stirred something in me that had been forgotten for too long. Studying the ordered lawns and shrubberies of the old Thornyhold, I felt myself seized, for the first time since my schooldays, by the old longing to paint. Not 'to be an artist', no ambitions after London exhibitions, or dreams of vast canvases hung on gallery walls, but a desire to record some of the beauty around me, to put Thornyhold, quite literally, back in the picture. I would start this very week, and soon, when my hand was in again, I would tackle this same view of the house as I had seen it – recognised it – with so much love on that first day. And with the work, somehow, stake my own claim to Thornyhold.

Meantime the garden, like the house, must be brought to order.

William had come from time to time, as he had promised, to help me with the garden. Between us we got the front strip weeded and tidied for the winter, and made a start on the kitchen garden and herb beds. Most of Cousin Geillis's harvest would be wasted, because I knew very little as yet about the picking and drying of her plants, but I could deal with the pot-herbs, and brought in rosemary and sage and thyme and sprigs of sweet bay, and hunted out the jars for my bramble jelly. There was no orchard fruit to gather (if the Trapps had taken it during the interregnum, that was fair enough) but there would be wild blackberries in plenty. If I could lay hands on Cousin Geillis's famous recipe book

117

I might find new ways of using what was left of the garden produce.

But search as I might, I found nothing except an ancient volume of country recipes collected years ago by the local Women's Institute. Whatever was special about my cousin's preserves would just have to be missed; the jams and jellies in the WI book made luscious enough reading, and for the present would have to serve.

So one beautiful day I gave myself a holiday, and went blackberrying.

William had given me rough directions. Through the wicket at the side of the house, along the woodland path, then up a lane, which was rutted but passable, and led eventually, he told me, to an ancient quarry set in pastureland. This, long since disused, was overgrown with blackberry bushes, and, since it caught all the sun, ripened them beautifully.

I tied a basket to my bicycle, and set off. It was a roughish ride, and it took me some three or four miles, but by road it would have been fully six or more. The afternoon sun shone down with real heat on the quarry, and the wind could find no way there. Rabbits fled at my approach, scuttling up the steep byways of the rock face, to vanish among the stones. There was water at the quarry's base, a pool surrounded by fine, sheep-nibbled turf. The sheep, indeed, were still there, but moved off at my approach. Their dismal bleating echoed from the quarry cliff, and was answered loudly and sweetly by a robin's song. There were no other sounds. The wild thyme was still in flower, and here and there harebells hung motionless in the windless air.

William had not misled me. The place was a mass of brambles, and the fruit was big and glinting-ripe. I got to work.

I had almost filled my basket when I slowly became conscious that the bleating of the sheep had not dwindled with the flock's disappearance. One voice remained, steadily complaining. Only faintly curious, but glad of a respite, I straightened up and looked around. No sign. The short turf by the water was inhabited only by a pied wagtail, making its darting runs after the insects brought out by the warm sunshine. The robin flew down to a bush nearby, and whispered its musical undersong. From somewhere deep among the banked brambles, the sheep complained.

And now that I was listening, there was more in the cry than idle grumbling. There was fear. I set my basket down and went to look.

She was caught, like Abraham's ram, in a thicket of thorns. In trying to push through, she had brought a dozen hooked boughs down to fix themselves in her fleece, and when she had tried to pull herself out backwards, others had gaffed and netted her like a fish. She was immovable.

She saw me, gave one last cry, and fell silent. I picked my way carefully in past the first barbed branches, and started to try and unravel her.

It was an appalling job. I had no gloves, and to do the job without injury one would have needed heavy gauntlets of leather. And secateurs, or even wire cutters, with them, for as I tore each bough away from the sheep's wool – which took all my strength but did not appear to hurt the sheep at all – the bough tended to spring straight back and catch hold before I had reached for the next one. And each movement brought lacerations of hands and arms. I was scratched and bleeding freely before I gave up and began to scour the quarry, sure that somewhere, some picnicker careless of the countryside would have thrown away a bottle or sharp-edged tin. I soon found one. Beside the remains of a camp-fire near the pool was a broken whisky bottle. I started to hack the brambles through with that, and haul them away, and in another ten minutes or so it began to look as if the sheep could be moved, but I was afraid that, once she found she could move, she might struggle away from me, and trap herself all over again.

"What on earth are you doing?" queried a startled voice, just behind me. I jumped and turned. A man had approached, his footsteps soundless on the mossy turf of the quarry's floor. He was slightly above middle height, with darkish hair showing a hint of grey, and dark brows over grey eyes. His skin was weathered to a healthy red-brown, and his clothes were workman's clothes, but his voice was educated. He carried a pair of binoculars slung over one shoulder, and in his hand was a crook.

He must be the shepherd, or the farmer. Relieved, I had just opened my mouth to speak when he repeated sharply: "What the devil have you been doing to that ewe?"

I gaped. Caught in my work of mercy, I had expected the shepherd to spring to my help, but he looked both startled and angry.

"What the devil do you think I'm doing?" I answered tartly. Then, following his look, I saw what he had seen. My hands were bleeding freely, and blood had dripped and smeared over the animal's fleece. And in one bloody hand I held that most horrible of weapons, a broken bottle.

I said, rather feebly: "It's my own blood. Did you think I was cutting her up for a stew?"

"Oh, my God," he said. "I see. But when you catch someone with a broken bottle in their hands and blood all over the place . . . I'm terribly sorry. Are you badly hurt?"

"Not really. They're not glass cuts; I was using the bottle to hack these beastly brambles away. She was stuck fast, but she's almost out now, and I'm scratched to death. Can you help?"

"Well, of course. You come out of that and let me."

He produced a clasp-knife from a pocket, and then, with the crook, started to haul back the remaining bramble stems that trapped the ewe. Some of them he cut, then he handed the stem of the crook to me.

"Hold them back with this, will you, please, while I haul her out? If I cut them all at once she'll probably bolt straight back into the thick of it."

I took the stick, and held back the bundle of thorns. He waded in among the remaining strands, then laid hold of the thick fleece with both hands, and threw his weight back. She came, and as she came, she started to struggle wildly, but he held her, and finally yanked her clear of the thorns. In her terror, she fought to bolt back into cover, but he managed to turn her round and give her a shove, till, calling dismally, she bolted, safe and sound, up the track where her sisters had gone. Apart from the bloodstains, and a very ragged fleece, she seemed none the worse.

"Well, thank you," I said.

"Well, thank *you*," said the shepherd. "But for you, she might well have died there."

"You'd have found her yourself."

"As it happens, yes, but it was the purest chance that brought me this way."

"And thank goodness for that. Even if I could have got her free, I doubt if I could have turned her. They're incredibly strong, aren't they? Here's your crook."

He took it. "Now, your hands. How bad are they?"

I held them out. "Scratches, but they'll heal. They've been bleeding so much that I suppose they'll be clean. Do you think the water's all right? I'd like to wash."

I knelt down by the pool and washed the bloodstains off. The scratches were many and sore, but only one of them was deep. This was still bleeding quite freely. He stood without speaking till I had finished, then handed me a clean handkerchief. I protested, groping for my own, only to find that I had none.

"Take it," he insisted. "Look, returning it is no problem. I live just over the hill there. Come up now and we'll put something on those cuts, and I'm sure we can find some sticking-plaster. Anyway, you'd like a cup of tea, wouldn't you?"

"Well –" I said, weakly.

"Did you get all the brambles you wanted?"

"Just about. I can easily come back another time, anyway." I regarded my hands. "I hardly feel like picking any more just this minute. Is this your land, by the way? Was I trespassing?"

"No, no. It's a public path, and in any case the quarry would be common land. Before it filled up, I believe the gipsies used to camp here. Let me take the basket. Oh, I see, you've got a bicycle."

"Will it be safe here if I come back the same way?"

"I think so, but we won't chance it. I'll take it for you. We go this way, and it's pretty steep, but much the quickest."

Wheeling the bicycle, he started off up the track the sheep had used. I followed. Once at the head of the quarry, I could see a low, grey farmhouse, set in its own shaw of beeches, with a sprawl of outbuildings to one side. Rooks were loud in the trees, and cattle were gathering near a gate where a farm road curled past the buildings and out of sight.

"You can go back that way," he said, pointing. "The track you were on joins it just over that brow. You live hereabouts, I take it? Or are you on holiday? You can't have been here long, or we'd surely have met, and I wouldn't have forgotten that."

His glance made it a compliment, and I laughed.

"I haven't been here a month yet, but I think you probably know a fair amount about me, all the same."

"What do you mean?"

I nodded towards the gate. A small figure slid through it and came running towards us.

"Dad! Miss Geillis!"

"It was William who told me about the quarry and the brambles," I said.

William's father scooped his son up under one arm and dumped him on the saddle of my bicycle. He regarded me across the handlebars.

"So you're our new witch," he said, smiling.

15

"Well," I said, "I'm Geillis Ramsey and I do seem to be taking over my cousin's reputation. That's almost the first thing William said to me, too. Has he been telling tales to you?"

"Inevitably. His flair for fiction is even better than mine.

I'm supposed to be the one who does the inventing round here, and at least I get paid for my efforts, but William's well on the way to outstripping me. However, he does seem to have introduced us, which is a good mark for him. How do you do, Miss Ramsey? I'm Christopher Dryden." As we reached the gate he tipped his son off the bicycle. "Run along in, will you, and put the kettle on." Then to me: "How are you enjoying Thornyhold?"

"I love it."

He propped the bicycle against the wall. "Not too lonely there?"

"Not at all. The Trapps have been very helpful, and William, too. I meant to come and see you soon anyway, to ask if it was all right for William to come over so often. Oh, and to thank you myself for the eggs you sent. It was terribly good of you."

"They were nothing. Eggs and milk are no problem here. We're still part of the farm, and the Yellands are very good to us."

"And it's all right about William? I love having him, and he's a great help, but perhaps you would rather he stayed at home?"

"Not a bit of it. I'm busy most of the time, and don't pay enough attention to him, I'm afraid. And he loves Thornyhold. I think he misses your cousin quite a lot."

"I gathered that. Well, that's fine, but I'm afraid poor William gets a lot of work to do when he does come over."

"He likes it. And I'm very grateful to you for letting him. I'm afraid that when I'm in the throes of a book I'm very bad company. I've tried to time my writing so that I'm free when he's on holiday from school, but it never seems to work that way. I've been hard at it all summer, and haven't had much time for him, poor chap. Shall we go in now? I'll show you where to wash, and – William, get that box of plasters and lint and stuff down from the bathroom, will you? – by the time you've dealt with those hands of yours the kettle should be ready."

William did as he was told, then vanished about some concern of his own. I rejoined my host in the farm kitchen, a big, long room with a low ceiling. The old fireplace was there, but its ovens were plainly disused, and an electric stove stood at the far end of the room. Two windows looked out over the pasture; the sills were deep in papers, which did seem to be in some sort of order. Down the centre of the room was a long, scrubbed table, with plates and cutlery set ready at the end nearest the stove; one guessed that between meals they were put straight back on the table as soon as they were washed up. The butter crock stood there, a tin of salt, a half-empty bottle of red wine and one of tomato ketchup. Bachelor living as a fine art; the kitchen was clean and workmanlike, and the clutter made sense for a busy man looking after himself.

Teapot and mugs stood ready. He made the tea and opened a round tin that held biscuits.

"Do sit down. Milk and sugar?"

"Milk, please, but no sugar. Thank you." I looked around me. "One thing about these old farmhouses, everyone lived in the kitchen, so it gets the sun and it really is a lovely room. Do you use that fireplace?"

"I light a fire most evenings, except in hot weather. William does his homework here. I work in the little room behind this – I think it used to be the farmer's office. It's as dark as the pit and looks straight out on the old pigsties."

"But with all the house to choose from –" I protested.

"Oh, it was first choice. You get no writing done at all if you sit at a table with a view. You'd spend the whole time watching the birds or thinking about what you would like to be doing out of doors, instead of flogging yourself to work out of sheer boredom."

"You're joking."

"I assure you I'm not. It's hard work, and doesn't do well with distractions. Just an occasional walk to clear the fog away."

"Like Bunyan, writing all that in prison. Only he probably never got out for a walk at all."

"Actually, I believe they did let him out now and again, but he did about twelve years all told. So he really could get on with the job."

"Well," I said, "as prisons go, you're lucky."

"I know that. But you see why I'm happy that William has taken to you so well. Your cousin was terribly good to him and he was really cut to pieces when she died. She was remarkable with children."

"I know." .

"Then you can imagine how pleased I was when he told me he had been over to see you, and you were smashing, too. I quote."

"And a witch, don't forget."

"Oh, of course. I do gather that your magic touch with his ferret is every bit as powerful as Miss Saxon's."

"I only used her medicine, and William told me which it was. How did you get on with the rest of the dose, by the way?"

"Fine. Only one small nip to show for it, clean through my thick driving gloves. And a running commentary from William, comparing my technique very unfavourably with yours."

I laughed. "It sounds as if Silkworm is himself again. Did my cousin do much, er, doctoring?"

"Yes, indeed. Ever since we've lived here we've heard people speak of her as a kind of local healer. Do you know this part of the country well?"

"Not at all. I'm only here because Cousin Geillis left Thornyhold to me."

"Well, in some ways, it's – this corner of the county, anyway is – still a fairly primitive sort of place. I expect you knew that your cousin had studied herbalism professionally at one time, and in fact what she did mainly was grow and make up the medicines and so on, to supply some big firm in London. But she was always willing to help local folk who asked her to, and she did a lot of animal doctoring, so she fitted very naturally into the Thornyhold setting as a witch – a white witch, of course! The local 'wise woman'. Didn't you know that your house has a history as a witch's house?"

"Really? Well, I know it's got its own magic, but – a witch's house? I always pictured a witch's cottage as being small and dark and windowless, with a smoky thatch and a cauldron over the fire, but Thornyhold is so – so eighteenth-century respectable! It's a charming house."

"So it is. But in the mid-nineteenth century the squire's widow from the big house retired there and took to witch-craft in a big way. She lived there for seventy years and died at the age of ninety-two, and the house has lived on old Goody Gostelow's reputation ever since."

"Good heavens! At Thornyhold? Then I hope she was a white witch, too!"

"Oh, yes. In fact the poor girl was highly religious, and had been driven out by her rake of a husband who was a pillar of some local hellfire club, and a satanist as well, it's said. So Lady Sibyl set to work to defend herself and her Dower House against the devil's works. Thornyhold was actually the agent's house, but the agent had married the lady's former nurse, and he and his wife took her in. No doubt Squire Gostelow, when he was sober enough, might have got round to turning them all out, but he died soon after and they were left in peace."

"Lucky for Lady Sibyl. But I thought you said she was a white witch."

"She had nothing to do with his death. Local chronicles have it that 'his various excesses caught up with him at an early age'. He was in his thirties. The estate passed to a nephew who seems to have been away most of the time; in any case he left well alone at the Dower House. The big house was burned down, in 1912 I think it was, and the last male of the family was killed on the Somme. Which left old Lady Sibyl – 'Goody Gostelow' by that time – still at Thornyhold, still defending herself against the devil's works, and living in peace till her death in 1920. What is it?"

"Nothing, really. Her initials, SG. There's an old water-colour, a picture of the house, in the drawing-room, and it has SG in the corner. I thought at first that the monogram was GS, but she must have done it."

"Probably. All young ladies were taught to sketch in those days, weren't they? Now you're smiling."

"I was taught, too, at school. I was planning to do some sketches of the house and garden as they are now."

"That house really does keep its continuity, doesn't it?"

"You're surely not going to tell me that Cousin Geillis drew, too? I never heard of it."

"Oh, no. All her time was taken up with the garden, and her herbs. That's what took her to Thornyhold, really. She saw it when she was plant-hunting in Westermain, and the old people – the couple who lived on there after Lady Sibyl's death – showed her round, and she found the place irresistible."

"She said something like that to me. No, thank you." This as he proffered the biscuit tin again. "But I'd love a little more tea, please, if there's enough? Just half . . . that's lovely. Thank you. What did you mean, the defences against the devil and so on?"

"You won't have noticed how the place is planned? I mean the garden?"

"Planned? Well, the herb garden, of course, but what else? What's so special?"

"It's defended against witchcraft and black magic. You've got yew and juniper at the south-west corner of the house, and there's ash and rowan, and a bay tree, and then the quickthorn hedge with some of the holy thorn of Glastonbury planted amongst it. And of course elder trees. Your cousin once showed me the lot. She was highly intrigued by the story, and took care to keep it as it had been."

"Trefoil, John's wort, Vervain, Dill,
   Hinder witches of their will," I quoted.

"What's that?"

"Cousin Geillis's pot-pourri. She guarded her still-room, too."

"Did she really? Well, that doesn't surprise me. She never said anything about this to you, then?"

"Well, no, she never told me the story of the house. She just said it 'seemed made for her' and she'd 'taken it on.' I see now what she meant. Actually, I didn't know her at all well. She came to see me two or three times when I was a child, and that was all. I was rather lonely and – and a bit unhappy, and it seemed as if she just turned up when I needed her. She used to take me for walks. I loved going with her, and I think I learned a lot. I don't mean about herbalism or anything like that, but she taught me to identify plants and flowers, and a lot about animals and birds, too. I did ask her once if she was a witch, but she just laughed. I think that, when I was a child, I thought there was some kind of magic about her."

And I know it now, I added, but not aloud.

"Where was your home?" he asked.

"My father was vicar of a colliery parish in the north-east. It was hideous, and the countryside was poor and scrubby. I was at school in the Lake District, and that was lovely, and I had a year at Durham University before my mother died, but I spent most of my time there working, and in any case I couldn't have afforded to go far enough away at weekends to smell the country air. Then my mother died and I went back to look after Daddy, and it was pit-heaps and graveyards again. So you see why Thornyhold is heaven for me. Some day I suppose I might begin to feel lonely, or bored, but just at present I love every minute of every day. It's just enough to wake to the birds, and to go to sleep in the silence." I stopped, setting my empty mug down with a bit of a rattle. "I'm sorry. You're too good a listener, and maybe when one lives alone, however much one likes it, one gets too talkative. Were you taking the air to clear the fog today, then? I thought you were the shepherd."

"Yes. I'd done my stint for the day."

"Then I'm not keeping you back from your work? I ought to go now, anyway. Thank you for the tea."

"Why must you? I assure you, I've come to one of those natural breaks in the book, where one can walk away and let things go on working in the subconscious. It's true, don't look so unbelieving. It means I can afford to tear myself away from my view of the pigsties, and go out on parole, as much as I like and you'll put up with."

He spoke convincingly, but the glint of laughter in his eyes brought my shyness back with a rush. I said uncertainly: "That's very nice of you, but I really ought to be going. There are the brambles to pick over, and I'd like to start the jelly tonight. And there's Hodge – the cat. He wasn't in when I left, and I locked everything up, so he'll be looking for his supper."

"You don't need to lock your doors hereabouts, surely? I don't think we ever do."

"I know, but ... Oh, well, I suppose it's a habit left over from home."

He looked at me quickly. "You've had trouble?"

"No, no. Not trouble. But ... I believe you know Mrs Trapp? From the lodge."

Some change in his expression. Indefinable, but like a ripple over still water. "Yes."

"She used to work for my cousin sometimes, and then the lawyers asked her to clean the house before I came here, so I suppose she does feel – I mean, she really does know the house better than I do."

"And she still thinks she can come and go as she pleases?"

"Yes. But in the country people do, don't they? Come in without knocking, and that sort of thing?"

"To some extent, yes. She used to come here quite often, the same sort of thing, very kind and helpful, but of course I can't do with interruptions at random, so I had to tell her so."

I was thinking what William had told me. I decided to be as direct as he had been. "Do you like her?"

That faint touch again of what could be embarrassment. "Like? I hardly know. As I said, she's very kind, but . . ."

"Do you trust her?"

"Oh, certainly. Ah, William's been talking, has he? I told you he had too much imagination. Well, the truth is, she used to bring all sorts of dishes, and she's a beautiful cook, but one couldn't help remembering the gossip."

"Gossip?"

He hesitated, then looked up, smiling. "Yes, why not? You live here now, so you'll hear it soon enough. Mrs Trapp is one of the local ladies who, as your cousin did, practise herbalism. A wise woman. A witch, if you like. I'm sure she would like you to think of her that way. Perfectly harmless, of course, but there are stories. She's supposed to have given her mother some dose or other which stole the old lady's wits away. Nobody blames her, in fact the general opinion is that Mrs Trapp was generous not to poison her mother outright; the old woman was a tartar. But now she's as mild as a kitten, and happy with it. Spends all her time in her rocking-chair by the window looking out at nothing, or doing crochet work and singing to herself."

"I – I think I saw her. Behind the curtain in the little lodge on the right."

"That's it. What I think really happens is that Mrs Trapp feeds her some sort of tranquilliser, and maybe exaggerates the dose a little . . . But the old lady is happy and comfortable, and very well fed, and Agnes and Jessamy have a bit of peace for a change." He laughed at my look. "But you see why I'm a bit wary now of her cakes and pies?"

"Ye-es. But what would she want to do to you?"

"I can't imagine. Before I heard the tales about the old lady I used to eat them and be thankful. I really discouraged her because – I told you – I can't do with interruptions, and she used to walk in at any time, with some dish, or some baking, that of course one had to stop and sample, and thank her for."

"Fudge," said William from the doorway, "and home-

131

made toffee. It was smashing, too. Dad hardly ever eats sweets so he gave it all to me. Would you like to come and see Silkworm now?"

"Is he all right?"

"He's fine."

"Well, do you mind if I look at him some other time?" I got to my feet. "I really ought to go. Thank you for the tea and the first aid."

"You're very welcome." My host had risen when I did. "William, take Miss Ramsey's basket out and fix it on her bike, will you?" Then, as the boy ran out: "Look, please don't worry about Mrs Trapp. She was a great admirer of Miss Saxon, and she'll wish you nothing but good, I'm sure. To answer your question properly, yes, she's honest. Did your cousin leave an inventory?"

"Yes. There was a copy of it along with the copy of her Will. I never checked it. Should I?"

"Only to set your mind at rest. You'll find nothing has been touched. Our Agnes may be no great shakes as a witch, but she's honest, of that I'm sure. Do you really have to go? I hope you'll come again, any time, we'll be happy to see you. Now William and I will set you on your way, and show you the road home."

16

It was love at first sight, of course.

I say 'of course' because (and later I could see and prove how right I was) no woman who was more or less ordinarily impressionable could have come within his field without responding to it, the unexplainable and extraordinary pull, not of personality, for when that is too strong it can, and often does, repel; nor of sexuality, of which the same can be said; but of what I can only call sheer magnetism, spiced with a combination of both. He was one of those people born – sometimes to their pleasure, more often to their bane – to be a lodestone, a bright particular star. Literature and fiction are full of *femmes fatales*, but there is also an *homme fatal*, an altogether rarer bird, and pity help the lonely and impressionable female who comes within range of him.

And when he asks her into his home, when his son takes to her and makes her free of his company, when he invites her to come and see him again any time she feels inclined . . .

Pity help poor lonely spinster Geillis Ramsey. I rode home through the gently darkening autumn evening, my feet pumping away at the pedals over the rough forest track, my head in the clouds of sweet imagination, my brain completely dormant.

Till the track dipped sharply to ford a muddy rill. I met it wrongly, splashed myself to the knees with black water, and came to, swearing.

As I pushed the bicycle up the next rutted incline, the brain took over once more. So I felt like swooning into his arms, his bed, anything? But he was married, with a ten-year-old son. He was a distinguished writer who had rented a lonely and uncomfortable house simply because he wanted solitude to write in. He had been polite to me because, mistaking my motives towards that silly, that ever-blessed sheep, he had startled me and been momentarily rude. Because he was grateful to me for taking William off his hands. He had a son, and he was married. Even if she had left him (how long ago? I must ask William) he was still married. And in my vicarage-written and already old-fashioned book, that put the whole idea out of the ring. My bright particular star was way beyond my wildest and most enchanted flight.

His hair was thick and dark brown, with just the beginning of grey. He must be, what? About forty, late thirties perhaps? He would be in *Who's Who* and I could look him up in the public library and get all his books to read. He was a couple of inches taller than me; just right; but he stooped a bit, probably with the hours spent over his desk. He liked solitude, and the countryside. He was content with the little that that rather bleak farmhouse offered. He was a loner, and so was I. He would be just as quiet, and a good deal more comfortable when he moved into Thornyhold with me . . .

He was married. Married. And even if *Who's Who* says he was divorced, what makes you think he would ever look at you, Geillis Ramsey? So come down to earth. You may be a witch-elect, but it would take a stronger toil of grace than you could ever weave to catch and hold a man like Christopher Dryden.

The white wicket gate was open. I coasted through it, past the protective clump of rowan and elder, inside the bastion of the quickthorn hedge, to dismount at the shed. Hodge was sitting on the back windowsill, and rose to greet me, stretching his front paws luxuriously, and showing a wide pink yawn.

"Anybody been around?" I asked him, and had my answer in the cat's unruffled demeanour. I let myself in, and he followed, purring. I fed him, then as soon as I had washed, and put fresh plasters on my hands, I started work on the blackberries.

At dusk, when they were simmering, there was a knock at the back door. Before I could get to it, I heard it open, so I knew who to expect.

"You're in, then," smiled Agnes Trapp.

"Yes. Do come in. How are you?"

"Fine, thanks." She came in, sniffing. "Brambles. You making jelly, then?"

"Yes. I really enjoyed myself. I love picking brambles."

"You got your hands pretty badly scratched, didn't you?"

"I'm afraid so." I stirred the fruit. She settled herself at the table.

"Who told you about the quarry?" she asked.

"William. How did you know I'd been at the quarry?"

She ignored that, merely replying: "Oh, yes. They live just over the hill from there. Did you know that?"

"I didn't know before today, but William's father came on me when he was out for his afternoon walk, and we got talking. William had told him about my being here at Thornyhold. I'd cut one of my hands rather badly, and he asked me back to the farm to get it tied up."

Silence. I stirred the fruit again.

"It seems a very lonely place, doesn't it," I asked her, "even for a writer? I mean, without anyone to look after the house?"

"As to that, I used to give him a hand now and then, but it's too far to go. There's a woman goes in now twice a week to clean up. Bessie Yelland, the farmer's wife from Black Cocks. Never sees him, she says. Writers are queer cattle, seemingly. Asked you in, did he?"

"Yes. I gathered he'd come to a stopping-place in the book. Did you know his wife, Agnes? Or did she leave him before he came to live hereabouts?"

"Leave him?" She sounded surprised.

I bit my lip. "I – perhaps I shouldn't have mentioned it. William told me. She left him, it must have been some time ago, surely. I don't know if it was for another man. Was there a divorce? William didn't say, and of course I couldn't ask him."

"Yes, I knew. But it happened before he ever came here. I don't know why it happened. I never heard tell of a divorce. Mr Dryden never talked about it."

I went back to the fruit, stirring.

Another silence, quite a long one. Then, in a different tone, "Did you find the recipe?" she asked.

"What recipe?" My mind had been a long way away.

"Why, for the bramble jelly!" She sounded impatient,

almost to rudeness. I glanced at her. She was not looking at me; her gaze was sweeping the kitchen, taking in the orderliness, the shining glass, the spotless enamel, the clean curtains and cushions, the flowers on the windowsill. There was a glitter in her eyes, a sort of force to her that I had not seen before. For a moment I wondered if my strenuous cleaning efforts could have offended her, but she had helped me herself, and had shown no sign of offence, even over the scrubbing of the pigeon-loft.

"You said you'd look out her recipe book for me," she said.

"Oh, yes, of course, I remember you spoke of it, but I'm afraid I haven't had time to look for it yet. I'm just making this lot in the usual way." I stirred the fruit again. "I think they're about done. I'll put them to strain now."

"Let me help you." Before I could protest, she was on her feet, and at the cupboard. "My, my, but you've been right through everything, haven't you? The place looks really smart and nice. This'll be the bowl, is it? No, let me."

I let her. Together we spooned the pulp into the jelly bag, and together carried bowl and bag into the larder, and left the bag suspended to drip. She took in the scrubbed shelves, the clean racks, the food lying ready for supper.

"Oh, you got yourself some fish. But you'd like some of my soup, wouldn't you? I brought a can of my leek soup for you. It'll heat up a treat."

"How very kind," I said, helplessly. "But you mustn't spoil me, Agnes, really! I've got to learn to look after myself, you know!"

Back in the kitchen, she busied herself taking down a saucepan and tipping the contents of a blue enamel can into it. She gave me quick, smiling glance, as sharp as a bodkin. "Looks to me as if you can do all right now, Miss Ramsey. You got this place lovely."

"Well," I said, and was annoyed to hear the almost apologetic note in my voice, "you know how it is. The rooms you'd done were fine, but when my own things arrived I had to turn the place out, and one does like things arranged in one's own way. And it is the best way to find out exactly what there is in the house."

"I'd have thought there'd be a list," she said, "along with the lawyer's papers. First thing they did was to send the valuation people along to go through everything." Then, as I was silent: "Well, wasn't there?"

"Yes, I believe there was. I haven't had time to look through it yet."

She set the pan gently down on the stove, and turned. The tension, whatever it was, had vanished. Mr Dryden had been right, I thought, and I had been over-wary. The thought of an inventory did not worry her: the reverse; it appeared to have relieved her mind.

She said comfortably: "She always was a tidy kind of body, your aunty. What about that still-room of hers? You done that yet?"

"Not yet. At least, not properly. I've done the room, but I haven't checked the shelves yet. I really will look through those books tomorrow. It's the likeliest place for her special recipes. In fact, there might be a list in the inventory, and if I find the book you want, I'll bring it down for you straight away."

"I'll take that kindly. Will you be going for more brambles for yourself?"

"I hadn't thought about it. But if you want some, I'd love to go over there again if this weather holds."

She pushed the lid back on her can with a rap and picked her cardigan off the back of the chair.

"Don't bother. There's a-plenty where we live. You've no call to go over there again. Enjoy your soup. It's our own leeks, and cream added."

And she went.

As the back door shut, Hodge came out from under the chair where he had been hiding, and went back to his saucer.

"Are you right, Hodge, or is Mr Dryden? How, tell me this, did she know I'd been over to the quarry? And how did she know, because I'll swear she knew already, that I'd been to the farmhouse? And why was she anxious to stop my going there again?"

Hodge made no reply, but lifted his chin from the saucer and watched me as I lifted the pan of soup from the stove. Watched me with interest and apparent approval, as I crossed to the sink and tipped the lovely-smelling soup down the drain. It was absurd, and after what I had been told today, it was probably plain stupid, but I was remembering the pie that had smelled equally delicious, and the night when, after eating it, I had dreamed an appalling dream. And now, in spite of what William's father had meant as reassurance, I was recalling the old woman rocking, rocking, behind the lace curtains in the window of the tiny lodge. If our Agnes was a witch I would not trust any of her concoctions, and if she was 'no great shakes as a witch' I would trust them even less.

"So that's that," I said to Hodge, turning on the cold tap to wash the remains of the soup away. "And perhaps we'll have a good night's sleep tonight, and no nightmares."

The moon was high, and the night a still-life of black and silver. I suppose it was tempting Providence to repeat my actions of that other night, but before getting into bed I crossed to the window to draw the curtains back, then opened the sash wide and leaned out to look at the night.

Hodge jumped to the sill beside me, and before I could stop myself I had taken hold of him, but tonight there was no magic in the air. No distant music, no wavering light. Only the rich moon of autumn, almost at the full, standing clear above the end of the forest ride, and laying a bright path across the river.

The owl hooted from somewhere near at hand. I looked that way. Nothing but the black mass of the forest trees, brushed here and there with the grey bloom of the moon.

For the new witch of Thornyhold, tonight was, blessedly, just an ordinary night. No light-edged vision. Nothing. And no sound now except the steady purring of an ordinary cat.

Under my hands Hodge stiffened, and started to pull back. The purring stopped abruptly. I let him go and he dropped silently back into the room and slid like a shadow towards the bed. The fur was ridged along his back and his ears were laid flat.

Seconds later, I heard what he had heard, the distant, insistent barking of a dog. For the first few nights of my stay at Thornyhold it had troubled me, but if some farmer or woodman kept his dog chained up, there was nothing to be done about it, so I had closed my mind to it, and had grown used to the sound, and presently after a few nights it had stopped, and I had forgotten it. Now it was here again, and sounding, on this still night, louder and much nearer. And now no longer barking, but howling, like a wolf baying the moon.

An eerie sound, an uncomfortable sound that brought the hairs brushing up along my arms, myself reacting just as the cat had done. I told myself it was nothing, an atavism, a primitive reaction to the wolf in the night just as the dog itself was harking back, calling dog to dog, wolf-pack to wolf-pack, enjoying the only freedom a chained dog could have, the pleasure of communication with its kind.

It was enjoying nothing. The howling broke off, into a sharp cry of pain or terror. Then a series of wild, barking yelps. Then silence.

I found myself at the front door, and running down the path to the front gate, before I even knew I had moved. Not that there was anything I could do. There was no way that I was going adventuring into the woods in the middle of the night. That was for heroines, not for sensible me. But something in sensible me had responded violently, and without thought, to the dog's scream of pain, so here I was at the wicket gate, groping in the darkness to find the latch.

The moon was clear of the trees, and beyond the shadow

of the thorn hedge the driveway was as light as a winter's day. I saw him even before I heard him, Jessamy Trapp, running towards me, his footsteps muffled on the moss of the driveway, his breathing ragged and sobbing. Then I saw how he was running, with one shoulder hunched, his left forearm held tightly to his chest and his other hand gripping it, so that his body was crooked, and he lurched as he ran.

He had not seen me. He was heading for the path at the side of the house, and the short cut to the lodge.

"Jessamy!"

He checked with a gasp of fright, turned, saw me, and came, slowing to a walk, still hunched over that arm.

"What's happened? What is it? Are you hurt?"

"Oh, miss . . ." It was not just breathlessness; he was sobbing, swallowing tears. He sounded much younger than his years. Like a hurt child, he held his arms out in front of him for me to see. He still clutched the left forearm with his other hand, and now between the fingers I could see an ooze of black. "He bit me. Bit me bad. It hurts. Got me in the arm, he did."

"You'd better come in. We'll clean it up and take a look at it. Come."

No questions. They could come later. He followed me into the kitchen, sat where I pointed, at a chair by the table, and waited docilely while I ran a basin of hot water. Thanking my lucky stars that Cousin Geillis had believed in conventional medicine as well as her still-room remedies, I lifted her first aid box down from its place, and proceeded to wash Jessamy's arm clean.

It was a nasty wound, the deep bruised punctures of a sharp bite. Jessamy, his tears dried now, and some sort of stoicism returning as shock dwindled, watched with shrinking interest, then finally with a kind of pride.

"It be bad, miss?"

"It's a nasty bite. Now tell me what happened. Not your own dog, surely?"

"No. No. Don't have no dog. Ma don't like them. Dirty things."

"Vermin. Yes. Well, whose dog, and why?"

"Just a dog. Stray dog, likely. Letting him out. But he bit me."

"Out of where?" I saw that, in a fist clenched against the pain of the bitten arm, he held a tuft of black hairs. "A trap, was it? Hang on now, Jessamy, this might hurt. Does someone set traps in the woods?"

A gasp as the antiseptic bit into the wounds. Then a vigorous nodding. "That's right. A trap. Gipsies set un, likely. I let him out, and then he bit me. Savage, he was."

"Where was this?"

There was a sort of hesitation in the look he slid sideways at me. A vague gesture of the uninjured hand took in the woods to the west. "Up there. In the woods. Over to the big house."

"Well, you can show me, tomorrow maybe." I was thinking, anxiously, about Hodge. Traps were something I would certainly have to see about. "You got the dog out all right? Why did he bite? Was he hurt?"

"Don't think so. Didn't see. He ran."

I finished tying the bandage. "There you are. That's the best I can do, and it should be all right for now. You'd better see a doctor in the morning."

"She don't have no truck with that sort. Does her own. She'd be main mad at me if she knew. Say it served me right."

"You should get it seen to, though. How do you feel now?"

"Fine. That hurts a bit still, but fine." The anxious child's look came back. "You won't tell her, miss? See, if I pull the sleeve down, she'll never know."

There was no point in arguing. He did look better. The pallor of fright had gone, and the wound was clean. I tipped the stained water away and lifted the top off the stove. "All right. Hand me the rags, will you? I'll burn them. And those dirty hairs . . . Is that all? There. Well, let me see it again in the morning, will you? We'll decide then about a doctor."

He flashed me that brilliant smile, so like his mother's, and smoothed the sleeve carefully down over the bandage, while I made him a mug of strong, sweet tea and cut him a slice of the cake I had baked yesterday. I did ask another question or two, but got no answers that made sense, and eventually it occurred to me to wonder just what Jessamy had been doing in the woods at that time of night. Visiting traps that he himself had set? It seemed likely. But nothing was to be done or said tonight. Tomorrow we should see. So I gave up, and let him eat and drink in smiling silence, till presently he left me to lock up and go to bed, once more in search of that peaceful and dreamless night.

17

"Do you know anyone who sets traps in the woods?" I asked
William.

He came soon after breakfast, with another gift of eggs,

144

and the declared intention of finishing the weeding of the herb beds. We went out together to the toolshed.

"No. I didn't know anyone did. They're not legal, are they?"

"Gin traps, no, thank goodness. But snares? Your father said you got gipsies here sometimes. They might try to trap rabbits."

"I suppose so. There haven't been any gipsies here, though, not for ages. They used to camp down in that quarry where Dad found you with the sheep, but it's too overgrown now, and they were given a site somewhere on the other side of the forest. An old lane that's not used any more since the road cut it off. I've seen them there. But not near us, Mr Yelland won't let them. Why?"

The shed door was ajar. I pushed it wider. "Because last night –"

I stopped dead. William, close behind me, blundered into me and started to say "Sorry", but that, too, got bitten off. We both stood like dummies in the toolshed doorway, staring down at something in the corner.

In Hodge's bed. Curled tightly among the sacks and newspapers, trying to make itself even smaller, and blinking up at us with scared, ingratiating eyes. A collie dog, thin and filthy and shivering with fright. Black and white. A ghost from the past, from a dream.

I don't think I even remembered Jessamy and the bitten arm. I was down on my knees beside the dog as once I had gone down on the flagstones of the vicarage kitchen. And the savage dog crouched and shivered, with his rat-like tail clamped tightly in to his body, only the tip free in a feeble attempt at a wag. A tongue came out, trying to lick. There was a frayed rope round his neck. It had been carelessly knotted, and the knot had tightened cruelly. The end had been gnawed through.

William was down beside me, stroking the dog's head. "He's dreadfully thin! He's starving!"

"Yes. Careful. I'm sure he's all right, but if you hurt him

he could snap." All the time I spoke I was patting, smoothing, feeling the dog's body, keeping my voice soothing and my actions gentle and slow. "William. Run to the kitchen and warm some milk. Blood heat. Try it with your finger. Break a slice of bread into it, little pieces, and bring it in a basin. Don't let Hodge out. And bring the sharp kitchen knife to get this rope off. All right, boy, all right, boy. Lie still."

William ran. The dog reached up and licked my chin. I talked, and handled him. He was dreadfully thin, his nose was cracked and dry, his coat tangled and filthy, but gradually the shivering lessened to brief spasms, then stopped, and he lay still. There was blood on the newspapers where he lay, and probing very cautiously I found, just at the root of the tail, a bare patch, raw and still bleeding a little where the dog had been licking at it, as if a piece of skin or a tuft of hair had been pulled out and the skin had torn with it. Jessamy's attacker, certainly, and if Jessamy had handled the wound incautiously as he set the dog free, then the 'nasty bite' was explained.

William came, carefully, with the basin and the kitchen knife. Keeping the blade out of the dog's line of vision, I managed to slide the knife in under the rope and cut it. It fell away. William put the basin on the floor, and I gently persuaded the dog towards it. He got up and crawled forward uncertainly, the starved body still crouched and cringing. We watched in silence while he lapped. Swallowing seemed difficult, but he managed almost all the bowlful before he turned and crept back into his nest.

"Shall I bring some of Hodge's food?" asked William.

"No. He's been starved too long. The bread and milk's enough for now. We'll let him sleep on it."

"May I pat him?"

"Of course. Talk to him while I get my bike outside. Take it slowly. I don't think he thinks much of the human race as yet."

We left the dog then, shutting the shed door on him.

"Was that why you were asking about traps?" asked William.

"Yes."

"But you didn't know about the dog, did you?"

"No. But in a way, yes. Listen." I told him about the night's adventures with Jessamy. "And if the dog was caught by the tail, and Jessamy hurt him trying to get him out, that'll be why he got bitten. The wound looks too bad for a snare, unless the dog was worrying at it himself. But whatever kind of trap it is, I'm going to find it and take it away."

"Can I help?"

"Of course. I'm counting on it. Jessamy said it was 'over to the big house.' How far is that?"

"Not far. About half a mile."

"Then let's go."

Though the 'big house' had certainly been pretty big, it was easy, even in the spectacularly tumbled ruins, to see that no trap, in the normal sense of the word, would be set there. Jessamy had either failed to understand me, or had seized on an easy explanation to save further questioning.

The front steps were still fairly well intact. They mounted in a handsomely splayed sweep to the main doorway, and in doing so bridged a sort of dry moat, a narrow courtyard where sunken half-windows had once lighted the basement rooms. Here, presumably, had been the offices; billiard room, gunroom, cloakrooms, and at the rear of the house the kitchens, pantries, boot-room, boiler-room. The cellars would be lower still.

"No one would set a trap here," said William, as we gingerly clambered up the steps and peered over the balustrade into the basement area.

"You wouldn't think so. If it – the dog – had got into the house itself, it might just have fallen in somewhere and got trapped that way."

"With a rope round its neck?"

"Well, no."

"I'll go down and see what's through that gap, shall I?"

"All right, but for heaven's sake be careful."

I watched while the boy climbed carefully down into the sunken area, across the wedged and fallen blocks of masonry, till he could lean in through what was left of a basement window.

"Can you see?"

No reply. Then, without turning, he beckoned. I clambered down beside him, and he moved aside for me. I peered in.

The shell of a small room, where cracks in the walls and ceiling let light in. A floor deep in plaster and fallen stone and splintered wood, long rotten. A wooden door jamb sprung from its bed, with a piece of frayed rope knotted round it. A chipped enamel bowl, empty and dry. Dog's droppings, many of them, in the small space round the door jamb. And even above their stink, the prison smell of fear and despair and the death of trust and love.

We said nothing. I had to bite hard on the words I would have liked to use, and I think William was swallowing tears.

We climbed out of the pit and up into the clear air, and padded in silence back to our bicycles.

William made no attempt to mount. He stood holding his bicycle, looking not at me but back at the big house.

"Can they claim him back?"

"They?"

"Whoever put him there. You told me Jessamy said it was gipsies."

I shook my head. "Whoever left that dog to starve hasn't a chance in – hasn't any sort of chance to reclaim him. They'd be lucky to avoid prosecution. No, if it was gipsies, we won't hear from them again."

"Will you keep him, then?"

"Oh, yes. But –" I hesitated. "Just for the time being, would your father let you keep him, William?"

148

"Me?" He looked pleased, but with a shade of doubt.

"Yes. There are a few questions I want the answers to, and until I get them, I think we must keep the dog pretty quiet. It's a queer sort of business, you see. I mean –"

He was there instantly. "You mean they would hurt him? Jessamy wasn't just letting him out?"

"I don't know. I just know that ... It's something to do with ... Oh, I can't tell you yet, William. Honestly, could you just leave it with me for now?"

I could not tell him that it was to do with a nightmare of witchcraft, and the memory of something like a promise made to me beside the River Eden. But my assumptions were the same as his own, and he knew it. I added, slowly: "All right. If you think about it ... The dog gnawed through that rope, and probably broke it itself. And once the rope broke, it could – and did – jump out of that place and run away. So, granted even that Jessamy climbed in to rescue it, what did he do to get himself bitten like that? There was that scream of pain I heard. If something hurt and frightened the dog so that it threw itself against the rope and snapped it, and *then* ran away ... Well, there it is."

"That wound? Yes. Oh, Miss Geillis!" He drew a breath. "Well, of course I'll take him. Straight away?"

"The sooner the better. Will your father mind?"

"Not if I tell him what's happened. It can't be today, because he's had to go to London to see the publisher. He'll be late back. But it'll be all right, I know it will. He likes animals, you know, he really does, but he doesn't have time, and a dog takes a lot of time, he says. I'll have to tell him about it, won't I?"

"Of course. And make it clear that I'll take the dog myself once everything's cleared up. You must keep him safe for now, and feed him up. I'm sure there's nothing wrong that kindness and good food won't cure, but I'll get him to a vet as soon as I can. I'll go into Arnside and get food for him, but for the moment, brown bread and milk and maybe an egg, beaten up or even scrambled. You can manage that?"

"Oh, yes!"

"Then let's get back, shall we? You're the expert on keys, William. Does the toolshed lock?"

"Yes."

"Then let's get back and lock it before I have any more callers."

Back at Thornyhold, we checked on the dog, which was fast asleep, locked the toolshed door, and took ourselves to the kitchen, where I made coffee for myself, and gave William a mug of sweet cocoa and a slab of the cake I had cut last night for Jessamy.

He had asked no more questions, seemingly content to leave the past to itself and to dwell on the exciting prospect of looking after the dog and bringing it back to health. I hardly listened. I was still half in, half out of that strange moonlight world of dreams and memories, where other mysteries remained to be solved.

"Who hereabouts keeps pigeons?" I asked.

"Pigeons?" William, interrupted in mid-flight about sheep-dog trials and the dazzling merits of collie dogs, repeated it in the tone of voice he might have used for pterodactyls.

His expression brought me back to earth and made me laugh. "Yes. Pigeons. Birds. With feathers. That say 'coo' and live in lofts. Or in attics like mine. You told me you used to help Miss Geillis look after hers."

"Sorry," said William, grinning. "What about pigeons, Miss Geillis?"

"Don't you think you could just make it 'Gilly'? Less muddling, perhaps? And drop the 'miss'?"

"I – I'm not sure."

"Try it. Go on. Gilly."

"Gilly."

"Again."

"Gilly."

"That's fine. Now, what I asked you was, who around here keeps pigeons?"

He knitted his brows. "Let me think . . . Well, for a start, there used to be pigeons nesting at the farm, not our house, the one where the farmer lives, Black Cocks, but I think they were wild ones, you know, rock doves. Dad says all the tame sorts were bred from them, so they take easily to nesting in boxes and things, because in the wild they go into caves and holes –"

"Not wild pigeons. Homers. Carriers."

"Oh, yes, well, there must be a few in the town. There's a big field just outside, by the river bridge, and it's divided into allotments; you know, little gardens. Lots of the people who have those keep pigeon lofts. Why? Were you wanting to start keeping them again yourself?"

"It seems I might have to. I've got two now. A second one came soon after I got here, with a message."

"*A message?*" His mug went down on the table with a rattle, and some cocoa spilt over the rim. "Came here? What did it say?"

"I'll show you."

I had tucked it away in the inner pocket of my handbag. I fished the slip of flimsy out. "Here."

I suppose it was a stupid thing to do. The truth was that, in my need for a confidant, I had forgotten how much of a child William still was. In so many ways he had the sense and humour and tough outlook of a boy twice his age, and I had just made him free of my name as I might do a contemporary. So I handed him the message.

He got up to take it. As he read it, I saw the healthy colour leave his face. His lips parted, quite bloodless.

I said, with quick contrition: "Oh, William, I'm sorry! I should never have let you see it . . . Here, sit down. It's all right. Whoever sent it, it couldn't have been nicer or more welcome. It came just when it was needed. The pigeon must be –"

"She can't have sent it. She can't be still alive. I was at the funeral. I went with Dad. I saw ... I mean, she was buried. I saw it."

"William, William! Don't! You make me feel terrible! I'd never have showed you the thing if I hadn't wanted a friend's advice. It was –"

"Dad didn't want me to go, but I – well, I liked her, and I wanted to be there. I didn't go when Mummy died because he said I wasn't old enough, but that was years ago, so he did let me go this time, and I saw it all."

"*William –*"

He was not listening. He was as deep in his own shocked thoughts as I was. "Do you mean she *was* a witch? A real one? I know people said so, and she used to laugh. She said she sometimes saw the future a bit, and she would tease me about that, what was going to happen to me, but it was always funny, I mean just fun. Wasn't it?"

"Yes, yes, of course it was."

"Was she really a witch?"

"I don't know. I don't know if there are such people. I do know she had some sort of magic about her, and there are lots of people who can see 'a bit into the future'. But whatever my cousin Geillis was, she was a good woman, William, and you were right to be fond of her. I only met her a few times, but I loved her. So stop worrying yourself about magic and spells. I don't know whether such things exist or not, but if they do, then trust in God and they can't hurt you. Okay?"

"Okay. I'm all right, really. But you – what's the matter, Miss Gilly? Gilly? Are *you* all right? You look kind of funny."

"Do I? It's nothing. Nothing at all. Only – I thought – I must have got it wrong, but you told me your mother had run away and left you. That's all. I was surprised when you said she had died. And sorry, of course. I'm sorry."

"So'm I. About telling a lie, I mean." He looked down into his empty mug. "I sort of made things up about it when it happened. It made it better in a way. But I shouldn't have told a real lie about it."

"It's all right. I understand. It doesn't matter."

"It might have made it awkward with Dad."

"Well, yes, it might. But it didn't."

There must have been something unconvincing in my tone. He glanced at me doubtfully, then left it alone. "Or if you'd talked about it to someone else who knew."

Agnes? Who assuredly knew, and who had failed to enlighten me. Why?

That could wait, too. I said briskly: "Forget it, William. Now, about this message. We'll forget magic, too, and work out how this could have happened, shall we? So let's get back to pigeons."

He pushed up his mug aside. "Yes. Birds. With feathers, that say 'coo'. What about them?"

He was recovering fast. I poured more coffee for myself and sat down again. "I don't know much about them. For instance, how fast do they fly?"

"They can do about sixty, but of course it depends on the wind and weather."

"*Sixty miles an hour?* Good heavens! Do you know if my cousin's birds were carriers?"

"I don't know. They were all homers, of course; you might say all pigeons are."

"But you never saw her send a message?"

"No. But that's not to say she didn't. There was a lot she did that I was never allowed to know."

"Have you any idea what happened to her pigeons? Where they went?"

"Someone came and took them away, that's all. Mrs Trapp told me they'd gone, so I needn't come to feed them any more."

"Well, the only explanation can be that my cousin left the message ready, with instructions for the bird to be released when I got to Thornyhold."

"Well, but that would mean she knew you'd be coming.

Knew she was dying, I mean. She must have written the message before she was taken away, before they took the pigeons."

"She did know," I said gently. "That was one bit of the future she was sure about. Long before she was even taken ill she wrote me a letter, and gave it to her lawyers to post on a certain date, and it said: 'When you get this, Thornyhold will be yours.' I think that knowing the future might be disturbing, but it can be good as well; knowing and not being frightened, having the time to make all one's arrangements, and knowing that there are good hands waiting for the things and people one cares about. Don't you think so?"

He was silent, but the strain had gone from his face and he nodded. I set my cup down and got to my feet.

"Well, this has been a pretty disturbing morning for both of us, all things considered. Let's forget it all now, shall we, and just get on with the job in hand?"

"Can I take a peep at him before I go?" There was no doubt in William's mind as to the job in hand.

"Just a peep. Don't wake him up."

"What are you going to call him?"

"I once knew a collie called Rover. What do you think about that?"

He wrinkled his nose. "A bit ordinary? What about Rags?"

"I think you're right. Never go back. Rags it is. Off you go then, William, and thank you for everything. Let me know what your father says."

I saw him to the back door. On his way down the path he turned. "Oh, I totally forgot. Dad said specially I was to ask if your hands were all right."

"They're fine. Please thank him."

"Okay. I'll be seeing you."

I watched him peer in through the toolshed window, then nod back at me, miming sleep. He waved, and went.

I stared after him till he vanished into the woods, then my gaze lifted. Above the treetops the high clouds seemed to form themselves into a huge question-mark.

18

I made myself some lunch, fed Hodge and the dog, and spent some time with the latter. He was more relaxed now, seemed pleased to see me, and managed to wag fully half his tail as he ate a mixture of brown bread and chicken scraps softened with chicken stock. When I let him out for a few minutes he showed no desire to run away, but did his business and then retreated into the safety of the shed. I locked the door on him again and went back into the house.

I had promised to look for the 'special' recipe book, and if I could find it and hand it over to Agnes, it might keep the Trapps away, at least until I could get the dog temporarily out of the way. I suspected that what Agnes really wanted was not a recipe for something like bramble jelly – what could be special about that? – but the secrets of some of Cousin Geillis's cures. As far as I was concerned, she could have them. One thing I was certain about, they would do no harm to anyone.

I had locked the inventory, along with the copy of my cousin's will, in the desk in the den. I got it out, took it into the drawing-room, and sat down to read it through.

It was arranged room by room. I started by skimming quickly through the contents of the room I was in, furniture, soft goods, pictures, ornaments ... As far as I could see without detailed checking, everything was there. Last came the contents of the big bookcase. This, if I was to be accurate, would require a detailed check, but for the moment a rapid glance down the list must suffice. When I had cleaned the room I had spent a long time over the shelves, and could more or less remember what was there. It was a rich collection; novels, one or two biographies (like me, she had little taste for them); a full collection of travel books, that is, travellers' accounts of exotic countries. Books about animals; three full shelves on birds; another on butterflies and moths, and two on trees, flowers and grasses. But the main – and most attractive – section was on gardens and garden plants. I glanced at some of the latter; the books on plants were a gardener's selection, not a herbalist's. There was nothing here that could be called a recipe book.

In any case Agnes Trapp had had access to these shelves, as to the cookery books in the kitchen and the few reference books in the den, so the still-room was really the only likely place.

I leafed through the inventory and found it, 'still-room contents', a series of formidable lists; page after page of chemicals or distillations, all those bottles and jars named and in order. A mercifully short list of furnishings followed, then, finally, three full pages of books.

But no trouble there; no trouble at all. The first title was underlined in red. The only one to be so distinguished. And its title made it sure.

Goody Gostelow's own Home Remedies and Receipts. Goody Gostelow, the old lady who had lived here for seventy years, whose reputation as a witch had passed right on to Cousin Geillis and now, after a fashion, to me. Goody Gostelow, expert on magic, who had made Thornyhold into an enchanted stronghold to keep out evil and allow the good to grow and ripen. Whose Home Remedies for healing had presumably been studied and followed by my cousin.

Whose recipes Agnes Trapp was so very anxious to see.

I checked that the doors were locked, then took a duster and went upstairs.

At first glance I could see nothing that might be Goody Gostelow's book, but there were dozens of volumes, some of them much used, some even ragged with handling, and it would be easy to miss a small book tucked inside another. I set to work, methodically, to lift the books out in sections, examine them one by one, dust them, and return them to the shelves. It was heavy work. And it was slow, not only because I cleaned each book before returning it to its shelf, but because the books were fascinating, and I lingered over many of them. Of its kind, it seemed to be a comprehensive and probably a valuable collection. I was no judge of its completeness, but there seemed to be everything, from a kind of primer of homoeopathy to a tome, heavy with thick paper, woodcuts and small print, which seemed – it was in German Gothic – to be a treatise on botany. I found trans-lations of Dioscorides and Galen, reprints of the herbals of

Culpeper and Gerard and John Parkinson, at least half a dozen books on the planning and planting of herb gardens, and several on wild plants and their uses, side by side with exotics like *Maori Medicines*, and *A Witch-doctor Remembers*.

And that was the crop. There were recipes in plenty, ranging from simple things like mint and comfrey tea to "wrap the kumaras in puriri leaves and bake slowly over hot stones, then dry in the sun for two weeks", but no sign at all of Goody Gostelow. The only real find of the afternoon was on the top shelf, when I lifted out three volumes of somebody's treatise on the edible and poisonous fungi of Europe.

Behind the books, dusty but still gleaming, was the crystal globe that Cousin Geillis and I had looked into on that day by the River Eden.

I stopped at four o'clock for a cup of tea and a visit to the toolshed, then got back to work. By the time I had finished, and the books were all back in place, it was growing dark, and my back and arms were aching. I had a bath, then fed the dog, and made supper for Hodge and myself in the kitchen. Afterwards, for the first time, I set a match to the drawing-room fire, and soon had a cheerful bright blaze, with the light dwelling on the pretty cretonnes and polished furniture and the glass of the bookcase.

As I went to draw the curtains Hodge, who had followed me into the room, asked to be let out of the French windows. I obliged him, then, after a moment's thought, followed him out and went round to the toolshed. This time the dog – I must try to think of him as Rags – met me just inside the door, and let me lead him round and back into the house. I sat down in one of the arm-chairs with a book I had noticed earlier, *Pigeons, How to Keep and Care for Them*, but kept my eyes on the dog. For a few minutes he wandered uneasily round the room, sniffing, exploring, with frequent glances back at me, and the tail ready to wave whenever he caught my eye.

"Rags?" I tried it, and he came, and was patted and soothed, and finally, with a sigh, he settled himself down beside my chair, nose on paws, blinking at the flames.

It was a long, peaceful evening. The dog slept, only rousing when I got up to put a log on the fire. I could not guess whether he was used to a house and a hearthrug, but he certainly took to mine with no hesitation. Finally came the sound I had been waiting for, Hodge's demand to be let in. I glanced at Rags. He raised his head, eyed the window and wagged his tail, but did not move. I crossed the room and opened the window. In came Hodge, stopped dead, blew himself up to a formidable size, and spat furiously. Rags lay still, wagging that ingratiating tail. The cat advanced. The dog shrank nearer to my chair, abasing himself.

Watching the duel of wills, I was satisfied. The dog obviously knew cats and liked them; the cat, the dominant animal, would take time to get used to the dog's presence, but knew himself to be in no danger. A week or two, and all would be well.

I sat for a while longer, watchful over my book, while the dog went back to a wakeful doze and Hodge stalked, with great dignity, to the arm-chair on the other side of the fire and settled, with frequent pauses to glare at the dog, to washing himself.

A movement on the table at my elbow caught my attention. The globe. I had set it down there and forgotten it, and the firelight was moving over it, light and shadow, colour and darkness.

> *Black spirits and white, red spirits and gray,*
> *Mingle, mingle, mingle, you that mingle may!*

It was bad luck to quote from *Macbeth*, wasn't it? But then that particular rhyme was not from *Macbeth* itself, but only quoted from some older witch-play . . .

Hodge, the witch's cat, with one leg still held rigidly upright, had stopped his washing and was staring at the globe. His eyes were wide and bright, but his fur lay sleek, newly licked and unruffled. He looked interested, no more.

I picked it up, held it between my hands, and stared into it myself.

They were still there, among the shadow and the flames; the flight of pigeons. It was like looking into one of those old paperweights, which, when shaken, loose a snow-storm. Flock after flock of pigeons wheeled and circled, then, while I watched, coalesced into one shimmering cloud of flight and sank slowly to rest.

Rags seemed happy to go back to his bed in the toolshed. I left him there with a biscuit and a bowl of fresh water, then set a saucer of milk in the kitchen for Hodge while I locked up. Hodge, still slightly edgy, but mollified by the dog's banishment and the soothing ritual of bedtime, stalked ahead of me up the stairs and vanished into my bedroom.

One part of the evening ritual remained. I filled the water-jug for the pigeons, and went upstairs to the attic.

I believe I had expected it, but all the same I stood there for several seconds, while the superstitious flesh crept on my arms. There were three pigeons now, on perches side by side. They shuffled and cooed. Nothing could have looked more innocent than these birds of peace, these messengers of the dead.

The new one was different yet again, blue-grey, its breast glimmering with iris. It regarded me placidly with garnet eyes as I reached out and lifted it from its perch.

There was a message on its leg. Of course there was. Gently I removed this, put the bird back, put food down and poured fresh water into the trough before I unfolded the screw of paper. The birds flew down to the grain, and the newcomer dipped its head to drink.

Standing directly under the unshaded electric bulb I unfolded the thin fragment of paper.

It was different writing. A thin printing in capitals: WELCOME TO THORNYHOLD AND GOD BLESS YOUR SLEEP, it said. No signature.

I crossed to the window, and stood for a long time looking out at the fading colours of the sky, where, on that extraordinary night, I had seen the owls and the beckoning light, and had flown through and over those high whispering trees. I had always been content to know that there was more in the living world than we could hope to understand. Now I found myself drifting on the peace of belief. Even if it meant that that 'nightmare' had been the truth, I thought I could accept it. *God bless your sleep*. Perhaps if I forgot the other long-past nightmares, and recalled the good things of my childhood and what I had been taught, He would.

19

I guessed that Agnes would not want to wait for me to take her the coveted book, and I was right. She came up soon after breakfast. Before the back door rattled and Hodge vanished upstairs the toolshed window had been obscured, the dog fed and admonished to silence, the globe was locked away in the desk with the inventory, and I was in the kitchen washing pots for the bramble jelly.

"Well, Miss Ramsey?" was her greeting. She had been hurrying. She was breathless and her colour was high.

I greeted her warmly. "Oh, Agnes, I'm so glad you've come! I was going to come down later, but I quite forgot to do this jelly yesterday, and I thought I'd better get on with it. Nearly two pints of juice – that's not bad, is it? And now I wonder –"

"You said you'd look out for that book." Sharp. Accusing.

"Yes. That's what made me forget the jelly. I found the inventory, and I've been through all the books in the place, along with the lists. It took ages. There is one that sounds exciting, and I wondered – but for the moment, can you tell me, please, about this jelly? I can't find any special recipe, so I'm just going by the one I know. A pound of sugar to a pint of juice, and I did manage to find a few windfall apples in the orchard –"

"It'll do." She almost snapped it. The flush had deepened, but not, I thought, at my reference to the stripped fruit trees. It was anger. But she left the matter aside for a moment to show me the gift which, as usual, she had brought me. She dumped a big basket of blackberries on the table with a rap that set the fruit jumping. "Brought you these. I told you there was plenty near by us. And I put some of our crab-apples in, too. Do as well as anything to make a good set."

"Well, thank you! How very kind." I seemed to be saying that, with various shades of insincerity, almost every hour on the hour. "That'll save me another trip to the quarry."

"That's right." Suddenly, from the look in her eye, quickly veiled, I knew that that was exactly why she had picked and brought the fruit. Why on earth should it be to her advantage to stop me going over there again? I shrugged it off mentally, and turned away from her, stirring the juice.

Behind me, she said, sharply: "About the book."

"Oh, yes. I gather you'd seen this book? I mean, you do know that my cousin had it?"

"Oh, yes."

"Well, the first one in the still-room inventory seemed the likeliest one to me. It was called *Goody Gostelow's own Home Remedies and Receipts*." I glanced back at her. "Was that the title you remember?"

"That'd be it!" The blue eyes shone with excitement. "That'd be it!"

"I thought it might," I said, stirring. "But I'm afraid it isn't there."

"What do you mean, it isn't there?"

"Just what I say. There's a list in the inventory of all the books in the shelves, and as far as I can make out, all the others are there, but not that one. Maybe she lent it to someone?"

Her voice rose. "She wouldn't do that! She couldn't! If she was going to let anybody take a look at it, that would be me. If it's gone to old Madge ... but she wouldn't do that! Not Miss Saxon!"

I looked at her curiously. My look seemed to bring her to herself. She said, more calmly: "The Widow Marget that lives over to Tidworth. No friend of mine. Nor no friend of Miss Saxon's neither, I shouldn't think."

"Then she probably didn't lend her the book. But if you know her, why don't you ask her next time you go that way?"

"I might, at that," said Agnes. She sat down at the table. Her fingers were plucking at her skirt. She looked sulky and deflated. For the first time since I had met her, I felt sorry for her, without quite knowing why.

I stirred the jelly. "Did you ever actually see the book?"

"Once. But Miss Saxon wasn't one for letting her recipes out, and she took it away before I could get anything much puzzled out."

"Did she never give you any of her recipes?"

"Oh, yes, the comfrey salve and some of the teas. But the rest she kept. She gave me a medicine once for mother's

164

cough that was sovereign. That was her word, sovereign. I'd rightly like a look at that one before the winter comes."

"Of course." I bent to sniff at the boiling juice. It smelled done. I spooned a little out on to a cold plate. "Agnes, you said you couldn't get it 'puzzled out'. Do you mean it was handwritten?"

"Oh, yes, it was in writing, and some of it very faint and scratchy. Terrible hard to read, it was. But I'm no great reader of books, anyway!"

The jelly wrinkled to a set on the plate as I tilted it. I lifted the jelly pan over to the table, and took the warm jars from above the Aga. "I did hear something about Goody Gostelow – Lady Sibyl. Mr Dryden told me. I was thinking that, if she lived so long ago, and with all the – well, the stories about her, the book might have some sort of value. So perhaps the lawyers have it, or my cousin may have put it in the bank, or something. Don't be upset. I'll find it, and let you know."

She looked mollified. "Well, I'll be glad. Not that it's desperate, but when people promise something, and people have looked forward to something . . ." She let it hang. "That jelly looks all right. Here, let me, I'll sort the covers for you. You did look on all the shelves?"

"What? Yes, I did. You know yourself that it's not here in the kitchen, or in the drawing-room or the den. I'm sure I didn't miss it in the still-room, but you can look for yourself if you like. That's the key there on the dresser."

My very readiness must have reassured her. She shook her head. "Not if you've looked. I'm not so handy with books, myself. It'll turn up, maybe. If you ask at the lawyer's, I'll maybe go and see the Widow Marget. There, that's the labels done. I'll help you pick these new brambles over."

She found a big bowl, tipped the blackberries from her basket, and sat down again at the table.

I finished pouring the jelly, and set the pots aside to cool. Four pots I got, and felt absurdly proud of myself as the sunlight, streaming through the window, made the rich colour glow more beautifully even than wine.

"Good enough for the jam tent at the show?" I asked her, laughing.

"I said you'd not got a lot to learn." Picking busily, she darted a look at me. It was a friendly one, and smiling. "That's done for the year, the show, I mean, but there'll be others. Some day, maybe, you'll go along o' me to meet the other ladies? We've meetings all year."

"Well, thank you. I think I'd like to." I laughed again. "But not to show my home cooking. Not yet, anyway."

"Time enough," said Agnes. Another glance. "Did you like my soup?"

"It was delicious. What was in it, apart from the leeks and the cream?"

"Just what comes to hand. Mushrooms and such, and wild herbs of my own recipe." A few minutes more, while I joined her in picking the fruit over. "You not finding it too lonesome here, then? You sleep all right?"

"Beautifully, thank you. That dog, Agnes, the one I was complaining about, it seems to have gone. Whose was it?"

"All the folks have dogs hereabouts. Maybe it's got shut in for a change."

"Let's hope it stays that way. One thing I've been meaning to ask you, have you any idea who took Miss Saxon's pigeons? William told me that someone came with a basket and took them away. Did you see them go?"

This time she nodded. "Chap that took them works over towards Taggs Farm, two mile past that to Tidworth. Name of Masson, Eddy Masson. It was him got her started, giving her a clutch. Never got keen like him, though, Miss Saxon didn't. She just liked to fill her place with such creatures. Used to take the ones that was no good, and give the best ones over to Eddy Masson again. She said once that when she went, he'd promised to take them. And took them he did, but I don't know if he'd keep them. Why?"

"I just wondered. I suppose the one that's still here was out and flying when the others were picked up. How many did she have?"

"Nine or ten." She laughed. "If you don't go to count the rest that used to come in for the food. Wild pigeons, squirrels, the lot. And not just in the attics. I've seen robins and such on the tea-table, and that dratted cat never moving to get rid of them."

"How dreadful. Now, you'll have a cup of coffee, won't you?"

Over the coffee we talked neutrally. She did not mention the recipe book again.

"Is there anything I can give you from here?" I asked, finally, as she showed no sign of leaving. "I was just going out into the garden. William has been helping me there, but I haven't got everything identified yet. I'll be dividing the plants soon, if there's anything you've got your eye on."

But she shook her head, took her leave, and went away down the drive.

As soon as I was sure she had gone I let Rags out into the walled garden for a run, then took him upstairs to the attic. The pigeons – still only three – cooed and rustled and flew up to their perches, where they sat shifting from foot to foot, watching us warily. The dog eyed them, but without interest. All he seemed to want, as yet, was sleep and food, and to feel secure. I left him with food and water and an old blanket, and locked the door as I went out. Then back to the toolshed to remove any trace of his occupancy. Until William came for him I was taking no risks.

After lunch I finished picking over Agnes's brambles. They were good ones, plump and very ripe. A few were too ripe, and these, together with the stalks and leaves, I put aside and threw out on the compost heap by the back gate. The rest of the fruit went into the jelly pan.

Just as it came to the simmer I heard a sound at the back door. Not Agnes again, surely? William, come for the dog? Or perhaps – the quick jump and thud of my heart told me who I had been hoping to see. But it was Jessamy, with a bulging carrier bag gripped in hands stained with· blackberries.

"Why, Jessamy! Come in. Are those for me? Your mother's just been here, and brought me loads! But how sweet of you."

He dumped the carrier on the draining-board. He was breathing hard, and his blue eyes, so like his mother's, looked· vague and strained. "Them's no manner of good. Don't 'ee touch 'em, miss."

"The brambles? Why? I've just picked them over, and they're beauties. What d'you mean?"

The dull, wooden look came down again over his face. He looked away. "Nothing. Nothing. But don't you be touching they. No manner of good. I picked un these instead. These be healthy berries. And I put elder in with they to keep the witchcraft away. Don't you fret about that, neither. I ast before I took the elderberries down."

"Asked whom? Your mother?"

"Nay. Nay." He looked scared. "Ast her that lives in the tree."

Oh mercy me, here we go, another touch of old England . . . Aloud I said, gently: "Well, thank you, Jessamy. Now will you let me take another look at that arm of yours? How does it feel?"

"Better. It be great."

He pushed back his sleeve and held the arm out. My bandages had gone, and a rag, crumpled but quite clean, had replaced them.

"You've not been to the doctor, then? Who put this on?"

"She did. I had to tell her about th' dog, you see, when I gave her the witch-knot. But she don't know I came here and you was still awake." He was agitated, trying to reassure me. "Never told her, miss. I never told her."

"That's all right," I said soothingly. "Don't worry. Just let me take a look, will you?"

The cloth came away with a mass of dark-green pulp. Under it the wound looked fine; clean, pale, healing fast. The bruising had already faded to a dirty yellow, the punctures cleanly scabbed over.

"This really is great, Jessamy! What on earth did she put on it?"

"Leaves. Some she grows out the back. And ointment, Miss Saxon's that was, some she made every summer wi' the same plant. Swore by it, she did."

"She was right. I won't put anything else on it. Let me bind it up again."

"Sovereign," said Jessamy, as his mother had done. He repeated it, like a child pleased to have remembered a lesson. "'In or out, that's sovereign.' That's what she used to say."

The scent of the stuff was familiar, evocative. Yet how? And when? It smelled of a damp meadow, the edge of a pool, a stream lapsing through green weeds. I could almost hear the rustle of Cousin Geillis's dress, feel her peering over my shoulder as I started to replace the poultice. *Comfrey*, that was it; *called knitbone, bruisewort, consound. The roots boiled in water or wine and the decoction drunk heals inward hurts, bruises, wounds and ulcers of the lung. The roots being outwardly applied cure fresh wounds or cuts immediately*. ("In or out, that's sovereign.") The recipe – Home Remedy or Receipt? – unreeled in my mind as if I had made it a hundred times. *For the ointment, digest the root or leaves in hot paraffin wax, strain and allow to cool* . . . And from somewhere faint and far back, a sentence that ran like a tranquil psalm: *Comfrey joyeth in watery ditches, in fat and fruitfull meadowes; they grow all in my garden*.

"Jessamy –" My voice sounded almost as faint and far away. "If you need any more of the salve, I'll give you some. There's plenty in the still-room."

"Thanks, miss. Thanks." He rolled his sleeve down. "And you won't touch they brambles? You didn't drink the soup. Don't you eat those, neither."

"How did you –?" I stopped, blinking at him, still bemused. I said feebly: "It was delicious. I did thank your mother."

A hiss from the stove, and the sweet-acrid smell of burning fruit recalled me sharply. I hurried to lift the pan aside. Behind me he said anxiously: "Don't tell her."

"What? Oh, the brambles. No, I won't tell her. But look, if that arm starts to trouble you at all, you must see a doctor, whatever your mother says. Do you want your carrier back?"

He shook his head, making for the door. Just before he went out he paused. "You will chuck they berries away, miss? That paddock's broth of hers don't do any good at all."

For quite a few seconds after he had gone, I stared after him at the oblong of empty light which was the doorway. Old England, indeed. I did not dare believe my ears. But Jessamy apparently saw himself as being in my debt, and it would do no harm to listen to him.

All right, then, preposterous though it was, Agnes had tried twice to drug my sleep. The first time, with the pie, she had succeeded; hence the nightmare. The second time, with the soup, she had failed. And now a third attempt, with the brambles. Paddock's broth, indeed. Poison? Highly unlikely. Then what? Something to drug me to sleep again while Agnes roamed the house? Looking for what? That book? Again unlikely. Even if that was what she had been searching for earlier, she had no reason now to doubt my promise to let her see it. She had already had the chance to see everywhere except in the still-room, and now I had offered her even that. So why?

I lifted the jelly-pan off the stove, and dumped it on the draining-board beside Jessamy's carrier bag. Jessamy meant me well, certainly, but I could not believe he was right about this. Even if for some reason Agnes wanted me to sleep soundly tonight, drugging the brambles would not ensure it. The jelly would, in the normal way, not be used for weeks, even months, and then in small quantities and at times she could not predict. Besides, I might well, as one did, give one or two pots away, or send them (as in fact I had intended) to the parish sale of work.

But – to get back to the first question – why drug me at all? The first time – the pie – was no more than a well-founded suspicion, but the soup seemed to be a fact. "You didn't drink the soup," Jessamy had said, and I had wondered how he knew. But I had already had the answer: "You was still awake." So they had not intended to come to the house that night, or surely Jessamy would have had to warn her that the drug had not worked. Agnes, I remembered now, had asked me if I had slept well, just as she had asked after that first night.

There was more. She knew about the dog. Jessamy had told her. And though she knew about the bitten arm and the dog's escape, she had not mentioned it when I gave her an obvious lead. The inference was that she had known Rags was in the big house, and had sent Jessamy there herself. Not to feed him; the bowl had been dry and empty. Not to release him, either; the rope had been gnawed and snapped.

So, if he was neither feeding the dog nor letting him go, why had he been sent? And there again I had the answer, in the dog's torn skin, the frantic leap that had snapped the rope and let him escape, the bitten arm, the tuft of hair left in Jessamy's hand. "I had to tell her about the dog when I gave her the witch-knot." I had no idea what a witch-knot was; something like an elf-knot, I supposed, a tangled skein of hair; but almost certainly Jessamy had used the term for the tuft which he must have hidden in his pocket when he handed me the soiled cloths to burn.

I left it at that. There was little point in any further guessing. I could ask him next time I saw him, and it was even possible that he might tell me. William had said that he was gentle enough, but he was afraid of his mother, and did as she told him. Well, that fitted. He had been no more than stupid with the dog: if he had thought to take scissors he could have got his witch-knot without the bite, and they would still have the dog.

They would still have the dog. That was the crux. Agnes could do as she liked with her spells, her paddock's broth, her witch-knots and her 'meetings' – covens? – up by the quarry, as long as no living creatures were made to suffer. I would not trouble with poor Jessamy. I would tackle Agnes herself as soon as I saw her, and get the truth out of her.

Perhaps the strangest thing about it all was that, though puzzled and uneasy because I could not see what was happening, I was not frightened. It was as if Thornyhold itself, embattled against evil, was infusing into the nervous, unsure girl I had been, some sort of strength (I hesitated to use the word 'power') which was a shield. The shade, or rather the shining, of Cousin Geillis's presence; doves that brought messages of peace; scented flowers and herbs that hindered witches of their will. *They grow all in my garden.* All that needed to be said, I had said to William: "I don't know whether such things exist or not, but if they do, trust in God and they can't hurt you."

I came back out of my thoughts and into the sweet-smelling, normal kitchen. The sunlight glowed in the four pots of jelly. Four was enough. I would tip Agnes's fruit out, and Jessamy's with it. And while I thought about it, I would get some of the comfrey salve, and put it on Rags's tail. If he licked at it, it would do him no harm. In or out, that's sovereign.

I hefted the heavy pan and carried it out to the compost heap. The birds were busy, with no apparent ill effects, on the discarded pickings. Agnes's brambles were surely as innocent as Jessamy's. In any case, sooner than hurt anyone's feelings, I would bury them all out of sight. I emptied the pan, took it back indoors and got the carrier-bag and tipped that, too, then went to the toolshed for the spade. I dug a hasty pit beside the compost heap and began to shovel the discarded fruit into it.

I was just finishing the job when I heard the front wicket clash, and moments later William's father appeared round the side of the house, making for the back door. He had raised a hand to knock when he saw me, and turned to greet me.

20

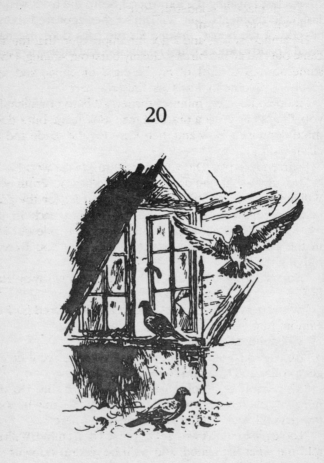

I straightened up to lean on the spade, and pushed the hair back out of my eyes with a blackberry-stained hand.

"Why, hullo! How nice to see you. I – I thought you might come over. Did William ask you to come for the dog?"

"Yes. It made a wonderful excuse."

"I beg your pardon?"

He smiled at me, and I got the impression that the sun came out and all the birds suddenly burst out singing. I took some sort of control of my besotted thoughts, and said feebly: "Do come in. I was just finishing here."

"If I'd come a few minutes earlier, I'd have done that for you. I'm not as good a practical man as William, but I don't mind deputising now and then. Give me the spade and I'll clean it off."

I surrendered it. "Did you come through the wood?"

"No, my car's in the drive. Didn't you hear it? From what William said, I reckoned it would be too far for the poor beast to walk. There. Do you want it put back in the toolshed?" Then, as his eye fell on the empty pile of sacks in the corner, with real anxiety: "The dog? You weren't burying the dog?"

"No, no! Only some fruit that had to be thrown away. He's fine."

"Thank goodness for that! I wouldn't have dared go back without him."

"William didn't come with you, then?"

"No. He's gone on his bicycle to Arnside to see if he can get a collar and lead and some dog food."

"It's terribly good of you to help out like this. Do you mind? Or rather, do you really not mind? It'll only be for a few days till, well, till things get sorted out here."

"Look, please don't worry. Of course I don't mind. William told me what happened, and we'll be glad to do what we can. Where is he?"

"Up in the attic. I was afraid they'd – afraid someone might see him if I kept him down here. I was just going up to see him, and put some stuff on that tail. Have you time to come in and have a cup of coffee? Or – heavens, I didn't realise it was that time! – would you like some sherry? I found quite a store in the sideboard."

"Indeed yes. I know Miss Saxon's sherry. Thank you."

175

He seemed to know where it was, too, and the glasses. While I washed my hands and put the jelly pan to rinse he found and brought sherry and glasses into the kitchen. He looked round appreciatively.

"I always liked this house. I'm glad you're letting it stay just the same."

"I love it. It felt like home from the very start. Shall we fetch Rags down now, and let him get used to you before he's handed over?"

"Good idea. He won't have had much of a chance yet to trust people. Did you find out where he came from?"

"Not yet. I don't really want to, because one thing's certain, I'm not handing him back. He's here to stay. The attic stair's this way, through the back kitchen."

"I know."

He followed me through and opened the staircase door for me.

"You know the house pretty well," I said.

"I came here quite a lot. I was very fond of your cousin."

As I opened the attic door I was met by a very different dog from the one that William and I had rescued. He came to meet me, and the whole of his tail was wagging. His body was still arched, tucked in over the shrunken belly, but the eyes were different, and they were eyes I knew, eager and loving. I knelt down to greet him, and held him while Mr Dryden made much of him. I left them together while I went to get grain for the birds.

"You knew she kept pigeons, of course? Did you ever come up here?"

"A couple of times." He was talking gently to the dog, which had tried to follow me, but allowed the man to hold him back. I saw Mr Dryden eyeing the birds as they flew down to the food. "Three of them?"

"Yes. Did William tell you about the message?"

"Yes, he did. I hope he was meant to? That is – you didn't mean him not to?"

"Oh, no. Was he still worried about it?"

176

"I don't think so. Puzzled, that's all, but I explained."

He got to his feet as I dropped the grain scoop back into the crock. Rags came sidling up to me, ears flattened, ready for a caress, then went ahead of us down the first steep flight with a stumble and a rush, and stood waiting on the landing, almost the picture of a dog eager for a promised walk.

"They recover fast, don't they?" said Mr Dryden. "I don't think you need worry. By the time he comes back to you we'll have him as fit as a fiddle."

"Can you manage the food, do you think? It's not always easy for the cat, and I've never kept a dog."

"We're living on a farm, remember. There's plenty. In fact the corn you're feeding to the pigeons was a gift from our hens."

"Really? I'm grateful yet again. What did you tell William?"

He turned to shut the staircase door. "What about?"

"The pigeon with the message. You said you 'explained' to him."

"Oh. Well, I should have said, 'explained as best I could'."

"Which was?"

"I gather I said much the same as you did. The only way it could have happened is for someone to have taken a bird and released it just after you got here."

"Yes, but what really worried him was that she wrote the message herself, and this must have meant that she foresaw her own death."

"Not necessarily, surely? She may well have pictured herself coming back from hospital, with you ensconced here to share it with her?"

I shook my head. "She knew. And she knew more than that; she foresaw my father's death as well." I told him about the dated letter that had been lodged with the will, and what she had said to me that day by the river. "I told William that even if she did foresee her own death, such things weren't so very uncommon, and in fact I knew Cousin Geillis would have been glad of the knowledge." I looked at him. "It would be nice to feel that way, but I'm not sure that I could. Could you?"

He shook his head. "She was a tougher character than I could ever be. But it fits. It rings true. William accepted it, anyway."

"Then that's all right. I asked Agnes who took the pigeons and she said it was someone called Masson who lives over your way. Do you know him?"

"Yes, he's Mr Yelland's shepherd. Yelland is the farmer who owns Taggs Farm. It was once two farms, but it was joined into one when he married Bessie Corbett, so now the Yellands live at Black Cocks and I rent the other house."

"Boscobel."

He smiled. "It appealed more than Taggs Farm."

"And Mr Masson?"

"He has a cottage a couple of miles away, at Tidworth."

"Do you suppose he could have released that bird on the date she gave him?"

"I suppose he might. If the birds were all there with him, he must have done."

We were back in the kitchen, and Rags rushed forward to explore Hodge's empty dinner-bowl. Hodge was on the table, washing. He spat once, a token hiss, as the dog came into the room, then went back to his washing.

I laughed. "No trouble there. Well, the pigeon mystery can wait till I see Mr Masson myself. Do sit down."

He poured sherry and handed me a glass. "Does it worry you?"

"Not a bit. Actually, I liked it. It was like her."

"Have there been other messages?"

"Only one, and that was better still. It came like a blessing from the air."

He was silent, sensing perhaps that I wanted to say no more. We sat watching while the dog scoured the empty bowl, then came over to us for attention. The cat washed, attending to nobody but himself.

I smoothed the dog's head. "Do you know of a stone circle hereabouts?"

He looked amused. "Well, there's Stonehenge."

"Oh, heavens, I suppose there is! But not as big as that. A little one."

"Actually, Stonehenge isn't as big as one imagines it from the pictures. Haven't you ever seen it?"

"No. I didn't realise it was so near. I'm from the far north, remember? No, I did wonder if there was a small one, something like the one near Keswick, maybe not far from the quarry? The quarry where we met?"

Even as I said it, something about the phrase stopped me short, confused. It was a lovers' phrase, and it seemed to go ringing on and on between us.

But he seemed to notice nothing. (And why indeed should he? You're on your own in this, Geillis Ramsey.) He was saying: "There's nothing like that hereabouts that I know of. Certainly nowhere near Boscobel or Black Cocks. But Stonehenge – you've really never seen it? Would you like to?"

"Love to. Once summer comes again, and I've maybe got myself a car and some petrol to run it on –"

"I have a car, and the tank is full, and the weather is gorgeous right now. How about this afternoon? It's not far."

"I – why, I'd love to. But – are you sure? What about the book? I thought you were head down in that."

"For once it can take second place. I was going to ask you today, anyway, if you'd like to go out somewhere; coming for Rags just made the excuse. We can take him home and have a sandwich or something –"

"I could give you something here, if you'd like it. An omelette? Thanks to you, I'm well off for eggs."

"Thank you, but no. William will be home by now, and he'll be watching the road for you."

I laughed. "For Rags, don't you mean?"

"Of course. We'll have a sandwich at Boscobel. Please say yes."

"Yes. It sounds lovely. Thank you, Mr Dryden. Will you have some more sherry while I go up and get the ointment for Rags, and collect a jacket for myself?"

The drive over to Boscobel began almost in silence. I remember the whisper of the car's tyres on the moss of the drive, the dapple of sunlight sliding over us as we purred under the trees, the flash of blue as a jay fled low across the bonnet. My companion did not speak, and whether it was the effect of his close proximity, and the sudden feeling of intimacy given by a closed car, coupled with the too-vivid knowledge of my own feelings, I found myself gripped by something of my old, crippling diffidence, and was glad of the dog's presence as a bridge to the silence. Rags seemed nervous of the car at first, and I had to make much of him as I held him down under the dashboard till we were past the lodge.

As the car threaded its way between the twin halves of the lodge I saw the curtains on our right – Agnes's side – twitch ever so slightly, and fall straight again. And on the other side the shadow rocking to and fro, to and fro, in the solitude of the tiny house.

We turned out into the sunlight of the road. Mr Dryden spoke at last. "They were there."

"Yes. I saw."

"Well, you can let him up now. Will he go on the back seat, do you think?"

But when I tried to ease Rags back across the gearbox, he refused to go, so I kept him where he was, on my knee, and sat back as comfortably as I could.

Mr Dryden glanced down. "Are you all right like that?"

"I'm fine. He doesn't weigh much, poor chap. He'll settle down soon. Do you know, Mr Dryden, it must be years, literally, since I had a run out, like this, just for pleasure. It's wonderful!"

"I'm glad. And do you think you could make it Christopher? Or even Christopher John? That's what I was always called when I was a boy, to distinguish me from my father. Whichever you like. Will you, please?"

"I – yes, thank you. And you know mine."

The car gathered speed. The hedges streamed by. "William calls you Gilly. I understand you asked him to. Do you like that, or Geillis?"

I smiled and echoed him. "Whichever you like."

"Geillis." He said it very softly, as if to himself, and a shiver went up my spine. I hugged Rags to me and put my head down to his. "Do you know," added Christopher John, "that it's a real witch's name?"

My head came up with a jerk. "Good heavens, no! Is it? I used to ask my mother where the name came from, but she never told me. Cousin Geillis's name, I mean. I was called after her."

"She was your godmother?"

"Sponsor, she called it. She wasn't – at least she made out that she wasn't – on terms with God."

(The second message: *Welcome to Thornyhold and God bless your sleep*? Who had sent it? Who?)

He was saying something about Edinburgh, and the witch trials there. "There was a Geillis Duncane. She's mentioned in the *Demonology*. And so, incidentally, is one Agnes Sampson. And I seem to have seen that lamb-like name cropping up elsewhere in the chronicles of witchcraft – as well, that is, as our own Agnes, who works at it with the best of them."

"And I'll bet she's the prettiest witch in the coven." I said it lightly, more for something to say than for any other reason.

"Pretty? Is she? I suppose she is."

Whether it was the indifference of his tone, the absent way he spoke as he steered carefully to overtake a couple of cyclists on that narrow road, but that was the moment at which the scales dropped from my eyes with a thud that I could actually hear, only it was the twisting thud of my heart.

181

I saw it all – no, not all, but many things that I ought to have seen long before.

Agnes Trapp had not drugged the blackberries. She had picked them because, quite simply, she did not want me to go over to the quarry again, and perhaps go up to Boscobel. And she had deliberately lied to me – or misled me – about Christopher John's wife.

The reason? So bemused and bedazzled had I been that I had not taken into account the fact that other women might be just as responsive to my *homme fatal* as I was. Like an arrow striking home, the simple truth thudded into my brain. Agnes was in love with him, too.

William was waiting, hanging over the gate.

As we approached he swung it wider, and we drove into the yard. I opened my door, and Rags jumped out. For a moment he stood looking doubtfully about him, ready, I think, to be afraid of another strange place, with its new sights and smells. Then the boy called, "Rags! Rags!" and boy and dog flew together.

We left them and went into the house.

21

We did see Stonehenge. In those days it stood unfenced, deserted, small in the middle of the great Plain, but as one left the road and walked to it across the grass the stones reared themselves to their awesome height, and the circle closed round with its own old magic.

This was certainly not the stone circle of my dream. There were harebells in the grass, and the lichens on the tall stones were beautiful in the sunlight, green and amber and furry grey as chinchilla. The breeze in the long autumn grasses sounded like the ripple of a slow river. Late though the year was, an occasional bird-call echoed over the Plain. Above us the sky arched, enormous, wisps of cloud breaking and forming and flowing through the blue like the creaming of a quiet sea.

There was no one else there. We walked slowly round between the massive menhirs, while Christopher John told me about the place. Nothing was known, he said, about its origins or the great men of our prehistory who had built it, but there was evidence to show where the stones had come from, and this, considering their size and the distances involved, was barely credible. Of course legends had arisen to explain the apparent miracle of the building. It had been erected in a night by Merlin, and King Uther Pendragon lay buried at its centre. The Druids had sacrificed their wretched victims there. Its builders had oriented it towards the rising sun of the summer solstice, and people still came sometimes to pray there, and watch for wonders. It was a calendar, a gigantic time-keeper of the years. It was a thousand-mile-stone on the path of some sky-haunting dragon . . .

None of it, truth or legend, was needed to enhance the magic of the place. For me, that was there in the clean air and the breeze on the grasses and the singing of happiness.

We had tea at Avebury, at an inn in the very centre of another circle so vast that the whole cannot be seen from any of its stones. Parts of it were lost in the fields round about, and a village with its roads and lanes cut here and there through the ring. We made no attempt to walk round it, but drove home instead by green byways, where Christopher John stopped the car once or twice to let me gather wild flowers and berries "to draw", I told him. "I used to do a lot, but I had to let it go rather, and I'd like to start again now that I've got the house straight."

And all the time, we talked. That fit of shyness had passed as if it had never been, and the earlier ease had come back. I forget now all that we talked about, but at length, on the way home, I began to learn about him. We stopped beside the river bridge over the Arn, with the ruins of the old abbey beyond the trees catching the reddening rays of the sun, and he sat on the parapet and talked while I gathered bryony from the hedgerow, and glossy berries of honeysuckle, and a handful of the exquisite late harebells that look so fragile, but are as tough as wire.

He had served through the war in the Western Desert: he said very little about that, except that he had known Sidney Keyes, the young poet who was killed in 1943, at the age of twenty, and who, had he lived, said Christopher John, would have been one of the greatest of our time.

"In fact is, even so," he said. "Do you know his work?"

"I don't think so. I'm afraid I haven't read poetry much at all lately. I used to love Walter de la Mare."

"'The sweetest singer, and one of the most profound thinkers of our age.'" It sounded like a quotation, which it apparently was. "He was my wife's favourite," he said. "She worked as poetry editor for the Aladdin Press. She and William stayed with her sister in Essex during the war, but she had to go up to London for a meeting, and there was a raid that night. She was killed, while I was sitting quite safely somewhere near Tobruk. William can just remember her." He went on then to tell me about her, Cecily, William's mother, dead these six years. He spoke of her with love, but without grief. Six years, and whatever the loss, happiness steals back.

"Or comes suddenly, like the sunrise at Stonehenge," he said, looking away through the trees, where the ruins, robbed of the last sunlight, showed ghostly grey. "Look, there's a spike of wild arum by the abbey gateway. What could you want better than that for colour?"

We got back to Thornyhold at dusk. Christopher John saw me to my door, unlocked it for me, declined to come in, and tripped over Hodge on his way down the path. I heard the car door open and shut.

I snatched Hodge up and kissed him, said: "Oh, *Hodge*!" and turned to run upstairs. Outside, the car's engine started, idled briefly, was killed. Hodge kicked me furiously and leaped from my arms as Christopher John came rapidly up the path again, carrying the flowers I had picked, and a small parcel wrapped in brown paper.

"You left your flowers. I'm afraid they got a bit squashed, but they might come round."

"Oh, dear! They were on my lap, and I forgot all about them. They must have slipped off and got trodden on. I'm terribly sorry."

"Don't be. It was a good thing, as it happens. Reminded me of something I ought to have brought back weeks ago. Miss Saxon asked me to keep it for you. Here it is now, with apologies. And thank you once more for a wonderful day."

Before I could answer he had sketched a salute, turned and gone. This time the car started with a roar, and went quickly away.

Hodge said something urgent from the baize door, so I pushed it open and carried flowers and package to the kitchen. Flowers first, into a jug of water. Hodge's supper next, or there would be no peace at all. Finally, to unwrap the package.

Whether by witchcraft or not, I knew already what it would contain. And it did. Lying there on the table beside the sherry bottle and the jug of wild flowers was *Goody Gostelow's own Home Remedies and Receipts*.

Of course I took the book to bed with me, and of course I sat up half the night, reading it.

Reading, that is, as much of it as I could. Agnes had been right; the crabbed, spidery hand and the faded ink made some of the words indecipherable, but a modern hand –

my cousin's – had translated the worst of the words, and had also pencilled in notes or even corrections to the old recipes.

For that is what they were. If I had expected a book of magic spells, I was disappointed. It was just what the title had promised, a book of recipes and home remedies. Some of them Cousin Geillis had obviously tried and used; here and there she had added notes: *This works well, but use sparingly, half the dose for a child.* Or: *Too violent. Try (indecipherable) instead?* and a further note: *Yes.* The comfrey salve was there: *For the ointment, digest the root or leaves in hot paraffin wax, strain and allow to cool.* I read it with a prickling of the skin at my own foreknowledge, and a smile at Cousin Geillis's note: *Culpeper's recipe. Sovereign, inside or out.* Against another recipe she had written: *It won't grow here. Italian. Ask C.J.*

The book was not set in order; that is, the recipes seemed to have been written down as they were acquired, or tried out, so that soups, pies, puddings and so on, were interspersed with pickles and wines, medicines and household cleansers. The medicines, and of course the preserves and wines, used plants, herbs, fungi, mosses, the barks and sap of trees – every imaginable product, not only of the garden, but of the hedgerows and streams and woods.

I read on, and as I read, an idea began to grow, and gradually took hold of me. To begin with I had assumed, with a good deal of misgiving, that I should try to follow in the steps of Lady Sibyl and Cousin Geillis and become, in fact and not merely in jest, the third 'witch' of Thornyhold. But what I had seen of my cousin's library, and the contents of her still-room – her professional life tidied away to make room for something new – had convinced me otherwise. Things had changed. Even to myself I would not acknowledge how, but I knew that the lifetime's study given by my spinster cousin would take more time and dedication than I, with marriage and a young family, was likely to have.

So our minds leap ahead of facts or even probabilities.

But mine made the leap, and I knew at last just what I had to do.

The talent you're born with. I would use it, my one real talent, and make drawings of all the plants and fungi, with descriptions, and notes of their habitats, and perhaps some day make an illustrated book of the sovereign remedies and recipes of Thornyhold. Christopher John would advise me. But whether it made a publishable book or not, I would do it for my own pleasure, and in the doing, perhaps, learn how to use in my own way the gentle powers of garden and woodland. I would start tomorrow to make a fair copy of Lady Sibyl's book, and perhaps even try out some of the recipes for myself.

I remembered then that I had promised to let Agnes see the book. That first, then. Tomorrow as ever was I would gather my new courage, take the book down to the lodge, and get answers to the questions I wanted to ask. But no mention, no hint at all, of brambles and the quarry and Boscobel.

Brambles. A thought struck me, and I picked up the book again. I checked through it, curiously. There was no recipe in it for bramble jelly.

Beyond the open window the owl hooted. Overhead some small clawed creature pattered among the remains of the pigeons' grain. Beside me, snugged deep in the eiderdown, Hodge purred suddenly, then switched off like Christopher John's engine. A big moth flew in, and beat crazily at my bedside light. I reached to switch off and give the creature a chance to get away and back into the cool night.

No recipe for bramble jelly. That had been Agnes's excuse for getting me to look for the book. If she had wanted some of the herbal recipes for herself, surely she would have said so. But there had been those elaborate lies about 'Miss Saxon's jelly was always the best', and the special recipe that must be in this book. And this was certainly the book with the difficult writing that she had not had time or chance to make out.

Conclusion? That the book contained some other recipe that she wanted, but did not want to talk about.

And on the heels of that conclusion, another. That whatever it was, Cousin Geillis had not wanted her to have it. Had perhaps found her examining the book, and so had taken the precaution of lodging it in Christopher John's safe keeping till my arrival.

I switched the light on again. The moth had gone. Hodge half-opened an eye in reproach, then shut it again, stretched luxuriously and sank back into sleep.

I reached to pick up the book. Its cover, never a very strong one, had split with long usage, and the backbone had broken, letting the stitching go. My action in stretching for the bedside lamp had tumbled the book aside, so that it slid, half opened, across my knees, while a loose page slid out free of the rest.

I picked this up and opened the book to replace it, glancing at it half-idly as I did so. It looked and felt different from the rest; a thicker, yellower paper, brownish ink, splotches and blots made perhaps by a quill pen, and in a different, older hand. A recipe supplied by an altogether different person from the virtuous ladies Sibyl Gostelow and Geillis Saxon. A recipe belonging to the book I had expected to find, the only recipe that could claim to be 'real' magic, and pretty certainly the one that our local witch wanted so very badly.

It was called, simply: *The Love Philtre*.

I think that my first emotion was recoil, then, woman for woman, a sort of pity. Afterwards, sharply, and still woman to woman, a flash of uncertainty: am I wrong about the way he feels for me? And finally, an incredulous: supposing the damned thing works?

I picked up the thick, tatter-edged parchment and read it through . . .

The Love Philtre. Take the wings of four bats, nine hairs from the tail of a newly dead or dying dog, the blood of a black pigeon, and seethe together with . . .

I omit the rest. But there already, with no questions asked or possible to ask, was the answer to another of my questions.

———◆———

I sat there in the dark for a long time, trying not to blame Agnes for what (I told myself) was an uneducated country-woman's attitude to animals. For Agnes, as for many of her kind brought up in the remoter countryside of the '40s, all wild creatures were vermin; a cat was tolerated only as it would kill mice or birds, even the robin; a dog only as it would work, or act as guard. She would think nothing of wringing the necks of my stray pigeons, or drowning the ownerless Hodge, or keeping the wretched Rags for her witch's cauldron. I could acquit her of the injury to Rags, inflicted by Jessamy in his unthinking simplicity, but it was impossible – and, surely, wrong? – to forgive the cruelty that had tied him up and kept him on starvation rations for the sake of that repulsive spell . . .

I was trying so hard not to blame Agnes that I found I was shaking. I told myself that my own deep and even obsessive love for animals was a personal thing, a product of my own unhappiness and lack of self-confidence. Animals were safer, and far kinder, than people. It was I myself, in my inadequacy, who was abnormal, not the simpler, more extrovert people with their robust attitudes to the natural world.

I thought suddenly of my father's curate, now himself long dead, and what he had done with my rabbit. Presumably he had bred the rabbits for food, and if a child had kept one for love, and subsequently returned it, it would go back into the category of meat. Fair enough. I ate meat myself. The wrong had been done, not to the rabbit, but to the child.

And my mother, with the dog? She had been the product of a tough pioneer society, hacking a living out of the New Zealand bush, where animals were stock or game, and there was no room, in the poverty of a hard-working life, for sentiment. Even the children would be regarded as working tools, and daughters in consequence as less desirable than sons. The wrongs of my childhood, if they were that, could, with this sweating effort of the imagination, be understood, and forgotten ...

So the obscene love philtre led me, through that long night, to the exorcism of my own miserable spectres, and, finally, to an exhausted kind of peace.

When at last I slept I dreamed, not of stone circles and dying dogs, but of pigeons flying against a high blue sky, and Christopher John smiling and saying: "Happiness comes back, in the end."

22

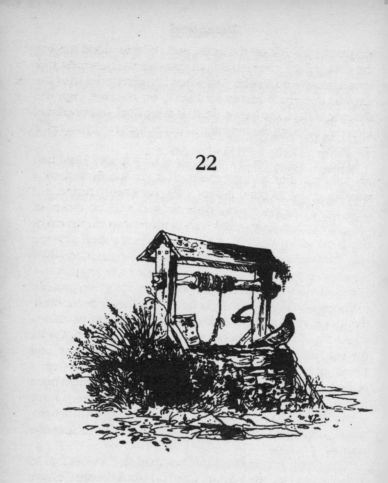

Since this is not a tale of midnight witchcraft, but a simple, a reasonably simple, love story, it is fitting that the final chapters should open on the morning of a glorious day.

Even the early sunshine warming the crisp air, the dew

shimmering thick on the grass, and the thin cloud misting the shine of the river, could not disperse the heaviness that lay on me when I awoke. And when I remembered what the day was to bring, I had to hold fast to my courage. Only the thought of Rags, the 'newly dead or dying dog', sustained me. I hurried through the morning's chores, then ran upstairs for the book.

I had no intention of letting Agnes have it until I had had my talk with her and got the truth from her. Even then, I was not going to hand it over with that ghastly recipe still in it. I took the parchment page out and, with no flicker of compunction, set a match to it and washed the charred flakes down the still-room sink. I put the book on a shelf with the rest, locked the door, and went downstairs to prepare, while my resolution held, to go and see Agnes at the lodge.

It is always better to meet the enemy on one's own ground; to choose the position to fight from. I had never been inside the lodge, had not been asked inside on the few occasions when I had stopped there on my way past. I did not want the coming interview to take place in front of Jessamy, and I was certainly not going to talk on Agnes's doorstep. I intended merely to tell her that the coveted book had been found, but that it was fragile and possibly valuable, so that if she wanted to look at it she must do so at Thornyhold, where she would be at liberty to copy out what recipes she wanted.

Afterwards, not to waste this beautiful day, I would go to Tidworth and see Mr Masson, who had taken Cousin Geillis's pigeons, and ask him about the birds that had brought the messages. See if the wild idea I had had about the second message could possibly be right. And (though I tried not to admit it even to myself) see if, as I passed the track that led to Boscobel, I might catch a glimpse of Christopher John.

I cut myself some sandwiches, put one of my pots of bramble jelly in the bicycle basket, and set off down the drive.

At the lodge I met the first check to my brave and cunning

plans: Agnes was not at home, and neither, apparently, was Jessamy. There was no answer to my knock.

But as I stooped to put the pot of jelly on the doorstep I heard Jessamy's voice just behind me.

"Why, good morning, miss!"

He had been, not in his own house, but in its twin on the other side of the drive. He had left the door wide. Inside I caught a glimpse of a tiny room, spotlessly neat, with a red checked cloth on a small table, a fireplace glinting with brass, and an old-fashioned rocking-chair where the old lady sat, looking surely twice as old as her years, like a Victorian picture, with an apron over her lap, and a white shawl round her shoulders. She nodded and smiled at me, and waved a hand. I smiled and waved back. Jessamy said: "Ma's not here, miss. Her's gone out."

"Do you know where she's gone?"

"Never said."

"And you didn't see? Did she go up through the woods?"

"Nay. Went towards town." He pointed in the direction of St Thorn.

"And she didn't say when she'd be back?"

He shook his head. "Went after breakfast. Never said. Did'ee make the jelly, miss?"

"Yes. It made a lovely batch. Thank you again, Jessamy. I brought a pot for you and your mother. How's the arm?"

"Better. That's healed right up."

"I'm glad. When your mother comes in, will you tell her that I found the book? Tell her to come up if she wants to see it."

"A book?" That vague, puzzled look. "Ma to look at a book?"

"Yes. She'll know what I mean. Just tell her I found the book." I picked up my bicycle. Gran was waving again, and I responded. "Tell her I'll be out till about tea-time, but to come up after that if she wants to see it. Thanks, Jessamy. All clear?"

"Aye." He lowered his voice. "'Tain't no use at all you

coming in to talk to Gran. She be pleased to see you, that's all."

"It's all right, I understand. It's nice to see her. She looks very well."

Another wave, and as I wheeled my bicycle out in the sunny road, I saw the rocking-chair begin its incessant swaying once more.

———◆———

There was no sign of Christopher John as I passed the mouth of the Boscobel track. Beyond it the road deteriorated into a rutted lane, obviously much used by cattle, which wound between hedges for another mile or so before reaching Tidworth. And there it stopped. Tidworth was remote, a tiny hamlet, with half a dozen cottages huddled round a green where white ducks were enjoying a muddy pond. A pillar-box outside one of the cottages, and some goods for sale in the window, indicated the post office. I left my bicycle at the gate and went in. There was no one in the shop, but the smell of baking bread drifted in from the back room, and the *ting* of the doorbell was answered by a woman who hurried in, wiping flour off her hands on to a large checked apron.

"I'm sorry to bother you when you're busy –" I began.

"That's all right, miss. What can I do for you?"

I hesitated, looking around me, wondering what to buy. There was very little on the shelves; rationing had hit this sort of tiny general shop hard, as people tended to take their coupons into the town where their custom might bring the odd perk with it of unrationed goods. And in a place like Tidworth people would have their own eggs, grow their own vegetables, make their own bread... My eye stopped at a stack of unrationed cocoa.

"May I have one of those tins of cocoa, please?"

She reached for the tin, but without taking her eyes off me. She was a tall, bony woman, dressed in black with a rust-coloured cardigan. She had greying hair pulled back into a bun, a strong-looking jaw, and black eyes that took me in with interest, more, with a sharp curiosity that surprised me till I recollected that strangers must only rarely come along this dead-end road.

"Was there anything else? That'll be one and fourpence halfpenny, please ... Much obliged."

"There – er – there was something else, actually ... I'm told that there's a Mr Masson who lives in Tidworth? I wonder if you could tell me which is his house?"

"Eddy Masson? Aye, he's got the end cottage. You passed it, it's the first one you come to on the road. But I doubt you'll not find him there. He'm rarely there except at nights, or Sundays. Works over to Farmer Yelland at Black Cocks."

Why had I not thought of that myself? To get to Black Cocks you had to go by Boscobel. I smiled at her.

"Thank you very much. I could call there on the way back. But – perhaps Mrs Masson's at home?"

"Not married," she said, and then, with a disconcerting flicker of amusement, "not yet.'"

"Oh, well," I said vaguely, "thank you so much." I turned with an odd sense of relief towards the door.

Her voice stopped me. "You staying in these parts, then?"

"Yes. That is, I'm not on holiday. I live here now, at Thornyhold. You must know it? I moved in in September, and I'm still just finding my way about. This is the first time I've been to Tidworth. It's very pretty, but a bit out of the way, isn't it?"

"They say that even the crows ha' to fly out backwards." She nodded, looking pleased. "There now! As if I didn't guess who you were as soon as you came into the shop! Miss Ramsey you'll be, as the Widow Trapp works for! Well, miss, I'm glad to know you."

She pushed up the counter flap and came through, holding out a hand.

Pigeon post, I thought. Pigeon post was nothing to the jungle drums of Westermain. But of course everyone within miles would know of me by this time. Would probably also know me by sight. They would certainly know all that I had done to the house; the 'Widow Trapp' would have seen to that.

The Widow Trapp. And the rival witch lived at Tidworth. The old-fashioned phrase set up an echo that made the guess a certainty. I took her hand. It was dry and bony and surprisingly strong. "How do you do, Mrs Marget?"

Her delighted reaction held a kind of echo, too. "There, now, didn't she tell me? Didn't I know the minute I laid eyes on you?"

"Tell you what? Know what?" She didn't answer, but shook her head, the black eyes dancing. She picked the tin of cocoa up and pressed it into my hand. "You're forgetting this. Yes, I'm Madge Marget, and you'll know my George, I reckon – that's my son. He's the postman, and he was telling me that old Miss Saxon's place looks a fair treat now, and the new young lady was the prettiest sight you'd see between here and Salisbury. So as soon as you come into the shop I says to myself, that's her, I says, with a look of Miss Saxon that there's no mistaking, and a right beauty, too, no offence."

"No – I – How could there be? Thank you."

She folded her hands under her apron, and leaned back against the counter, obviously ready for a long chat, but I thanked her again quickly, with some sort of excuse about being in a hurry, and made for the door. As I opened it I found her close behind me. A hand came over my shoulder, pointing.

"That's Eddy Masson's house, a-down there by the stacks. He keeps them there."

"Keeps what?"

"Those."

And the finger pointed to where, high over the big elms, a flight of pigeons circled, dipped, and wheeled away in the direction of Boscobel.

23

Mr Masson's cottage stood a little apart from the road, and if I had not been told that he had no wife, I could have guessed it from the generally neglected look of house and garden. The wicket gate was rotting, and hung on one hinge.

I pushed through it and picked my way over the weedy cobbles to the door. This stood open, and gave straight on to the living-room, where the remains of breakfast still stood on a table covered with newspaper. A pair of carpet slippers lay where they had been kicked off, in front of the fireless grate.

Another glimpse of bachelor living, and nothing to compare with Christopher John's competence. The only thing they had in common was staring at me from the cold stove. A pie-dish, blue and white, containing the uneaten half of a pie. A pie-dish I recognised. Agnes, it seemed, spread her charities widely.

Purely as a matter of form, I knocked at the door, waited the conventional half-minute for a reply, then, as if looking for the back door, trod through the weeds round to the back of the cottage. There, at the foot of what had once been a garden, stood the pigeon-house. As I approached it I heard a sound from the air above me, and looked up, just as the flight of pigeons came home. Twenty or so, at a guess, grey and white and black, wheeling against a blue sky. I stood still. They circled once, twice, a third time lower and more tightly, then one by one they dropped to the landing-sill of their house, and went in.

It was apparent that all Mr Masson's spare time and care was given to the pigeon-house. Though the exterior paint was fading and peeling the woodwork was sound, and the glass and mesh of the windows looked almost new. The door, when I tried it, was securely locked, but by standing on tiptoe I could see through the wired glass of the front.

Most of the birds were feeding. A few flew up in momentary alarm as they saw me, but they were used to being watched, and quickly settled back to their strutting and pecking. Most of them were grey, like the first of Thornyhold's messengers, but there were dark ones among them, and a few of the soft red, and one pure and lovely white. They were all, as far as I could see, ringed, but none of them had the distinctive metallic ring of the carriers.

Not that that need mean anything, I thought, as I plodded back to the gate. For all I knew they might wear special rings to carry the tiny rolls of paper. So I had every excuse in the world for going to Black Cocks to see Mr Masson, and the best excuse in the world for passing Boscobel's gate – and maybe calling in to ask how Rags was getting on?

I told myself angrily that I needed no excuse. He had surely made that sufficiently obvious. Was nothing, even the patent liking and admiration – all right, attraction – he had shown for me, going to cure me of the self-effacing instinct built into me by that repressed childhood, the shyness that vanished utterly once I was with him, but which paralysed me from approaching him?

In the end, it didn't matter. There was no sign of him at Boscobel, and his car was not in the yard. Nor could I see William's bicycle. And of course no dog.

I pedalled by, and on to Black Cocks.

* * *

The first thing I saw there was Christopher John's car standing just outside the farmyard gate, with William's bicycle leaning against the wall near by. And after all, no courage was required. All that was needed, it seemed, was his nearness. The singing in the air again, the brightness, the lift of the spirit that spelled delight. I propped my bicycle beside William's, and let myself through the gate.

At first glance the yard looked deserted, except for hens scratching and clucking among the spillings from the stacks. There were some pigeons among them, which flew up with a rattle of wings, and I saw that they were wild birds, ring-doves that flew high before tilting into a circle and making for the tall elms beyond the farmhouse.

"Hullo? Is anyone there?"

My voice sounded thin and lost in the emptiness of the yard. The sun beat down on the roofs of the buildings, and flashed from the car's windscreen. Cattle lowed somewhere, and I heard a chain clank. No other answer.

"Christopher John? William?" Then, remembering where I was: "Mr Yelland? Mr Masson? Is anyone around?"

Still no answer, not even a dog barking.

But he was here. I knew it. Knew it even before my eye was caught by a flight of pigeons that wheeled, dipped, circled the elms where their wild cousins hid, then flew away. Grey, rosy-red, and white, the Tidworth flock was out again. The sun glinted on their tilting wings, making them the snowflake wings of the crystal. He was here. He must be here. If Cousin Geillis had been right about me, I knew he was here . . .

Geillis, you lovesick fool, pull yourself together. It doesn't take a witch to know that! His car's here, isn't it? All right, then, he and Rags and William, and probably Masson, too, have gone off with the farmer somewhere. And at that moment, as if in answer, I heard a distant barking, and the bleating of sheep, then a long, sweet whistle, and what sounded like a shout. The sounds came from some way beyond the buildings that edged the stackyard.

I gave up, and tried what I should have done for a start; went to the door of the farmhouse and knocked there.

At first I thought I had drawn another blank, but just as I raised my hand to knock again, a girl came hurrying through from the back premises somewhere, wiping her hands on her apron as she came. "There now, I thought I heard someone shouting! I was in the dairy, washing up. You bin here long?"

"No. I only knocked once. Are you Mrs Yelland?"

"Nay, then." She shook black curls, and a dimple showed. "If you want her, she's over to Taggs Farm giving a hand there. Twice a week, she goes, and she won't be back till tea-time, but you'll be going back that way, likely, and —"

"Actually, it was Mr Masson I wanted a word with. I believe he works here?"

"He does that. I ha'n't seen him today, nor Mr Yelland, not

201

since breakfast. They're over to the thirty-acre, gathering."

"Gathering?"

"Moving the sheep. You can hear them. But if you'll wait a bit, they'll be in for their dinners. Another half-hour, maybe. There's fences to mend. You like to come in?"

"I – no, I won't, thank you very much. May I wait outside, please? It's such a lovely day."

"You're welcome, I'm sure. Well, I'd better be getting back to the dinner. 'Bye then." And she bustled back into the house.

I went slowly through the empty stackyard. During my absence the ring-doves had returned, and were busy again among the hens. This time, as they flew up, they went no further than the open door twenty feet or so above, in the barn wall, where they sat on the sill, watching me warily.

It was the sort of half-door, or unglazed window, that opened at floor level on a loft, for loading. And where there was a loft, there would be a way up. I left the baking sun of the stackyard for the gloom of the big barn, and peered round me. Straw was stacked at one end of the barn almost up to the cross-beams, and at the other end right up to the floor of a half-loft. A solid flight of wooden steps led up to this. I climbed the steps to reach a clean boarded floor, lit by a brilliant slant of light from the door. The pigeons had gone. I crossed to the doorway, and knelt there to look out over the roofs of the buildings towards the pastures.

The men were there. In the distance I could make out a small figure that could be William, with a couple of men, and three dogs and a flock of sheep. But not Christopher John. Even at that distance I would have known –

He was not at that distance, nor any distance. As I knelt there, shading my eyes against the sun, I saw him below me, not fifty yards away, just outside the yard gate, with his hand on the door of his car. Then I saw him catch sight of my bicycle. He checked, turned, and cast a look around him.

I drew a breath to call out, then, as if a gentle touch from the air had sealed my mouth, I made no sound. For ·

Christopher John, after that one swift look, whipped open the car door, slid into the driving seat, and almost before my held breath had gone out, was away and out of sight down the track to Boscobel.

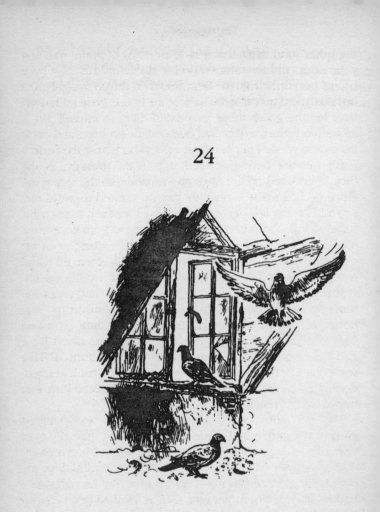

24

Now, of course, I could not possibly stop at Boscobel. But when I passed the gate and allowed myself a swift look sideways, I could see no sign of his car. I did catch a glimpse of a woman, whom I took to be Mrs Yelland, carrying a box into the house, and there was a sack, perhaps of grain, standing where it had been dumped on the doorstep. He must have brought supplies from the farm, and then driven straight on. If he had parked his car at the back of the house, he would surely have left the goods there, or carried them in himself. No, it looked very much as if he had dumped the packages and made his escape in case I might call on my way back from the farm.

He needn't have bothered, I thought drearily, as my bicycle bumped off the track and turned into the side road. Once he had made it obvious that he wanted to avoid me, I would be the last person to go near him even to ask why. In any case, Mrs Yelland's presence would make it even more impossible for me to stop and ask him what the matter was. Even when – half a mile later – I realised that he could not have known that I had seen him take that avoiding action at the farm gate, I simply concluded that he had taken the same action at Boscobel in case I should call on my way home. All the old fears and uncertainties came crowding back, to settle, dark and formless, like a weeping cloud. How had I ever dreamed that my love could be returned? That someone like him would ever look my way? What had I said, done, that could have so annoyed – no, disgusted him, that he would not risk meeting me?

My eyes stung, and I lowered my head and pumped away at the pedals as I made myself go back mentally over yesterday, that peaceful and lovely day, when I had thought – been certain – that he loved me. Had the strength of my own feelings deceived me – scared him? But he had said – had looked . . . No, forget that, Geillis. He had been charming and friendly and kind, and I had forgotten to be shy. Perhaps because he had spoken at some length about William, and then about his dead wife, I had read too much into that kindness. So forget it. He had been kind, that was all, to William's friend and lonely neighbour. It came to me like the final, shameful stab of self-betrayal, that he must be used to the effect he had on women. He had seen it working on me, and had decided to draw back.

Then so must I. The next move must come from him. And if it did not come, then it did not come.

The decision, inevitable as it was, came on a flash of pride that steadied my miserably churning thoughts, and brought me back to something near common sense. As the same moment I became aware, for the first time since I had left the Boscobel track, of where I was. I had sailed downhill past the Thornyhold gates without even seeing them, and there at the hill's foot was the River Arn, and the bridge where Christopher John and I had sat yesterday, when all was happiness and the sun was shining.

Well, it was shining today, too. I dismounted at the bridge, took my packet of sandwiches and fruit out of the bicycle basket and, still sustained by that stiffening pride, sat down in the same place on the parapet to eat my lunch.

I suppose, being lovesick, I should have left most of the food, but I was hungry, and enjoyed it, and the warmth and the beauty of the autumn trees, and the flowers in the hedgerow where I had hunted for them yesterday. There was more wild arum growing in the grass beside the crumbling gateposts of the old abbey. The spike I had picked yesterday had been spoiled when I dropped the flowers in the car, so when I had finished eating I wheeled the machine the few yards to the gateway, picked the wild arum and dropped it into the basket with the empty lunch-packet, and turned for home. This was the time for that fresh start that I had promised myself; I would get out my painting tools and begin this very afternoon.

But then I hesitated. Less than ever, after this morning's distress, did I want to tackle Agnes. She was quite capable of hurrying up to Thornyhold as soon as she saw me pass the lodge. I would keep away until I felt more able to face her.

I propped my bicycle by the gateway and went in through the high hedges to the field where the ruins stood.

As Mr Hannaker had said, there was nothing much to see. This was not a national monument, with shaved turf carpeting a noble nave, and carefully pointed pillars lining aisles open to the sky. St Thorn had been a small foundation, but the remains of the church showed spacious lines, with one pointed arch, still intact, framing the sky. Nothing was left of the abbey buildings except, outlined here and there in the grass, the bases of the old walls, long since plundered for their stones by the local builders and farmers. The bigger stones from doorways and pillars – and from graves, too, by the look of them – had been cleared more recently, and set back against the hedges, presumably to make the place into pasture. That cows were pastured here was very obvious.

I picked my way into the remains of the church. Nettles grew everywhere, and the grass was long and rank in the shadows, but the centre was grazed clear, where the worst of the debris of fallen masonry had been shovelled aside to make way for the cattle. It was very quiet. No cattle were about, and no birds sang.

I stood in the sunlit nave and looked about me. Towering above me, with the fragments of its tracery still clinging, was the arch that could be seen from the road. The only other remains of any size were the two massive jambs of the west door, and lesser columns to either side where the north and south doors had opened on cloister and garth. Some of the pillars that had lined the aisles still stood, but most were reduced to grass-grown stumps. Nothing else, except, near the west end, a flat slab of stone – what my father would have called a 'resurrection-defier' – that must once have marked an important grave. All meaningless now, deserted, sad. Beyond the broken stones stretched the empty field. Even the sunlight could bring nothing back; it was a place for darkness.

It was indeed. I recognised it now. It was not the same, of course, but it could have been the setting of my dream. The standing stones of cleared graves and broken pillars. The empty sky beyond the uprights of the west door. The flat stone half hidden in the grass. The feeling of desolation.

"Well, Miss Ramsey, fancy seeing you here!"

I spun round.

Agnes Trapp leaned her bicycle against the gatepost opposite my own, and came towards me, smiling.

The sight of her banished all other preoccupations from my mind. So powerfully had I already gone in imagination through the interview I had planned with her that I half expected her to tackle me with it straight away, but all she said was: "You come in to look at the old place, then? Pretty, isn't it?"

"Ye-es. Actually, I came to get some flowers and things. That yellow one growing on the wall is quite rare."

"Flowers? Han't you plenty in the garden, then?"

"Wild ones. I want to draw them. I used to do quite a bit of flower painting. I thought I'd like to start again. Agnes –"

"Yes?"

She had been looking about her as we talked and now turned back to me, with a kind of smiling complacency that made me wonder, suddenly, if she was here by chance, or if the jungle drums – Jessamy or the Widow Marget? – had set her looking for me, to find me here on her own ground. I took a deep breath, and with it a fast hold on my courage. This was certainly not the place I would have chosen, but something told me it was now or never. I left the shadowy precinct of the church, and walked over to where, in sunlight, lay a log; no old unhallowed stone, just a fallen tree, clean and dead. "I was hoping to see you today." My voice sounded calm and pleasant. "I called at your house, but Jessamy told me you'd gone into town. I wanted to tell you that I found the book."

"You did?" She looked pleased. More than pleased; she sparkled. There was something about her this morning, a shine of pleasure, almost of gaiety, and with it something of that force I had seen in her before. Well, I had not chosen my ground as I would have wished, but this would have to do. I sat down on the fallen log.

"Yes. I was right about it. My cousin had given it to someone for safe keeping because, as we thought, it is actually rather valuable. So you'll understand that I'd rather not let it out of the house, at any rate till I've let some expert or other take a look at it."

"But she told me I could have it! She –"

"I know. Let me finish. It's there at home, and if you want to, you can come up and look at it and copy out anything you want. One thing, though –"

"What's that?" Quick, almost defensive.

"There isn't a recipe for bramble jelly in the book."

"You been through it all, then?" Sharply.

"Not really. I just glanced through for that one, because you'd told me it was special. It's definitely not there."

I saw the spark of laughter jump to her eyes. She sat down beside me on the tree-trunk, a yard or so away. "Oh, well, there, I must 'a seen it somewhere else. But there's others I remember I'd be glad to have."

"Then that's all right." I smoothed a hand along the stripped tree-trunk. The feel of the warm wood was real and somehow reassuring. "Any time. Just let me know."

"Today? After supper?"

"If you like. I'm going home soon."

A pause. I saw her eyeing me with some curiosity, but, I thought, totally without suspicion or enmity. "Did you only come here after the flowers?" she asked.

It was my opening. "Yes, and to look at the old church. But now that I've seen it, I'm a bit puzzled. I feel as if I'd been here before, but I know that's not true."

Her smile broadened, and she gave a nod of satisfaction. "I thought you'd feel that way."

"Why? Agnes, why did you drug me that night, when you left the pie for my supper?"

If she was startled, it was for no more than a second. Then she nodded again, triumphantly. "I knew it! As soon as I laid eyes on you I said to the others, 'She's all right,' I said. 'She's likely. She'll be one of us, give her time.' And I was right.

There was no fooling you, was there? You knew straight away."

"Not straight away. But soon enough. What was in that pie?"

"Nothing to harm, nothing to harm. Just to let you know we were here, and you were welcome."

I was silent for a moment. "So that's what it's all been about? You did say once that you'd like to take me along to your meetings. I gather that they're held here?"

She was looking at me with a new expression, in which I thought I could see a touch of awe. "Do you tell me that you saw this –" she waved a hand – "these? That first time, without even getting out of your bed?"

"Something very like this place." I added, slowly: "And one or two people I'd know again."

"Then you have got the power! You've got it already! You're one of us, Miss Geillis Ramsey!"

"*No, I'm not. You drugged me, and I had a dream, and it was something like this churchyard, that's all.*" That was what I started to say, but, as if that gentle hand had stopped my lips again, I paused, and said, instead: "My cousin was here, too. Miss Saxon. She helped me to leave. And next morning a pigeon came in with a message from her, wishing me well."

The ground was mine now. She went white. "But that – that cannat be true, miss, it cannat! She wasn't here. She's dead."

"So?"

"She never was here. She never would come." She took a gulp of air. "And like I told you, the pigeons all went over Eddy Masson's way."

"So?" I said again. Whether or not I had what Agnes called 'the power', such power as I had found I would exploit while I could. "You're not suggesting that Mr Masson sent me the message? I'll show it to you when you come to Thornyhold this evening. You know Miss Saxon's writing, I suppose?" I settled myself more comfortably on the log.

"Tell me this, please. When I woke first after that drugged dream, I thought that you and Jessamy were in my bedroom, and I found later that you could have got into the house by the scullery window. Well?"

She was looking down at the grass at her feet. She nodded. "We didn't do no harm. Jessamy got in that little window and let me in. We came to see if you was all right after the medicine, that's all. You don't always know, the first time."

Gran. Yes. It fitted.

"And to shut the window up."

"Ah. That was you."

A nod. "You went flying, am I right?"

I said nothing, but she took it for an answer.

"Well, to stop you really going through the window. There's some as do."

No great shakes as a witch. Poor Gran with her overdose. It seemed I had been lucky. I kept my voice level and hard. "Did you look through the house while I was asleep?"

"Nay. What was the use? I'd looked already." She hesitated, then the blue eyes came up, guileless. "I won't say I didn't look for the key, but I couldn't find it."

"The still-room key?"

"Aye."

"And the soup, which I may tell you I didn't drink –"

"You didn't drink that?" She said it, I thought, admiringly. "How did you know not to drink that?" Then, with a spark of her old self: "Did another bird come and tell you?"

I laughed, and that disconcerted her, too. "No. Not that night." Not to give Jessamy away, I moved back on to half-truths. "I was awake when that dog cried out, and I saw Jessamy running past the house. Did the dog bite him?"

"Aye. Wouldn't take the food, but broke its rope and bit him –"

"Don't bother, Agnes." This time I let the anger show. "I know what happened. Do you think I can't see? I went to the big house in the morning and found where you'd kept the dog. And I called it to me, and it came."

"That dog? Came? To you?"

"And it will stay with me. Where did you get it?"

"It was straying. Gipsies, likely." She sounded surly and subdued, and I had no reason to doubt her. "Would 'a got shot otherwise, a collie straying in sheep land."

"Well, it's mine now, so you'll let it alone. I won't ask what you were doing with it, because I know that, too. But you'll not touch it again, neither you nor Jessamy. Understand?"

Another nod. She shuffled her feet in the grass.

"Was Jessamy badly bitten? Dog bites can be dangerous."

"Not bad, and I put the bruisewort on, and the salve your aunty made."

"Was that the recipe that you wanted from Lady Sibyl's book?"

A look upward at that, slanted and sly. I saw a dimple, and the pretty mouth pursed as if to stop a smile. "No, miss."

"Then what?"

"There's one for a cordial from the plums, and I saw some for sweets that your aunty used to make for Gran. She has a real sweet tooth –"

"For *sweets?*"

Unguarded, the syllable was totally disbelieving. She flashed me a look, then smiled, and dipping into the pocket of her coat, brought out a small round box made of wood-shavings, the sort that used to hold Turkish delight at Christmas time. She opened it. Inside, nestling in a white lace paper doily, were small squares of fudge.

"I make a lot," said Agnes. "Not just for Mother, for all the sales. Try some. 'Tis my own recipe, this one, and got a prize last time I put it into Arnside Show. Help yourself, miss, do."

Try some.

Try tackling a known witch on her own ground, and end up sitting with her on a log eating home-made fudge. Try not eating it. I looked at the box, then, helplessly, at Agnes.

"Thanks, but I don't really – I mean, it looks lovely, but I don't care terribly for sweets –"

She laughed merrily. "So you think it's got something in

212

it that'll set you flying again? Nay, nay, there's nothing here to hurt. Look, I'll eat it myself, to show you."

She took a piece, popped it into her mouth, crunched, chewed and swallowed. "There!" She got to her feet and stood in front of me, all at once solemn. "Miss Ramsey, if I done wrong I'm sorry. We all have our own ways, and I thought the world of your aunty, but I knew, we all knew, that she would never come along with us here. All right. But 'tis no manner of harm we do, just a little fun and a few secrets and something to look forward to come the right times . . . Well, I thought when I saw you, *she* might be different, I thought, and she's likely, so I gave it a try, nothing to hurt nor harm. Never hurt nor harmed yet, except my own mother, and you wouldn't call that harm if you'd 'a known her before . . ."

"Agnes —"

"No, let be a minute. I've not done yet." She nodded, still solemn, and went on. "All right, so maybe you don't like what Jess did to the dog, but you know he's not clever, and he knows no better."

"Would you really have drowned Hodge?"

She stopped, disconcerted. "Drowned Hodge?"

"Did you try? You couldn't have done it in the well, not after that bird fell in and she put the grating over, but what did you do to him to make him hate you so?"

"There, now, you see!" It was triumph. "You knew that, too! But you're wrong about Hodge. He was her cat, and a cat's tricky to mell with. I never did nothing to Hodge. He went, that's all, after she went. Oh, Miss Geillis, Miss Geillis, won't you come with me, just the once, and see?"

"No, I won't. Whatever I know, or have, it's going to stay right inside Thornyhold, and my animals are staying there with me, and nothing of the other sort is to come near us again."

There was a silence, while we measured one another, eye to eye. My heart was thumping, and my hand, flat on the tree-trunk, was damp. But it was Agnes's gaze that fell.

"Well," she said at length, on a long breath, as if relinquishing something. "You mean it, I see that. All right. I promise. Neither hurt nor harm, you and yours." She took another sweet, and held out the box again. "So take a piece, miss, and we'll say no more, except that I'm main sorry if there's been any upset."

What could I do? She was already swallowing. I took a piece of the fudge, and put it in my mouth. It was coffee-flavoured, and very good.

I stood up. "Well, I'll get home now, I think. I – I'm glad we've had this talk, Agnes, and got things straight. I'll expect you this evening, shall I? Are you going back now?"

"No," said Agnes. She was standing very straight. The sparkle was a glitter. Her eyes were brilliant, her face rosy. She looked very pretty. "I'm off to Taggs Farm. Boscobel he calls it. I left some of the sweets there yesterday, while you and he was out sweethearting, and now I'm going over to see them working."

I stared at her. The barely swallowed sweetstuff made me feel sick.

"What are you talking about?" It was a frightened croak. Some of her wretched drugs ... sweets ... see them working. Then, sweets, he doesn't eat them, he'll give them to William. *Too violent. Half the dose for a child.* "What have you done?"

"Nothing you won't get over! But it's my turn now! I was going to wait till I'd seen the one in her book, the love drink, but after yesterday and the way he looked at you I wasn't waiting any more, and that drink wasn't the only one I knew! So I made the sweets and took them over, and the minute he lays eyes on me, Miss Geillis Ramsey, it's me he'll want, me! And don't you think he'll ever have cause to regret it, neither!"

She shoved the box of sweets back in her pocket and laughed in my face. I said nothing, I must have been staring at her, mouth open, like an idiot, but it was not distress that struck me dumb. She was still talking, flushed and exultant, but I did not hear a word of it.

What she had told me was crazy, it was shocking, but the very shock tore clean through the whirling clouds of the morning's misery, and blew them to shreds. My thoughts settled, clear and still. *Christopher John.* If Agnes was telling the truth, and I thought she was, then nothing I had said or done had alienated or alarmed him. In the sane and daylight world he loved me, and had made it plain. All that had happened this morning was that he had succumbed to some filthy drug of Agnes's concocting, and I knew from my own experience what effect her efforts could have.

So if she had something of witchcraft at her fingertips, then how much more could I, Geillis of Thornyhold –?

I stopped short. That way, no. It didn't need the sudden chill of a cloud across the sun, as tangible as that touch from the air, to turn me back from something that I, and Cousin Geillis with her greater powers, had rejected. But the new self-confidence remained. "In the sane and daylight world." My own phrase came back to me. It was still that. He and I belonged there, not to the sad and silly world of drugs and nightmare dreams, and in the real world he loved me. He was highly intelligent and articulate; he knew about Agnes; surely, then, all I had to do was tell him all that had happened, and we could talk it out?

Her voice rose, shrill and triumphant. "Yes, you may well stand there, my lady! So you won't join in with us, oh no! Then you can just stay outside and see what we can do when we want to! And now I'll be on my way!"

"Agnes! Are you out of your mind? Agnes! No, wait, Listen –"

I was shouting at the air. She was already through the gateway, had grabbed her bicycle and mounted. By the time I reached the gateway she was fifty yards away, pedalling furiously. The dappled shadows swallowed her pounding form, and she was gone.

I seized my own machine and yanked it out on to the metal. I swear I had no thought of beating her to the encounter, the fairytale meeting that her shaky magic had planned. It was William I was afraid for, with the image of Gran, the echo of Christopher John: *no great shakes as a witch* . . .

But she was pretty competent with a bicycle. As I whirled mine round on the road and made to mount, I saw that both tyres were flat to the ground. And the pump, surprise, surprise, was nowhere to be seen.

A car slid to a stop beside me.

"Is anything wrong?" asked Christopher John.

25

"What on earth's the matter?"

Before I could even speak he was out of the car and I was in his arms. The bicycle went clanging to the ground. Even if I had wanted to I could not have spoken through the kiss.

Centuries later, coming to through the things he was saying
– "My dearest girl, my dear, what is it? You look shocked,
awful. Have you had an accident on that damned bike of
yours?" – I managed to take breath and say, shakily:

"No. No, I'm all right. Christopher John, where's William?
Was he to be home for lunch?"

"No. I had to go to St Thorn, but I left him at the farm.
Why?"

"Did you get a package this morning, a box of fudge?"

He looked down, surprised. "Yes. How did you know?
Why? What is all this?" Then, quick as if lightning had run
between us: "Oh, my God. Agnes?"

"Yes. You told me, no, William said you hardly ever ate
sweets, so I thought you might have given them to him."

"No, I didn't. I gave the box to Eddy Masson. He was
working with the sheep at Black Cocks, and he'd eat sweets
all day if he could get them. For heaven's sake, what's in
them?"

I do not know what trailing vestige of loyalty, woman to
woman, kept me from telling him. But I would not have
exposed even a real enemy to the man she longed for and
could not have. (Most certainly, now, could not have.) And
Agnes, in spite of this last crazy push, was not really
an enemy. Standing there in the road, in Christopher
John's arms, I could allow myself to see the funny side of
it all.

"What are you laughing like that for? A moment ago I
thought you were in tears."

"Nothing. I'm happy. You were saying?"

"I was saying I love you. And what's in those sweets that
makes it so urgent . . . and now so funny?"

"I don't know. But there's something. She told me so. She
was here, you see, and we had a bit of a scene, and then she
dashed off on her bike and I was going after her to warn
you and William because I don't trust her recipes, and then
I found that." I gestured towards the fallen bicycle.

"Yes, I saw your tyres. I take it she did that? That's not

quite so funny, then. I think we'd better be getting up to
Boscobel as quickly as we can."

A furious hooting drove us apart. He had left his car right
in the middle of the road, with a door open and the engine
still running. Behind it, pulling up with another flurry of
hooting and a squeal of brakes, was the taxi from St Thorn,
that knew the way.

Mr Hannaker's face came, grinning, out of the window.

"Look, mate, I don't want to spoil the fun, but I've got a
fare to pick up and – oh, it's you, miss. Nice to see you
again."

"And you," I said weakly. "How do you do, Mr Hannaker?"

"You settling in all right, then? Getting to know a few
folks?" He spoke quite gravely, but I laughed as I went to
pick my bicycle up and move it out of his way.

"As you see. You were afraid I'd be lonely."

The grin came back, broad and cheerful. "Well, miss, good
for you. See you around."

And as Christopher John moved his car the taxi crawled
round it, pipped the horn twice for 'thank you', and vanished
round a curve in the road. I pushed my machine in through
the gateway and hid it behind the hedge. Then we were
away, fast, in the taxi's wake.

Past the lodge gates, and round another bend or two, and
the road stretched ahead of us straight and empty, save for
the taxi half a mile or so ahead.

"No sign of her," he said.

"She'll have turned off at the lodge – the short cut through
the woods. Can she get there before we do?"

"On that track? Not a hope. But what's the hurry?"

"I suppose there isn't any, really, now. Only I was worrying
about William. If Mr Masson gave him some –"

The car surged forward. After a minute he said: "The stuff
was addressed to me. She didn't say why? No hint at all as
to what was in it?"

"None at all." That, at least, was truthful. "But she –
she seems to like experimenting with these silly spells or

whatever they are, and she makes mistakes. You know that; you told me. And – well she tried something on me, once, and I gathered from what she just told me that she wasn't too sure of the result. She did say the sweets were harmless, but William's only a child, so whatever's in them would be far too strong for him anyway."

"Yes. Well, we're nearly there."

The car turned, a shade too fast, into the side road, whipped along between the hedges, and at last into the track that climbed towards the beeches of Boscobel.

As we reached the crest of the hill we saw Agnes, bumping at great speed along the field path that led from the quarry to the farm. Bent low, scarlet in the face, her skirt billowing as she pumped away at the pedals, she was no longer a figure of menace, but of bucolic comedy. She did not, mercifully, see Christopher John. All her attention was on the obstruction that lay between her and the farm gate.

Farmer Yelland's sheep, all hundred and sixty-four of them, milling and bleating and bobbing around like froth awash on a millrace, with a couple of collies weaving and dodging to hold them together right across Agnes's path. They flowed round the bicycle and stopped it. There was one with a ragged fleece that got tangled with one of the pedals, and stuck there, complaining bitterly and very loudly.

Agnes was calling out, but nothing, above the earth-shaking, earsplitting full orchestra of the flock, could be heard. She was not shouting at us. Four-square and thigh deep in his flock, standing stock still and staring at her as if he had never seen her before, was a big man holding a crook. He was chewing.

Agnes dropped her bicycle. It vanished under the tide of sheep. Eddy Masson's crook came down and hauled a lively gimmer out of the way. He waded towards Agnes through the flood of sheep.

"Oh, my God," I said shakily. "It works. It really works. And she had some, too."

"What?" He turned, leaning close to me. "What did you say? I can't hear a thing in all that racket."

I smiled at him. The sun was on his hair, showing up the grey. There were wrinkles at the corner of his eyes, and heart-stopping hollows under the cheekbones. I had never seen anyone . . . never felt . . . Here, out of the whole world, was the only man . . .

"Nothing," I said. "I was wrong about the sweets. There was nothing in them to hurt. Nothing at all."

But I still wonder what would have happened if the taxi had come along that road in front of Christopher John.

Bucolic, yes, but an eclogue, a gentle pastoral. The sheep were moving off now, away from the house. Agnes and Mr Masson walked slowly after them, heads close, talking. Neither glanced back. As the car slid up to the Boscobel gate I saw the shepherd's arm go round her.

Christopher John braked, and I got out of the car to open the gate. As he drove through and round to the side of the house William came running from the back yard. He had not seen me. He ran straight to the car.

"Dad! Dad! That pigeon you brought over this morning –"

Christopher John, getting out of the car, caught hold of his son and steadied him. "Hang on a minute. Did Eddy Masson give you any of those sweets I gave him?"

"What? Not a bite, the greedy pig. Why? But Dad, the pigeon! Mrs Yates put it in the study, but Rags got in and upset the box and it got away. It'll have gone over to Gilly's by now, and you never put the message on it!"

Here Rags, hurtling round the side of the house in William's wake, caught sight of me and came running. William, turning, saw me there. A hand went to his mouth.

Christopher John put an arm out and pulled his son against him. "It's all right, she's a witch, didn't you know? She knows it all already."

"*Do* you?" This, wide-eyed, to me.

"Almost all of it," I said, smiling. "But I'd like to see the message, if I may?"

Without a word, Christopher John slipped a hand into his breast pocket and took out a tiny, folded piece of paper. I opened and read it. Like the first message, it was in my cousin's hand.

Love is foreseen from the beginning, and outlasts the end. Goodbye, my dears.

After a while I looked up. "Of course you know what it says."

"Yes. She showed me both the messages when she left them with me and told me when to send them. It was her way of blessing you – both of us." He saw the question in my eyes and nodded. "Yes, she told me, long before you came here, what would happen. She was comforting me for Cecily's death. She told me that William and I would be healed, and from Thornyhold. As we have been."

Here William, as Rags leaped to lick his face, caught and held him close. The three of them stood there in the sunlight, hopeful, smiling. Rags's smile was easily the broadest of the three.

It was not possible, standing there facing them, to take it all in, but the paper in my hand made one thing plain. Made fact out of fairytale, and put magic in its place as a natural part of my 'sane and daylight world'. Cousin Geillis had foreseen this long ago, and seen, perhaps, on that day by the River Eden, how her own death would be linked with my coming to life, with the climb of that shy pond-creature out of the dark into the sunlight. It might be that my vision of the doves in the crystal had given her the idea of using her adopted waifs to carry her blessing back to me, and incidentally forge the first bond between Christopher John and myself. The touch of fantasy was typical of the fairy-godmother relationship that she had had with me. Typical, too, was the way I had been left – forced – to choose my own path through the enchanted woods, where she must have known I would be led to venture.

Christopher John was speaking, something about what had happened at Black Cocks this morning.

"I'd asked Eddy Masson to bring another of the Thorny-hold pigeons over to the farm, and I'd just put the box in my car when I saw your bicycle there. That confounded bird was making all sorts of noises, so I drove straight off home with it, and then I had to go to St Thorn to pick up a parcel there. Where were you? I hope you didn't see me running away?"

I shook my head, not in denial, but because I still found it difficult to speak.

"I was planning, in any case, to drive over to Thornyhold tonight," he said, "and then send that second message over later on . . . Her blessing, and *envoi*. I was only afraid that I might be assuming rather too much, and a great deal too soon, but I – well, I rather trusted to our talk this evening to put that right."

Too soon? And I had been afraid it might be too late. Still slightly bemused, I fastened on one phrase he had used. "That second message, you said? She only left two? But this one today makes three. So where did the other one come from?"

That heart-shaking smile again. "A blessing from the air. You said so yourself." He held out his free arm and gathered me to him, with William and Rags still held close to his other side. "When William rushed home that first day and told me all about you, and later, after I'd met you and talked to you myself . . . Well, I could see that Miss Saxon was perfectly right about the fate I was headed for, but I couldn't let her make all the running, could I?"

I laughed, reached up and kissed him. "Give William some credit, too! You must know quite well that I'd take anything on just to get him and Silkworm to come and live with me."

"That's what I was counting on," said Christopher John.

There is not much more to tell.

We are still at Thornyhold, though our children, William and the two girls, left home long since. None of their families live very far away, so we see them often.

Agnes married Eddy Masson, and went to live at Tidworth. She was, so said the jungle drums, devoted to her husband, and happily occupied her time waging war with the Widow Marget. At any rate, she never tried to come into our lives again, but remained a distant and pleasant neighbour. Gran died soon after the move, peacefully in her sleep, and Jessamy, to everyone's surprise, married a young woman whose good sense and kindness soon pulled him out of his slough of stupidity, and they produced three children who were all healthy, dirty, and perfectly sane, and crowded happily into the two lodges at the Thornyhold gate.

So the witch-story turned into comedy, and the midnight enchantments faded, as they usually do, into the light of common day. The only reason I have told it is because a little while ago I overheard one of my grandchildren, turning the pages of my first illustrated herbal, say to her sister:

"You know, Jill, I sometimes think that Grandmother could have been a witch if she had wanted to."